THE VINTNER'S LEGACY

D1615777

Also by Kristen Harnisch
The Vintner's Daughter
The California Wife

The Vintner's LEGACY

a novel

KRISTEN HARNISCH

WENHAM
LAKE PRESS

Published 2022 by Wenham Lake Press, LLC
Printed in the United States of America
ISBN: 979-8-9856509-4-5

For my beloved brother, Matthew Lacroix

Cast of Characters

Adeline Chevreau Donnelly, their daughter
Gemma Donnelly, their daughter
Rourke Donnelly, their son

VOUVRAY, FRANCE

CHEVREAU/LEMIEUX FAMILY
Luc Lemieux, Sara and Philippe Lemieux's son
Jacques Chevreau, Luc's step-grandfather and Marie
    Donnelly's uncle
Marguerite Thibault Chevreau, Luc's grandmother

TOURS, FRANCE

CHEVREAU FAMILY
Pierre "Pip" Chevreau, Adeline Donnelly's grandfather
    (Jacques Chevreau's brother)
Mim Chevreau, Adeline Donnelly's grandmother

HELLO GIRLS/U.S. ARMY SIGNAL CORPS
Virginia Hunt   **Gertrude**
Barbara   **Gloria**
Giselle   **Sadie**

U.S. ARMY SIGNAL CORPS
Private First Class Bartholomew Martin
Sergeant Archibald Rivers
Corporal Houle

MARCHAND FAMILY
Capitaine Pierre Marchand, French 10th Colonial Division
Brigitte Marchand, his wife
Ondine Marchand, his daughter
Michel Marchand, his son

KÖLN (COLOGNE), GERMANY

SOMMER FAMILY
Leutnant Heinrich Sommer, German Army 231st Infantry
    Medical Corps
Anna Sommer, his wife
Werner Sommer, his son

NEW YORK, NEW YORK

SISTERS OF NOTRE DAME
Reverend Mother (formerly Sister Paulette)

U.S. ARMY MEDICAL CORPS NURSES
Sally Dunn
Harriet Hussmann
Anna Ring

THE WESTERN FRONT

SURGEONS

Lieutenant Colonel Clive Jenkins, M.D.

SOLDIERS

Corporal Shepherd Holmes, U.S. Marine Corps
Private First Class James Book, U.S. Army

REAL HISTORICAL CHARACTERS

Lieutenant Colonel Eugene Kilgore, M.D.,
Commanding officer, Base Hospital No. 30
Major Alanson Weeks, M.D., Surgical Team No. 50
Captain John Homer Woolsey, M.D., Surgical Team No. 50
Colonel Paul Malone, U.S. Army, 2nd Division,
23rd Regiment commander
Major Charles Elliott, U.S. Army, 23rd Regiment,
3rd Battalion commander
Major Edmund Waddill, U.S. Army, 23rd Regiment,
1st Battalion commander
Major Berton Sibley, U.S. Marine Corps,
6th Marine Regiment, 3rd Battalion commander
General James Harbord, commander of 2nd Division Marine
Corps at the Battle of Belleau Wood

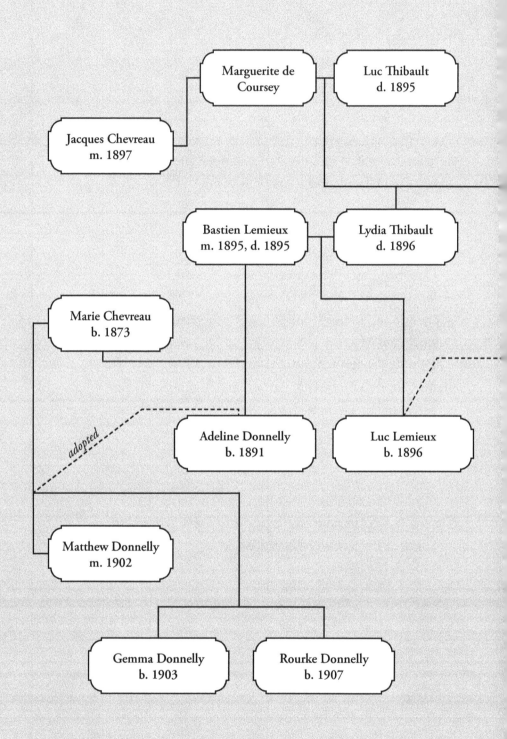

Thibault-Lemieux Family Tree in 1917

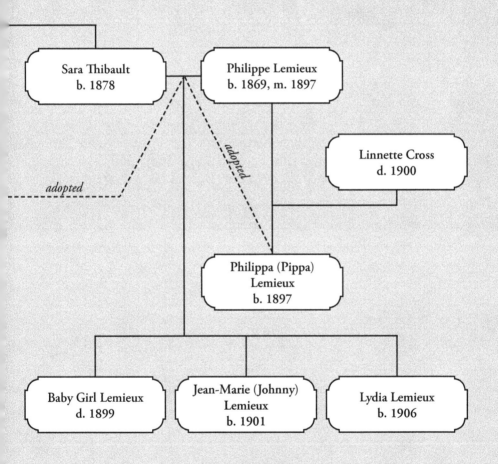

CHAPTER 1

June 14, 1918

ON THE OUTSKIRTS OF BOURESCHES, FRANCE

Mortar shells whistled and whizzed over the half-meter-wide dugout where Luc Lemieux cowered. They landed far too close, rutting the earth and spraying dirt. The narrower the trench, they said, the less likely a soldier was to suffer a direct hit and be blown to bits.

Luc dozed in snatches until a wet sensation, like a sprinkle of morning rain, woke him. The sweet and spicy scent of lilacs mixed with horseradish settled in his foxhole. Then his nostrils began to burn as if someone were singeing the tender flesh inside with a lit match.

Tin mess pans clattered. "Wake up! Gas! Gas!"

Luc clamped his eyes and mouth shut. Holding his breath, he scrambled to his feet and reached for his canteen. He swigged water, gargled, swished and spit. He splashed more water on his face, then tipped his head back, the liquid streaming into his nostrils. Blowing hard, he tried to expel the poison from his nose. Luc pulled his gas mask from its satchel, fastened it over his face and secured his helmet. He sprang from the dugout and charged back down the Gobert ravine with only the silvery haze of moonlight to guide him.

Men without masks wobbled and sank around him, clutching their necks and twisting violently as they choked on the blisters that swelled in their throats. Their limbs flailed as they tried to feel their way out. Blinded men huddled together, a labor of moles shuffling en masse away from an advancing enemy they could not see. Luc and the able-bodied soldiers of the 23rd Infantry ran west, away from the edge of Bouresches and the noxious fumes and the Huns who would soon barrage them with bullets.

Luc's tongue poked a painful boil inside his right cheek. Had he stopped breathing and donned his mask fast enough to prevent the gas particles from blistering his lungs? He recalled his basic training: gas was heavier than air and settled in low-lying areas. In the dark, the glass eye cups of his mask obscured his vision, so he used his hands and feet to navigate up the rocky slope of the ravine to higher ground. He clawed his way to the top in a few minutes and sprinted across the flat, grassy farmland.

When he reached a tight cluster of trees, Luc slumped to the ground. Beneath his mask, hot and dank with perspiration, he battled to breathe through the respirator. Panic crept up his throat. His hands flew to the mask, but the gnawing voice of his sergeant stopped him: *Never remove your mask until you are certain the gas is gone.* Luc concentrated instead on breathing threads of oxygen through the respirator. Threads eventually expanded to ribbons of air, and Luc's heart settled back into a semi-normal rhythm.

What else should he do? He was separated from his battalion and he could not see any of his comrades from this vantage point above the ravine. A bitter bile flared in his gullet. He swallowed hard to push it back down. He must survive, for Maman, for Papa, for all of them. He must return—for Ondine.

There was only one thing left to do. Luc signed the cross. *In the name of the Father, and of the Son, and of the Holy Ghost. Amen.* He toppled over on his side. He had no choice but to wait until dawn—if dawn ever came.

CHAPTER 2

Six Months Earlier, December 24, 1917

TOURS, FRANCE

The harvest of souls had begun three and a half years ago, just days after Luc had arrived to claim his inheritance of the family's Loire Valley vineyard, Saint Martin. Five hundred kilometers away, the blood of his adopted countrymen now spilled in the fields and seeped into the soil of northeastern France.

If the newspaper reports were accurate, the Hun butchers had slithered like a steel snake through Belgium and northern France, looting villages and slaughtering women and children. The Americans were the Allies' last hope. Now that they had started moving their supply depot to nearby Tours, Luc was determined to deliver another ten barrels of his 1916 vintage to the generals—and leave with a post in the U.S. Army.

The wagon rattled along the cobbles, parting a throng of pedestrians, until its wheels glided up the newly paved road that led to the stark limestone and brick buildings of the American Expeditionary Forces' Service of Supply headquarters. The hundred-window façade of the Chief Surgeon's Office stretched along the right side of the courtyard ahead. In an open wood shop directly to Luc's left, metal blades sliced like sharp teeth through freshly milled pine planks. The buzzing and squealing muffled all other street noises. Luc hunched his shoulders but tipped his hat when he spied one of his Vouvray neighbors inside. A barrel-maker skilled in the use of saw and plane, Louis Bertrand now assembled regulation pine caskets for the army.

Twenty meters down the road, on the steps of the Signal Corps base post, the willowy Virginia Hunt lingered with a bulky, brass-buttoned wool trench coat draped over her shoulders. Her pink lips sucked long drags off a cigarette and the steam from her breath mingled with wisps of smoke to form a small cloud. Blond tendrils escaped from beneath her dark army cap, accentuating Virginia's ice-blue eyes and peachy cheeks.

Luc gulped. He wasn't sure which he craved more—the cigarette or the pleasure of Virginia's company. He set the brake and slid a burlap bag from beneath the seat.

"Mademoiselle Hunt," he called as he stepped down.

Her melancholy expression brightened. "Weekly delivery, Lemieux?"

"*Bien sûr*. Merry Christmas," he replied with a wink, handing her two bottles in exchange for the cigarette she proffered. These girls led such dreary existences in service to their country that he felt duty bound to give them small luxuries, like his Vouvray chenin blanc.

"*Merci.*" She tucked the bottles into the crook of her arm.

He lit his cigarette and peered inside the open door. A row of nine young American female signal operators sat in front of a long switchboard, headsets secured, rapid-firing French commands like machine guns. They jammed plugs into holes so fast he could hardly follow their hand motions. These women could connect five emergency calls in the time it took a man to connect one, and shift on a dime from speaking English to French, Virginia had boasted.

"How are the Hello Girls?"

Beneath sweeping, dark lashes, her gaze narrowed. "Determined to help our boys stop the filthy Boches and end this war."

He smiled admiringly as the smoke warmed and relaxed his chest. He was twenty-one, but he guessed she must be a few years older to be so poised.

She flicked her cigarette butt onto the step and squashed it with her spit-and-polish black boot. "You have any family? A sweetheart?"

"My grandparents live with me in Vouvray . . . and my parents are back in California with the rest of my family." No time for a sweetheart with a vineyard to run and French soldiers to feed every night.

Her gloved hand touched his arm. "Don't let them send you to the front, Lemieux." She hesitated, as if she wanted to say more, but instead lifted her face to the colorless sky. Its gray heft squeezed his skull. The biting wind told of a storm brewing. "*À la prochaine, mon ami,*" she said, slipping back inside.

7

He inhaled one last long drag. His mother had said the same thing, of course, when he had set sail for France before his eighteenth birthday, the August day on which he inherited the vineyard and half of his great-grandfather LeBlanc's estate. What was it about him that made women want to protect him? Sure, he was lanky, but he was also taller than his father—and strong from working the land. Shouldn't *he* be the one to shield *them*?

He drove his wagon past the soldiers and civilians who pulsed through the streets. As he neared a patch of jaundiced grass, Luc steered the mules left and sidled the wagon to the curb at the Chief Quartermaster's stores. The wide, black lacquered door that led to the supply rooms burst ajar, its thick steel padlock swinging and creaking against the wood panel. The quartermaster's men emerged in olive drab uniforms and white starched aprons as if choreographed.

"Is that Lemieux?" a corporal with a clipboard called out.

"Yes, sir." Luc hopped down and doffed his cap.

"The *poilus* giving you any trouble?"

"No, sir." As if the French soldiers who billeted for one or two nights had any strength to cause trouble, many of them as wobbly as newborn foals by the time they reached Saint Martin for a rest from the front. "We're pleased to serve the Allies, sir."

"How many do you board each night?" Spectacles teetered on the bridge of the corporal's pointy nose, lending him the air of a stern schoolmaster.

Luc flattened out the crumpled parchment and handed it over. "Only about ten soldiers each week, sir, but they eat a lion's share." Even with the Americans' help, he lacked enough to feed the *poilus* as they headed home from the front. Luc now had no means to export wine overseas or over land, and he hoped his mother and father in California fared better at their Napa ranch.

The corporal handed him a stack of francs, ration cards, a case of canned sardines and ten baguettes. As grateful as the soldiers would be for these—and for Luc's chenin blanc, which they assured him was far superior to the swill they drank in the trenches—the *poilus* who bunked in the caves at Saint Martin treated him as if he were an *embusqué*, shirking his duty to fight. Even Virginia and the Hello Girls operating the phone lines did more for the war effort than he did.

"Sir, I still want to enlist." Luc jumped up into the wagon bed and placed the cash and foodstuffs in the strongbox near the front end, next to the wool blankets his grandmother packed in case he was stranded overnight somewhere. He started to roll the barrels down two parallel planks to the awaiting supply men.

"Patience, Lemieux. We have hundreds of thousands of men and tons of supplies we're moving to the front right now."

"Yes, sir."

The last barrel flew down and the corporal stopped it with one hand and a steel-toed boot. He scribbled on his clipboard and ripped off a receipt for Luc. "Next week, then?" he confirmed.

At three in the afternoon, the sky cracked open and sharp sleet pelted Luc and his team of skittish mules, soaking their skins and delaying their arrival home by at least an hour. A mantle of gloom descended and the team tramped forward, guided only by Luc's single, swinging lantern.

As fatigue bowed his head, Luc finally saw the house windows in the distance, hung like a chain of bright gold tiles in the dark. As he drew nearer, the scent of burning wood fires reached his nostrils, triggering a deep sense of relief. Beyond the house, candlelight glowed from the windows hewn into the massive ledge of tufa rock. Tonight, hundreds of barrels slept in the cellar on the first floor, while more French soldiers would sleep in cots on the second floor of the centuries-old caves.

Grandmère would be preparing a stew with a few of the rabbits that Jacques, Luc's honorary grandfather, had removed from traps this morning, and the bread would complement the supper. He reached back to grab the items from the strongbox and was surprised to see that the blankets were strewn about the wagon bed. As he lifted the lantern for a closer look, two pairs of frightened eyes stared back—and two pairs of hands with dirty nails clutched half-eaten baguettes.

———

The Americans were fortunate that Ondine and Michel were not German spies. The pair of teenagers had hopped an army freight train outside of Paris two days ago and were about to sail into one of their military depots—completely undetected. The train lurched and lumbered along the tracks, spewing sulfuric smoke from its stack like an old, tired gypsy might from his pipe. While her brother peppered her with questions about how they would escape unnoticed, Ondine wedged her small torso between the heavy sliding doors of their freight car. She winced as the car jostled and a door bounced against her petite shoulder blade.

Waiting for the brakeman's footsteps atop the roof of the rail car and the squealing brakes, she stole another look out. The depot and loading dock were only four hundred meters down the tracks. A brightly colored American flag billowed above, snapping in the breeze. She could not make out the station sign from this distance. A hive of American soldiers, sporting ugly olive uniforms and shouting commands in English, hustled with hand trucks to meet the train.

Ondine had observed the setting and rising sun and guessed they were headed southwest, far away from the Germans. She knew the cargo was destined for some sort of American medical or supply outfit, for their companions on the trip had been large wooden crates marked *Property of U.S. Army* and *Fragile: X-Ray Machine*. She could not read English, but she knew enough to identify "U.S. Army" and "X-Ray." She and Michel had slept soundly on the hard, shifting floor, even though the night air chilled Ondine's skin. At least this time they did not have to endure the wailing of mothers and children, and the thick stench of human *merde* and vomit, or sleep standing up between her Lille neighbors with their hot onion breath and wandering hands.

The screech of wheels alerted Ondine to their imminent stop. Ahead, a thick, vivid yellow-green hedge of laurel ran parallel to the tracks, tall enough to conceal their hunched figures. It was their only hope.

"Quickly, Michel!" she hissed. Her brother scuffled to his feet and caught hold of Ondine's extended hand. "When I say, jump as far as you can over that hedge. As you hit the ground, form a ball with your body and roll on your side. Watch your head."

There were only seconds left until they reached the jump-off point.

"Now!" Ondine cried. The two hit the ground hard, tumbling into a thicket of prickly shrubbery.

Michel groaned. Ondine examined her brother's legs. "I'm fine, just scratched up a bit," he said, rubbing his leg. Narrow streaks of blood formed on his raw hands. Ondine's wool stockings had suffered, showing larger holes and runs. The week-old angry red scrapes on Ondine's thighs and deep purple bruises on her wrists had started to recede, but her innards still ached with shame. She found it hard to breathe at times.

She tightened her shawl around her shoulders and wiped her runny nose. A look of concern flashed across Michel's features, but Ondine raised a finger to her lips. She did not want his pity. It summoned the horror of that night.

Ondine poked her head up from behind the hedge. The train loomed two meters away, stretching in both directions. Doors slid open with a bang and footsteps scurried as cargo was unloaded. Now would be the perfect time to round the end of the train and make their escape.

Michel's eyes darted in the direction of the caboose. "What do I say if someone stops us?" he whispered.

"That we are orphans and have no home and no food. We look so slovenly, they have no choice but to believe us," she replied.

"Do you believe Père is dead, too?" Michel whispered, his chapped lips trembling.

Ondine sighed and squeezed his shoulder. "Of course not, but if we want food and shelter, we need to say he is—for now."

At the mere mention of food, Ondine's stomach twisted and gurgled. They hadn't eaten since Paris two days ago, when they had pilfered a bag of peanuts from a street vendor as he haggled with a sour-faced customer.

Ondine tracked pairs of boots moving, shuffling right and left, rolling equipment and supplies to trucks lining the street. When she sensed an opening, Ondine tugged Michel's collar and the two sprinted across the tracks and down an incline, ducking behind a clump of bushes. No one came after them. Ondine exhaled. When the *camions* revved their engines and pulled away, Ondine and Michel followed amid the lingering dust. They walked a kilometer or so past ramshackle homes until they reached a cluster of austere stone buildings. A sign on one read *AEF Service of Supply*.

Sharply dressed men and women, most in uniform, rushed past with hardly a glance. Ondine was unsure of her next move. Should they beg by the roadside? No, they would be carted off to some asylum for war orphans where they would lose any small freedoms they possessed.

They were strong and able to do chores for their keep. The pink scales of itchy skin on their necks and scalps that had worsened since they had left home would stay hidden beneath Ondine's kerchief and Michel's cap. They would find work and she would see Michel settled. He would help the Allies defeat the Huns, just as Ondine had done back in Lille.

A voice chirped in thickly accented French. Ondine and Michel turned to see a brunette dressed in a dark skirt, matching baggy jacket, a wide-lapelled shirt collar, black leather gloves and boots. A jaunty angled cloth cap with white piping covered the top half of her wavy hair, which had been chopped just below her earlobes. She addressed Ondine, asking her name and if she were looking for someone.

A familiar panic struck Ondine and her lips involuntarily sealed shut. Michel wrung his cap and replied in French, "We are from Lille, *mademoiselle*. I am Michel. This is Ondine, my sister. We are looking for some food and work."

"We are orphans from Lille," Ondine wanted to say, but the words stuck in her throat and then evaporated in a white cloud of breath. Her eyes grew wide and expectant. Perhaps this well-dressed, fine-smelling young American lady would look at her face and not her soiled shoes and stained dress. Mère had always said Ondine's eyes were her best feature, she remembered with a pang of sorrow.

L'américaine slipped a hand into her pocket and pulled out a bar wrapped in plain paper. *"Voilà! Chocolat!"* she said triumphantly. "I'm sorry I don't have more to give you right now." The woman tapped her gloved fingers on her lips. "There is not much work here for children, but . . ." Her voice trailed as she glanced over her shoulder. Outside one of the buildings was a wagon pulled by two mules. *L'américaine* leaned in and said softly, "See that wagon over there? It's owned by a kind gentleman farmer who lives just a few kilometers from here. He might have some work for you." Her lips swept into a smile, revealing a row of straight, white teeth. For a stinging moment, all Ondine could see and hear was her beloved Mère.

Michel thanked *l'américaine* and they continued down the road. The gentleman farmer was speaking to a uniformed man in a crisp, white apron and unloading barrels from the wagon. The farmer was surprisingly young—not much older than Ondine, she guessed—with straight posture, broad shoulders, lithe limbs and clear skin. Something must be wrong with him. Why was he not fighting for the Allies?

The farmer turned and shook his head, as if laughing at himself. The skin around the corners of his eyes crinkled and the flesh of his cheek rounded and blushed a healthy shade of pink. He secured the tailboard. Fresh dark green paint decorated the wagon boards, and a low-slung canvas bonnet protected the cargo from rain and sleet. The mules, though on the smaller side, looked well fed and watered. As the young farmer collected a purse from the aproned soldier, Ondine could almost hear the coins jingle from across the street. He was rather handsome and seemed relaxed, not stern and fearful like the men of Lille. Then again, the enemy had never invaded his town, so why would he have reason to scowl?

As the young man slid into the driver's seat, Ondine signaled to Michel and they sprinted toward the back of the wagon. As it pulled away from the curb, they hooked their arms over the tailboard, pushed their feet off the running board and hoisted themselves into the back. Ondine waited for shouting, for the farmer to stop his wagon and check for stowaways, but neither happened.

Ondine spied a stack of folded blankets. Then, quietly lifting the lid of the large jockey box bolted to an interior board, the two discovered a jug of water and foodstuffs. Michel nodded enthusiastically in answer to Ondine's silent question about whether they should eat the loaves.

With blankets wrapped tightly around them, Ondine closed her eyes and prayed. She prayed God would forgive her. She prayed for her mother in heaven, and her father somewhere on the front, and for *l'américaine* who had shown them kindness. She prayed that this farmer would do the same.

Ondine awoke when the wagon lurched to a stop. Sleet pelted the bonnet of the wagon. The biting air caused her to tremble and clench her chattering teeth. She shook Michel and handed him the rest of the bread they had started to eat before their stomachs revolted. Within moments, a bright light blinded them.

———

SAN FRANCISCO, CALIFORNIA

Sara Thibault Lemieux sat at the carved mahogany vanity table in Marie and Matthew Donnelly's guest room. Roses twined across the wallpaper, and draperies spilled into pools of silk on the carpets. Sara appraised herself in the mirror. Strands of silver streaked her chestnut hair and her waist had thickened just enough so she could pinch a healthy inch or two. Her fingers were long and lean, but the skin that covered her hands reminded Sara of a dragonfly's diaphanous wing. She slathered on some lanolin cream but doubted its efficacy. She was not sure when a thief had filched her youth and sketched dainty lines around the corners of her eyes and lips, but at least her cheeks remained smooth and supple. Almost forty years old, she was a vintner and mother of four, but she was powerless to ignore the gnawing, hollow sensation in her gut.

She glanced at the palm-sized photograph propped against the jar of cream: Luc at seventeen, before he left for France, just weeks before France declared war on Germany. Dark, cropped hair framed his face. His midnight gaze, dimpled chin and full shoulders lent him a determined, if not overconfident, air. Three and a half years was such a long time in the life of a young man. Sara ached to see him again, to hear his throaty laughter, to warn him as young men must be warned—repeatedly.

According to Luc's letters, the Saint Martin vineyard was thriving under his stewardship, but the Germans were advancing into France faster than anyone had imagined, and she feared it might not be long until they seized Paris—and finally the Loire. What would happen to Luc or her mother and Jacques? Or to Adeline and Matthew Donnelly as they cast off for their journey across the Atlantic to the front lines? The world was spinning off its axis, frenzied with war.

The deep timbre of her husband's voice jolted Sara back to the present. "Sara, it's time." He leaned against the doorjamb. Grey flecked his sideburns, but sandy hair swept over his forehead, belying his forty-eight years. Despite his bitter disappointment at being too old to serve in the regular army, Philippe had rallied the family and insisted they take the ferry over to San Francisco, to bolster the Donnelly family before Marie and Matthew's daughter Adeline set sail for France with the University of California's Base Hospital No. 30 the day after Christmas. Matthew Donnelly would follow in two months' time.

Philippe knelt behind Sara, squeezed her waist and make a silly face in the mirror. Sara laughed at her own severity. A pleasant aroma of mint and spiced cologne wafted from his skin, lifting Sara's spirits. They had been married for twenty years now, and Philippe knew better than to try to cheer Sara with trite platitudes.

"Are the children downstairs? Where's Pippa?" It was a question she asked regularly, for her stepdaughter often whiled away the winter days drawing, painting or reading in solitude.

"All are seated at the table, with scrubbed faces, dressed suitably and waiting for their tardy Maman." She jabbed him in the side before they hurried down the curving staircase and into the dining room. Thick red velvet ribbon and boughs of evergreen curled around the railings from top to bottom, and the fresh, sweet scent of pine needles streamed through the hall. The Christmas tree nearly brushed the vaulted ceiling. Gold and silver ornaments from the family's travels festooned its branches and, at its peak, a Victorian angel spread her arms and wings wide. In the dining room, a crystal chandelier's incandescent bulbs bathed the table and its occupants in soft light. Sara's throat constricted. This could be Adeline and Matthew's last Christmas at home for a long while.

The two families had bartered with shopkeepers to serve a meal that Adeline would savor. Despite the Donnellys' family wealth and their Queen Anne–style turreted home on Nob Hill, they still observed meatless Tuesdays and wheatless Wednesdays like every other American family who saved food for the boys fighting in the Great War. This Christmas, poultry in a cream sauce, potatoes, carrots, green beans and bread hot from the warmer accompanied tangy melted butter and a 1915 chardonnay crafted by Sara and Philippe at their Eagle's Run vineyard.

Sara and Marie had forged a sisterly friendship over the past twenty-one years and, in that time, even when they all thought Matthew might be lost in the earthquake of 1906, Sara had never witnessed Marie in such a frantic state. Her puffy eyes and red-mottled complexion revealed the fear only a mother could understand. Earlier in the day, at Christmas Mass, Marie had excused herself after Communion. Sara followed her out to the narthex, where Marie spilled her grief into the folds of Sara's handkerchief. This is what it was to be a mother. For decades, you throw all your energy, all your hope, into caring for your children, but time and circumstance always snatch them away—sometimes forever.

In the case of Adeline and Luc, they would be living in a war-ravaged country with a new set of rules for survival. Had Marie and Sara aptly prepared them?

Marie and Matthew sat at the table's head, a trio of stained-glass windows behind them, with Adeline to Marie's right. Adeline had always been a petite beauty like Marie, with eyes as ripe and round as chestnuts and brunette curls that framed rosy cheeks. She was the smaller, more contemplative counterpart of her half brother, Luc. The two shared a father—Philippe's deceased brother, Bastien—whom Marie and Sara tried hard to forget.

Around the table, Marie's other daughter, Gemma, and son, Rourke, both took after Matthew with fair, Irish skin and hair, light blue eyes and a penchant for mischief. Even on this solemn evening, the two were giggling with Sara and Philippe's two youngest, Johnny and Lydia.

"The front pages of the *Chronicle* are all about the war, but the back pages are all about the Dry forces. Do you have any news?" Matthew squeezed Marie's hand while he sipped his chardonnay.

"They want to institute a wartime prohibition, and I'm fairly certain they'll succeed," Philippe replied.

Aurora, a longtime friend to both families and a grape-farming expert, chimed in. "And if they do, they will decimate the state's grape trade and cripple its economy."

Matthew gaped. "It is ridiculous that the state of California would place its entire wine industry at risk and eliminate so many jobs."

"Around these parts, it's not the winemakers they oppose as much as the Sonoma Highway saloons and houses of ill-repute they want to shut down." Philippe stabbed his roasted potatoes. "The vineyards are disappearing, replaced with hundreds of thousands of prune trees and acres of currants."

"What does that mean for Eagle's Run?" Marie asked.

In the past year, the prices for the 1916 vintage had soared and they'd sold every bottle and barrel before they even began the fall 1917 harvest, which was twice the tonnage. With the income, they had been able to pay off the mortgage on the winery.

"We now have to decide if we stay the course and continue to harvest grapes, or if we rip them out and start over with a new crop."

"What about the income from the orchard and your contract with the archdiocese for sacramental wine? Surely that would keep you until a prohibition is over?"

"Perhaps, but who knows how long it could last?" Sara said. She was no stranger to the shifting sands of the wine industry. Even the California Wine Association was selling off its assets, a clear signal that prohibition legislation was inevitable.

Philippe had already lost a large part of their contract with the archdiocese many years ago, and the orchard income wasn't extensive enough to provide for the four of them and their cellar man. And what about Luc? They might need to send him some cash if the war didn't end soon and he remained unable to export his Saint Martin wines.

Philippe waved away their concerns. "Don't worry, we'll sort it all out. Now Adeline, tell us, did the army give you any details about your trip? Will you be traveling with your fellow nurses?"

She seemed startled to be asked such a direct question but recovered quickly. "I sail from Fort Mason tomorrow with the nurses of the 30th. We'll sail through the Panama Canal and up to New York. I believe the journey takes about six days. In New York, we'll train and prepare until the medical and dental officers join us. Then we'll all set sail in April for Brest, France."

"Brest?" Philippe asked. "Not Saint-Nazaire, where our troops arrived in June? Brest is so far north. Where do you go after that?"

"We have been assigned to Royat-les-Bains, isn't that right, Papa?"

Matthew's expression brightened. "Exactly. I've been assigned to Surgical Team No. 51 and Adeline will be working with Surgical Team No. 50 at the same base hospital."

No one would dare mention it, and perhaps Adeline was blissfully unaware, but one of the riskiest parts of this whole endeavor was the week's journey across the Atlantic, where German U-boats lurked, waiting to torpedo passenger ships, as they had the *Lusitania.*

"I do hope we're able to work together, don't you, Papa?" Adeline's expression cheered.

"Absolutely. We make a great team, don't we, *ma petite fleur?*" Even if his accent was atrocious, Sara loved Matthew for the way he attempted to speak his wife and adopted daughter's first language and the way he cared for Adeline as if she were blood kin. Sara tried to do the same for Pippa.

"And Tante Sara, if I have a day or two off, I hope to visit Luc and the family in Vouvray." Adeline lifted the last piece of meat off her plate. Marie heaped on more chicken and potatoes, as if it were her daughter's last meal.

"Royat? Isn't that where the thermal springs are?" Sara inquired. Adeline nodded. Sara did not want to disappoint her, but Vouvray was hundreds of kilometers northwest of Royat. "He would be delighted, I am sure!"

"Has Luc joined up yet?" Matthew inquired.

If Philippe had his way, their adopted son would be charging at the Germans with his Springfield rifle. *Men.* How could they be so shortsighted, so hungry for glory? Their false sense of duty distracted them from any sense of self-preservation.

"According to his letters," Philippe replied, "he has begged to enlist, but they have turned him away. They need his knowledge of Tours and his friendships to procure supplies and billets for the soldiers. He's of more use to them now as a local wine man, apparently."

"So, wine sales have rebounded?"

"Not exactly, but the army is moving their supply depot to Tours and Luc is selling them his excess inventory of chenin blanc," Sara chimed in.

"Wine production has dropped since the war started. Luc has no exports anymore—all his wine goes to the French and American armies now," Philippe added.

"Uncle Jacques and Maman are in good health, still helping with the harvest and feeding the soldiers that come through," Sara said.

"They have kept Saint Martin up and running for the past twenty years, haven't they?" Matthew asked.

Sara nodded. Her mother had married Marie's uncle, Jacques Chevreau, after Sara's father had died in a mudslide in 1895. Sara, with the help of Philippe, Jacques and Maman, had kept her father's vineyard and legacy alive for Luc.

Now, Sara was helpless to control the fates of Luc, Adeline and Matthew, and prayer was far too passive an endeavor for a woman who rose at six and worked until suppertime. Since Luc had left, she had squirreled away enough cash for the family to travel to France and back. With the German U-boat attacks on passenger ships and the war in France, it was too dangerous to make the crossing now. She would bide her time, because she knew that someday soon, the Americans would use all their might to defeat the Boches and make the seas safe for travel again.

Aurora Thierry, a dear friend of both families who celebrated with them this evening, marked every occasion with a toast. She clinked her glass with her fork and a hush fell over the table.

"Aren't we all so fortunate that in the midst of a great war, we can come together to celebrate our Savior's birthday?" She raised her glass. "Here's to Adeline and Matthew, who will soon be healing our boys who have sacrificed so much in the name of freedom."

"*À votre santé!*" they chimed in unison. Amid this bittersweet cheer, a small projectile flew across the table and hit Adeline. Her eyebrows scrunched together, and she rubbed her forehead. Rourke held something in his lap and Sara's son Johnny shook with silent laughter. The silver bowl of cocktail nuts had somehow walked its way over to the boys' side of the table.

Sara flashed Johnny a stern look, but by then, Rourke had already launched an attack on his other sister, Gemma, catapulting a spoonful of shelled nuts in her direction. Gemma did not bat an eyelash before chucking a dinner roll so hard it left a pink blotch where it smacked Rourke's cheek. Adeline also whipped a roll with considerable spin, hitting Johnny square in the jaw.

"Matthew!" Marie nudged her husband. But both Matthew and Philippe were laughing too hard to say anything. Marie threw up her hands in exasperation.

After the kitchen staff cleared the table and everyone had complimented the cook on the hearty meal, Matthew turned to Pippa. She had remained quiet throughout the meal, which was not unusual. Sara's adopted daughter rarely smiled. As she had once confided in Sara, she thought her smile was freakish and lopsided, a result of the scar from her cleft lip surgery long ago.

"Pippa, my dear, I think this would be the perfect time for your presentation of gifts," Matthew urged. The corners of Pippa's mouth tugged into a grin. She quickly hid it from view behind her hand, but Sara didn't care, for this smile swirled up to brighten Pippa's blue eyes. She was stunning, with a sheet of fuss-free blond hair and skin as smooth as a porcelain doll's.

"What's this?" All at the table murmured in surprise.

With a conspiratorial glance at Matthew, Pippa walked to the sideboard and removed four postcard-sized gifts wrapped in brown paper and scarlet ribbon. She handed one each to Matthew, Adeline and Marie, and one to Gemma and Rourke to share.

Pippa's cheeks burned crimson. "Portraits."

Marie unwrapped the covering to reveal an ink sketch of Adeline and Matthew. Gemma and Rourke received a similar rendering. Matthew and Adeline's parchments displayed a sketch of Marie, Gemma and Rourke. Sara marveled at Pippa's talent and precision. Since her surgery at age four, Pippa had studied people's faces with an almost intrusive obsession. She had started drawing as soon as she could hold a pencil and always carried one with her, slipped into her bun, behind her ear or in her sash.

Marie rushed over to Pippa and swept her into an embrace. When it was time for Adeline to offer her thanks, she squeezed Pippa so tightly, Sara thought she might suffocate her. Her heart faltered, skipping a beat. Adeline and Pippa had always been close confidantes, despite their nearly seven-year age difference. What would Pippa do without her?

———

Adeline stared at the ceiling in her bedroom, clasping Pippa's treasured gift to her chest. The carefully rendered sketch of her family members captured the uniqueness of each: the twinkle of mischief in Rourke's eyes, the sweep of Maman's hair that hid the scar at her scalp, the posies held by rose-lipped Gemma, Papa's wide grin, only partially hidden by his fashionable mustache.

The cast-iron radiator clanked, warming the night socks she had draped over its ornate scrollwork, and reminding her of the comforts of home she would have to forgo in France. Fear of the unknown welled in her belly, but she shoved it down. It was an honor to serve with the men and women of Base Hospital No. 30.

There was a soft rap at the door. "Addie," Maman called.

"Yes?" Adeline opened the door. The lilac scent of her mother's perfume triggered a flood of memories. She wanted to cry but instead bit her lower lip.

Adeline's arms wrapped around her mother's small frame. Her fingertips memorized the texture of the rich silk brocade dress, her face nuzzled into the familiar, springy nest of hair, her heartbeats fell into time with Maman's. For the first eleven years of Adeline's life, it had been just the two of them. Maman had risen from an unwed, pregnant eighteen-year-old, spurned by her lover, to a mother and midwife in the slums of New York's Lower East Side, and then on to become one of California's first female surgeons. Though now married to a fellow surgeon and heir to the Donnelly iron fortune, Marie Chevreau Donnelly was still the daughter of Pip and Mim Chevreau, humble tavern owners in Tours.

Maman used her thumbs to wipe Adeline's tears away. Her own eyes glistened as she sat on the bed, pulling Adeline toward her. Holding her hand, her gaze trained on the bedspread, Maman began.

"You know how proud we are of you. I have no doubt you will be a great success. Conditions will be much worse than they are here in our hospital. You will see many die, but you cannot take it to heart. Your job is to save the lives you can, and help the others breathe easier during the time they have left." She lifted Adeline's chin with her fingertips and looked her in the eye. "You must eat and walk in the fresh air, even if it's for five minutes a day, understand?"

Adeline nodded. She was almost twenty-seven, but her mother insisted on treating her like a child. Maman pressed a wooden crucifix into her hand, threaded on a sparkling gold chain.

"But this is your favorite—the one Uncle Jacques carved for you!"

"Indeed, and just as it protected me on my journey to America so many years ago, so it will protect you on your voyage to France."

How could she summon the courage to leave? Adeline's desire to stay bloomed like a flowering, fragrant garden in her chest, edging out any notion of patriotism.

Maman squeezed Adeline's hand. "And you must let the memory of Jess go. He would want you to find happiness, in your work, or with a new fellow." Three years ago, Jess Sumter, the young man who worked for Sara and Philippe and was stepping out with Adeline, had been struck and killed by a truck on Main Street in Napa. Since then, Adeline had thrown herself into her nursing work, demanding to assist with more and more challenging surgeries, like amputations and abdominal procedures, working herself to the bone.

What no one suspected was that Adeline did not miss Jess. Her regret, her sadness, persisted not from grief, but from guilt. She had quietly broken with Jess two days before the accident. He was distraught and distracted and not looking when he walked in front of the truck.

She missed the idea of Jess—the companionship and the laughter—but not the tongue-lashings or bruised triceps when he threatened her.

"Yes, Maman, I *have* let him go." Now she had a chance to serve her country, to make amends.

Mother and daughter sat on the edge of the bed, clasping hands. Adeline wanted to ask her one last time about her blood father, but Maman's moist eyes and slumped shoulders revealed a sentiment so sharp, Adeline could not bear to distress her further.

She had not visited France since she was a child, fourteen years ago. This time, she would discover the truth about her father. According to her mother, Bastien Lemieux had been a roué who had abandoned Marie and tortured Luc's mother and Sara's sister, Lydia, until Sara killed him in defense of her own virtue. If this man's—this rapist's—bad blood coursed through her veins, shouldn't she try to learn more about him?

How much did her half brother Luc know about their father—or care?

CHAMPAGNE, FRANCE

Leutnant Heinrich Sommer fingered the envelope perched on his ribcage. His bent arm served as his pillow, a straw pallet as his bed. Around him, the other officers of the Kaiser's 231st Division medical corps rustled and snored, rising only to relieve themselves in the narrow, subterranean river that served as their urinal.

The dank, musty air of the chalky limestone cave streamed into his lungs, spurring a phlegmy cough. A thin army blanket was no barrier against the chill that permeated his bones.

Heinrich counted eleven months and nine days since he had reported to Zossen Camp near Berlin from medical school in Köln. Anna had not sent any letters or drawings from Werner since June, when she had given a miserable account of ration lines and rice bags filled with bugs. Heinrich had delighted in the crayon sketch of flowers and bumblebees, drawn in his son's shaky four-year-old hand, just before the French attacked on the eighteenth near Nauroy, sending bayonets and helmets and arms and legs flying.

The envelope on his chest was crinkled and smudged with dirt, but still sealed. The scrawling script revealed it had been hastily addressed, not what a soldier would expect from his wife at *Weihnachtszeit*, when one anticipated the small kindnesses of the season: chocolates, lebkuchen, or perhaps some gloves or a few packs of the coveted Salem Aleikum smokes for bartering.

Heinrich pressed his palm against Anna's letter. He remembered his last Christmas in Köln: the ornate spires of the Gothic cathedral, a thousand candles forming a brilliant halo on the altar, the easy weight of Werner as he wriggled in his father's arms,

Anna's soft moans as Heinrich had made love to her on freshly laundered sheets.

He would linger with these memories for just a while longer—until he mustered the courage to read Anna's note.

CHAPTER 3

December 25–26, 1917

VOUVRAY, FRANCE

L uc had expected to find them gone this Christmas morn, but the boy and girl were curled up together in quilts, asleep in front of the fire's dying embers. He stacked four logs and poked the kindling until the flames blazed and the adolescents stirred.

They had fallen asleep the night before, reluctant to share their names. Luc squatted down next to the boy, and with the promise of more food, gently coaxed information from him. His name was Michel. His sister's name was Ondine. The girl did not speak, but the silent bow of her head revealed a deeply lodged sorrow. They were from Lille, a town in occupied northern France, close to Belgium.

Grandmère set plates of bread, pots of strawberry jam and honey and three mugs of hot chicory on the table. Before turning to prepare a Christmas breakfast for the two soldiers in their keep, she encouraged the children. "Best eat while the bread's hot, *mes petits*. You must build your strength for a thorough washing today. Then we'll fix up a proper room for you," she added with a quick, commanding glance at Luc. He abandoned any notion of returning them to Tours. Luc might own Saint Martin, but Grandmère still ran the roost.

Luc drew out a chair, to which Michel guided his sister and then took a seat across from his host. The pair scratched their scalps and necks intermittently. The azure blue of Ondine's eyes was striking, but it was the communion of her heart-shaped face, pale blond hair and brows, cavernous cheeks and cracked lips that unnerved Luc. Arms crossed, she cradled an elbow in each palm and clamped her mouth shut.

Luc glanced at the boy. "How old are you?"

"Fourteen. Ondine is seventeen."

"How did you arrive here?"

"We stowed away in your wagon, sir."

Luc smirked. "Yes, I know. I mean how did you travel this far from Lille?"

The boy shifted in his chair and bit his thumbnail until the cuticle started to bleed. With a long glance at Ondine, Michel stuttered, "The Boches b-b-bayoneted Mère." Ondine's fingers trembled as she reached for Michel's hand.

"Père is at the front," he continued. "We haven't received a letter in months. The Boches sent us away on trains—the women and children. We didn't know where they were sending us. We escaped when the train derailed outside of Paris."

"So why didn't you stay near Paris? Why did you travel this far south?"

The boy cocked his head, as if he thought Luc might be daft. "Everyone knows the Germans will reach Paris by spring." He squeezed Ondine's hand. "The Americans. The Americans are in Tours and the Germans aren't. The Americans are the hope of France," he announced, blazing with patriotism.

Luc could not disagree. The spindles of his chair creaked in protest as he leaned back.

"What is your father's name?"

Michel straightened and puffed out his chest. "Capitaine Pierre François Marchand."

"An officer?" Luc asked in surprise.

"Yes."

"What division?"

Michel shrugged. Ondine's head lifted, as if she wanted to speak.

"He's at the front?"

"We believe so."

Grandmère hovered behind Ondine. "We are so sorry that you lost your mother. She must be an angel now, to guide you two this far, to us. You're safe now. Eat, eat." Michel slathered jam on two pieces of bread and handed one to Ondine. She seemed to be in a trance. Was she slow in the head?

Luc knew his grandmother was right, inviting the children to stay, but she should have consulted him first.

"Do you have any family south of Paris?" he persisted.

"Not that we know of, sir."

33

His better angel—along with a withering glance from his grandmother—reminded him that if it had not been for the generosity of the Sisters of Notre Dame in New York, he might have died, alongside his mother, shortly after his birth. He raked a hand through his hair and met his grandmother's challenge. "You can stay here and earn your keep—until we find your father. I'll make inquiries the next time I'm in Tours."

Ondine pressed her palms together and lifted her face. Her expression of hope and gratitude was almost too much for Luc to bear. He cleared his throat, ashamed that he could have even thought of turning away these two. Humanity was another casualty of war.

"Jacques, these two have traveled all the way from Lille to Vouvray. Wouldn't you say that makes them exceptionally brave?" Grandmère asked. When Michel puffed out his chest, Luc stifled a laugh.

Jacques, who had slipped in from collecting firewood, replied robustly, "Indeed, indeed." He grasped Michel's wrist and extended the boy's arm to reveal scaly, pink splotches. "Lice?"

The boy's cheeks flamed red and he nodded. "You too?" Jacques gently inquired of Ondine.

"Ondine, too. We all had it, that's why the Germans sent us away. Some got worse, like tu-tu-tuber-cu-losis."

"That's what we soldiers must endure, son. I was afflicted with the same critters when I was fighting the Prussians in '71."

"You fought the Germans in '71?"

"Yes—and now is our chance to take back Alsace-Lorraine and restore the Republic."

Michel nodded solemnly. Jacques whispered something to Grandmère and said, "Madame Chevreau will wash you down while Luc and I tend to the soldiers. Then we'll meet back here for a proper Christmas dinner."

———

Luc and Jacques served the two *poilus* hard-boiled eggs, bread and jam, along with hot chicory and tea in the set of rooms carved out of tufa rock behind the main house. The creamy white limestone extracted from these caves had built the elegant *châteaux* and cathedrals in this Valley of the Kings. The Thibault-Lemieux family now used the caves to house its wine—and guests.

The four men sat at the small table by the hearth, fire burning high and bright, and wished each other a *Joyeux Noël*. The soldiers ate hastily, eager to board the only boat this day that would take them the 130 kilometers or so down the Loire to their families in Angers.

"How long have you two been in the fight?" Luc asked.

The lieutenants, dressed in their sky-blue uniforms with regimental patches, exchanged a glance. Renauld, a big-boned man with a barrel-sized chin, replied, "Since 1914. Last year at this time, we were up to our necks in the blood-soaked mud of the Somme."

"Swept right over the first German line," the skinny, clerkly one named Curley added, using a ragged nail to pick a thread of meat from his incisor.

"Remember how we came through the fog and captured the German machine gunners? As soon as they saw us, they waved their hands frantically and started shouting, '*Kamerad! Kamerad!*'" Renauld exclaimed with an exaggerated German accent. "They couldn't wait to surrender!"

Jacques shook with laughter.

"And tell them about the tanks, Renauld."

"Tanks?" Jacques's face lit up as he leaned forward. "You saw them?"

"The Mark tank. First time it was used in battle." Renauld spread his arms as wide as a pterodactyl's. "This thing was a giant rhombus rolling over barbed wire, trenches, through machine-gun fire, everything. Even had wire mesh on top to deflect grenades."

Curley elbowed his friend. "Tell 'em about Combles!"

"The one that got stuck?"

Curley nodded, his jaw slack with anticipation.

"Before it got stuck in the middle of a field, it helped take Combles, squashing all the Germans in its path."

"And then?" Luc asked.

"Broke down on its way back." Renauld had shoulders the size of fieldstones that tensed and released unconsciously while he spoke. "The English tried to rescue the crew, but the Germans surrounded them first. Poor bastards decided to set their own gas tank on fire. Flames jutted out the armor slits and black smoke billowed from the machine."

Curley's nose wrinkled in disgust. "All you could smell was the roasting flesh."

Jacques's head dipped.

"What fools!" Luc cried.

Renauld's body snapped into a tight, straight line. "Some might call them heroes. They saved the biggest military secret of the Allies, they did."

"While killing themselves and destroying their families' lives," Luc retorted.

Luc caught a whiff of tobacco and onions on Renauld's breath as he leaned toward him. "A shirker like you shouldn't judge the actions of the men fighting to save our country and your property, while you—what? Pick grapes and make wine?" he scoffed.

The heat of embarrassment crawled from Luc's chest to his neck and prickled his cheeks. "Forgive me, gentlemen. We are grateful for your bravery."

Renauld punched him in the shoulder. "Grateful, but not man enough to fight beside us, *n'est-ce pas?*"

Jacques rose to his feet. "Luc didn't mean any disrespect. We'll wait outside while you finish your breakfast in peace. We'll take you down to the dock in ten minutes."

After bidding the soldiers *adieu* and *bonne chance* at the nearby river dock, Luc and Jacques trudged back to the house through the fields and grapevines. The grapes slept; the new buds would not break until early April.

"The Americans turned me down again," Luc confided.

Jacques picked up a fallen tree limb, snapped off its branches and employed it as a walking stick to steady his gait as he maneuvered the gradual incline to the house. "They'll come to their senses eventually. Instead of thinking about what you need, think about what *they* need. They're trying to mobilize an entire army— millions of soldiers, nurses, physicians, horses and mules. How are they going to deliver all those supplies to the front lines? Who's going to do it for them? Someone who knows the roads and speaks fluent French could be very useful in that capacity, don't you think?"

With a bad back and failing sight, Jacques was too impaired to work outside of Saint Martin, but Luc could always count on him to deliver his own succinct brand of wisdom.

"What about the harvest?" Luc asked.

Jacques stopped short. "I've been harvesting those grapes since your mother was a mite, and though I'm no spring chicken, now I have Michel and Ondine to lend a hand."

Luc hesitated before asking his last question. He knew Jacques would be unflinchingly honest, for he had fought the Prussians and lost, and still carried the invisible scars. "Do you think I'm ready?" Luc ventured.

Jacques grimaced. "Wrong question. No one is ever ready to go to war. The question you should ask yourself is: Are you willing to trade your life for liberty—to win freedom for the generations of French men and women who will come after you?"

The idea of a higher purpose energized Luc but also dashed any illusion of his own invincibility. What if, in war, God ripped out all the remaining chapters from his book of days? Would his last weeks on earth be weighty enough to take the place of all his future promise?

He choked back all doubt and seized the audacity of youth. "I am."

Jacques clapped him on the shoulder. "Then you're as ready as anyone, son."

Once Michel finished bathing, Madame seated him in front of the hearth. He looked like a newborn swaddled in an oversized blanket. The cowlicks in his shaggy hair swirled and stuck upright at the crown of his head, lending him an impish air. He glanced up at Madame with the gratitude of a puppy. Satisfaction welled within Ondine: she had delivered Michel to a safe place where he would be cared for.

Madame instructed him, "Stay here. I'll be right back to comb out and trim your hair, young man." Perhaps it was her brisk tone or her aging skin, which reminded Ondine of a wrinkly rind of goat cheese, but Madame wielded more authority over her brother than Ondine had ever hoped to have. She was relieved to have someone else serve as Michel's mother for a day.

To Ondine's surprise and delight, Madame emptied most of the sullied water from Michel's bath onto the flowerbeds outside and refreshed the tub with several pots of hot water heated on the cookstove. Holding the buckets of steaming water, she hastened down the hallway, her thickly pleated wool skirts swishing back and forth. Ondine recognized the sturdiness of a woman who had worked the land and hearth in equal measures.

Ondine stood in the bedroom, the metal tub and fireplace at one end, the bed and dressers at the other. A photograph of a bride graced the bedside table, its silver frame glistening in the sunlight that flowed through the leaded glass panes of the room's only window. Ondine stole a closer look. The bride had perfect skin, curled wisps of hair at her temples, a bouquet of wildflowers clasped in her hands. She possessed Madame's fair skin, light eyes and long fingers, but this was not a younger Madame. The plain white dress and lace veil were stunning but outdated, so the wedding could not have been a recent affair. *Who was this girl?*

Madame returned with two more buckets of hot water, which she dumped into the tub. Ondine wanted to help but, again, struggled to speak the words required. Madame handed her a cake of soap, a square cloth and a wool blanket. She instructed Ondine to disrobe, throw her clothes and kerchief into the flames, and then bathe, giving her body and hair a thorough scrubbing. Ondine's spirits buoyed unexpectedly at the suggestion that she should burn the clothes she had been wearing for over a week. Before she left, Madame added another log to the fireplace and poked the stacked wood until it blazed. With a curt nod to the tub, Madame closed the door.

Grateful that she was allowed privacy, Ondine dipped a toe, then a leg, then slid her entire body beneath the surface of the steamy water. Pinching her nose shut, Ondine concentrated on the gentle motion of the water caressing her earlobes and massaging the pads of her sore feet. What if she were to breathe the liquid in and let it fill her lungs like a water balloon? Would they burst?

She popped her head above the surface, sputtering like a fish. The heat seeped into her knotted muscles, slowly teasing them apart. This was the first time she had been able to properly wash since—since they had left Lille—and Ondine decided she would treat her bath with the reverence of a baptism or a spiritual cleansing if that were possible. Could a simple bath exorcise the demons that now dwelled inside her?

Ondine dunked the soapy cloth and moved it gently against the scabbed streaks on her thighs. As she carefully washed her intimate parts, her face flushed with humiliation. Though the soreness of her bruises down there was a memory now, it was a vicious memory, one that shredded her insides with panic, stealing away the calmness that she had been able to summon in her younger years, when her mother was alive and her father was home and there were no Germans in Lille.

Ondine moved the sudsy cloth to the unscathed parts of her body, down her arms and between her toes. She recalled how she would shriek mock protestations when Mère tickled the tender skin between her toes, how she would giggle until she cried, and how her insides had felt like warm butter.

An abrupt knock on the door interrupted Ondine's musings. Without expecting a reply, Madame swept into the room. "Carry on, my dear," she said, diverting her gaze to the other side of the room. "I am just searching for something to dress you in." She paid no mind to Ondine's hunched figure and rummaged through a trunk near the bed's footboard. "This should do nicely," she announced, shaking out a blue wool frock. "Though it may need hemming. Sara is probably a good ten centimeters taller than you, my dear." She sniffed the fabric. "Smells a bit musty, but it will have to do until we can sew you a new dress." *A new dress?* She did not deserve this woman's kindness. She did not deserve any luxury at all.

———

Luc and Jacques burst through the kitchen door just as Ondine lowered herself cross-legged onto the floor beside Michel. Their jovial presence filled the small space, but the scrape of their boots against the slate entranceway set Ondine's teeth on edge. Madame chided them. "Boots off, boys!"

Ondine followed Monsieur Luc's movements as he shook out the snowflakes that clung to his thick, dark hair. Her own scalp still stung from the metal comb Madame Chevreau had raked through every strand of her hair, but it was the sort of pain she welcomed—the sort of pain that banished unwanted vermin and connected her to her body and allowed her to begin healing.

Monsieur Chevreau pecked Madame's cheek and stole a slice of bread from the sideboard. She shooed him away with a fuss. "Look what we have here," he said, drying his beard and hair with a kitchen towel. "You two clean up just fine," he observed.

Michel wore breeches, a collared shirt and a fisherman's knit sweater, and Ondine wore the blue dress, which hung loosely off her figure. The faint scent of mothballs hung in the air, soon to be overpowered by the sweet and spicy fragrance of mulled wine.

"Luc, bring in the old vines for burning, and Jacques, would you please dump the remaining bathwater?" Madame Chevreau asked, holding out a bucket. Michel stared at Madame as she spoke, as if the commanding yet pleasant lilt of her voice were just the elixir to slake his thirst. She placed a hessian sack overflowing with holly and white flowering dogwood on the sideboard. She spoke softly as she handled the flora. "I have lost a husband and a daughter—Lydia was her name. You may have seen her photograph in the bedroom." She glanced at them knowingly. "She was Luc's mother and died the day he was born."

Michel gulped. "We are sorry, madame. Did she die here with you?"

Ondine nudged Michel, flashing him a withering look. Madame answered simply, "No. She died in New York. I wasn't able to say goodbye." She continued her handiwork, but her shoulders curled inward and she sniffed. Madame snipped the ends of the branches with her gardening shears. "When I clipped these branches, they started to die. We will enjoy their beauty over the holiday, and then I'll have to toss them, with their wilting berries and flowers, into the compost pile." She arranged the sprigs of holly and dogwood, along with a few fragrant pine branches, in the center of the table. Ondine and Michel rose to admire the decorations. Madame continued, "But will these beauties meet their end in the compost pile? Of course not! They will return to the earth, where we all return one day, but their spirit—their essence and beauty and the memory we have of them—will never die. We will remember the pleasure they gave us long after they are gone from our home."

When the two men returned, the younger slid several gnarled branches on top of the fire. He beckoned Michel to his side and handed him a bottle of chenin blanc. "Will you do the honors, Michel?" Monsieur Luc's eyes twinkled with mischief.

"*M'sieu*? You want me to drink this before the meal?" Michel looked wary.

Luc laughed. "No! Sprinkle it on the grapevines in the fire and you'll ensure a strong harvest next year!"

Michel smiled, uncorked the bottle and doused the wood with wine. The fire flared, climbing far up the chimney.

Madame clapped her hands together. *"Voilà!"* she said. "Now, Luc and Michel, the birds are hanging in the scullery."

Luc cringed, and Michel laughed.

"Luc, you and Michel pluck them clean, then bring them to me," she ordered.

A recipe card fluttered between Madame's fingers. "Do you read and write?" she asked Ondine, who nodded. *Mais oui*, she thought, but the words did not follow. Her frustration must have shown. Madame squeezed her shoulder. "You have made a *bûche de Noël*? Perhaps with your mother?"

Ondine nodded and her eyes brimmed. The recent loss of Mère gutted her, for more reasons than Madame could guess, but Ondine liked that Madame talked about the dead. Talking about the dead brought them closer, more than a photograph ever could. Talking about the dead seemed to beckon their souls back to the realm of the living. While Ondine remembered Mère, chocolate frosting clinging to her fingertips and flour in her tendrils of hair that came loose from her sunny chignon, Madame ducked down and reached into the cupboards, passing the flour, sugar and chocolate to her new *sous chef*.

Ondine was so engrossed in making, baking and decorating the chocolate yule log cake, and cutting root vegetables for the main dish, that she forgot to think, forgot to grieve.

When Ondine bit into the savory, juicy poultry, warmth spread through her. The crusty bread with fresh butter and the canned beans were so delicious on her tongue she feared she might weep. *How can this half of France be untouched by war when her city was sacked and now controlled by the enemy? Was it simply bad luck?*

Michel said, quite like a young gentleman, "Thank you for welcoming us into your home." Under the table, Ondine tapped her foot against his leg. Michel quickly added, "We will work for our keep and help in any way we can."

Luc glanced at his grandmother and Jacques. Jacques nodded and Madame replied, "We appreciate that, and we expect you to stay until your father can be located."

A few sips of wine loosened Michel's tongue, and he did not stop talking until Ondine presented the *bûche de Noël*. Luc had bartered the sugar, flour and chocolate from the quarter-master's corporal last week in exchange for a case of chenin blanc. Ondine bowed her head, unable to meet his warm, dark gaze when he complimented her on her artistry. Madame explained how Ondine had used the tines of the fork to texture the frosting, so it looked like genuine tree bark. Mère had taught her. Robbed of her speech, Ondine nodded in thanks but fidgeted about, laying the knives and forks and fresh dessert plates on the table.

The conversation resumed, words swirled in the air, jests boomeranged between the two men, and compliments to the women on the cooking and the decorations abounded. The atmosphere was convivial. It was as if the household had been expecting them all along. Ondine worried how long it would take for her and Michel to outstay their welcome.

———

NAPA, CALIFORNIA

The day after Christmas, Sara rose early, eager to feed her family breakfast but reluctant to begin cleaning the winery equipment in preparation for the January racking. She knew that all their efforts could be in vain. They could rack the wines and prune the vines this winter and even pick the grapes this fall for the 1918 vintage, but if a prohibition were passed, they wouldn't be able to make or sell any wine.

The 1917 vintage had finished fermenting and soon *soutirage* would begin. Sara and Philippe and their cellar man, Mac Cuddy, would rack the reds several times. This fining process of drawing the wine off the lees several times each winter clarified it, softened the tannins and rounded out the taste. *Cabernet sauvignon* was one of their bestselling reds and was in high demand at the San Francisco hotels. What would happen to their finances if a prohibition dried up demand?

Sara stacked griddlecakes on the table. Lydia and Johnny bounced into the kitchen, gleefully ravenous, while Pippa glided in, dressed in her field boots and work dress, scanning the pages of a book.

Philippe's voice boomed upstairs. "Johnny, I almost tripped over Fred." He appeared with Johnny's copper tabby in one hand. "You must let him out in the mornings," he reprimanded as he released the feline onto the floor and nudged him gently toward the door.

"Good morning." Philippe greeted Sara with a kiss on the cheek.

Neither the clanking of silverware nor the sweet smell of syrup seemed to stir Pippa's appetite. While the others chewed their hotcakes and gulped their coffee and juice, Pippa's nose stayed wedged between the pages of her book. "No books at the table, Pippa," Philippe chided.

"Sorry, Papa," she replied. He took the text and handed her a full plate. "Thank you for breakfast, Maman."

"Tomorrow morning it's your turn, Pippa," Sara reminded her.

"Oh yes, but this morning I simply couldn't release myself from da Vinci's genius! Do you know he wrote backwards, so one could only decipher his writing if it was held to a mirror? Or that *La Joconde* was never finished?"

She picked at her food while Lydia and Johnny finished and began bellyaching about the start of school in two days. "May we be excused?" Johnny flashed a grin at Lydia.

Philippe checked his pocket watch. "You have ten minutes until you need to start your chores," he replied. Their chairs shrieked against the floor as they rose to go. "Wait a second." He reached into his pocket and pulled out two large, shiny marbles. "Another small gift for you mibsters."

"Wow! A new shooter! Thanks, Pop!" Johnny bounded for the door, the heavy marble bag swaying in his pants pocket.

Lydia fingered the big, yellow-and-black-striped orb. "A bumblebee for me?" She wrapped her arms around Philippe and nestled her face and dark mop of curls into his neck. "Thank you, Papa," she trilled. Her lips curled into a sweet smile.

Philippe beamed and squeezed his youngest daughter. "Go have fun!"

Sara pulled her shawl tighter and cupped her hands around her warm mug, sipping her coffee, and secretly dreading the workday ahead. As she aged, her joints ached more, as if they required more oil, and she tired more quickly. She found it frustrating, yet she had to keep busy. Otherwise she would fritter away the hours worrying about Luc and Adeline.

Philippe and Pippa were deep in conversation. Sara hadn't heard a word. "What's this?" she asked.

"I was telling Papa that I would like to apply for a job in town. And earn a proper wage."

Philippe's expression darkened. Sara was wary, too. While she applauded Pippa's growing independence, she feared the worst.

"Where would you apply?" Philippe asked.

"At the Art Emporium—it's a new shop they've created in the back of Hudson's Dry Goods. They pay twenty-five cents per hour and I would receive a discount on my art supplies."

"How do you know all this? Have you already interviewed?"

Pippa swabbed her syrupy plate with the last square of pancake. She spoke softly, but deliberately. "I inquired."

"You could earn more working for us. What if we paid you?"

Pippa's fork clattered on her plate. "I just turned twenty years old. You can't keep me hidden forever."

"Is that what you think? How could you think that's our intention?" Philippe bristled.

Sara rested a hand on Pippa's shoulder and shot Philippe a warning glance. "I think Pippa is trying to say that she is an independent woman and would like us to treat her that way."

Pippa lifted her chin. Philippe stared at the two of them. "Next, she'll be wanting her own apartment in downtown Napa!"

Pippa's smile spread, sparking life in her dove-white skin and pert little nose. "Papa, don't be ridiculous! I just want a job is all." She laughed.

"You have a job, working with us in the family business."

"And I am so grateful for it. Picking and pruning grapes has strengthened my fingers." She wiggled ten dainty, ink-stained digits. "But I am an artist, Papa. I need to be around other artists if I'm going to improve."

Pippa was pouring on the charm as thick as the syrup on her hotcake, but Sara admired her pluck. Perhaps a job was just the boost of confidence she needed to break free of her shell.

Philippe tugged on his collar as if it were choking him. He stood and stacked his dishes. "How do you plan to make a living as an artist? This isn't the sixteenth or seventeenth century. No one is going to offer to be your patron and pay your way."

"I am talented and hardworking and willing to take small jobs here and there—like the one at the Art Emporium—while I create my portraits and landscapes and eventually sell them."

Sara interjected, "She has won every major art competition in the county since she was ten, Philippe. The girl is talented."

"Of course she is, but how . . ."

"Pippa, how many hours per week would they need you to work?" Sara asked.

Pippa perked up. "Thirty hours a week, Maman. Of course, in September and October, I'd work the night harvest and switch my store hours to the afternoons. And I would find time to riddle the bottles, or I could teach Lydia. She's old enough to take over and she would welcome the responsibility."

Sara knew Philippe could not toss up any other objections. After all, Pippa had finished her schooling three years ago, and short of taking art classes here and there, she was not interested in nursing or secretarial school. She had never been an enthusiastic student.

"I suppose you could try it for a time *if* they offer you the job." Pippa bit her lip and wriggled in her chair. "You already have the job?" he cried.

She shrugged. "I didn't see the point of working you into a lather for no good reason, Papa, so I interviewed and made sure I had the job first." She jumped up and pecked him on the cheek. "Thank you, Papa!" She patted Sara's head. "And you too, Maman, for helping me fight my corner!" she added before vanishing through the kitchen door.

Philippe crossed his arms, exhaling loudly. "What just happened?"

"I think you were bamboozled by your eldest daughter."

He chuckled. "I believe you're right." His tone grew serious. "But you know why I worry."

"I do, but when I was seventeen, I had to leave my home for a new country. When I was eighteen, my sister died, and I had to care for her newborn son and travel alone with him from New York to Napa! When I was twenty, I was already married to you."

"True, but Pippa is different."

Ire began to creep up Sara's neck. *Different because she has an awkward smile, or different because she was born of Philippe's mistress?* "She is a perfectly pretty girl with a slightly unbalanced smile. The customers will get used to it—it's part of Pippa's unique charm. Besides, in time, it will become like oxygen to her fire."

He leaned over and tucked a strand of hair behind her ear. "What on earth are you talking about?"

"These adversities will only fuel her potential."

A glance of sorrow flashed between them. Sara and Philippe knew of adversity: though she had saved her sister Lydia's life, and her own, her actions had cost Philippe his brother Bastien.

"Perhaps, but she's not as strong as you are." He stood up and began to clear the rest of the dishes.

"Not now, but she will be in time."

He bent over to kiss Sara. "I doubt *I* am strong enough for that."

"Have you thought any more about the vineyard?" she asked.

Philippe dropped back into his chair. "The rest of the county, hell, half of California, is ripping up their vineyards and replanting with currants and prunes. We should seriously consider doing the same."

"I think we should wait. At some point, either before or after prohibition, the demand for wine or wine grapes will spike, and so will prices. Do you really want to be stuck with acres of currants and prunes when that happens?"

"Sara, this is serious. The California Wine Association is already liquidating its assets and making grape juice. The Drys are gaining power. Who knows how long the prohibition will last once it starts? Every state in the nation where women can vote— except for California—has voted in favor of a prohibition! The Drys will just grow stronger when more women have the vote!"

51

Philippe was right, but there must be another way. They had worked too hard to make this vineyard and Saint Martin profitable, and now the Thibault-Lemieux wines—their chenin blancs and chardonnay and zinfandel and cabernet—were world-renowned for their quality. They had cultivated dedicated customers in San Francisco, New York, Chicago, New Orleans, Los Angeles and Atlanta. How could they give it all up now?

"Sara." He clasped her hands and lowered his voice. "We have to think of the future. We have to plant crops that will sell, so we can give our children what we had."

She recoiled. "What I *had* at seventeen was a beautiful home in Vouvray, and a father I adored—"

"Sara, don't," he commanded as his fingertips dug into her flesh.

"And a vineyard I was going to inherit—and your family stole it all!"

He released his grip on her. "And you took my brother's life in kind. I forgave you and returned Saint Martin to you and helped you raise Luc, our nephew—why do you still hold my family's crimes against me?"

He flashed her a look of disgust and walked out.

Sara's stomach churned. Why had she said that? Twenty years and she had never spoken of that horrible time in their lives. Despite it all, they had fallen in love, and forgiven each other, and made amends. Why did she choose this moment to attack him? They needed to band together.

Sara blew her nose, retied her hair, and wandered around the ranch until she found Philippe by their stillborn daughter's grave.

As she approached, he stiffened, hands on hips. He was still lean and muscular, although he had lost some of his bulk, but not his broad shoulders. His hands were calloused, but long and elegant, and she still craved the intimacy of his touch. She linked an arm through his and rested her head on his arm. "I'm sorry. I don't know what came over me except that I feel threatened, just like I did all those years ago. We are nearing the last chapter of our lives, and I won't accept defeat. I will not allow some irrational crowd of scaremongers to take our business and our income and everything we plan to leave to our children."

Philippe sighed. "We may not have a choice."

Sara's mind sifted through the random and sometimes inane ideas she had pondered but had kept to herself. "How much do you estimate it would cost to rip out the vines and replant with these other crops?" she asked.

"A few thousand dollars."

"Give me one month. One month to come up with a new plan that doesn't involve ripping out the vines. Then, if you don't like my ideas, we can come up with some sort of compromise."

"One month, but only because your ideas have saved the vineyard in the past." He pulled her into a bear hug that squeezed out her tension and renewed her excitement. "One month, but then we'll have to take action."

———

"Stop fidgeting, dearest," Pippa admonished her younger sister that evening. Lydia was her only hope for a sketch model. Lord knew Johnny was as restless as the wind. "Think of the Mary Janes

I'm going to give you as payment for your modeling services."
Pippa's gaze flashed to the yellow-and-red-wrapped rectangular
candies in the clay pinch pot she had sculpted and painted in
the fifth grade.

Poised on the trunk at the foot of her bed, Lydia bolted up
straight, clasped her hands in her lap, crossed her ankles and
smiled. "Don't tell Maman," she whispered through gritted
teeth.

"Our secret, of course. Just don't break a tooth!" Pippa moved
the side of the pencil lead in a circular motion, trying to convey
the bounce of Lydia's chocolate curls. Pippa estimated they had
only another half hour of good light filtering in, so she would
have to work quickly.

Lydia giggled, and her curls jiggled. She raised a hand to her
heart. "Promise."

"Relax your shoulders a tad, Bear," Pippa instructed, calling
her by the pet name Johnny had invented for their little sister.
He claimed it was because their baby sister had been soft like a
teddy bear, but Pippa believed it was due to Lydia's unyielding
baby's growl when agitated. Pippa dropped her own shoulders
to demonstrate. Lydia followed and her facial features loosened
as well. Fortunately, she had developed into a delightful child.

Now, at age eleven, Lydia was far from a bear, or a teddy
bear. She was taller than all the boys in her grade, and lanky like
Maman, with the same arresting sea-green eyes framed by delicate brow lines that arched at the slightest amusement. She was
named after Maman's sister, Lydia Thibault Lemieux. According
to Maman, the pair shared a mane of ringlets and a singular *joie*

de vivre. Pippa believed the similarity ended there, for Lydia's elongated face, hands and feet were all Maman's.

With short flicks of her pencil, Pippa sketched Lydia's mouth, taking care to boldly shade the full lower lip and barely shade the upper lip.

Lydia studied her sister just as intently. "Am I beautiful, Pippa? I mean, with my wild hair and all."

"You are more than just beautiful. You are intelligent. And your 'wild' hair isn't so wild, but the hallmark of an adventurous spirit," Pippa replied.

"Like your scar."

"My scar?" Pippa's cheeks flamed and her philtrum tingled. She bit her upper lip.

"Your scarline is a hallmark," Lydia clarified. "It defines you as a woman of substance. Otherwise, you would be too beautiful and that would not be fair to the rest of us."

Pippa raised an eyebrow. "Have you been reading Tante Aurora's *Ladies' Home Journal* again?"

Lydia shrugged. "I may have glanced at a page."

"Lydia!"

Lydia leaned forward and squinted. "Have you seen the latest taffeta day dresses? Mother-of-pearl, there's a war going on! Who is silly enough to ruffle around in taffeta or georgette crepe for that matter? I am a woman of economy. Plain old gingham with pockets suits me just fine, thank you."

Pippa stifled a laugh. "Quiet! I'm trying to sketch your lips."

"Sorry." Lydia gave her sister a chimp-like grin.

"That's too phony. Look over my shoulder, out the window,

and pretend you're gazing upon the loveliest, rainbow-colored bird you have ever seen."

"A rainbow-colored bird? Is there such a thing?" Lydia asked.

Pippa huffed. "No, but if there were, what would you feel upon seeing it?"

Lydia looked perplexed.

"Wonderment." Pippa tapped the paper with her knuckle. "Wonderment is the look I'm trying to draw here, okay?"

"Okay! Sheez." Lydia transformed her features into a childlike expression of surprise.

"Close enough," Pippa murmured. She fussed over the curve of Lydia's eyes, drawing and then erasing them several times. Her pencil marks did not yet capture the competing emotions Lydia held. She sighed in frustration.

Lydia perked up. "Don't be discouraged, Pippa. You'll come close, but you'll never be able to draw my eyes perfectly."

"Why not?"

With the dramatic air of Sarah Bernhardt, Lydia lifted her chin and gazed off into the distance. "Because eyes, as everyone knows, are the windows to the soul. The soul, by definition, is elusive and ethereal."

Pippa scooped up the stash of candies and chucked them at her sister, one by one. Lydia held up her hands to deflect them, then dropped to her knees, scrambling to pick them up. Pippa set aside her drawing pad and joined Lydia. She tickled her sister until Lydia begged for mercy, laughing and offering Pippa a Mary Jane if she would only stop.

———

FORT MASON, SAN FRANCISCO

Adeline strode up the gangplank, the last touches and scents and smiles of her family seared into her memory. For six months, she had been preparing to depart for war with the other sixty-four nurses of Base Hospital No. 30. In June, they had learned to march, salute and suck in their bellies while standing at attention. They had paraded up Market Street in their white uniforms, garnering quick support from their fellow San Franciscans, who would later send an unending stream of afghans, pillows, socks and supplies to their unit in Royat.

Since they had received their orders in November, the nurses had spent every weekday outfitting the hospital with the bandages, X-ray equipment, splints and surgical tools they would need. These women were her family for the duration of the war. Adeline clutched her knapsack close to her side, flipped her wide collar up and braced against the wind as she turned onto the deck. The nurses lined up, waving and cheering as the sailors cast off. The gigantic red, white and blue Stars and Stripes fluttering above their heads was the only streak of color against an iron sky.

The ship would dock at Ellis Island in six days. While the other nurses had been disappointed to learn of their temporary assignments to other Atlantic coast camps before they departed for France, Adeline clutched her orders with secret delight. She was assigned to pass the next few months at Rockefeller Hospital. She inhaled the crisp air and sighed. New York City was her hometown. She had grown up in a convent on the Lower East Side. Would she be able to find it? Would they remember her from her last visit?

CHAMPAGNE, FRANCE

Heinrich kept Anna's letter tucked in his pocket all Christmas Day. When the holiday had finally passed and daybreak called again, Heinrich rolled off his cot and walked to the cave entrance. He stood in a column of sunshine so warm and bright it made him squint. There, with only the mourning doves warbling in the nearby field of grass, he tore open Anna's letter.

Dear Husband,

You have been away nearly a year now, and I have been working all this time. You have only come home once on leave.

The new Pfennig benefits are laughable. I have only bread and cabbage to eat. The 30 Mark war benefit is not enough. One pound of bacon costs 9 Marks and a shirt 10.

This is the last letter I will write you, for I am marrying another man. This other man will provide for me. I will give your son to the orphanage, for who knows when you will be home again?

This is the best solution, for otherwise I should have to take our lives. Together we would all perish. Separately, we may have a chance to live, though a miserable existence it may be.

Anna

CHAPTER 4

New Year's Eve 1917–January 1918

VOUVRAY, FRANCE

Along with the ten hectares of grapes at Saint Martin and the renowned quality of its chenin blanc, Luc was most proud of the repairs he had made to the old dovecote in the back woods. When Maman had described the farm and property he was inheriting, she had not mentioned the hexagonal two-story structure, which stood only fifty paces from where Luc's grandfather and namesake, Luc Thibault, was buried.

Neither Grandmère nor Jacques knew much of it either, having spent all their time cultivating grapes and making wine; Grandmère assumed it had been built centuries ago, when an elegant but small château had stood on the property. An old ink sketch showed the rectangular stone edifice with two turrets and two outbuildings on either side. In the foreground, the members of the original aristocratic family stood, surrounded by pigeons in cages.

Luc now approached the pale yellow limestone structure with a ladder in one hand and three tin buckets strung over his left arm. When Luc had first inspected it, the *pigeonnier* roof, constructed of slate over a wooden frame, needed to be patched, and the interior required a thorough cleaning, new nesting pots and a new pair of shutters for the second-floor opening. The two oak doors needed a fresh coat of paint as well.

In town, he had sought out the local pigeon breeder, who came out to inspect the dovecote. Pigeon eggs and flesh provided food, of course, but the real benefit for a farmer like him was their dung. Their droppings could be collected, composted with soil and cut grass, and used to fertilize the soil around the vines.

He had finished all the repairs before his first bud break at Saint Martin in April 1915, in between pruning the vines and protecting them from frost. The hardest part had been locating one hundred small terra-cotta pots that he could slide into the original *boulins* in the *pigeonnier's* interior brick wall to provide nesting space for each pair of birds. Once he had found a supplier, he arranged the pots, stuffing each with a handful of straw. He purchased twelve pairs of birds to start.

After nearly three years, Luc's *pigeonnier* was overrun with fowl. As he scraped dung off the floor and into an empty bucket, he decided that, in addition to harvesting the eggs, it was time to use the bird flesh to feed the soldiers—and the family.

Dead leaves crunched beneath his boots and the buckets rattled as he trudged toward the main house. Everywhere he turned, beautiful, statuesque white birch trees swayed gently beneath the silver heavens. He guessed there would be snow by tomorrow morn, New Year's Day. As he passed his grandfather's headstone, he ran a hand over the textured top edge as his sign of respect. He reached the clearing that overlooked the house and vines.

Near the outdoor pump, Ondine stood like a statue, arm outstretched and lifted, looking toward the sky. Within moments, two chickadees fluttered down, rested on her hand and pecked. As soon as they flew away, the girl dug into her apron pocket and pulled out more seed. They came again, perched this time on her shoulder, her head, her thumb.

Luc approached her. "They like you," he encouraged with a grin.

The faint smile vanished. She dropped her head and gripped the handle of her bucket so fast its hinges squealed, splashing the water on the frozen ground. She hurried into the house without a word.

"Good morning to you, too," Luc mumbled. What was he doing here? He should be with people his own age—but they were off fighting the war. He sure as heck wasn't going to spend New Year's Eve playing card games or watching Grandmère quilt another square, bored out of his skull. He knew just the remedy.

It was eight o'clock when Luc drove up to Chevreau's tavern in Tours in the runabout he had purchased for the equivalent of $280 when Ford had first opened the factory in Bordeaux. He was saving up for a Peugeot Type 1525 truck to replace his mules and wagon. With ample space and usable load to transport his wine barrels, the truck remained a dream until the war was over.

Army jeeps littered the street outside the popular tavern. He could not yet wear a U.S. Army doughboy uniform, but he figured he could at least dress smartly in his trousers, white shirt, vest, sack coat and new derby.

Since the Americans had arrived, Chevreau's had become a favorite watering hole and Pip and Mim—Jacques's brother and sister-in-law—had even hired a band to play the blues, ragtime and that newfangled music from Louisiana called jazz. When Luc entered the establishment, he was swept away by the rhythms. With a wave from the bartender and a flurry of interest from the six Hello Girls who sat at a table, Luc instantly felt welcomed. Chevreau's tavern was a slice of America in war-frayed France.

The shadowy room smelled of sweat and stale beer, with an occasional burst of sweet berry wine or flowery perfume. He walked to the bar and ordered a brandy. In America, he would have ordered beer, but French beer wasn't nearly as well-crafted as French wine. This fact didn't seem to bother the Americans seated around him.

He sipped his drink and turned just in time to see Virginia Hunt approach. Her blond waves rippled across her forehead and she was wearing a bouncy white silk blouse—definitely not army regulation.

"Luc! Come join us! The girls want to thank you for the wine." She was never coy. She said what she meant, even if it lacked propriety. Luc found this refreshing. He followed Virginia back to her table.

Two of the women he had met before: Barbara, an attractive brunette, and Giselle, a knockout redhead. The other three were rather homely, but one named Gertrude had an infectious laugh, another called Gloria a razor-sharp wit, and the third, Sadie, had quite a talent for holding her liquor, he discovered.

"Where you from?" Sadie asked.

"Down the road, in Vouvray."

"No, I mean, you're American, right?"

"Oh, yeah. From Napa, California. Moved here almost four years ago."

"No kidding! We're from Sacramento. Any family hereabouts?"

"Just grandparents and friends."

Barbara ground her cigarette into the ashtray. "And a few new charges if I'm not mistaken, eh, Luc?"

"What do you know about it?"

She shrugged. "I may have mentioned that you needed some farmhands."

She had no right to meddle, but instead of pointing this out, he tossed back his brandy.

"I knew you were a decent fella, and that you had family in these parts. Orphans need a family."

"They're only temporary orphans. Their mother is dead, but their father is fighting at the front."

"You still trying to enlist?" Barbara asked.

"I'll serve my country in any way I can. For example, entertaining you lovely ladies this evening. It's a tough assignment, but I'm equal to the task."

They laughed and ordered another round of drinks. The plucking of the string bass and the tinkling of the piano keys dazzled Luc. Virginia gave a whoop, jumped on the seat of her chair, and before Luc could resist, pulled him up with her. The wall-to-wall crowd danced, rippling like a single organism, the bartenders eager to slake its thirst.

A few hours later, Luc headed to the bar to close out their tab and Virginia followed him. "You could so easily break my heart," she purred, "but I won't allow it."

He barely heard a word. His gaze was trained on those plump, red-stained lips and the tingle of her silk-stocking-clad calf as it rubbed against his leg. The place was so dim and smoke-filled and its patrons so inebriated, Luc doubted anyone would notice.

"May I take you to dinner Saturday night? I know a quiet place nearby." His hand found her waist. "Their French cuisine is the best . . ."

She tossed back her head of blond curls and laughed. "My God, you're adorable." Her fingertips grazed his cheek. "How old are you?"

"Twenty-two," he lied, stretching his age by eight months. Was she poking fun at him?

"You don't have a sweetheart? I find that hard to believe, with your good looks." She sucked a drag off her cigarette and then brought it to his lips. The smoke filled his lungs and the nicotine sailed through his veins.

He shook his head and allowed himself a smile. "The vineyard and the soldiers we billet keep me busy."

"That white wine of yours is aces," she said, nodding to the girls at the table, most of whom were sitting on soldiers' laps, talking in low whispers as the bandleader prepared the crowd to count down to midnight. "The girls love it."

"It's chenin blanc—grows nicely in this part of the Loire. My family has been making it for nearly a century," he added with pride.

"Don't your relatives own this place, too?" She eyed the exposed dark wood rafters above them.

"Friends," he corrected. The family history was too complicated to explain, and he doubted Virginia would care.

"So, you must know every nook and cranny."

"I sure do."

As midnight neared, the crowd chanted, "Ten–nine–eight–seven . . ."

"Would you like the grand tour?" he asked.

"Six–five–four–three," they shouted.

She nodded, blue eyes sparkling with mischief.

"Two–one!" The place erupted into applause. Everyone had partnered up by then, shouting and singing and swaying.

Virginia moved closer. Her hot, sweet, alcohol-infused breath mingled with his. When her lips found his, the rest of his body ached with yearning. Sure, he had kissed girls before, but not a real woman like Virginia.

Clasping hands, the pair slipped down the back hall and around the corner to the storeroom. He led her to the back, where the barrels of wine were stacked high and afforded a degree of privacy. They probably had a few minutes before Pip or Mim or the bartender would come back to retrieve more booze.

Virginia wrapped her slender fingers around his neck and kissed him hard again. He pulled her near, his hand climbing up the long row of buttons to where her white blouse dipped to reveal her creamy curves. Her hand caught his, and he was afraid she would brush him away, but instead she unfastened two pearl buttons and placed his hand on her warm flesh. He gently squeezed and probed and pressed against her.

Her tongue wrapped around his. She fumbled with the buttons on his trousers. "They won't let you in the women's dormitory," she whispered. "We have to finish here. Now."

Finish? He'd assumed they were just starting. With that, the door burst open and footsteps pounded. Pip yelled out commands in French, and barrels roared as he rolled them across the floor. When Pip saw the two of them standing there, red-faced and moon-eyed, he slapped his forehead and cried, *"Mon Dieu!"* He ran a hand over his bald scalp, as if searching for his lost mane of hair. Grumbling, he turned away.

Virginia stiffened and buttoned her shirt. The scents of Luc's spiced cologne and Virginia's flowery fragrance lingered in the air. As intense as his need was for her, he was strangely relieved that Pip had interrupted their liaison.

Virginia started to giggle and nuzzle Luc. "I suppose our fate is to be star-crossed lovers," she sighed.

"Hopefully not," he said, touching his lips to hers. He didn't want their liaison to end but didn't want to consummate it in his friend's tavern storeroom either. "Meet me for dinner Saturday night."

"How is this going to work, Luc? You're a nice fella, and sure, we can go out to dinner, have a few laughs. But where do we go after that? To my dormitory with my roommate? To your house with your grandparents?"

Like a lightning bolt, his father's words echoed in his head: *There are girls you marry and there are girls you don't. It's fairly easy to tell the difference.* Luc's throat was as dry as dust when he contemplated Virginia's baby blues.

She patted his cheek, swung her luscious hips around and sashayed back out to the bar.

The snow had started to fall heavily by the time Luc tried to leave, so he instead passed the night on Pip and Mim's hard storeroom floor. By morning, the streets were silent; a veil of fresh snow covered the wheel tracks and hoofprints of the night before. Luc closed his eyes, turned up his wool collar and stuffed his bare hands into his pockets. The brisk air swept away the hot, smoky tavern of the night before. In this moment, he could almost forget that a war raged only five hundred kilometers away.

———

Ondine did not understand her affliction. Since that last night in Lille, she had not been able to speak to anyone except Michel. She wanted to, but as soon as the words formed on the tip of her tongue, the horror of that night stole them away.

The windows in the room she shared with Michel were sealed tight. The shutters were closed to shield them from the morning light and muffle the roosters' crowing. The night was silent, save for the shuffle of Luc's feet as he wandered the house late into the evenings. What did he have to worry about?

"Ondine?" Michel whispered. His tone was bright, almost hopeful. A lump of anguish rose in her throat. No brother, no son, should see what Michel saw that night. She could have endured it all alone, but the fact that her brother had watched them assault her and murder Mère magnified her pain a thousandfold. How could he even bear to look at her, never mind speak to her? They both knew it was all her fault.

"Yes?" she answered.

"It's nice to hear you, Ondine." His words carried a smile. Her chest swelled with sorrow. "Do you like it here?" he asked.

"They seem to be good people," she said.

"Does Madame treat you well? Do you feel safe?"

"I think I do."

"Good. Good," he replied earnestly. His voice had deepened since their arrival a week ago. He looked a few centimeters taller, too, though she couldn't judge as they lay in the dark. Clearing his throat, Michel added, "I'll take care of you now, Ondine. I promise."

She wiped her wet cheeks. Michel never pushed her to speak outside this room. He understood her struggle, even though she was not able to define it. She croaked, "Thank you, Michel. I know you will."

"*Bonne nuit*, Ondine," he replied hoarsely.

"*Bonne nuit.*"

Mère and Père had raised Ondine to believe that all men had good, or God, in them. When the Germans shelled Lille for ten days in October 1914, destroying thousands of homes and killing hundreds of civilians, Ondine thought they must have made a mistake.

When the Germans marched into town after the bombing and ordered the mayor and prefect to designate sixty hostages to be imprisoned in the citadel or positioned as human shields at the airfield and weapons stores, Ondine's hope wavered. When the Germans ordered all the remaining men over seventeen to work for the Kaiser, when the Germans infiltrated their daily lives, billeting in French homes, demanding food and linens, forcing the women to launder their clothes or serve as their secretaries, Ondine's anger flared. Finally, when the Germans started shipping prominent Lille citizens to the work camps in the fall of 1915, the injustice of it all struck at Ondine's heart. She could no longer idly watch as her mother and the other adults of Lille cowered in the enemy's shadow.

The morning after the trains pulled out of Lille, carrying their friends and neighbors to the camp, Ondine rose as usual at four-thirty. The German officer, Hauptmann Koller, who slept in her parents' bedroom, growled and sputtered in his sleep as Ondine slipped out of the bed she shared with her mother and tiptoed past Michel's room and out of the house.

Ondine milked their cow, Lisette, every morning, but that day was different. Before tending to Lisette's ballooning udder, Ondine waded into the knee-high grass in the adjacent pasture, where she had spied two mysterious baskets the previous morning while weeding the vegetable garden. The flame of her single candle flickered against the pitch dark. A single candle, she surmised, would be less conspicuous than her usual lantern to a patrol passing this time of night. Ondine stumbled over the first basket, and then found the second nearby, both with small parachutes and notes attached, reading *Please open* in French and Flemish. With the baskets tucked under her arms, Ondine hurried into the barn.

She lit her lamp. Her heart hammered against her ribcage. Each basket contained a pigeon and a note. The notes were written in French and Flemish again, assuring the finder of an Allied victory and asking for information. The first: *How many Germans guard the Dix-Huit Ponts at night and during the day?* The second: *How many prisoners are held at the airfield?* Ondine rolled the tiny pieces of paper and slid them deep into her right sock, beneath her heel. She watered the pigeons and fed them the packet of seeds tucked in their baskets. With a quick glance at the house to ensure that the *Hauptmann*'s bedroom lamp was not lit, Ondine hid the pigeons in their baskets beneath the mound of hay in the loft and started to milk Lisette.

Within seventeen hours, Ondine had answered the notes, secured them to the metal message holders on each pigeon's leg and released the birds after nightfall as instructed. It was thrilling that her information might help the Allies whip the Germans.

For two years she answered the notes, flouting the German warnings that any citizen found aiding the Allies in this manner would be shot instantly. Ondine was never foolish enough to write her name or address on the return note, but nonetheless, the Germans eventually discovered her and raided the house. Although they found no evidence, Ondine's punishment had been swift and deadly.

She shivered, shrinking from the memory, curling her knees inward. She stared into the darkness, gulping the cool bedroom air into her lungs. Michel's breathing was steady and deep from where he slept across the room.

Did he ever dream of that night? Of leaving Mère alone in her river of blood? Of being torn from her side and piled into the livestock car and rumbling through the northern countryside? That night, Ondine had vowed to survive just long enough to deliver her brother to safety. With their parents absent, the two men here, along with Madame as a strict mother figure, could raise Michel into a man.

Luc's lean, sturdy figure, fine dark eyes and persistent employment suggested he was a reliable sort, but his restlessness concerned her. Half of Ondine resented him for his life of ease, but the other half reveled in its tranquility.

As quiet and peaceful as this night seemed, Ondine's insides roiled. Her cuts and bruises had healed, but her soul had splintered. Ondine feared there was no way to repair it.

To ease her mind into sleep, Ondine resorted not to prayer, but to her precious numbers. Since the invasion, she had not attended school, but she practiced in her head to keep her wits sharp. She missed her numbers. They either added up, or they didn't. They were divisible or they weren't. There was no uncertainty in the numbers.

———

NAPA, CALIFORNIA

At seven o'clock, Sara headed downstairs to wish Pippa good luck. Judging from the clomping of their boots and the clanking of dishware in the porcelain sink earlier that morning, Johnny and Philippe had already eaten. Sara walked toward the kitchen wearing her wool frock and a kerchief secured beneath the bun at the nape of her neck. She guessed that Johnny was mucking the stables and Philippe was inspecting the vines.

Sara loved her narrow but tidy kitchen at the rear of the house they had called home for twenty years. The children moaned about washing the dishes, but Sara loved dunking her hands into the hot, sudsy water and greeting the steam that rose to warm her nose and ears. Next to the sink stood the new Glenwood K wood and coal cookstove that Philippe had purchased this past fall. What a jewel! It was large enough so she could easily prepare dinner for ten and even take some pleasure in the process. However, Sara's real passion was winemaking, not cooking meals.

Just around the corner, a hallway led to the pantry, the water closet and the newly installed icebox, situated where the larder used to be. In summer, when the family was toiling in the vineyard, Sara would make two pitchers of lemonade, store them in the icebox and mete out the cold, sweet nectar as a reward—or a bribe, in Lydia's case. The icebox and range were the largest of many luxuries Sara and Philippe had delighted in since the record sale of wine last year. However, experience had taught Sara to question her good fortune, to wait for the other shoe to drop, so to speak. Would prohibition destroy the booming wine business they had built together? Would Luc go to war?

A chorus of *"Bonjour, Maman!"* distracted her as she walked into the kitchen. Sara's attention shifted to her daughters, seated at the table. Their physical appearances could not be more divergent. Lydia, in her white cotton nightgown and brown wool socks, had a shock of brunette curls that only Liquid Silmerine could tame. Her striking eyes harbored a spark of mischief and her lips danced with secret amusement at the strangest things, for she possessed a hearty sense of humor. Tall and lanky, Lydia at eleven was a hair taller than Pippa at twenty.

Pippa, on the other hand, possessed a shapely frame and skin with the luster of a pearl. Her petite features—the cornflower-blue eyes, pink pout and fine flaxen hair—were captivating but still a bit distressing to Sara. Though Pippa looked upon the world with a quiet wonderment and an amiable disposition, her presence was a constant reminder of Philippe's previous liaison with Linnette Cross, Pippa's birth mother. Since Linnette's death in 1900, Sara had cherished and shielded Pippa like her own flesh and blood. Philippe's love and loyalty belonged to Sara, but she could not shake the fear that one day Pippa might engage in her mother's wantonness. "Bad blood" was the phrase most commonly whispered in the early days of Pippa's adoption. Since Pippa had become a young woman, Sara had watched for the signs. Did depravity run in her blood? Was it shameful to think it might?

"Maman, come sit and have coffee," Pippa beckoned cheerfully, patting the seat of the wooden chair next to her. Sara admired Pippa's ensemble: a neatly pressed navy ankle-length skirt with gold buttons and a wide-collared white lace blouse. A tie of cranberry red added a splash of color, and Pippa's newly shiny brown leather day shoes tapped a tune as she buttered her toast.

"You look smart, Pippa."

"You think? I want to look pretty, but capable. You know, businesslike."

"Would you like my red velvet ribbon to wear in your hair?" Lydia chimed, tapping her feet and slurping oatmeal off her spoon.

Sara's heart melted. Lydia had offered her treasured red ribbon. Sara ruffled her younger daughter's tangled hair, a veritable squirrel's nest of chaos.

Pippa replied, "I love your ribbon, Lydie, but I don't know if they allow them. Mr. Hudson has a strict dress code for his employees." Sara flashed Pippa a smile of appreciation for sparing her sister's feelings.

Lydia murmured around a mouthful of toast, "You should ask them."

"I will, dearest."

"I'm sure you'll be a smashing success," Sara said.

"Really, Maman?" She kissed Sara's cheek, leaving a smudge of butter. "Oops, sorry!" Pippa dabbed a napkin at Sara's face. "I have to hurry if I want to be on time."

"Actually, you have plenty of time. Your father is driving you in the Chevrolet."

Pippa's head whipped around. "I thought we had decided I could walk!"

"We had discussed it, but your father insists on driving you and picking you up at five."

"But, Maman . . ." Pippa slumped, drained of enthusiasm.

Her protestations tugged on Sara's heartstrings, but she could not give in, for more reasons than she could say. "Your father and I have already decided."

Pippa blinked, as if willing Sara to change her mind. Despite her obstinance, her tone had been conciliatory, almost timid. She could not have been more different from Sara at the same age.

74

"Maman, I'm twenty years old. I don't smoke cigarettes, I don't drink spirits, I don't even go to the county dances. Don't you trust me to walk a few miles in the morning?"

"Of course, we trust you. It's others we don't trust." At that moment, Philippe rolled up outside the window.

Pippa pulled on her mittens with a huff and trudged outside. With a creak and a whoosh of the door, she disappeared from Sara's view. When Pippa did not appear on the other side of the motor car, Philippe glanced at Sara, his sandy eyebrows raised in a question. Sara shrugged and mouthed, "Where did she go?" Yet, as the words passed her lips, Sara felt a pang in her chest.

She peered out the opposite window, which faced the orchard. Her gaze followed Pippa until she reached its edge, where two wooden crosses rose from the earth beneath two pear trees that flowered in the spring—a flurry of white petals. Next to the grave of Sara and Philippe's first daughter was their makeshift memorial for Pippa's mother, Linnette. *Would Pippa's wound ever heal? Would Sara and Philippe ever be enough?*

Sara squinted to see Pippa crouch down and brush the leaves, pine needles and winter debris from the patch of ground surrounded by small white stones. When she returned, she slid into the motor car, hugging her lunch pail and satchel like a kindergartner on her first day of school. She exchanged a few quick words with Philippe and in no time, he had her smiling again. With a plume of dust, they rambled down the driveway toward town.

———

"Papa, pull over there." Pippa pointed to the cobbler's shop located a block before Hudson's Dry Goods.

75

To her horror, the car rumbled on. "I need some tools. You won't even know I'm there."

Pippa adored her father—and especially the fact that he had changed into his Sunday best, a single-breasted herringbone suit and black bowler hat, before driving her to town—but if he walked her into her work place on the first day, she would surely wilt from embarrassment.

"Just give me the money and your list, Papa. I'll purchase the tools before you come 'round to pick me up tonight at *five*." She emphasized the time, for she suspected he had a notion of coming earlier.

After a little grumbling, he eventually acquiesced, pulling the car to the curb half a block before Hudson's. He handed her a list and ten dollars.

Leaving him without the usual kiss on the cheek, Pippa stepped out and approached the store. Papa watched from the car, of course. Hudson's picture windows gleamed in the morning sunlight. As Pippa drew closer, her gaze widened to absorb the kaleidoscope of color inside.

The bell jingled overhead as she entered. She hoped her red tie was not too bright for her first day. Since the war, clothing had become so drab—perhaps to show solidarity with the boys at the front—but no one appreciated a splash of color more than Pippa.

She walked through the front section of Hudson's between two aisles of shiny metal hardware and housewares. Shell-pink trim enlivened the olive-green walls and shelves. She wondered if Mrs. Hudson had chosen the color palette, or if Mr. Hudson were trying to attract female customers. Regardless, the pink made the place welcoming—reminiscent of a parlor.

Pippa greeted an older gentleman tending the store before passing beneath the elaborately carved, pink-trimmed archway on the far wall and into the newly created Art Emporium at the back of the building. A brass-encased cash register, an ornate focal point nearly the size of a small stove, dwarfed its table in the center of the room. The sharp scents of ink and bleach mingled with the nutty smell of drawing paper. Shelves filled with art books and paper stock topped rows of cupboards on three walls. An exit door and picture window cut the far wall into three sections, where drawing stands were poised and ready for purchase.

A raven-haired, reedy stock boy turned to greet her. "You must be Miss Philippa Lemucks." He climbed down the ladder, wiped his hands on his starched white apron, extended a hand and smiled. There was something unnerving, yet intriguing, about his blue gaze. His black pupils were slightly different sizes.

"I'm Billy Hudson, Mr. Hudson's nephew. I'm working here this summer before I head to school in the fall."

"Nice to meet you, Billy," she said. "And you may call me Pippa. Pippa *Le-myuh*." He flushed and she felt a stab of regret for correcting him. "Most French surnames are tricky," she added congenially, trying to project her voice. Maman had advised her to speak up to her employers and ask questions; she was too soft-spoken at home.

"My uncle told me I should show you the ropes. You know, how to work ol' Natty, stock the shelves, help the customers."

"Ol' Natty?"

He turned and waved an arm at the brass beast that dominated the center of the room. "Ol' Natty is our cash register—the National brand." He shrugged. "Kind of silly, but we nicknamed her Ol' Natty, since she's been here for ten years. She's part of the family."

"Oh, I see." Pippa glanced around. "Your uncle isn't here?"

"He's at the train depot, picking up a shipment of pens and paper from San Francisco."

"What type of pens?" Pippa asked, thrilled at the prospect of having her choice of the finest drawing implements.

"I dunno, steel-tipped, I'd imagine. Do you draw?"

"Yes. Portraits mostly. Noses are the trickiest for me." She silently rebuked herself. She had the tendency to share too much with strangers—a nervous habit.

"Nostrils are the hardest for me," he admitted.

She laughed, in part because he had a funny way about him, but also because she wanted to draw his attention away from the scar below her own nose. "You draw as well?" she asked.

"I sketch—before I sculpt. Just last week I was shaping the head of Zeus in soapstone. Broke the poor fella's nose clean off. I'm still working on perfecting my touch."

Pippa's gaze narrowed.

He blurted, "My touch with the hammer and chisel, I meant." He pivoted toward the cardboard boxes behind him. Exhaling loudly, he suggested, "Let's start by unpacking the rest of these." When his gaze met hers, his right eye shifted, but his left eye remained inert. She controlled the urge to jump back in surprise.

After hanging her coat, satchel and lunch pail in the closet, Pippa followed Billy's instructions to the letter. As she trailed him around the store, she admired his neat appearance. Beneath the apron, he wore navy-colored britches, a crisp white dress shirt, a gray cardigan and a snappy paisley bow tie. His flat hair was slicked back, and his face was clean-shaven. His nose, in stark contrast to hers, was long and hooked, but lent him a capable, efficient air.

Pippa had never seen so many art supplies—some she had only read about. They organized stacks of white and ivory sketch paper, boxes of sepia and logwood ink, pens, chalk, crayons, pastels, oil paints and varying sizes of horsehair paintbrushes, from fine to thick. She ran her thumb over the satiny tips before she stacked them neatly in the merchandise drawer. By the time they had finished for the day, she knew the location of nearly every item they sold. Tomorrow, she would try to memorize their prices.

She observed Billy handle the customers, all of whom were frequent patrons. He introduced her to each one, taking care to pronounce her last name properly. When he punched the numbers on the cash register and cranked the arm, she hovered nearby, making a mental note of the order of operations. Pippa had never excelled at arithmetic, and she dreaded having to hand-calculate figures. This brass beast was nothing short of a miracle and she was determined to learn how to use it.

At noon, Billy locked the back door and drew the shade. Pippa's cheeks flamed. "What are you doing?" she asked in the most casual tone she could muster.

He cocked his head in confusion. "Closing for lunch."

Relief swept over her like a cool breeze. "Oh, yes, of course."

He grabbed his lunch sack from beneath the counter. "During the spring, I eat my lunch in the park and take a stroll, but since it's bitter cold outside today, I thought we could just eat here. Unless you have an errand to run?" He motioned to two stools against the wall.

Pippa did not want to intrude on Billy's lunch break, but having no other option, she agreed. "No, I just have to make sure I purchase some tools for my father from Mr. Hudson before the day ends."

"He should return soon. If not, Jim will still be manning the front store. He can help you."

"I would be most obliged, thank you."

Billy unwrapped his sandwich and the sulfuric scent of chopped egg and mayonnaise hung in the air. "You probably wonder why I'm not fighting over there," he asserted after swallowing a bite.

Of course, she had wondered that instantly, but instead she replied, "It's none of my concern."

"Glass eye." He tapped his left eyeball with his index finger. It made a subtle clicking sound.

Pippa leaned closer, unable to resist the perfectly matched, speckled blue iris. Even the white of his artificial eye was eerily authentic, with fine pink capillaries running through it. "Really? It's awfully pretty," she noted.

"My brother accidentally shot me with a BB gun."

Pippa winced. "That must have been so painful."

"Naw, I was too young to remember. The irony is that now he's over there fighting for freedom and I'm stuck here stocking shelves. No offense . . ." his voice trailed off, as did the hint of bitterness at his fate.

Pippa didn't know how to respond to that, so she simply bit into her buttered bread. After years of enduring the scrutiny of her schoolmates and strangers because of the scar that ran from her lip to her nose and set her grin askew, Pippa would never reject someone because of his appearance.

"I sat for the artist for an hour while he painted it."

"He's very talented," Pippa noted. In awkward situations like these, it was probably best to just tell the truth.

Billy cleared his throat and swigged from his milk bottle. "I think I should go back to wearing a patch. Then people wouldn't look at me so strange, trying to figure what's different."

"Sometimes I wish I had a patch, or just a bag with two eyes to wear over my head," she mused. As soon as the last word escaped her lips, she regretted her remark.

Billy's expression softened. "Why?"

Pippa shifted uncomfortably on the hard stool. "My scar," she muttered.

"That tiny ol' thing? Aw, now you're just joshin' me." Billy sipped his milk, but when Pippa stayed silent, he gazed at her in confusion. "You're serious?"

Pippa shrugged. "Yes." Beads of perspiration formed beneath her collar. She had shared too much again, even if Billy was an open, easy person to talk to. Her fingers curled in, gouging the soft white bread she held. She wanted to disappear.

He leaned back, scrutinizing her for a few moments. "Are you fishing?"

Her head snapped up. "What?"

"Fishing. For a compliment?"

Her bewilderment left her tongue-tied. She did not know if she should be pleased or indignant. While Billy waited for a reply, he shined a green apple on his apron.

Just then, Mr. Hudson strolled in from the hardware store. He was shorter than Billy and regarded Pippa from beneath two white-tufted eyebrows. "Ah, Miss Lemeeks. How is your first day going?"

"Very well, thank you." She wiped her mouth with her cloth napkin and shoved the remnants of her lunch into the pail.

"Just swimmingly, Uncle. And it's pronounced Le-myuh," Billy agreed, winking ever so slightly with his good eye. "Pippa Lemieux."

<hr />

NEW YORK, NEW YORK

When she wasn't tending to cases of measles and mumps, Adeline spent her twelve-hour shifts sweeping the narrow aisles between the cots and mopping the white-tiled corridors of Rockefeller Hospital. After their first five shifts and a full night's rest, she ducked out to tour the city with Sally Dunn, Harriet Hussman and Anna Ring, the three other nurses of the 30th assigned to the hospital with her. They strolled through Central Park, where they were stunned to find a German U-boat, captured by the U.S.

Navy and on display to convince patriotic New Yorkers to buy war bonds. They wandered through the park's meadows and past its sculptures, with Adeline describing every landmark in both English and French, for she had been assigned to instruct her fellow nurses in the colloquialisms of the French language so they would be somewhat prepared when they eventually arrived at the hospital in Royat-les-Bains, south of Paris. Finally, Adeline convinced Sally, Harriet and Anna to try ice skating, and they swirled around the crowded rink, laughing and linking arms like adolescents.

When icy snow began to prick their cheeks like needles, Adeline and her new friends hung up their skates, bought bags of roasted peanuts and chestnuts and ducked into the subway to ride back downtown—this time to one of Adeline's favorite childhood landmarks, the Union Square Theater.

Philippe had taken Adeline and her mother there when she was younger. Although she couldn't recall any of the acts, memories of the colorful costumes and the smell of roasted peanuts and the belly laughter from that afternoon filled her with joy.

Now, as they approached, Adeline was surprised to see that the theater, once home to multiple vaudeville shows, had been converted to a moving picture house. The archways and Shakespeare medallion were less majestic than Adeline had remembered and, although the ceilings inside had been painted gold and ivory and the two large cupolas still loomed, the vast room had the appearance of a rich aristocrat down on her luck. Adeline hid her disappointment from her fellow nurses, for the three of them bubbled over with excitement at any excuse to break free from the hospital.

When Harriet and Anna balked at the fifty-cent tickets, for they had not yet been paid their monthly salary of thirty dollars, Adeline slid a ten-dollar bill from the roll of cash Maman had given her before she left. This kind of qualified as an emergency. They needed to lift their spirits before another week of emptying bedpans and bathing patients.

After viewing Mary Pickford's latest silent film, *Stella Maris*, the foursome had no choice but to return to their dormitory, so they wouldn't miss the dinner hour. They plopped on the cots. Sally, technically their superior, rubbed her toes. "I'm frozen to the core, Addie, but what a delightful day!"

"How on earth do you know your way around?" Harriet asked, raking her fingers through her fiery orange hair.

Adeline shrugged. "I was born here and lived here until I was eleven. And I come here with my parents from time to time."

"Oh really? This is my first trip out of Petaluma! I used to attend the hog fair from time to time," Harriet added with a wry grin.

Anna perked up. "I think Addie is the most cosmopolitan girl I've ever met." She wrapped a towel around her hair and rubbed the ends.

"Indeed," Sally chimed in. "What on earth are you doing here? You certainly don't need the cash."

Adeline, still uncomfortable with her stepfather's wealth, replied, "I grew up in a surgery. It's second nature to me. I just want to help our boys."

"You're not in it for the paycheck?" Anna joked, rolling a stocking down over her toes. The thirty dollars a month they were promised had still not materialized.

"Naw, she's in it for the men in uniform, right, Addie?" Harriet clucked. "Did you see those handsome fellas staring at us in Central Park?" She whistled. "And the one with the beautifully coiffed mustache? I would guzzle that tall drink of water, let me tell you!"

Anna smacked her with a feather pillow.

"Hey!" Harriet cried.

"Your romantic streak is going to land you in heaps of trouble over there, Harriet. No fraternizing with the patients, understand?" Sally said.

"Not even the Frenchies?" Harriet asked dreamily, swooning over the pillow she now hugged to her chest.

Adeline chuckled, but Sally frowned and wagged a finger. "Look but don't touch, ladies."

Anna fell back onto her cot and sighed. "The story of my life."

CHAMPAGNE, FRANCE

Heinrich buttoned his *feldgrau* tunic, turned up the collar of his greatcoat, fastened his Red Cross armband and secured his steel helmet. As the lowest-ranking medical officer, it was his duty to scavenge for medical supplies. He walked through the German-occupied territory, scanning the cold, desolate landscape.

The earth was a bald corpse. The 231st Division had arrived just after the action, but the scars of war were striking. Artillery blasts had burned Champagne's forests and vegetation and gouged its chalky soil. Vultures preened and swooped over slumped, decomposing British and French cadavers, abandoned as their comrades retreated in defeat.

The scent of death invaded Heinrich's nostrils. He tied his handkerchief tightly around his nose and mouth. His mind flashed back to Nauroy and his stomach clenched.

"A good soldier kills without thinking of his adversary as a human being," their *Hauptmann* had shouted, urging the infantry on. When Heinrich had plunged his bayonet into the chest of a young French soldier to save himself, he had nearly vomited from shame. One of his comrades had been able to strangle a French captain and joke about it later. But Heinrich's young *poilu* had been forced to fight, just like him. He had a mother, a father, perhaps a sister who awaited his return home. At another time, in another place, they would have shaken hands and been the best of friends. Yet here on the battlefield, both sides raged like mad dogs.

Heinrich trudged beyond the dead and then past the living of his division, hiding in their machine-gun nests waiting for their next orders. Clouds of cigarette smoke hung in the air over their narrow trenches.

He headed toward what looked like a tent in the distance, with its canvas flapping in the breeze. Along the way, he squatted and pressed his palm into the dusty, barren earth. He closed his eyes and thought of the farm where he was raised. He remembered the sweet smell of hay and the tangy scent of freshly mowed grass. The ground in Champagne, once known for producing the earth's premier wine grapes, now quivered beneath his touch and reeked of decay.

As Heinrich neared the tent, he spied abandoned stretchers and boxes of supplies strewn across the dirt floor. Instinctively, he raised his hands and shouted, *"Kamerad? Je suis docteur."* He was not actually a doctor yet, but rather a medical student who had been called up to serve in the Kaiser's infantry for six months before becoming a medical officer, or what the British would call a probationer surgeon. He peered into the tent and saw no one.

He surmised that this had been a British dressing station. He rummaged through the boxes and struck gold in the form of rubber gloves and real bandages. For months, the surgeons of his division had operated on soldiers with their bare hands and bandaged them up with cellulose and scrap paper. When soaked in blood, both had fallen to pieces.

Heinrich stacked the boxes of gloves and bandages on a stretcher and carried it back to the cave where the medical corps had established their station. He should have celebrated these spoils of war, but instead his thoughts turned once again to Anna and Werner.

As much as he wanted to rail in anger at the Fates, Heinrich blamed himself, not Anna, for her inconstancy. Hadn't he always suspected her faithlessness? Had she not been pregnant with Werner five years ago, he never would have married her. He had only been twenty-one at the time, a first-year medical student. His Catholic faith along with his own code of honor had dictated that they marry so their child would not suffer the stigma of being born a bastard.

And what had that earned him? He was now a wifeless cuckold, and worst of all, he had no notion of where she had taken their son.

When Heinrich ducked back into the cave, Oberstleutnant Schröder, the medical lieutenant colonel, was issuing instructions to his soldiers. He glanced at Heinrich. "We're retreating north in a few days to Givet for more training. What's that?" he asked, pointing to the stretcher packed with supplies.

"British bandages and rubber gloves I found."

"Well done, *Leutnant*."

Givet was located on the northeast border of France. From there, it was only a half day's journey to Köln. Heinrich cleared his throat. "*Oberstleutnant*, I would like to request a two-week furlough," he said.

"Whatever for?" Schröder's gaze narrowed beneath his black, caterpillar brow.

"I'm supposed to be a one-year volunteer, and my year of service was up on the fifteenth."

Schröder scoffed. "And my birthday was last week, but no one baked me a cake."

Heinrich cringed. He was not about to divulge that he was a cuckold, so he fibbed. "My wife is ill and can no longer care for our son. I need to go home and make arrangements."

"Surely there is family nearby who can take care of these details?" Schröder scribbled on his clipboard.

"No, *Oberstleutnant*, there is not."

Schröder exhaled loudly. "I'll petition command for your furlough as soon as we reach Givet, but it's not guaranteed."

Heinrich's chest filled with longing and excitement at the prospect of holding Werner again. Would he be able to find his son? Would Werner even remember him, absent these last twelve months?

CHAPTER 5

February 1918

VOUVRAY, FRANCE

Winter twilight descended in shades of yellow and aqua. Stars sprinkled like salt crystals across the sky. The Loire River flowed wide and frigid and deep at the edge of the Saint Martin property. Skiffs and barges jockeyed for space on the water. The clang of the buoys carried through the bare trees. Smoke from the kitchen chimney streamed high into the night air. Michel's stomach grumbled aloud. Any food was welcome after a day of chopping and hauling birchwood. With fingerless gloves and paring knives, Michel and Luc sat atop the woodpile, whittling branches into figurines.

"Did you know there is a Le Loir and a La Loire near here?" Luc asked.

"Are both rivers?"

"Not exactly. La Loire—the female—is the wide river you see before you. Le Loir—the male—is a tributary that flows from the female."

"Isn't that opposite the Bible? I mean, shouldn't the female flow from the male, like God created Eve from Adam's rib?"

Luc bumped Michel's shoulder. "I'm sure we men would prefer it that way."

Michel sighed. After a few minutes of silence, his voice trembled and he sputtered, "My papa—Père doesn't know Mère is dead. They just—and then—and there was no time to send word. They just carted us off and left—left her there." Horror-stricken, he stared at the yellow grass beneath them as though he was reliving the grisly scene.

Luc swallowed hard. He had nearly upchucked when he had encountered his first dead body during the San Francisco earthquake eleven years ago, but that had been a stranger, not his own mother. "There's nothing you could have done to save her, Michel." He placed a hand on the boy's shoulder. "We will write to him."

Michel nodded and ran a gloved hand across his dripping nose. "What does your father do when he's not soldiering?" Luc ventured.

"He works at city hall, in the Chamber of Commerce. He helps with the trade between France, Belgium and England."

"How long has he been gone?"

Michel shrugged. "He missed my last three birthdays, so since I was eleven." When Luc had been that age, he had trailed Philippe through the vines to inspect and pick the grapes, to the winery to stir the fermenting tanks, or to San Francisco to make deliveries, like that day they were caught in the great earthquake and fire.

"We'll write two identical letters. One we'll keep and send to the Lille City Hall when the Germans have retreated, and the other we'll send immediately to his regiment."

"But I don't know where they are."

"Don't worry, I have friends who can help."

At that moment, the supper bell rang. Ondine emerged from the house and passed into view, but she could not see them, for they sat behind her with their backs against the stone wall. She struck out toward the river.

"Does she speak?" Luc wondered aloud.

Michel squeezed his eyes shut. "Only to me." He jumped down and headed into the house.

The poor kid. Luc continued to whittle down a branch into a serpent-like creature. He did not possess any talent, but the mere act of scraping bark and peeling tree flesh calmed him. Luc's stomach rumbled at the thought of Grandmère's vegetable soup and the thick slice of bread that awaited him, but there was a sort of frantic energy about Ondine's gait—and the surprising fact that she did not carry a lantern at twilight—that compelled Luc to stay and watch.

Seemingly unaware of his surveillance, she stopped at the river's edge next to a pile of stones. She tied the two bottom corners of her apron to its sash, fashioning a sling. Luc slid off the woodpile and walked closer, squinting to focus on Ondine's slight figure. She slid three large stones, one by one, into the apron sling.

When Luc realized what she intended to do, he launched down the hill and sprinted to the shoreline, his heart punching against his ribcage. He did not shout her name, fearful that she would react by plunging herself into the inky water before he reached her.

He closed the distance between them, feet thudding and breath panting. Ondine stumbled and splashed into the water. Luc followed, the icy water prickling his extremities. He dug his fingers into her shoulder and hooked his other arm around her waist. Although he stood over a head taller than the girl, he had to summon all his strength, flexing his calf and thigh muscles to lift her legs from the mud of the riverbed. The two crashed onto the shore. Luc's back hit the frozen ground; Ondine's collapsed onto Luc's torso; the rocks in her apron, tumbling to the side, scraped his hipbones.

Her legs splayed out as she struggled to regain her footing. She sunk her boot heels into the gritty riverbank, trying to push herself up, squirming and grunting like a penned animal. Luc tightened his hold on her, but her ribs were so delicate beneath his arm, he feared they might snap like twigs. "Ondine, no. Ondine, stop!" he urged, heaving with exertion. He placed a palm on her forehead and gently guided her back down to him. She rested her head against the interior curve of his shoulder, her mouth wide, guzzling air. Her chest expanded against his and her muscles twitched.

"*Bâtard!*" A voice cried out in the dark. *Michel?* Fists pummeled Luc's nose and cheekbones before he could raise a hand.

"No, Michel! No!" Ondine implored, her fresh voice a strange mixture of sweetness and strength. Luc clawed at the murky sky until he was able to grab hold of Michel and arrest his attack. Someone finally pulled the kid off him.

A lantern rocked high above Luc's head, illuminating the scene and Jacques's stern expression. Luc threw an arm over his eyes and moaned. He could feel the hot blood trickling from his nose and pooling in his mouth. He sat up when he started to hack uncontrollably.

Jacques tossed him a handkerchief. Grandmère arrived soon after and helped Ondine up. "To the house, now. All three of you." Jacques grabbed Luc's hand and pulled him to stand. Mud stained Ondine's face. She stared at Luc. Pain clouded her soft blue eyes. Her shoulders sagged. She was defeated, surely, but more importantly, she seemed relieved.

The silent threesome washed for dinner and sat at the kitchen table. Luc assessed his injuries: nose throbbing and still bleeding, scrapes all over, rolled ankle swelling to the size of a baseball.

Root vegetable soup bubbled on the stove, its savory scent wafting to every corner of the kitchen. Luc glanced at his empty bowl and then at Jacques, who sat across from them, rubbing his whiskered chin. "What in the dickens were you doing, Luc?"

Michel straightened and pointed at Luc. "He attacked Ondine!"

Ondine guided Michel's wrist down to rest on the table. Shaking her head, unable to make eye contact, she shivered. "Luc pulled me from the water when I was . . . I was about to go under. He saved me." She curled her hand around Michel's. "He did not harm me," she murmured. Her words formed a silvery string of song that captivated Luc. He yearned to hear more.

"Why?" he asked tenderly, as if no one else was listening.

She sealed her lips shut, rose and fled from the room.

While Jacques filled the men's bowls with thick soup, Grandmère took a tray up to the room Ondine shared with Michel.

The kitchen was silent, save for the clicking and occasional chime of the grandfather clock and the slurping of soup, which the men never would have attempted if Grandmère had been seated at the table.

"I'm sorry, Luc." Michel dunked his bread. With a mouthful, he explained, "I thought . . . I was sure . . . It looked like . . ." He hung his head, unable to go on.

Luc set his spoon down on the rim of the bowl. "You have seen things no fourteen-year-old should." Michel's sorrow now—and the flash of rage earlier—confirmed what Luc had feared. The Germans must have raped their mother, in front of Michel and Ondine, before they killed her.

Jacques coughed. "War turns simple men into senseless killing machines." His fist punched the table. *"Liberté. Égalité. Fraternité!"* His face pinched as if he were sucking a lemon. *"Quelle farce!"*

After a half hour, Grandmère had still not returned. Michel's chair legs scraped the floor. "I must go check on Ondine."

By the time Grandmère entered the kitchen, Jacques had washed the dishes, swept the hearth, examined Luc's swollen ankle and propped it up on pillows. He was just returning from the caves where they kept a second icebox filled with blocks in winter. With a few strokes of the ice pick, he had a pile of crushed ice, which he gathered into a square of linseed oilcloth and set atop Luc's ankle.

94

Grandmère released a sigh. Her face was a ghostly white. Jacques held out a chair and then rushed to the cupboard to pour a glass of cognac. She curled her fingers around the glass of deep golden liqueur.

Luc and Jacques exchanged a worried glance. Grandmère sipped. "Ondine has confided in me that she suffered an unspeakable crime at the hands of the Germans who also killed her mother." She sipped the liquid in silence. "We must treat her with great care. You two must say nothing—and no more talk of the war, understand?"

Heat rushed through Luc's limbs and outrage ripped through his chest, causing his heart to thump in triple time. Wild, violent images flooded his mind. Grandmère patted his leg. "Luc?"

"Is she . . . ?" He could not bear to say the words.

"She is not with child."

"How can you be sure?"

"It has been two months since. We women have a way of knowing these things."

Jacques gazed out the window. A rumble cleared the emotion from his throat.

An uncomfortable silence fell over the table. Unable to endure it, Luc begged, "What can I do?"

Grandmère's voice strained with emotion. "Pray. And treat her as you would your own sister—with the utmost care."

———

Michel approached Luc the next morning. "Ondine is mortified." Michel rocked on his heels with his hands shoved into dirt-rimmed pockets. "She wants me to apologize to you. She wasn't thinking clearly, she says."

"Sit," Luc beckoned. He pushed a bowl of canned peaches toward Michel. "Eat."

Michel plunged his fork into the plump, juicy orbs of sunshine like a fortuneless boy mining for gold. He used his sleeve to wipe his mouth and the fine fuzz of whiskers that now sprouted across his upper lip. He possessed the temporary ungainliness of a boy who had suddenly awoken to larger feet and hands and musculature—a boy who had just lost his mother and now had to enter manhood without a father.

"You saw all of it, didn't you?" Luc asked.

Michel stared into his bowl and chewed.

"You were powerless to stop it," Luc asserted.

The fork clattered against the dish. "They held the blade to my throat, and I squeezed my eyes shut so Ondine wouldn't see me." The whites of Michel's eyes shot with blood when he whispered, "I braced for her cries, her screams, but there was nothing. She did not make a sound. Not a sound as they . . . again and again. When they stopped, I covered her and held her, so she couldn't see Mère." His eyes pooled with tears. "Ondine didn't even whimper."

"She stopped speaking altogether," Luc said.

"Yes."

Black, oily grief spread across Luc's chest. "I have three sisters myself. If someone were to hurt them like that, well, I don't know what I'd do."

Michel clenched a fist. "You would hunt them and gut them like the pigs they are."

"I probably would," Luc admitted hoarsely.

96

———

Luc did not know much about healing wounds of the soul, but he remembered how fear had once sunk its fangs and claws into him and held tight for months. When he was ten, he had witnessed the panic and dead bodies and tumbling buildings of the great earthquake and fire. With his father recuperating from a leg wound and his mother recovering from the birth of his sister, he had worked in the vineyard ten hours a day and ached from his scalp to his little toe by the time the dinner bell rang. He had been too tired to fall prey to his darker thoughts, and there's something about digging your hands in dirt that frees the mind and soothes the soul. Every day he set one foot in front of the other, blazing a trail that left fear by the roadside.

With Jacques and Grandmère's help, Luc set a grueling schedule for Michel on the farm. Breakfast at six, lantern lit by six-thirty, inspecting the vines before pruning.

"The below-freezing temperatures have been good for the vines. No disease." He ran a hand down one trunk.

Luc handed Michel a pair of secateurs and demonstrated how to use them. He pointed to one of the extraneous canes. "Clip here."

Michel did as he was told, but when he tried to clip the next cane, Luc stopped him. "We keep the young canes—their shoots will yield fruit this year. These new canes we also keep. They will lie dormant until the new shoots grow."

Michel's brows scrunched. "So only the one-year-old canes produce fruit?"

"Exactly."

"The vines look like old crones," Michel said with a chuckle.

"Ha! I suppose so. That's because we prune them using a method called *taille en éventail*. It keeps the vines short and allows sunshine and air to flow more evenly through the leaves and fruit."

It took years to master the proper technique of pruning, but Luc allowed the boy to practice on a block of the vineyard that had not yielded much fruit in past years. The two worked side by side. When Michel groaned, Luc would offer tidbits of advice, for Michel was an eager learner. "This may seem like tedious, unnecessary work, but the pruning we do now will determine the quality and quantity of the next vintage," he instructed, smiling to himself, remembering his own frustration when Papa had taught him how to prune. It was important for a man to learn a trade.

They broke for lunch. Once inside, Michel winced as he peeled off his gloves to reveal blistered fingertips and chafed palms.

Grandmère placed a jar of salve on the table. "Wash your hands with soap and water, then apply a healthy amount," she instructed.

Luc clapped him on the back. "We'll make a *vigneron* out of you in no time! And you, Miss Ondine," he said, ripping off a piece of bread with his teeth. "Mmm. After we eat, we have some tenants who require your attention." A tangy scent filled his nostrils, fueling his appetite.

"Jacques already fed the soldiers some stew," Grandmère interjected with a wary look. The poor *poilus* were headed back to the front after spending Christmas with their families. One felt obligated to fatten them up and let them drink as much fine wine as possible.

"Not the soldiers. You should both come," Luc added with a mischievous grin. Ondine had spoken little since she had tried to end her life. Given all that she had endured, Luc assumed she would be more relaxed if his grandmother accompanied them.

After two bowls of thick stew and a loaf of bread, Luc handed Michel off to Jacques to taste the aging wines, discern different flavors and learn the basics of blending while he led the women into the forest.

Ondine and Madame trudged behind Luc through the forest at the western edge of Saint Martin. They passed through a small iron-gated cemetery with a solitary headstone. Madame touched her arthritic fingers to her lips and pressed them to the top edge of the stone. "My first husband," she explained. Ondine paused to read the stone. Luc Thibault was only forty-nine when he died. "He was caught in a mudslide. Jacques was with him but couldn't save him. He brought him home to us, though."

Madame threaded her arm around Ondine's waist and guided her onward. Beneath the dark wool shawl that covered her white crest of hair, the older woman reminded Ondine of an owl tucked inside its hollow.

A two-story, hexagonal structure emerged, its pale-yellow limestone facade measuring six or seven meters wide. The building, a shaft of sunlight amid the winter gloom of the forest, had a wind vane and oxidized copper spire that pierced the sky.

Could she dare to hope? Luc tugged on a pair of thick, arched burgundy-painted doors. *"Voilà! Le pigeonnier!"*

Ondine froze, startled by the revelation. *How could he have known?*

Madame and Luc coaxed her inside. The pungent aroma of hay and dung, along with the whir and purr of the birds, was overwhelming. She covered her eyes and bowed, curling inward, as if struck.

"Ondine?" Madame, sounding concerned, rested a hand on her trembling shoulder.

Ondine shook her head. Her mouth opened and shut several times before she found the words. "How did you know?" she whispered, her tone aching with gratitude.

"Know what, child?" Madame raised a quizzical brow.

One of the hens flitted and landed on the floor. Ondine's hands hovered above it, then swooped down and snatched it up. She held the hen's keel in her palm, securing its legs with her index and middle fingers while her thumb and pinky and ring fingers encircled the bird's body. Her moist cheek grazed its feathers. "Michel told you?"

"Michel knows nothing of it," Luc said, scratching his head and appearing lost.

It did not matter. Luc had unwittingly given her the most delightful gift. Ondine twirled to face them. Afternoon sun beamed through the crack in the door and a troupe of dust motes danced about her. She thought her heart might burst out of her chest.

"I cared for pigeons in Lille," she announced.

Luc rocked back on his heels with a relieved expression. "Then you'll help me with them?"

"*Mais oui*, but you need to feed them better than this! *Mon Dieu*, they are athletes! They need protein and vitamins, and this," she said, expertly corralling the pigeon in one hand while allowing the feed to slip through the fingers of her other, "is wholly inadequate." Her lips pursed. "You should be feeding them a mix of peas, maize and rice. I'll write down the percentages for you."

"You read and write and calculate?" he asked, as if the thought had never occurred to him. Just because she couldn't speak for a while didn't mean she was a dunce. Luc folded his arms and grinned widely. "I don't know if they are athletes, but they do lay a lot of eggs," he agreed.

Tapping a finger to her upper lip, Ondine asked, "You eat some of the eggs, no?"

"Yes, but they come too fast for me to use them all," Madame replied.

"I have thought of selling the dung, but I need it for the vineyard," Luc added.

"Why don't you sell the birds when they're young, say, four weeks old?" Ondine nuzzled the bird she held before placing it back in its nest.

"I could sell the birds at the market in spring. The chef at the restaurant in Vouvray is renowned for his roasted squab and potatoes."

Ondine's head snapped up. *"M'sieu!"* She laughed so hard, she had to grapple to catch her breath. "Your pigeons are much more valuable as messengers than as your next meal!"

"You mean they are . . . homing pigeons?"

"Of course!" she cried. She pointed to the birds. "You have mostly blue cheques, like this one here." She moved on to another row of nests. "But here I see you also have red cheques, blue pieds and some dark cheques."

He had heard of homing pigeons, but he assumed they were a special breed, or a bit of war folklore. "Don't we have to train them or something?"

"You're a Thomas," she said disapprovingly.

"Thomas?" Madame asked.

"Doubting Thomas." She held Luc's wrist with her gloved hand and pulled him over to the wall of nests. "Cut me a piece of that twine," she commanded, pointing to the loop of rope that hung from Luc's belt.

She selected another bird and cooed softly to him. "Tie a small piece of twine to his leg. Wrap it tightly, so it doesn't fall off. He'll probably fly close to a kilometer and a half per minute." Luc did as he was told but looked at Ondine as if she had lost her mind—again.

Ondine held the bird she dubbed *Mon Chou* and marched out of the dovecote toward the house. With the flick of her head, she instructed Luc and Madame to follow. "Madame Chevreau, go warm yourself by the fire for a half hour, then return to the *pigeonnier* at precisely"—she turned Luc's wrist to read the time—"at precisely one-thirty and wait outside until you spot our friend here."

She headed into the kitchen to fetch a covered basket. Luc ushered her into the passenger seat of his Ford. He walked to the right fender and pulled the choke while cranking the lever. He stepped into the car and inserted the key. After adjusting the timing and throttle stalks and hand brake, he hopped back out of the car to crank the lever again. The steps were still faster than saddling, watering and feeding a horse. Within a minute or two, they were off.

"Where to?" he asked.

"Anywhere fifteen minutes from here—your choice," she replied confidently.

When Luc headed due east, instead of southeast along the curve of the Loire River, Ondine suspected he was issuing a silent challenge. When they passed through the sloping farmland and vineyards, finally parking beside a winter-bare copse, she was certain of it. "In there," he insisted.

The colonnade of oaks, Scots pines and giant sequoias swallowed them whole. They walked to its center, where deer rustled, and toads croaked. Before releasing *Mon Chou*, Ondine poured water from jug to bowl and urged him to drink. He lapped up the water while she stroked his feathers. "Godspeed," she murmured, before releasing him into the air. *Mon Chou* bolted like a racehorse from his gate.

Luc's jaw dropped. "He's so fast!"

The pigeon darted through the narrow slices of air between the trees and burst into the spacious golden farmland of the Loire Valley—headed due west.

"Back to the car!" Ondine shouted, lifting her skirt so she could run the distance. *"Tout de suite!"* The crisp air smacked her cheeks and chilled her ears as she ran to the motorcar. Luc only overtook her on the last two strides, even though his legs were much longer.

They bumped along the dirt road home with noses red as cherries, tears leaking from the corners of their eyes. She didn't understand this strange, exhilarating feeling, but when he flashed a smile, she knew he felt it, too. The wind swirled and seemed to gather up their miseries and hurl them helter-skelter across the countryside. In this moment, they were young, and every experience was fresh and untarnished.

Within fifteen minutes, they arrived back at Saint Martin and bolted for the *pigeonnier*. Madame stood in its center, pigeons swirling overhead. *Mon Chou*, with the circlet of twine still tied to his leg, sat on the heel of her palm, pecking at the mound of seeds she held.

Madame's expression danced. "He flew in five minutes ago."

Ondine clapped her hands together. *"Voilà!"* she cried. "You, *m'sieu*, have your own army of homing pigeons," she announced with a flourish of her hand. Sixty pairs of blank, blinking eyes stared in their direction. "Well?"

"What do we do now?" Luc wondered aloud.

"When the hatchlings are four weeks old, we transport them to Tours and sell them to the Americans. The Americans will train them at their new home—and these pigeons always return home."

"They use them on the front lines?"

"Thousands of them. The British are the experts, of course. They are the ones who taught us before the invasion. The pigeons transport messages to headquarters in Paris, Chaumont and now Tours all the time. These birds are faster and more reliable than any other method—even dogs."

"But how do they *know* which way to go?"

"It is innate." She tapped her fist to her heart. "They always find the flight path home."

———

NAPA, CALIFORNIA

Sara's nerves had not flared this badly since the moment twenty years ago when she had to tell Philippe the awful truth—that she had killed his brother in self-defense. Once he understood the circumstances, he had forgiven her. Since then, they had married, lost a child, adopted two and Sara had birthed two more of their own. They had expanded their American and French wine distribution network to cities across the country. They had upgraded the winery's crushing and bottling equipment and purchased new redwood tanks in 1914. They had acquired more acreage north of Eagle's Run in Rutherford and west in Sonoma, planting them with zinfandel, riesling and more sweet varietals in high demand from the archdiocese. Throughout it all, her singular ambition had been to leave land and property for their children. Now, she and Philippe had to tackle the trickiest obstacle yet: What could they do to protect their business from the looming prohibition and preserve this legacy for the next generation?

Inhaling sharply, she approached Philippe as he cleaned his plate of eggs with a triangle of toast while reading the latest edition of the *Napa Register*. Lydia and Johnny had already left for the schoolhouse and the house was quiet, save for the clicking of the fire in the cookstove and the ticking of the clock. Sara slipped into the seat opposite her husband. He was wearing a collared work shirt, dungarees and work boots.

He perused the headlines, his sight still as sharp as a falcon's, while she now required spectacles to read. His fingers, chapped and calloused from the recent pruning, gently clasped hers. He smiled roguishly and kissed the back of her hand.

"What are your plans today?" she asked, feigning nonchalance.

"Whatever plans I have can wait, Mrs. Lemieux."

She arched an eyebrow. "Wasn't this morning enough to satisfy you?" The memory of their frenetic coupling before the house sprang to life heated her cheeks. It bordered on scandalous, the way they still desired each other after so many years and so many children, but if it remained their secret, what was the harm?

He leaned over and softly bit her earlobe. "Never." He chuckled. She punched him lightly on the shoulder. "Okay, back to business if you insist. I'm inspecting the vines today. Care to join me? With the warmer temperatures and dry soil, we might have an early bud break."

Sara grinned, sinking back into her chair. Bud break, *veraison* in June and the harvest in September were her favorite times of the year. Bud break heralded the beginning of the growing season. The chardonnay vines would break first, awaking from their winter slumber and pulling the water up from their roots. The buds that developed last year would swell and eventually produce shoots. Sara glanced out the window at the vineyard. A luxurious carpet of mustard flowers erupted in a riot of yellow, orange and gold between the rows of bare trunks. The cover crop, originally planted in California by the Franciscan missionaries long ago, bloomed just before bud break as an extra layer of protection against worms, insects and late-winter frost. They would soon mow it down to provide nutrients for the growing grapes.

"I would love to come out with you," she replied enthusiastically. "But before we do, I have some ideas," she said bluntly, pulling a small leather-bound notebook from her pocket.

The newspaper rustled as he folded it. "Here comes trouble," he jested.

The muscles in her throat constricted. Why did she always feel shy about presenting her ideas? Legally, they shared ownership of Eagle's Run, and they ran their global operations together, along with Luc, to whom Sara had gifted the Saint Martin vineyard. What rankled Sara was that Philippe had the legal right to control and manage their joint property, even if he did consult her most of the time.

"Could you please refrain from making snap judgments before you hear me out?"

Philippe recoiled. "So serious, my love." He folded his arms and leaned in. "Is this about pulling up the vines and replanting?"

Sara straightened her posture. "Yes, in part, but there's much more to consider." She flattened her hands on the table to steady them. "From what I can determine, we provide approximately forty percent of the archdiocese's wine. We are their largest supplier and growing."

Philippe nodded encouragingly. "For now, but you know the other winemakers are desperate for more of a share."

Sara reached into her apron pocket and pulled out a letter, addressed to them in elegant black script. "We have to protect our share." She waved the opened letter between them. "From Monsignor O'Brien." Philippe snatched it from her hand and scanned its contents. They had first met Monsignor O'Brien in 1898, when he began serving as the archbishop's ecclesiastical wine procurer. Sara and Philippe liked to take credit for schooling him in the finer points of winemaking. Since then, they had kept up a friendly correspondence with the priest as he took on new assignments throughout the archdiocese. O'Brien, in turn, always recommended the "highest quality" Lemieux family wines both in and outside of the Church. Parish orders for Lemieux wines had increased tenfold since they had befriended the priest.

When Philippe finished reading, he dropped the letter on the table and swigged the rest of his coffee. "Monsignor wrote to ask us for a favor, not the other way around." His eyes narrowed.

Sara smiled mischievously.

"What do you have up your sleeve?" he asked.

"Monsignor is now the assistant to Archbishop Hanna. St. Isidore's Agricultural School is in debt, and he wants us to advise them on how to repair their vineyards. He says here, 'One of the St. Isidore's vineyards is bright and clean; however, they have ten acres in dire need of replanting or pruning.' What if we go a step further and offer to buy the land and teach the boys all we taught him?"

"What about replanting that land with prunes or currants?"

"We could look into that," she replied neutrally. "But if we bought the property, we would solidify our relationship with the archdiocese and give St. Isidore's an instant infusion of the cash they need to house and feed the boys. In return, we would ask for a letter from Archbishop Hanna testifying to the purity of the altar wine made at Eagle's Run, which could eventually include wine from the grapes at St. Isidore's."

"Ah, now *that* is an interesting idea." He shuffled to his feet and refilled his coffee mug, offering Sara a sip as he returned to his seat. "I'm just not sure if I want to part with our savings right now."

"It would cost us more to rip out our vines and replant other crops, wouldn't it? This way, we purchase another ten acres of vineyards, but the boys would maintain it under our supervision. It achieves Monsignor O'Brien's objective of training them to farm and our objective of finding a way to sell our wine legally during prohibition."

"And to not destroy our vines . . . at least not yet," Philippe added. "I could put Johnny in charge of instructing them. He's around the same age as the older boys at St. Isidore's. We can call on Reverend Crowley next week, when we're up visiting the Rutherford ranch." Crowley was the prefect of the agricultural school in Rutherford, which had housed orphaned boys from the San Francisco diocese since 1906.

"A brilliant plan!" Sara agreed, but her flattery was transparent.

Philippe cast her a sidelong glance. "Why shouldn't we replant some of our less fruitful acreage with other crops to insulate us against the prohibition?"

A rapping at the kitchen door and a flash of silvery-orange hair through the glass door panes brought Sara to her feet. "Oh, it's Aurora," she said, grateful for the interruption so she could construct her counterargument.

Philippe stood up and slid a chair out for their longtime friend and neighbor. "Oh, my dears, good morning!" the grandmotherly figure proclaimed in her sing-song voice, unwrapping her blue scarf from her neck and plopping down without ceremony. "I do hope I'm not interrupting," she said as an afterthought.

"You are always welcome, Aurora," Philippe replied sincerely. Aurora had been a mother figure to both of them since they had lived at Eagle's Run and was like a grandmother to their children.

"You are a very sweet liar," Aurora gushed, patting Philippe's cheek. "I have a proposal, my dears."

Sara and Philippe exchanged a wary glance. Philippe laughed. "Your last proposal left me with a herd of drunken hogs."

Sara giggled, nudging her friend.

Aurora's eyes rounded in shock. "How was I supposed to know the apricots were fermented? All right, I will admit it was ill-advised to feed them the refuse from the cannery." Her expression soured.

"The poor animals staggered around for four days, grunting and sleeping!" Philippe retorted, smiling. "Let's hope your next proposal is better thought out."

With a flick of her hand, Aurora dismissed his criticism. "It concerns Pippa and Lydia, and of course, you too, Sara, if you agree and would like to join us." She cleared her throat. "The National Woman's Party is mobilizing in the District of Columbia. Wilson is a coward who says he supports women's suffrage but wants us to temper our demands until the war is over. Imagine that, a president who has the nerve to send our sons to war without giving us a say-so! He claims that he wants to 'make the world safe for democracy,' but this is no democracy—it's a hypocrisy!" Aurora's face flushed with outrage. Sara couldn't agree more.

"Don't fly into a full tizzy, Aurora." Philippe poured her a glass of water from the tap. "What exactly do you have planned?"

"Philippe ..." Sara's tone issued a warning.

Philippe raised his palms in defense. "Listen, you know I'm in favor of sensible women having the right to vote, but half of you are hysterical over alcohol and since you won the vote here in California, we're facing a prohibition that will ruin the business we've fought so hard for."

Aurora's hand flew to her hip. "Half of us may be 'hysterical' voters, but half of you men are drunks. Tit for tat."

Philippe's mouth twisted in defeat. "Your proposal?"

"Seventeen states have given women the vote, including New York, but there are still some holdouts. We are mobilizing around the country to support our sisters to make sure President Wilson supports a national suffrage amendment. A dear friend is leading the National Woman's Party activities in Connecticut, and she's planning a rally in Hartford in mid-May. I am going to support her." Aurora's eyes twinkled with excitement. "I want to invite Sara, Lydia and Pippa to join me—to witness history in the making!"

Sara glanced warily at Philippe. "It sounds like a wonderful plan, Aurora, but Philippe and I would have to discuss the details."

"Of course, of course, dears. I need to book passage soon, so do let me know."

"Pippa won't be able to go, unfortunately, because she can't take time off from Hudson's," Philippe reminded them.

Aurora's shoulders sank, but Sara was excited that Philippe did not thoroughly object. "Lydia and I will definitely consider your proposal. We would back in time for the grape ripening, and a change of scenery could be just what we need."

"Fair enough!" Aurora replied.

"Before you go, perhaps you can help us settle something," Sara said. Philippe's nod was barely perceptible but gave her his consent to bring Aurora in on their tête-à-tête. After all, Aurora was a regional expert in grape farming specifically and agriculture in general. "Philippe and I were trying to decide what measures we should take to protect us from the prohibition. We will of course rely on our sacramental wine business, but should we replace the grapevines with another crop or wait and see?"

"You've worked so hard, replanting the vincyard after the fire all those years ago. I can see your reluctance."

"We expanded the orchard, too, but that's still a minor portion of our income," Philippe added.

"It just seems a shame to start replanting when we don't know when prohibition will begin or how long it will last," Sara added.

Aurora sprang up from the table. "May I?" she asked Sara before slathering strawberry jam on a biscuit. Between bites, she said, "Judging from the 1916 vintage, which was half destroyed by frost, and the 1917 vintage, which was record-breaking, I estimate an average crop this season." The biscuit muffled her last few words.

"Sounds right."

"A national prohibition will not pass until next year, so you should crush, bottle and ship before the first of January."

Sara wagged a finger, homing in on the possibilities. "Philippe, perhaps we should open that New York distribution office we have been talking about."

"Now? Why would we incur that expense now when the future of the wine business is so uncertain?"

"To expand our sales of sacramental wine to the eastern archdioceses. We can't ship any of our Vouvray blancs out of France," Sara asserted.

Aurora washed her biscuit down with a gulp of black coffee. "European shipments to New York and the eastern states have stopped entirely. During the last six months, three million gallons of California wine have been shipped out to fill the gap."

"Yes, but now with so many states ratifying the proposed bone-dry amendment, a national prohibition is inevitable."

Aurora dabbed a napkin to her mouth. "It sure as heck is. Ever since the Napa wine men, yourselves excluded, refused to separate themselves from the saloons and hard spirit makers, the Drys have gained traction and are gunning for a full prohibition—on beer and wine, too!" Aurora shuddered at the thought.

Philippe returned to the matter at hand. "Once shipping our non-sacramental wine becomes illegal, what will we do with a New York office?"

"We'll ship wine grapes." Sara scribbled on the blank page of her journal. "I read that four thousand carloads of California wine grapes were shipped east this past season—and Napa, as far as I know, shipped none."

"Our grapes are too delicate to last the journey east," Philippe replied.

Aurora shook her head. "The chardonnay grapes will never last, even in refrigerated cars, but the black grapes, like your zinfandel, should fare just fine."

"We have seventy acres of zinfandel here and another twenty in Rutherford that yield approximately four hundred fifty tons annually, and grapes are selling for fifty dollars a ton, excluding shipping costs."

"Is that the latest price?" Philippe leaned in and rubbed his forehead. "But the demand for wine grapes could drop when prohibition is passed."

"If the national prohibition is modeled after the Sheppard bill, then it will allow private citizens to legally make and keep wine for home consumption," Sara said hopefully.

Aurora chuckled. "My dears, there are about six hundred thousand Italians and one and a half million Jews living in New York alone—all of whom drink wine daily. Demand won't vanish overnight."

"Wouldn't the prohibition limit how much wine they could make?"

"Maybe, but the Prohibs can't enforce that law. What are they going to do? Arrest over two million people?"

"You're right, they'll go after the big fish," Philippe reasoned, his expression brightening. "We should open the New York distribution office right away. I could travel east with you and set it up. If we left in early May, we could return within five weeks."

Aurora clapped her hands together and cried, "What an adventure we'll have! Oh, I must buy a new traveling suit." She grabbed her scarf and coat and disappeared in a flutter, only to return thirty seconds later. Popping her head through the door she added, "Oh, I almost forgot! Keep your award-winning cabernet grapes but rip out the chardonnay after this year's harvest! Replant with prunes or currants—anything but grapes!" she cried. *"À bientôt!"*

Sara's head was spinning with the possibilities. She turned to Philippe. "So, we agree to inspect St. Isidore's vines with an eye to purchasing the land?"

"Yes, but once the prohibition is in full swing, we should replace the chardonnay grapes with another crop."

Sara's chest tightened at the thought, but Philippe and Aurora were right. "Agreed," she said reluctantly. And then it hit her. She slapped her palm on the table. "I know how we can open a New York distribution office for little expense and with full approval of the Church."

"*Ah, bon*, but whom could we trust to run it?"

Sara smiled slyly. "I know just the woman for the job."

———

The bell above the store entrance jingled. A young woman glided through Hudson's Dry Goods, her skirt brushing past narrow rows of shelves stocked with nails, screws and hammers, her head twitching like a chickadee's. She passed beneath the archway that joined the hardware store to the Art Emporium. Pippa snapped into action, since Billy was ringing up another customer at the cash register. "May I help you, ma'am?"

The woman shifted, her gaze darting to the art books, the drawing boards and then to the meticulously organized line of paint bottles.

"I haven't painted since I was a girl," she admitted awkwardly.

Pippa was afraid the woman might turn and flee the store. She understood that impulse all too well. "What would you like to paint?" she coaxed.

"You'll think it's frivolous."

With a light wave of her hand, Pippa dismissed her hesitation. "Not at all. Go on."

"My roses." The woman clutched an exquisite repoussé purse, which she twirled absentmindedly between her fingers. "You see, during the winter months when I'm shut in, I so desperately miss the scent and color of my roses."

"Would you like to recreate them on canvas?"

"Yes. The spring has been drier than usual . . . that is, my roses only bloom once a year, and with the dry spring, perhaps for only a few days this year, so I would like to capture their essence."

"A capital idea." Pippa stepped closer and murmured, "The best reason to paint is to record the beauty of this world. It's so fleeting, especially in these times, don't you agree?"

"Yes, that's exactly what I meant." Worry lines appeared on the woman's youthful forehead. "Do you think I could learn to paint again?"

"Of course! All it requires is the right materials, practice and a whole lot of patience." Pippa laughed lightly. "What kind of paint do you propose to use?"

"Oil."

"A nice choice, especially for bold color." Clearly the woman had an eye for fashion, and Pippa hoped to boost her confidence.

"You will want some canvases, medium, a few types of brushes and of course some paints. What color are your roses?"

The woman perked up. "Vibrant pink."

"My favorite," Pippa said, placing different sizes of canvases on the counter. She hovered over the paint selection. "For pink roses, I would recommend white, blue, gray, green, black, sienna, pink and red. Oh, and perhaps some yellow and orange for sunlight." Pippa swept them into a basket for the customer.

"So many?"

"Don't be intimidated. With oils, you will be layering on the paint." Pippa glanced up. Billy was still helping the other customer, but the store had been rather quiet today. "Do you have a few minutes to spare? I could show you how it's done, Mrs. . . . ?"

"Mary. Miss Mary Mansfield. Would you be so kind?"

"I would be happy to."

Pippa whirled an easel around and secured the canvas. She dropped dollops of paint onto a piece of paper and poured some medium into a teacup. Selecting a variety of brush sizes from the drawer, she tucked a rag into her apron string.

"Pippa, what are you doing?" Billy's tone was pleasant, but his teeth were clenched.

"Showing Miss Mansfield how to paint a rose," she replied with authority. Billy quieted down. Pippa would pay for the materials herself if Mr. Hudson insisted. If he expected her to sell art supplies, then certainly she would need to show the customers how to use them.

"Here we go." Pippa dabbed a half-inch brush in the medium and then into the gray. "I like to start with an outline of the flower, so we know where it will be on the canvas." She painted two shapes that resembled large, spherical, cumulus clouds. With the rag, she wiped the brush clean. "Then, before I paint the flowers, I like to paint the background leaves and garden."

"Oh, is that right?" Miss Mansfield peered over Pippa's shoulder.

"It's up to you, but I like to save the blooms for last." She swirled green and then the sienna on the canvas. "The trick to painting the background is to hold the brush loosely, toward the back, and use a crisscross motion, like so." She handed the brush to Miss Mansfield. "Now you try."

She held the brush tentatively between her fingers. Pippa nodded encouragingly. As Miss Mansfield brushed the canvas with paint, her feet began to tap gently. As her flourishes became bolder, so did the clatter of her boots on the wood floor.

"Ha, ha! What do you think?" she asked excitedly, pulling the brush from the canvas.

"Perfect. Now add a touch of the orange and red, as if the leaves are basking in the sunlight. Not too much, perhaps a dab or two here."

Miss Mansfield's brush and feet moved again in tandem, dancing across the canvas and the floor. "How is this?"

Pippa chuckled. "Excellent. Now clean the brush and I'll show you how to paint the roses."

Billy observed from behind the cash register, and when Pippa glanced his way with an air of satisfaction, she was pleased to see a look of dumbfounded amusement on his face.

The two women huddled together as Pippa's hand shaped the petals of the rose and its deep mauve center with a finer brush.

Miss Mansfield took over, careful to hold the handle near the tip, as Pippa instructed.

"Steady. No dancing when you're painting these small details," she warned playfully.

As Miss Mansfield detailed the rudimentary rose on the canvas, she exclaimed, "I had forgotten how much I love this!"

A rush of pleasure overwhelmed Pippa. "You're a natural. May I wrap up your supplies for you?"

"Oh, yes. Is there anything else I will need?"

"Perhaps one of our new artists' smocks." Pippa held it up and, with a nod of approval from Miss Mansfield, placed it in the basket. "When you are done with your painting, come back to visit us and we'll find just the right hook to hang it in your home."

"I will, I promise. Thank you, Miss . . ."

"Everyone calls me Pippa."

As soon as Mary Mansfield left the store, glowing and carrying her purchases, Billy about-faced from stocking the shelves. "That was incredible."

"What?"

"You handled that customer with such ease. She left so happy—and with a huge bag of supplies!"

"Just doing my job."

"You're so confident," Billy said wonderingly.

"Only when it comes to drawing and painting, I assure you."

"No. I think you're much better at selling things than I am."

Pippa's face warmed with pleasure at the compliment. "My parents sell wine, like most folks around here. My mother always reminds us, 'We are not selling wine. We are selling Napa.'"

"Which means?"

"It means we're selling the experience—the dream. We're not just selling art supplies here. We're selling the joy of color, of creativity. The paints and brushes are just the instruments to achieve those things."

"I suppose you're right." He scratched his head and his face brightened. "What are you doing tomorrow?"

"Chores in the morning, but I'm free in the afternoon."

"I'd love to show you something I am working on."

Her spirits soared. "A sculpture?"

"Yes, in my studio," he added with pride.

His own studio? She would give anything for a room dedicated to her drawing and painting. "Where should we meet?" Just the thought of spending time alone with a young man was rather daring.

"I could meet you here and we could walk to my parents' house, say, tomorrow at one o'clock?"

"Perfect." How would she tell her parents? Should she even ask their permission? After all, she was an adult now, and Susie Taylor, her neighbor of the same age, attended dances and movies with boys and she never had a chaperone. As Pippa churned over the alternatives, another customer lumbered toward the counter.

"Pippa?" Though she had not seen the man up close in three years, she recognized Boone Sumter, Jess's father. He stared at the nametag affixed to Pippa's apron a little too long. He had aged since his son had died.

"Yes, sir. How may I help you today?"

"My how you've grown! You look just like Linnette. I would recognize that face, that hair, anywhere." No one had ever named her birth mother in her presence, save for Papa and Maman. She treasured three distinct, if disjointed, memories of Linnette Cross: silky golden hair, soapy-smelling skin and the musical lilt of the only word she remembered her mother speaking: *Pippa.*

"You knew my mother?" she asked brightly.

His jowls jiggled as he chuckled. "The same as every other man in town, until your father laid claim to her. She was a genuine beauty, your mother was." He removed his hat to reveal the few strands of hair that clung to his glossy head. A chipmunk's tail of a mustache, waxed and curled at the corners, hung beneath his nose. His grin exposed a graveyard of angled, yellow teeth. "She was the finest high-falutin' whore for miles."

Pippa began to teeter. She gripped the edge of the table and swallowed hard. A brilliant white crept from the edges of her vision to its center. Driblets of perspiration dotted her forehead and scalp. She sucked in a deep breath and squinted, trying to pull the figure of the customer back into view. In a high-pitched distressed tone, she asked, "Why are you here, sir?"

The man leered, his gut hanging over the edge of the table. The bitter, sickly smell of chewing tobacco filled the small space between them. "Your papa found you, your new mother called you her own, but that doesn't mean you can put on airs, pretend you're respectable and not the bastard of a whore."

"Pippa?" Billy appeared from behind the closet door, where he was unpacking some of the new stock. "May I help?"

How much had Billy heard? How much did he—and his uncle— already know that she herself did not?

"Yes, Billy, thank you." Pippa's flesh crawled as she backed away from the ugly man. She gathered her coat and lunch pail and made a beeline for the front door.

She felt Mr. Hudson's eyes bore a hole in her back as she navigated between the rows of shelves. "Pippa?"

With her hand firmly wrapped around the brass doorknob, and the promise of a brisk February breeze on her face, Pippa answered, "I'm sorry, Mr. Hudson. I'm unwell." She stumbled out of the store and marched blindly through town until she reached the road toward Carneros.

She walked blindly for over an hour until she reached Las Amigas Road. She could not face her father. If she returned home, Maman would probably defend Papa, Lydia would ask too many questions and Johnny—Johnny was the one person who probably wouldn't give a fig. By the time she realized the sun was setting and that Papa would probably be waiting outside Hudson's in his idling Chevrolet truck, she was in front of Tante Aurora's farmhouse.

She knocked, but only Barney, Tante Aurora's collie, greeted her. "Where is she, Barney?" Pippa rubbed the wrinkle of furry flesh between his ears.

He replied with a bark and a whimper, which Pippa took to mean that Aurora was out. She plopped herself down on the porch swing, where she had sipped many cold glasses of lemonade with Tante Aurora and talked about art and literature and the seven wonders of the world. Barney hopped right up by her side. She bent her head over, nuzzling and crying into his fluffy fur.

A few minutes later, Pippa spied two headlights in the distance. The wheels of Tante Aurora's Cadillac crunched the driveway pebbles. "Pippa!" Aurora exclaimed, arms waving in the air as she shut the motor car door. She took one look at Pippa and scooped her into her fleshy embrace. She guided her into the parlor, where the wood-burning stove ticked, mercifully toasting the air in the room. Pippa slumped down on the long, blue, silk-and-mahogany settee. Barney, who must have sensed the angst that hung in the air, lounged on the oriental carpet below its carved feet.

"Oh, my dear, you look like you have been squeezed through the wringer. And your hands!" Her warm fingers kneaded Pippa's palms until the blood flowed again. "You need a blanket and a hot toddy," she announced and disappeared into the kitchen. The beauty of Tante 'Rora was that she knew when to leave one to oneself.

Pippa leaned over, propping her head against a cushion. She stared at the papered wall covered with framed photographs. There was a tintype of Tante 'Rora's husband and their young son, both of whom had died years ago. The rest of the photos were of Pippa's own family—many taken by Maman since she had acquired her prized Kodak camera for Marie and Matthew Donnelly's wedding.

Pippa's favorite photographs were the ones snapped in December—of her and Adeline at the Playland carousel and in front of the Cliff House in San Francisco. Adeline had taken her on a "mystery tour" of the city when she turned twenty. She had written clues on notecards and then Pippa had tried to guess their destinations. Addie was always ribbing Pippa for being a "country bumpkin" and encouraging her to explore the city more.

Six years Pippa's senior, Addie had also been born out of wedlock, which was perhaps why there had always been an unspoken

123

camaraderie between them. The day before their mystery tour, Addie had presented Pippa with five silk and cotton dresses. When Pippa refused them, Addie rolled her eyes and exclaimed, "What am I going to do with a bunch of dresses in the hospitals of France? By the time I return, they'll be out of fashion. You'll have to find some parties to wear them to while I'm gone."

Pippa knew she had been born out of wedlock, but this new revelation—that her mother had been a wanton woman—was the wildest yet. Was she even Philippe's daughter? If her mother had been a prostitute, how could they be sure? For goodness sakes, Boone Sumter, presumably one of her mother's paramours from back in the day, could have been her father! She shivered in disgust.

At least Addie's mother, Marie, though scorned by Papa's brother, was now a successful surgeon—one of the few women in her field. Something a daughter could be proud of.

Pippa's stomach somersaulted and she suddenly craved the steaming mug of bourbon and honey her honorary aunt placed before her. She threaded her fingers through the handle and allowed the heat to permeate her hands. Maybe if she concentrated on this moment, she would not have to face what might or might not be the truth and what that meant about who she was. She drained the mug of its warm elixir—and apparently drifted off to sleep.

She awoke to a darkened room and Maman kneeling beside the settee, trying to coax her awake. Pippa kept her eyes shut. She was not ready to speak. When Barney's scratchy tongue licked the length of her cheek, she knew the jig was up. *Meddling mutt!* She shooed him away with one hand and sat up.

"Hello, Maman." Pippa spied Tante Aurora leaning on the doorjamb. "Thank you, Tante," she said softly.

"Are you ill?" Maman asked, the back of her hand held to Pippa's forehead and her gaze fretful beneath the lamp's light. "Did something happen at the store?" Her voice quavered. *She knew! Pippa would bet her life that Maman was an accomplice in this deception! Did Tante Aurora know, too? Was there a grand conspiracy designed to protect Pippa from her past?*

She stood, pushed past Maman and marched out the door toward Eagle's Run.

———

"Why didn't you tell me?" Pippa stared up at her father.

Her father, who had returned home frantic only to find Pippa seated in the parlor with Maman, replied, "We thought you had enough to deal with, and no one except for the orphanage and Sara knew the circumstances of your birth."

"And Tante Aurora, yes?"

"Yes. She was—is—my friend," Philippe replied.

"Maman, could you please leave Papa and me to talk—alone?"

"Of course," she murmured, flashing Papa a sympathetic glance that made Pippa want to scream.

Pippa faced her father, whose countenance was alarmingly calm. "What *exactly* happened?"

"I married Sara in December of 1897—"

"The month I was born."

"Yes, but I didn't know about you."

"Wait, let's start from the beginning. When did you meet my mother?"

Across from Pippa, seated on the hassock to her armchair, Philippe intertwined his fingers and rested his elbows on his knees. "In 1895."

"*Where* did you meet her?" Clearly, she would need to be more specific. He was not in the mood to elaborate.

"Outside the Clinton Street House in Napa."

"House or *brothel*?"

He exhaled loudly. "Brothel." He sat back. "Where is this sudden curiosity coming from?"

"This isn't sudden! I've always wanted to know the details of my birth and your relationship with my mother, and, until today, I thought I did!"

"We told you everything we thought you were prepared to hear."

"I'm twenty years old, Papa. I have been an adult for two years now. You should have let me decide."

"You're right."

Pippa rose and circled the room, unable to look at her father and think straight at the same time. "So . . . you paid my mother for her . . . services?" she stammered. Her stomach seized with queasiness.

"Pippa, it wasn't like that. Your mother and I were friends. I wanted to protect her from that life."

"Then she *was* a common whore?"

"No!" His reaction was a bit too indignant to believe.

"Oh, then I suppose she was a 'high-falutin' whore' like the customer in the store told me today?"

"What? Who said that to you?" he snapped.

126

"Boone Sumter. He knew my mother. I have a right to know if people are going to spread rumors, or in this case, truths, about my parentage!"

Her father massaged his chin, his fingers and thumb moving over the shadow of whiskers that scraped her cheek when she hugged him goodnight. "Linnette had a good heart and she adored you. She told me about you nearly two years after you were born—after I married Sara."

Pippa was relieved to hear him speak her Christian name. "And what about Linnette? Did *you* adore *her*?" Her fear of his answer slid like a stone from her throat to her stomach.

He paused, constructing his next sentence. "I loved many things about Linnette. Her sense of humor, her beauty, her kindness . . ." His list trailed into silence. "But I fell in love with Sara and that's why I broke with Linnette."

"So, you were using Linnette for . . . companionship?" she quavered.

"I was young. I made mistakes, as you will."

"I will not fornicate with someone I do not love!" Pippa hated uttering such explicit words in the presence of her father, but it was the truth. His only reaction was to hang his head. He could not even look at her. Her heart pulsed wildly, and she sank back down into the armchair. "I'm a mistake, then? Why didn't you marry and make me legitimate?"

His tone was strangely soothing. "As I said, by the time I found out that you existed, I was already married to Sara." He moved closer, knelt on the floor and took her hands in his. "You have always been a blessing." Papa's eyes welled with tears.

Pippa withdrew her hands and crossed her arms. "And how did Maman feel about all this?"

"She was angry. She felt betrayed, but as soon as she met you, her heart thawed. She has loved you like her own daughter for seventeen years."

Pippa knew that was true. A rush of gratitude filled her chest, bolstering her courage. "Does Luc know? What about Adeline?"

"Yes, but only because the children at school teased you when you first arrived."

"Because of my speech impediment?" She recalled those tender days, and how Maman insisted that she go to school and learn with the other children because she was just as bright and as scholarly as Luc.

"No. Unfortunately, the Sumters spread the rumor that you were born out of wedlock."

"It's not a rumor. It's the truth."

"Still, it was unkind, and your brother Luc would have none of it."

Luc, a year and a half older than Pippa, had always protected her from the jeering bullies at school. "What did he do?"

"He punched the kid." Papa's lips twitched into a slight smile.

"Wait, was that Jess Sumter?"

Papa nodded. "But Luc and Adeline and the other children don't know about Linnette's past, only that you are my child and your mother died when you were three, so I took you home with me and Sara adopted you. Luc is adopted, too, so it didn't seem strange to them."

"You didn't know that Linnette was with child when you broke with her? When you married Maman?" She had to be sure.

"No."

"Linnette wasn't good enough for you, was she?" Pippa's chin trembled with emotion.

"No, that's not true." He touched his warm, rough palm to her cheek. "We weren't a suitable match in the long run. She knew nothing of farming or grape growing or my life outside of my time with her."

Pippa drew in several jagged breaths. She was perspiring so profusely, she had to wipe her clammy hands on her sullied store apron before she continued. "Papa," Pippa whispered. Twisting her apron string around her index finger until it bulged red, she finally drummed up the daring to ask. "How can you be sure I'm your daughter?"

A stiff silence penetrated the room. "Because Linnette never went back to that life after me."

"She told you that?"

"Yes. When I met you for the first time, the poor conditions you lived in confirmed it. I was so ashamed of my behavior. From that day on, I sent money for your care every month—and when I learned Linnette had died, I searched until I found you in the orphan asylum."

"But how could you be certain—that I am yours?"

"Oh, Pippa, is that what this is all about?"

She clenched her jaw. She had never questioned these things before, but now she felt like a smudge on his polished life.

"The moment I saw your bright blue eyes, it was like looking at my own reflection," he said in earnest.

"Truly?"

"Where do you think you get your nose? You have a smaller, more delicate version, but it's the exact same shape as mine!"

"Oh," she replied, sliding a finger from bridge to tip. "I suppose it is, Papa."

He clasped her hand in his and kissed it. "No more doubts, okay?"

She nodded, happy to confirm she was her father's daughter, but still sick to her stomach over her mother's profession. "But what do I say, Papa? To people like that man?"

"You say, 'I am Philippe Lemieux's daughter and any gossip you have regarding my parentage may be directed to him, thank you.'"

Pippa frowned. "I can't say that!" The audacity sent her mind into a tailspin.

"Or something like that. Hold your head high. Your character—the young lady you become—is more important than the circumstances surrounding your birth. Look at Adeline, for example."

But Addie's Maman wasn't a whore. Pippa shoved her misgivings aside as Papa pulled her into his arms for a quick embrace and a peck on the cheek. "That's my girl." His smile did not quite light his eyes, but she would have to accept his platitudes—for now.

The next day, Pippa avoided breakfast and lunch. Instead, she discarded three crinkled yellow and red Mary Jane wrappers on the windowsill.

130

She feigned illness, but of course her parents knew better. She paid Lydia a quarter to clean the chicken coop and collect the eggs for her. When Maman strolled in at half past one, she flitted around the sisters' room, hanging Pippa's dress and collecting her undergarments for the laundry. She threw open the drapes, allowing the glowing winter sunlight to penetrate even the darkest corners of the bedroom Pippa shared with her sister. Pippa winced.

"Rise and shine, my love. You have a visitor."

Pippa bolted upright. "Who?" she squeaked.

"Billy Hudson." Maman sat at the foot of the bed. Her green gaze softened. "He says you had a date at one o'clock to see his art studio. You can't hide anymore, Pippa."

A shiver ran through Pippa's chest. She yanked the quilt up to her underarms and stared down at its patchwork of yellow and green flowers. "Maman, he heard everything," she whispered, guessing that Papa would have told Maman the details of their conversation the night before. If he hadn't, Maman would have dragged her out of bed much earlier.

"What other people say about you is none of your concern."

"What do you mean?"

"What other people say or think about you doesn't matter. What you think—what God thinks—are all that matter."

"But Billy heard the whole thing. He knows about me, Maman. About my past."

Maman's mouth twitched with amusement. "Darling, you don't have a past. Your parents do." She cupped Pippa's knee. "And Billy doesn't seem to care either way. I think he's quite smitten."

How could she feign pleasantries at a time like this? "The woman who birthed me was a whore," Pippa croaked, shuddering at the violence of the words.

"Her name was Linnette Cross. I never met her, but she loved your father and you dearly. She cared for you until she died."

Pippa was unconvinced.

Maman sighed. "When I—" She stopped and, with uncharacteristic hesitation, continued. "When I was younger than you and growing up in France, I had to defend myself against your uncle—Luc's real father. He beat my sister and then tried to force himself on me and I . . . I killed him."

Pippa gasped. "How old were you?"

"Seventeen."

"And Luc knows?"

"Yes."

How was this admission supposed to help? Her father was a Lothario and her adoptive mother a murderess? Pippa kept her thoughts to herself, for she did not want to seem disrespectful, but . . . maybe people were right. Maybe God had marked her with a cleft lip because her parents had gravely sinned. Pippa thought her mind might explode with the magnitude of these revelations.

Maman continued, despite the look of horror on Pippa's face. "I did something I deeply regret. Your father treated your mother in a way he deeply regrets, but we are both so grateful that you were the result."

"Papa forgave you? For killing his brother?"

"Once he understood I was defending myself and my sister. He knew Bastien was not a good man."

Pippa sat in silence for a moment, the heat of shame rising in her cheeks. "I can't face Billy. I just can't."

"You can and you will," Maman persisted, rifling through Pippa's drawers and picking out a fresh chemise and bloomers. She inspected Pippa's hanging dresses. "This one ought to do," she said, holding out a blue wool that matched Pippa's eyes.

"Life continues, Pippa. If I hadn't owned up to my mistakes, and your father hadn't forgiven me, we wouldn't be here now—with a family and vineyards to leave you children."

Pippa took the dress from Maman. She supposed she could not argue with Maman's logic, at least not under her parents' roof, but she still felt the sharp stab of resentment.

"Now, clean up and get dressed. I'll offer Billy a cup of coffee." Maman smoothed Pippa's disheveled hair, just like she used to do when Pippa was little. Her mother's long, elegant fingers glided over Pippa's forehead and temples and the crown of her head.

"Yes, Maman."

Maman gently closed the door behind her. Pippa inspected her reflection as she ran a brush through her hair. Her puffy eyes were indeed her father's, but her blond hair and alabaster skin were most likely inherited from Linnette. She brushed her teeth and powdered her nose and the thin, pink scar line that ran down to her lip. She did not need to pinch her cheeks, for a high color rose across her bosom and neck and face. Pippa gripped the banister as she edged down the stairs. She cringed, hearing Billy and her father laughing downstairs.

Billy's chair scraped the floor when she came in. "Hello, Pippa." Standing nearly as tall as her father, Billy looked like a film star with slicked-back pomaded hair and a starched white shirt.

"Hello, Billy," she replied softly.

Her father cleared the plates and mugs from the table. Apparently, Billy had been treated to cake and coffee.

"Billy was just saying you two are planning to tour his studio this afternoon. I told him your sister Lydia would be happy to serve as chaperone." Was Papa teasing? Probably not.

"Papa, that's a little old-fashioned," she warned. She pulled her apron from the basket near the stove with silent thanks to her mother for laundering it.

"My parents will be home, if that is acceptable, sir. In fact, they have invited Pippa for supper if you'll permit it."

Papa was silent, but his gaze was steady as he sized up Billy. Pippa's irritation with her father reached an unprecedented level. *Would he dare to interfere with her friendship when his dalliance with Linnette had been so dishonorable? Would he dare to question her trustworthiness, or Billy's, when he himself had kept this secret for twenty years?* The clenched fists by her side or the scowl on her face must have communicated her ire, for Papa simply said, "I'll pick you up at seven o'clock, Pippa, if that suits."

Billy's Adam's apple bobbed in his neck. He sputtered, "Of course, sir. Our house is the little blue one on the corner of Laurel and Monroe Streets. Thank you, sir." Unable to wait one more excruciating moment, Pippa guided Billy out into the midday sunshine.

"How did you know where I live?" she asked, stepping up into Billy's father's buggy.

"You wrote your address down on your employment application. Mr. Hudson gave it to me. I hope you don't mind, but I figured you might need a distraction after you left so suddenly yesterday." Billy pulled a lap robe from the storage compartment behind the seat and tucked Pippa in. In an endearing show of concern, he made sure the blanket covered her from the waist all the way down to the tips of her boots.

Pippa slid her gloved hands beneath the blanket while Billy untethered the horse, slid into the seat beside her and urged the bay onward with a shake of the reins and a clucking sound. "I suppose you heard everything that horrid man said." Pippa ventured.

Billy ran a hand through his hair and exhaled loudly. He studied the road ahead. "I wish I hadn't, but I did."

A wave of nausea rose up. "I hope you don't think less of me." She fixed her eyes on the houses, barns and sheep that dotted the farmland off Duhig Road.

"Would I be here if I did?" He nudged her playfully with his elbow. Pippa sighed with relief.

Adjacent to the stable where the Hudsons kept their single horse was a smaller workroom. The barn door slid open to reveal figures on makeshift tables of pine planks and sawhorses. Exquisite wood carvings of bent-back men and supine women were startling and sensuous all at once. Their musculature was so lifelike. Some of their faces were shrouded, others carved with wild expressions of pain, joy or sadness, conjuring the same depth of feeling as Michelangelo's *Pietà*. Pippa was mesmerized by the sophistication and detail of his work.

"How long have you been carving?"

"I started about eight years ago. I wanted to train the one eye I had left," he said with self-effacing candor. "Now I'm starting to sculpt more, though I can't afford jade or bronze, so for now, plaster casts have to do." Billy dusted off a stool and offered Pippa a seat.

"Today, if you're willing, you can help me make one."

"Really? How?"

"I've made a clay sculpture from observing my subject, and now we can use plaster of Paris to make a cast of it."

Pippa jumped up from her seat and rubbed her hands together. "Where do we begin?"

Billy removed his jacket and tie, rolled up his sleeves and donned an apron. He indicated the large pot of water on the stove. "Once the water is warm, we mix the plaster of Paris." He handed her the plaster powder and a bucket. He whirled around the small space, collecting a spatula, hammer and chisel, metal shims, oil soap and a brush. Lastly, he handed Pippa a few squares of burlap and two clamps.

The squeaking of door hinges startled her. A sprightly, plump woman carrying a tray shuffled in. The scent of fresh hot bread filled the small space, causing Pippa's stomach to rumble. She had not eaten anything but a few candies since lunch the day before and she was suddenly ravenous. "Since my son has not seen fit to introduce us, I thought I would use the excuse of bringing you some refreshments."

Taking the obvious hint, Billy replied, "Pippa, this is my mother. Mama, this is Pippa Lemieux."

Mrs. Hudson placed the tray of bread, hard cheese and salami and raisins on the table. "I have visited your family's vineyard and even purchased their wine. The chardonnay is my favorite," she confided. "So nice that Billy has someone his own age to work with. He was quite bored working with his uncle—until you came along." Her cherubic cheeks glowed. "Nice to meet you, Miss Pippa. We sup at six, you two."

Billy sidled up to his clay sculpture and waved Pippa over. As she neared, she was struck by its familiarity. "Is that . . . ?"

"You? Yes," he answered sheepishly.

She swallowed hard. "But how?" she wondered aloud.

"It's not perfect. I sketched you from different angles during the day and then I shaped the clay last night. Perhaps I should have asked your permission, but I was afraid you would refuse."

"You were right."

"It was either you or the old biddy who sits on the stoop at the end of the block."

Pippa laughed. "Then you probably made the right choice."

He moved a step closer. "I wanted you to see what I see."

Pippa examined the clay head. Its likeness to her own reflection in the looking glass was uncanny. She leaned in, noting the thin ridge of clay that ran down the philtrum to the upper lip. Far from being repulsive, the imperfection gave the sculpture an intriguing focal point. Instinctively, Pippa touched her own scar.

Billy's long, graceful fingers skimmed the terra cotta sculpture's cheek and jawline. Pippa's breath faltered. Could she dare to hope that Billy would one day caress her own skin with the same tenderness?

"Beautiful," he said.

Pippa blushed. She filled the uncomfortable silence that ensued by tugging the lid off the plaster powder. "How much should I measure out?" she asked, her heart thrumming in her ears.

Billy reached over and cradled her elbow. His blue gaze locked on her face. "Beautiful."

"Thank you," she whispered breathlessly.

"Dump all of it in the bowl," he answered cheerfully, dipping a ladle into the water pot. He added an equal amount of water to the powder while Pippa mixed it.

He slid ten metal shims into the clay, fanning them out around the midline of the head and dividing it into two halves, front and back. He presented a brush to Pippa. "We'll start with the back of the head. Apply a thin layer at first, so we don't have any air bubbles," he instructed. Once they had coated the first half with three layers of plaster to a thickness of an inch, they washed their hands and sat by the warmth of the stove to eat. The crusty bread, along with a few crumbles of cheese and a slice of salami, sated Pippa's hunger.

Billy touched a cloth napkin to his lips and flicked a few crumbs off his lap. "Were you surprised by what that man said— in the store?"

"I was." Pippa nibbled on a semicircle of crust.

"When did your birth mother die?" Had anyone else made such an abrupt inquiry, Pippa would have fled the room. However, Billy's tone was so conversational and his manner so nonchalant, she felt safe to answer—on one condition.

"Can I trust you not to share what I tell you? Not even your parents. You know how people talk."

"Of course." He popped another raisin in his mouth.

138

"I was two. My father searched for me and found me in an orphan asylum in San Francisco."

"He had met you?"

"Yes, but he was already married to Sara, my adoptive mother, when he discovered I existed."

"I'm sorry about your mother."

She was not sure if he was sorry about her death or her unfortunate profession, but regardless, she appreciated the sentiment. "Me, too."

When the first half of the cast was dry, in about an hour's time, Billy removed the metal shims and chiseled three small indentations in the plaster where they would connect the front half.

Working until half past four, they coated the front half of the clay head with three more layers, taking great care to flood every crevice with plaster, eventually connecting the wet half to the dry half. By five thirty, the second half was dry and Pippa's clay likeness was encased in snowy white plaster of Paris.

"Now, we want to create a support for the plaster head. Could you please pass me those four metal rods and some burlap squares?"

Pippa complied while Billy stirred another bucket of plaster. "I had no idea the process was so lengthy."

"This is the fun part." Billy sat on the stool wadding up the burlap squares, his long, sinewy legs stretched beneath the table. Despite his loss of one eye, his movements were dexterous and fluid. "This is the first cast I've made outside of school, so it should be simpler for the next one."

"Where did you train?"

"San Francisco. Take a piece of the burlap and give me your hand," he said, palm extended. His lithe fingers cradled hers and he guided their hands into the bucket of warm, wet plaster. She had never stood this close to Billy before. He could so easily have ruined the moment by going too far, by insisting she sit on his knee or by curling his arm around her waist, but he did neither. He pulled her balled hand out of the plaster and showed her how to fasten one end of the metal rod to the top of the head by wrapping the wet burlap around it. She then attached the bottom of the rod at the base of the cast in the same manner. Pippa repeated the task independently for the other three rods, until they were all secured to the head.

"What's next?"

"Once it dries, we crack it open, remove the clay, and then we'll have our negative."

"Negative?"

"Yes, just like when you take a photograph, we've created a mold that's a negative of the head. Then we wash out the inside, clamp the two plaster halves together again, turn the mold upside down and fill it with plaster. The result will be the positive—or rather, a replica of the original clay head but in plaster."

"That sounds very complicated. I rather prefer my pencils and paints."

"You just like the instant gratification," he teased. "Creating new things requires patience."

"You have plaster on your cheek," she pointed out, dabbing the corner of her smock in water and rubbing off the smudge.

He gently clasped her wrist and bent down, his face hovering above hers. She lifted her chin to meet his kiss. His lips were unexpectedly supple and his taste, deliciously rousing.

"About our sculpture," Pippa murmured, "let's not show my father just yet."

His arms encircled her, and she pressed her cheek to his chest. He smelled of spice and soap and sulfur from the wet plaster. "No, let's not."

———

NEW YORK, NEW YORK

On Sunday, her day off, Adeline stepped out into the streets of Manhattan, determined to find the convent where she had lived as a child. She attended Mass at St. Patrick's Old Cathedral and then walked to the flagstone steps and carved wooden doors of the convent on Mott Street, now wedged between a grocer and a shoeshine parlor. Two long windows faced the street; spines of ice decorated their panes. Her extremities had numbed by the time someone responded to her rapping at the door.

As soon as Adeline announced her name, the young nun ushered her in through the dark wood-paneled entryway to the right-side parlor. The postulants and novitiates most likely all knew that Marie Donnelly was one of their most generous benefactors. For years, Adeline's mother had sent healthy annual donations as a token of her appreciation—and directed that the Sisters of Notre Dame use the money whenever possible to care for unwed mothers and their children.

Children conceived in sin. Children born out of wedlock. Children rejected by their fathers. Bastards. Adeline was one of these children, and this place had shaped her from her first breath. Maman had married Matthew in California when Adeline was eleven. Then she started to wear dresses with crinoline and lace, and she moved to a carpeted home with running water and indoor toilets, all provided by her stepfather's fortune. She attended the most exclusive girls' schools in San Francisco and gloried in summer steamship travel abroad. She had even won over her stepfather's disapproving father, Rourke Donnelly, senior, who now held her in the same regard as a blood granddaughter. No one dared to whisper about her parentage, or her mother's humble beginnings as a tavern owner's daughter, or that her Tante Sara had killed Bastien Lemieux, her real father, in self-defense. No one dared to impugn the rich and powerful Donnelly family. Yet, beneath the glittering white comforter of wealth, she knew what she was—and where she had come from.

She had always hoped that Uncle Philippe would marry her mother, for he had always been so kind to them both. After his brother Bastien had proved to be a cad, Philippe had secured passage for her mother to America, and he had arranged for her to stay and give birth to Adeline at the convent. Until Matthew had come along, Philippe was the only father figure Adeline had known.

She sighed contentedly as she regarded the parlor furnishings. It had been seventeen years since she and her mother had left for California but the hassock where Uncle Philippe had sat when he had visited was still there—but reupholstered in a gold brocade.

The parlor door squeaked open. There was something familiar about the Reverend Mother's demeanor, but Adeline could discern nothing more, for her black veil, white bandeau, wimple and robes covered everything but her face, and her hands were tucked behind her scapular.

"Welcome, *madame*, or is it *mademoiselle*?" she asked in the native French of her order.

"I don't know if you remember me, Mother, but—wait, are you, were you Sister Paulette?"

The Reverend Mother's gaze drifted to Adeline's crucifix and she burst into a smile, revealing a row of small, straight teeth. Her hands fluttered in the air and came to rest in a prayerful position. "Adeline? Adeline Chevreau?"

"Yes, yes!" Adeline cried, buoyed by the mention of her birth surname.

"Of course! I should have known you from your curly dark hair and your fine eyes! Welcome! What brings you here, my dear? Your mother should have sent word." She patted the chair across from her, gesturing for Adeline to sit, and the two of them began to chatter like magpies.

Adeline explained she was going to war. "My mother didn't know I planned to visit. When I discovered I would be stationed nearby for a few months before we ship out to France, I had to come find you."

"No matter, you're here now. Tell me, what news do you have from home? Of your mother and father, and of Sara and Luc and your uncle Philippe?" She was breathless with excitement.

Adeline explained that her stepfather would be sent to war in two months' time and that her mother would be holding down the fort, so to speak, at the couple's surgery in San Francisco, while mothering little Rourke and Gemma, too.

"Luc has been in France these past few years. He returned to Saint Martin, and I hope to see him when I'm abroad."

"Would you do me the favor and bring something to him?" Without waiting for Adeline's response, she led her deep into the stone convent. The place was snugger than she recalled. The severity and silence of the corridors brought back a flood of memories for Adeline. She would shuffle but never run through its hallowed hallways, whisper but never laugh aloud. Yet, as she ambled behind Reverend Mother, she recalled pressing her hot cheek against the cool stone on blistering summer days and biting into a red apple she had picked from the garden, reveling in the hypnotic melody of the *Ave Maria*. Calm swept over her. She was safe here, if only for a few minutes before she headed back out into the city streets.

Reverend Mother handed Adeline a brightly colored comic book entitled *Charlie Chaplin's Comic Capers*. She giggled. "Convent contraband, you know, but Luc will love it!" Adeline laughed, then rolled up the book and slid it into the pocket of her overcoat.

On the way back to the parlor, they passed the room at the back of the convent where Lydia had died giving birth to Luc. Adeline had only been five at the time, but the room reminded her of the rusty smell of blood and the heavy heat waves rippling through the air that August afternoon. Adeline stopped short. "Reverend Mother, did you know anything about my father—my *real* father?"

She frowned. "Your mother hardly ever spoke of him. She did say that he refused to take responsibility for you. That's why your uncle Philippe helped her come to America."

"And Tante Sara, did she say anything when she was here?"

Reverend Mother shook her head. "Sara was on the run from the authorities at the time. We only knew that Lydia was her widowed sister. When she wrote me a year later, after everything had been resolved between her and Philippe, she confessed her real name and the story of how she arrived here." She looked sideways at Adeline.

"I know that Sara killed my father. She said it was in defense of her virtue. Philippe and Maman, although they weren't there, believed her side of the story."

Reverend Mother considered this before speaking. "Perhaps they knew your father's character. According to Sara, he treated Lydia harshly. It was unbearable for them."

Adeline nodded. Unbearable, certainly, but did she really have to *kill* him? "How did my mother eventually discover Sara and Lydia's identity?"

"Why, your great-uncle Jacques, of course."

"Uncle Jacques?"

The Reverend Mother pointed to Adeline's collar. Adeline's hand flew to her cross. "Your mother saw the cross that hung around Sara's neck—it was the same as the one that her uncle Jacques had carved for her when she was a girl. She guessed that Sara and Lydia were trying to escape Bastien—your father."

"And she kept their secret?"

"Indeed."

Adeline lowered herself into a wingback chair. It was unreal to think how these families' lives had intertwined over the years, all because of one man—the man who, for Adeline, was an unknown, a missing link in her personal history. Adeline was struck with an idea. "Where did they bury Luc's mother?"

"Let me fetch my cloak, and I will take you to the spot." She clutched her rosary to her chest.

The two strode down to the very end of Mott Street, to a sliver of grass between two triple-deckers. They walked through a small iron gate to six grave markers. "Here." Reverend Mother pointed to the stone with Lydia's name. It was practically new, although she had died twenty-one years ago.

"Your mother and Sara sent us the money for the headstone ten years ago."

"Has Luc seen this?"

She shook her head. "Perhaps one day he will return."

———

GIVET, FRANCE

Heinrich bided his time. Though they had arrived at the new camp on the Belgian border a week ago, he had not heard back from Schröder about his request for a furlough.

Fever and respiratory ailments had increased among the troops, who were now engaged in mobile warfare training from dawn until dusk every day. Heinrich kept busy caring for the feverish and asthmatic—and kept watch for the perfect moment to again request a leave of absence to find his son.

The division drilled incessantly. From inside the first aid tent, Heinrich could determine which maneuvers the soldiers practiced just from what he heard and what he smelled. Acrid smoke from faux bombs blew after mock battles, short blasts meant the demolition squad had just detonated charges along the barbed wire, and the whistle of a rocket announced that the assault troops had passed through the wire and reached their target.

This morning, the troops had been practicing moving equipment and companies of infantry with their signal, trench mortar and flamethrower detachments. When Heinrich heard the terrifying whoosh and roar of the newest *Flammenwerfer*, he ducked out of his tent and stopped short. A hundred meters away, a soldier with a gas cylinder strapped to his back clenched a nozzle between his hands. From its metal jaws surged a fifteen-meter wall of fire, sure to roast any living thing in its path. The thundering noise would drown out the victims' screams, leaving the flamethrower's operator ignorant of the suffering he inflicted. Heinrich's countrymen had developed a weapon to unleash the flames of hell here on earth. His stomach somersaulted in horror. Sweat beaded on his brow and trickled down the nape of his neck. He retreated into the tent and gulped air until he finally stopped trembling.

———

Shortly after the noon hour, the crunch of marching boots halted, and shouts flared outside the tent where Heinrich worked.

"Did you ask to be excused from duty?" a voice growled.

Heinrich stepped out into the sunlight. A column of soldiers surrounded a two-wheeled limber. Attached to the limber's four-foot wheel was a drooping private, who quailed as a sergeant cinched the thick ropes around his wrists.

"Did you ask to be excused?" the sergeant bellowed again.

"Yes, sir." The soldier's chest hunched. His head dropped.

"Did you receive permission?"

The man whimpered now, but without tears. His chapped lips trembled as he answered. "Not yet, but I—" The butt of the sergeant's Gewehr 98 cracked sickeningly against the soldier's skull.

Heinrich edged toward the limber, heart hammering like a jackrabbit's. When he neared, he smelled and then saw a brown stain spreading across the back of the private's britches. He could feel the weight of his comrades' stares.

Twenty paces to his left, the colonel in charge of the drills scrutinized the scene, but no verdict was readable in his expression. He caught Heinrich's eye for an instant, long enough for Heinrich to discern that the superior officers present did not intend to step in.

"Sergeant," Heinrich called, raising his hand. "This soldier is ill and must be treated immediately."

The sergeant's expression soured, but when he saw Heinrich's shoulder straps, he snapped to attention and saluted. "He is being disciplined, *Leutnant*."

"For what reason?"

"He left his marching position without permission."

"It is obvious he had every intention of securing permission, but nature called first. He is obviously dehydrated and suffering from diarrhea. Release him at once."

The sergeant grumbled and looked to the nearby colonel, who gave an almost imperceptible nod. The sergeant spat on the ground, flicked his penknife open and sawed through the ropes around the private's wrists. The soldier fell into Heinrich's arms.

"Thank you, Sergeant," Heinrich muttered. He bolstered the private as they shuffled toward the first aid tent.

The colonel strutted over to Heinrich as he was about to duck into the tent with the private. His upper lip curled in disgust at the sickly smell surrounding them. He leaned in and whispered in Heinrich's ear. "About that leave of absence you requested, *Leutnant*. It is now denied."

CHAPTER 6

April 1918

The Germans had launched a spring offensive to drive deeper into the heart of France. By Luc's estimation, he only had a week to enlist before the Americans mobilized every last available man and surged toward the western front to stop the Huns from reaching Paris.

Luc arrived at the base in Tours with a basket of four of his strongest squeakers, not yet four weeks old. Ondine had chosen them herself. She had fed, watered and bathed them and packed them in paper and straw in the basket they had used to transport *Mon Chou*.

With an introduction from the corporal at the quartermaster's headquarters, Luc gifted the Signal Corps pigeoneers with the four birds and, in turn, secured a supply of bird feed: a mixture of mostly Canadian peas, with some rice, Argentine corn and milo maize sprinkled in. Of course, the pigeoneers had already received six hundred birds as a gift from British fanciers, the experts in carrier pigeons. The king himself had loaned his pigeons to help with the British war effort. Yet, here Luc stood, still seeking a proper war post.

He cleared his throat, remembering Ondine's instructions. "Before I go, gentlemen, do you have any fine mosquito cloth I could take with me?"

"You know about pigeon care?"

"Yes, sir," Luc fibbed.

The sergeant handed him a wad of cloth. "Say, why are you wearing civvies? Why haven't you enlisted?"

"I keep asking."

"Failed the physical?"

"No! Nothing like that."

"I'm about to receive shipment of three new mobile lofts. Come back next Tuesday." He raised his finger, as if he were about to finish his thought, but then disappeared behind a row of Ford Model T trucks that had been converted to pigeon lofts, two levels high, looking like something a troupe of circus performers would use to travel across the French countryside.

If he could convince the American pigeoneers to accept him and bring him to the front, then this bird detour might amount to something.

————

"I need you to teach me everything you know."

Ondine stared at Luc.

"About the pigeons!" He motioned up toward the loft.

"Now?"

"Before Tuesday."

Ondine's cheeks puffed to the size of crab apples before she released an exasperated sigh. Gold strands of hair ruffled beneath a rake of tiny fingers.

"D'accord." She threw out an open palm. He was unsure of the gesture and awkwardly reached for her hand. She recoiled, blushing, as though he had overstepped.

"The cloth, please, *m'sieu.*" When he handed it over, she ripped off a piece and stuffed the rest in her apron pocket.

Ondine sifted the bird feed through the mosquito cloth into a tin pail. "You must remove the dirt and dust. And look here." She picked out a black seed. "Don't ever give your birds bad or spoiled seed. It will end in infirmity or death. Fresh water?" she asked.

Liquid sloshed as Luc lifted the bucket for her inspection. She handed him a sardine can and buckshot.

"Place the buckshot in the can and rattle it," she instructed with a decisive flick of her head. The clatter reverberated and seventy-two pairs of flickering bird eyes instantly shifted, locking in on Luc. "From now on, that's how you signal them it's time to eat. Same rattle every time, so they know it's you."

"Er, *oui, mademoiselle,*" he responded, like an obedient schoolboy.

———

The following morning, raindrops pattered against the window-panes. Luc dressed and knocked softly on Michel and Ondine's bedroom door. Usually, Michel was up and dressed and appeared within moments of Luc's signal. This morning, nothing. Luc pushed open the door just enough to stick his head in. A heap of tangled quilts coiled across Michel's bed. Across the room, his sister slept on her back, her white gown buttoned up to its ruffled collar. Her hair rippled across the pillow, a blanket twined around her midsection, and a black sock shielded her eyes. Her snowy calf dangled from the edge of the mattress, sparking an unexpected surge in Luc's desire. He recalled the sensation of Virginia's pendulous breasts pressed against his chest. Unsettled by these yearnings, he quickly turned and headed for the front door.

In the caves behind the house, a candle flickered in one of the windows. Their guest soldier was awake—and probably entertaining a young visitor.

As Luc knocked on the cave's door, he could hear Michel's warble, the adolescent pitch and frequency fluctuating without warning. The sharp smell of coffee and cigarettes greeted Luc as he walked into the warmth.

Michel stood facing the soldier, who sat at the table flicking ash from his cigarette into his now empty porridge bowl. Michel, on his tiptoes, stretched his fingertips, nearly touching the low rock ceiling. "My père is about this tall, maybe even taller, with dark blond hair, a moustache and a scar beneath his right eye, where he was injured in a fight when he was ten. He has blue eyes and he sings in a deep voice, that Maman says sounds like the boom of a cannon. When he's working, he's always singing or humming. He can't help himself," Michel recalled with a wistful smile.

154

The soldier greeted Luc and thanked him for the hospitality. Luc took the seat opposite without a word, not wishing to interrupt. Dirt or blood still smudged near the lieutenant's hairline and crusted around his fingernails, as if he hadn't used the wash basin yet.

Michel dropped to a cross-legged position on the tufa cave floor, chin in hands. "Tell me what it's like, sir. In the trenches. I'm a man now. I need to know."

The soldier extinguished his cigarette in the bowl and shot Luc a hard look.

"Michel has seen the atrocities of war firsthand," Luc assured him.

With a crinkled brow, the soldier sat back and lit another cigarette. He offered it to Luc, who declined, preferring to wait for a smoke with his coffee. Michel reached for it instead and sucked a long drag. His eyes flew open and he erupted into a fit of coughing.

The men laughed. When Michel's hacking finally abated, the lieutenant spoke. He stripped his words of emotion—whether for his own benefit or Michel's, Luc could not fathom. "When the hail melts, we wade through the icy water of the trenches, stinging our toes, calves, knees. The shells whistle over our heads and we are kept awake some nights by the flashes of lightning from the cannon mouths. During the day, the machine gun sounds, *rat-tat-tat rat-tat-tat!*" He mimicked a gunner's stance, with his hands grasping a phantom weapon.

Michel gulped. "What do you eat?"

"The best thing I ate was a bowl of *ratatouille*, warm and filling, given to us by a farmer's wife when we billeted in their

155

barn. Jam and bread are always a treat, but usually we eat canned sardines and hardtack, rice and bits of meat if we are lucky.

"And the flies!" he exclaimed, slapping his knee. "Those fat, venomous flies that hover, night and day. On my sojourn home, I won't miss the ticks, the rats and all manner of vermin that attack us on the front."

Michel cleared his throat and, to Luc's surprise, asked, "And what do they do with the bodies?"

The lieutenant's expression softened when he met Michel's persistent stare. "We bury them after every battle, usually where they fall, with a wooden cross as a marker, if we have time. If not, we write the soldier's name, date and cause of death on a piece of paper and stuff it into an empty wine bottle, which we turn neck down and stick into the dirt beside him."

This was the best scenario of burial for a dead man. According to the other soldiers who had billeted at Saint Martin, the rising sun was to be feared, for it revealed the cadavers—still clasping their *flingots* in hands stiff with rigor mortis—and shapeless body parts flung across farmland. Each morning, as the soldiers tended to the injured and the burials, every living man carried a cutlass for finishing off the near-dead.

"So, the fields and the farms . . ." Michel's expression twisted as if he were trying to puzzle out another answer besides the horrific, obvious one.

"Are now cemeteries, many of them."

"But how do the dead men's families . . . ?" Michel whispered.

"The officers or the man's friends will write the families, tell them where to find their man." He ran a hand through his thinning hair, stopping to tease out an insect and drop it to the floor. "Rotten bastards, they send us into German fire to be mutilated by shells and they don't give a damn. We're like ants taking an enemy anthill."

Michel's expression darkened with confusion. "But why would Clemenceau and Foch not try to prevent the deaths of their countrymen and call an end to the war?"

The lieutenant met Michel's gaze. "Because war destroys any shred of kindness in men—and we all revert to our primal instincts."

———————

Afternoon sunshine stole through the crack between the dovecote doors, bathing Ondine and the birds in light. With a quick glance and calculation, she confirmed that all birds were present and accounted for. She stretched her wool shawl taut around her shoulders and began to sweep the floor. The hinges of the door squealed and Ondine shuddered.

"C'est moi," Luc reassured her, careful to close the door behind him. He wore his chore jacket, breeches and boots. He was at least four years older than she, but in that moment, with a tousle of mahogany hair falling carelessly over his forehead and his impish grin, he looked barely eighteen. Ondine imagined how the late-day stubble on his cheek might tickle beneath her lips. She swallowed hard, banishing the notion.

"You and Michel have finished working in the vineyard?"

"Yes, for today."

The meter of space between them seemed too close in the tight confines of the dovecote. Ondine instinctively pulled the corn husk broom upright against her shoulder, its brush resting near the tip of her clogs.

"He works hard?"

"Of course," he replied, taking a step forward and gripping the broom handle. Ondine held fast. "Allow me?" he said with a tug.

"No, thank you. I like the repetition. Besides, you don't do it properly."

Luc laughed. "Well then, you had best show me how it's done."

Ignoring him, she commanded, "Go down to the riverbank, scoop up some dry sand and bring it back here." She reached for the ceramic bowl from Madame's kitchen and handed it to him.

"What for?"

"The floor. When I'm done, we need to sprinkle a fresh coat of sand. Grit is good for the birds' digestion."

She set aside the broom and pushed both doors open. The birds darted out as if she had announced recess at the school-yard. Ondine swept out the debris and bird droppings from the dovecote while the pigeons fluttered around her, a timid squeaker resting on her shoulder and another circling her, anticipating his next meal. Ondine would spend all day with these winged crea-tures if she could. Their sprightly affection blunted the serrated blade of memory lodged inside her.

Upon his return, Luc dutifully sprinkled the sand and filled the nests with fresh hay. The birds continued their cheerful uproar on the *pigeonnier* roof. Ondine stepped out into the sun and took off her apron to shake it, releasing a spray of dirt, pebbles

158

and hay to the ground. She turned to face Luc, hands on hips. "You're going to war."

Luc blanched. "How did you know?"

"A new light in your eyes." She folded her apron, clutching it in both hands. She could not hold back anymore. "You think going to war makes you a hero, but you are a fool," she said softly beneath the whir of their feathered friends.

"Are you saying I shouldn't fight to protect this country?" he countered.

"This country did not protect Lille. For over three years we starved, lucky to have a scrap of dog or horse to eat."

Silence stretched between them. She had to tell him the truth before he left. "Do you know why I wanted to drown?" she whispered.

His gaze fell and his hands slid into pockets. Ondine could not bear his pity. "For Michel. I wanted to erase his memory of what happened. I wanted him to forget me and Mère, and maybe reunite with Père. It is my fault that I'm ruined, that Mère is dead, but Michel—he could go on to have a family, a future."

Luc beckoned her back inside the *pigeonnier* and offered her the stool to sit on. His demeanor was so calm, his touch at her elbow so gentle, that she acquiesced. He squatted down before her.

"Ruined?" His dark eyes probed hers.

Her cheeks tingled and her heart raced. "I know Madame Chevreau has told you what happened to me."

"Yes, but you were a victim of those men, of their . . . inhuman violence."

A familiar rage stirred in her belly. "All men are violent. Otherwise they would not kill or rape or set cities afire."

Luc exhaled. "Perhaps, but *you* are not *ruined*. You are innocent."

"I am defiled," she insisted.

"You are innocent."

At that, she smiled wryly. "You think?"

"I know."

"You think the Germans just wandered in one night, drunk, and decided to hurt us? No, they planned the attack on my family."

"But why?" Luc backed away and Ondine stood. She always thought more clearly when she walked around.

Ondine crossed the floor to the nests, grasped a red cheque and nuzzled the young bird beneath her jaw. "They attacked us because I was trading messages with the Allies."

"Spying? At seventeen?" He looked at her as if she were mad.

"Michel doesn't know. I started when I was fourteen."

"What are you talking about?"

"You don't believe me? Why? Because I'm not a man?"

"No, because how would you be able to sneak out and carry messages twenty kilometers east to where the French were fighting?"

"I wasn't carrying the messages."

Luc glanced around. "The pigeons? How could they fly without getting shot?"

She nestled the hen into the hay. "I would release them at night, and they would home to the Allies' lofts in the morning."

"But how . . . ?"

"The Allies would parachute baskets of birds into occupied territory. To the birds they would tie messages requesting information. What were the Germans doing? Who had been shot, relocated, taken prisoner? Things like that."

"And how did you obtain the information you sent them?"

"My mother was forced to work at the restaurant La Paix, where many of the high-ranking soldiers dined. I would ask her questions. Then I would write the information on rice paper and fold it into a tiny square, which I would place in the message holder on the pigeon's leg."

"What kind of information?"

"Shift positions, mostly. Where guards were posted, for example."

Luc gaped.

"Two years ago, the Dix-Huit Ponts in Lille exploded."

He stared blankly.

"The munitions depot," Ondine clarified. "The blast left a crater a hundred and fifty meters wide and thirty meters deep. How did this happen? The Germans said it was unstable explosives that spontaneously detonated. The accident killed thirty Germans and, unfortunately, many families who lived close to the depot."

"And you . . . ?"

"I told you, I sent them information."

"How did they find you?"

"I don't know. I never gave my name or location because sometimes the Germans would drop their own pigeons, with the hope that we would give ourselves away. It was almost two years later when they burst through the door." She bit her lip to stop its trembling. "We didn't have the chance to bury Mère. What if Père comes back to find her there, rotting?" She turned and pressed her forehead against the limestone wall and held herself, desperate to curb shivers of sorrow.

The pressure and heat of his hands curling around her arms soothed her, grounded her. "I am sure your neighbors gave her a proper burial."

"What neighbors? They were all sent away with us—on the train. She is dead and Michel is motherless because of what I did."

He turned her shoulders to face him and pressed her head to his chest. She did not resist, enticed by his scent of sea and salt and hay.

She was partially responsible for the deaths of the German guards at the munitions depot—and for the deaths of innocents who lived nearby. That Old Testament verse, justifying the Germans' retaliation against her, always floated near the periphery of her vivid, violent red dreams. She whispered, *"You shall not show pity: life for life, eye for eye, tooth for tooth, hand for hand, foot for foot."*

Luc's embrace tightened. His hot breath ruffled her hair. "I will hunt them and kill them and lay them at your feet."

———

NAPA, CALIFORNIA

Sara, Philippe and Johnny decided to take the steamer up the Napa River to Rutherford. As they pulled away from the pier, the signs of spring were everywhere. The wharves along the waterfront, the tannery and the lumberyards all bustled with activity. Cherry trees bloomed, and the large, silky buds of the magnolia trees had sprouted. The air was fresh and fragrant.

Sara was genuinely pleased with their new arrangement with St. Isidore's. In February and March, Philippe and Johnny had visited and instructed the boys on how to prune the old, dead or diseased wood and compost the soil in the vineyard. For his part, Monsignor O'Brien had agreed to write a letter naming Eagle's Run as one of the San Francisco archdiocese's highest quality sacramental wine suppliers, an endorsement they hoped would win them business from the New York archdiocese.

After their journey up the river, the threesome disembarked and walked the mile to St. Isidore's Agricultural School for Boys. At sixteen, Johnny was the spitting image of Philippe, with sandy hair, blue eyes that sparkled with mischief and a motor that ran at full throttle until his head hit the pillow each night. Sara had high hopes for channeling that energy here at the agricultural school, where the boys rose at six, attended class all morning and farmed until suppertime, with a break in the nearby swimming hole when the weather was warm.

Johnny, however, did not seem too keen on spending his afternoons and weekends teaching indigent boys to prune vines and grow grapes when he could be go-carting with his friends or meeting girls at the picture show in town.

"When will I be able to come home?" he whined, kicking dirt with the toe of his shoe.

Philippe clapped him on the back. "When we return from New York in six weeks' time, when *veraison* starts."

"What if I have a question about the vineyard?"

"You can call Mac, but we've taught you everything we know about grape farming. You're a natural, so just use your instincts."

"What if I can't do it, Pop?" he mumbled.

"If you make a mistake, try something different. There's no shame in it."

"I'm in charge?"

"Of the ten acres of vineyard, yes. You are the expert."

Johnny's petulant tone grew more serious. "Pop, I've never farmed Alicante Bouschet."

"It's simply a cross between *grenache* and *petit bouschet*."

"The combination will make a terrible red!"

Sara laughed. Apparently, Johnny had acquired some grape knowledge along the way. "Not terrible, just not memorable," she said, smirking. "Besides, you won't be making wine, just picking and shipping the grapes."

"Their skins are the heartiest and will transport well back east," Philippe explained. "They'll fetch around fifty dollars per ton."

"What do Father Crowley and the boys get out of the deal?" Sara was surprised to hear her son think like a businessman.

"We purchased the land, which gave them money to fund the school for another few years. Also, you'll be teaching those boys some valuable skills."

"And, if those ten acres of vines can yield just thirty tons of grapes, that's fifteen hundred dollars." Sara believed it was important for Johnny to understand how much the opportunity was worth.

"Phew! That's a lot of money." Johnny stopped abruptly when they arrived at the front gate of the school. The granary with tower clocks, the stately schoolhouse and dormitory, and even the red and yellow barns, housing chickens, cows, pigs and horses, all created a cheerful ambiance.

"I hear the new baseball diamond is finished," Philippe said, winking at Sara. He pulled a new ball of stitched horsehide from his satchel and flipped it to Johnny.

"Thanks, Pop!" he cried.

"I'll make you a deal, son. For every ton of grapes over thirty, I will pay you ten dollars of profit."

"Truly?" Johnny's eyes were the size of saucers.

"Yes, but it's our secret, okay?"

Johnny tossed the ball up and caught it. "What secret?" He grinned and headed toward his new temporary home.

———

After eight hours of taking inventory and stacking shelves at Hudson's, Pippa's back and calves ached mercilessly, but she was so content to drive home in Billy's buggy, she didn't give a fig. When they arrived at Eagle's Run and Billy tried to step down, Pippa touched his arm. "Not yet," she pleaded.

"I don't want your parents to worry. Surely, they will have heard us pull up," Billy said, bumping his shoulder against hers. With the slight chill in the air, his warmth was heavenly against her arm and thigh.

"I can see the shadow of Maman's face in the window," she announced sourly.

Billy chuckled. "She cares about you is all. Besides, your father will tan my hide if he sees me . . . well, you know."

"Sees what?" Pippa asked coyly, leaning in. She hoped for one last kiss before he handed her down, but Billy balked.

"Nothing would please me more, but I want to earn your parents' trust." He squeezed her hand clandestinely, with a furtive glance toward the house.

"That's not particularly exciting, is it?" she teased, still aglow from their earlier stolen kisses as they rambled down the Old Sonoma Highway. She had become so flustered and desirous, she'd had to insist they forge on to make it home before nightfall.

Billy jumped down and, with both hands on Pippa's waist, lowered her to the ground. At that very moment, Papa rounded the corner, wiping his wet hands on his dungarees.

Pippa cringed. Papa had always been handsome and athletic, but today, in his work clothes, he looked, well, like a farmer.

Billy did not seem to notice. He walked right up to Papa and shook his hand. "How are the grapes looking, sir?"

"Small," Papa replied wryly. He could have been a little more friendly, knowing Billy might be nervous.

Billy plunged his hands into his pockets. "Sir, if it's all right with you, I would like to take Pippa to town this Saturday for the picture show."

"What show is that?"

"Hearts of the World."

"Oh, the one with Lillian Gish?" Pippa asked excitedly.

"Mrs. Lemieux and I were just talking about how much we wanted to see that show. Could we make it a foursome?"

166

"Papa!" Pippa cried.

Papa elbowed Billy as he headed for the front door. "I'm just joshin'. Yes, you can go, but have her back by nine." Papa seemed particularly amused. Pippa, less so.

"Yes, sir. Goodnight, Pippa." Billy tipped his boater and, with a flick of the reins, raced down the drive, leaving a cloud of silt in his wake.

NEW YORK HARBOR, NEW YORK

Adeline marveled at the sheer size of the USS *Leviathan*, which stretched the length of almost three football fields from bow to stern. The aptly named *Vaterland* ocean liner, built for Germany's Hamburg-American Line, had been stranded in the United States when the war broke out in 1914, and the Americans had seized the ship in 1917. The Navy stripped the thirty-six-hundred-passenger ship of its Ritz-Carlton-themed finery and fitted it with enough bunks, toilets and mess halls to accommodate seven thousand troops and two thousand sailors for the week's journey across the Atlantic from New York Harbor to Brest, France.

Most startling, however, were the strange patterns of paint on the hull. The bow reminded Adeline of a shark's white teeth, the center of a zebra's stripes, and the stern of a gift ribbon tied in a bow—all white, bold markings against a dark background. This newfangled "dazzle" camouflage, borrowed from the Brits, was intended to obscure the ship on the high seas and make it difficult for the Huns' U-boats to estimate its range and speed and therefore target it.

Until Adeline boarded her temporary floating home as one of sixty-five nurses, with twenty-five officer physicians, one hundred fifty enlisted corpsmen and one hundred thousand dollars of American Red Cross supplies that comprised Base Hospital No. 30, she had not truly fathomed the depth of America's commitment to winning this war. Thousands of troops streamed up the gangplanks, hauling sea bags and beaming with pride, into the belly of the ship.

Someone called her Christian name. She whirled around. "Papa!" she cried. Forgetting herself, she stood on her tiptoes and pecked her stepfather on the cheek. In his drab olive high-collared wool uniform, Matthew Donnelly cut a fine figure with his newly trimmed sideburns and twinkling eyes. His skin was smooth and cool and reminded her of their tearful Christmas farewell.

Her stomach sank. "How are Maman and Gemma and Rourke?" She searched his face. As a surgeon, he was skilled at hiding emotion.

"Brave, but terrified for us," he replied, his tone edged with melancholy. "How was New York?"

"Frigid, but instructive. At Rockefeller Hospital, we had so many boys from Camp Merritt with influenza. If the doctors found fluid in the lungs, they immediately inserted a needle to draw it out. Doesn't that sound a bit aggressive? Turns out, most of those poor boys died after the procedure." She gripped his arms. "Make sure you tell them! Don't draw off the fluid unless it's frank pus and you're sure you have to solve it surgically!" she pleaded.

"I'll tell them," he promised. "You are your mother's daughter!" Marie Chevreau was known for her sharp mind and fascination with all things surgical.

"And yours," Adeline replied tenderly. She glanced down at his hands. His wedding band was gone, most likely on a chain around his neck, dangling near his heart. Surgeons and soldiers could not wear jewelry to war. "Will I see you during the voyage?" she asked with renewed enthusiasm.

"I'm not sure, but I expect we will regroup when we arrive in Brest. *Bon voyage, ma petite puce!*"

Although he hadn't quite mastered extending his lips enough to properly pronounce the French "u" sound, he was progressing nicely. "Have you been practicing your French with Maman?"

"I'm flattered that you noticed," he said, grinning. With a quick salute, he turned to rejoin the team of physicians from the 30th, who were assembling further down the railing.

On April 24, amidst a deafening roar and a flurry of farewell waves, tugboats escorted the *Leviathan* from New York Harbor.

Within four hours of setting sail, with nothing but white-capped indigo waves on all sides of them and God-knew-what beneath, the chow bell rang. Men and women surged into the mess hall, life jackets secured, mess kits in hand. Steaming coffee sloshed in Adeline's tin cup and a slice of beef, potatoes and an apple tart mounded her two interconnected plates. Adeline watched, fascinated, as the clean-cut young men of varying ethnicities and colors filed through the chow line, swapping stories, their shiny faces smiling at the prospect of a hot meal. Though she tried to push the disturbing thought from her mind, she could not help but wonder: How much of this fresh pink and bronze American flesh—how many of these beautiful boys—would die on the battlefield or end up on her operating table?

Within seventy-two hours, Adeline was staring at the bottom of a bucket in the tight, swaying cabin she shared with three other nurses. Intermittent sips of water and sour pickles were all she could ingest after emptying the contents of her stomach.

On her metal bunk, she curled toward the wall and pulled her blanket to her chin. She concentrated on the hum and vibrations of the engine room below her and eventually sank into a deep, dreamless sleep.

———

EN ROUTE TO THE MARNE RIVER, FRANCE

The marching was interminable. Heinrich's feet were so swollen, he did not dare remove his boots for fear he might not be able to wrestle them back on. Strange, what the body craves. At that moment, he would have sold his soul to wiggle his toes and dunk them in the cool, glistening waters of a stream.

He tried to make the most of the incessant tramping by challenging his mind to remember every detail about his son. When Heinrich had left for the war in January 1917, Werner had just celebrated his fourth birthday. He was now five. Would his hand still feel like a ball of soft dough in Heinrich's palm? Would his sweet smile still reach up to light his blue eyes?

Heinrich had no family to speak of. The only living child born to a cobbler and his wife, he had lost his parents when he was nineteen. It was silly—a grown man with a son of his own pining for simple childhood comforts—but the memories of earthy-sweet tanned leather, the fresh-cut wood that smelled of the forest and the sugary delight of his mother's streusel cake on his tongue made him long to return to his parents' workshop. When he thought of Werner in a house full of strangers, aching for his mother, unable to recall his father, he wanted to race back to Köln.

CHAPTER 7

May 1918

Luc reported to the U.S. Signal Corps pigeoneer training ground the first Tuesday of the month. As soon as he signed the paperwork, he received his orders and cotton uniform, along with a poncho, two sets of underwear and socks, two pairs of hobnailed trench boots, a cap, a campaign hat and a helmet. His personal items consisted of a blanket, half a tent, a tent pole with metal pins, one towel, one bar of soap, a toothbrush, shaving soap, razor and handkerchiefs. His gas mask bag hung over his shoulder and rested on his opposite hip. A mess kit, canteen, a meat can and a condiment can, filled with a three-day ration of sugar, coffee and tobacco, filled his haversack. All told, he would carry at least sixty pounds on his back, hardly a challenge for a man who carried the same weight in grapes in a wicker basket strapped to his back during every harvest.

Since he had missed the basic training that most of the men had endured back at Camp Devens in Massachusetts or Camp Merritt in New Jersey, the non-commissioned officer in charge, Sergeant Archibald Rivers, took it upon himself to show Luc the ropes. He issued Luc a pistol and magazine pouch, a Springfield .30 caliber rifle, a cartridge pouch and a sheathed bayonet to mount on that rifle. Once the sergeant was reasonably certain he could handle the rifle and pistol and hit the targets, he schooled Luc in the use and disposal of hand grenades and simulated a gas attack, in which Luc had to doff his helmet and pull on his gas mask and a horse's gas mask in less than ten seconds. With that cursory training accomplished, the sergeant led Luc to the lofts.

Sergeant Rivers, whose muscular frame and steel jaw seemed to be wasted managing birds when he could be battling Germans in the trenches, stabbed a finger at a two-story mobile loft. "These pigeons will help us win the war," he said solemnly. "Where telegraphs, telephones, signal lights, flares and dogs all fail, the pigeons succeed. Can human runners or dogs pass through walls of fire? Of course not! That's the beauty of these birds—they fly high above this ugly mess to dispatch crucial messages."

Luc stifled a laugh. Never in his life had he known anyone to take birding so seriously, not even Ondine.

"These birds range from six to eight weeks in age. They traveled here by rail, so we had to separate the sick to make room for these here healthy ones." He swung the door open. "Plenty of sunlight and air is needed, weather permitting."

"When do you feed them, sir?" Luc asked.

"You will feed them every morning at oh-six-hundred and then again at sixteen hundred hours. We have a strict ten-minute feeding time. No more. Give me your palm," he instructed.

Luc extended a hand and the sergeant dropped a handful of hard peas into it. "For rattling the chow can, sir?" Luc recalled. He shoved the peas in his pocket.

The sergeant pulled the shredded toothpick from his lips and pointed it at Luc. "You're a quick one. I like that." He stabbed it in the direction of a nearby pump. "Fresh water is a must. If you're near the battlelines, search for a freshwater source, and never keep soiled bathwater near the birds." These birds' high-falutin' accommodations definitely surpassed those of the soldiers. The sergeant smacked his clipboard against Luc's chest. "Feeding time is inventory time. Record every bird, the band numbers, color, special markings and anything regarding the condition of the bird." They approached another truck loft where a soldier crouched down, inspecting a flat tire.

"You and Martin here will be responsible for this loft."

As Martin stood, his legs and torso unfolded to stretch from the roots of his feet to the ceiling of the truck's cab. He must have been close to seven feet tall, with a streak of grease across his cheek, a buck-toothed grin and gangly arms that dangled at his sides. Martin wiped his greasy hands on the rag that hung from the pocket of his breeches and saluted the sergeant. He then clasped Luc's mitt with a giant's strength, nearly crushing his knuckles.

"PFC Bartholomew Martin, at your service, private," he said brightly. "The fellas call me Marty."

"Private Luc Lemieux," Luc replied in kind. He shuffled uncomfortably, not knowing whether to salute or stand at attention, since he wasn't in uniform and Marty wasn't wearing any headdress. He opted for the latter.

"A French frog?" Marty asked good-naturedly.

"French ancestry but American born."

"Marty," the sergeant said with a chuckle, "finish plugging that tire. We're going to borrow a bird." The bed of the truck had been fitted with a two-story-high loft with ten cages on each level. Each cage contained two pigeons. He reached into one and pulled out two red cheques. "Let's see you toss them," he commanded Luc.

Luc recalled Ondine's instructions. "One at a time, sir."

"Ha! Indeed. Release!"

Luc threw the bird gently as Ondine had taught him. The pigeon beat its wings and took flight, circling above them.

"These birds have already been liberated?" Luc asked, hoping to impress.

"We let them loose six days after they arrived. Most of them returned every day." He waved to Marty and commanded, "Show Private Lemieux around and find him a cot in the barracks, and give him your *Privates' Manual*, will you? Lemieux, we mobilize next week, so memorize it before we leave."

When the sergeant was out of earshot, Marty glanced at Luc. "You read?"

"Yes."

"English *and* French? Lucky son of a gun," Marty added wistfully.

176

One week later, Luc took the afternoon to attend to personal matters before his company mobilized the following day. At the U.S. Signal Corps building, Luc rapped on the door and then poked his head inside. Typewriters click-clacked and the women of the corps barked instructions in French to the men in the trenches, over lines that snaked across the front through grass, up tree trunks and around fence posts. The girls punched plugs into ports and toggled switches up and down from morning until night. Within moments, Luc was confronted by a six-foot-tall linebacker of a lady whom the Hello Girls had dubbed "The Enforcer." With one meaty palm on the open door and the other on his shoulder, she pushed Luc out.

He leaned against the iron railing and waited, hoping one of the girls had caught sight of him. In a few minutes, Barbara appeared.

"I'm shipping out tomorrow," Luc announced. He handed her a burlap sack filled with two wheels of his grandmother's home-made chèvre and a bottle of chenin blanc. "Ondine and Michel— the stowaways—their father is Capitaine Pierre Marchand. I can't recall his regiment, perhaps he's with the Sixth Army. If you could ask or keep a listen for his name on the lines . . ." his voice trailed. He knew it was a shot in the dark. "If you hear anything, please send word to the farm. His name and the directions to Saint Martin are wrapped in the cheese."

"In the cheese?" Barbara laughed, peering into the sack. "Espionage suits you," she teased.

As he turned to go, Barbara stopped him. "Wait," she insisted. She ducked back inside, and Virginia returned in her stead, squinting as she stepped out into the brazen May sunlight.

"I told you not to enlist," she scolded him.

"I couldn't resist," he said, a smile tugging on his lips. "Don't worry, I'll be in the rear, tending the pigeons." He chuckled to cover his unease.

Virginia shook her head. "The Germans will find you. Even the field hospitals are bombarded with Howitzer shells and gas every day. Keep your head down, your rifle handy, and for God sakes wear your gas mask." Her finger slid down his jawline. "I'd be devastated if anything happened to this face."

Her ripe plum kiss on New Year's Eve had set his head spinning. Luc ached for more, but here on the steps of the Signal Corps building, he could hardly indulge that fantasy. Virginia tucked a note into his upper coat pocket and stepped away. "Until later, soldier," she whispered. Before he could utter a word, she was gone.

As Luc retraced his steps to the barracks, the sun nestled into the crown of a giant black chestnut tree. Dread settled in his bones. What would his fate be? Would he ever return? Struggling to curtail his darker thoughts, he contemplated Virginia's lips. He pulled the crinkled paper from his pocket and read the immaculately neat script: *Meet me after chow outside the women's dormitory.*

———

At nineteen hundred hours, an elegant, white-robed arm pulled him inside the women's barracks. Virginia clasped his hand and guided him up the dark stairs, a single candle lighting their path. He could not help but admire her shapely backside as she climbed the stairs. His heart thrummed inside his chest. When they reached her cell of a room, he glanced around. "Where is your roommate?" he asked upon seeing the other twin bed.

"On assignment in Paris for a few days. That makes me a lucky girl," Virginia cooed. "Drink?"

"Sherry?"

Reading the bottle label, her faintly freckled nose wrinkled. "Some sort of *vin blanc*."

Luc stepped closer. "You drink this swill? That's no better than the *pinard* they give the French soldiers. Good thing I brought my own."

He poured two glasses of chilled chenin blanc, perfect for a summer's evening. Blades of the fan whirled, slicing through the trapped heat of the afternoon like a knife through brie.

Virginia smacked her lips. "You really make this wine?"

He laughed.

"Shh." She pressed a finger to his lips.

"Do you doubt it?" he whispered.

"You're so young."

"My family has been making wines at Clos du Saint Martin for nearly a century. My great-grandfather, my grandfather, my mother and now me."

She sipped and smiled, her cherry-colored lipstick smudging the glass rim. "It's delicious, but so different from the whites at home." Lines appeared on her forehead as she searched for a description that seemed to elude her.

"Most of the white wines from America—chardonnay, for example—grow in warmer climates, so they are more full-bodied with a higher percentage of alcohol. These Vouvray whites are more acidic, but lighter and more refreshing, especially during the summer months."

As Virginia closed the distance between them, her sweet scent swirled in the air, invading his nostrils and stealing his words. "Will they miss you at the barracks?" She ran the back of her hand down the front of his shirt to his belt buckle.

"Call to quarters is at nine fifteen," he said hoarsely, his throat like sandpaper.

She glanced at his wristwatch. "So, we have two hours together?"

"About that," he lamented, ducking his head, his lips lingering close to hers.

She cocked her head, her blond tresses dangling above her shoulder. "Do you think I'm easy?"

"I honestly don't know what to think, Virginia." His fingers swept a few loose tendrils from her temple.

"Then don't. Just feel," she commanded, slipping his hand into her belted robe. His fingers sank into her warm, abundant flesh. He breathlessly teased her nipple to a point. She moaned softly. Her lips, wet with sweet wine, kissed him with a fervor equal to his own.

"Are you sure? What about—?"

"You needn't worry about a child."

He had to ask. Ever since he had discovered what a cad his father had been—deserting Marie and Adeline to fend for themselves then six years later marrying Luc's own mother, already pregnant with him—he had vowed to be a different kind of man. Of course, he had never actually made love to a woman the way a husband would his wife. He had managed to do everything but the most intimate of acts, all with his neighbors' daughters in the secluded, fumbling haylofts of Carneros.

"I want you to know that I would never walk away from my responsibilities," he said.

Virginia giggled. "So earnest! Don't worry, the doctors told me I can't have children. My loss is our gain tonight. Besides, if you go off to war tomorrow, if you don't return . . ." With a well-timed sigh, she issued her sultry challenge.

Luc scooped Virginia into his arms. As her thighs tightened around his waist, the robe rippled off her shoulders, revealing two perfectly formed, creamy white orbs. He eased her onto the bed, and with her hands tangled in his hair, he laid a trail of kisses from her taut belly to the delicate sinews of her milky neck. She called his name again and again, feeding the fire of unspeakable lust.

He at last surrendered to swells of pleasure as she rocked beneath him. With only a sheen of glistening moisture between them, Virginia arched her hips and squeezed his hand, her lips rounding to form a small, tight *O*.

An hour later, Luc stared at the ceiling, wondering how he would summon the willpower to leave her bed when all that awaited him was pain and perhaps death. The recent rush of ecstasy notwithstanding, he doubted every decision that had led to this moment.

Virginia rolled on top of him, nestling her heavy, snowy breasts into his chest. He pecked her on the lips and attempted a smile.

"Why the long face?" she asked.

"Sorry. I suppose I am rather too serious."

"You're allowed. After all, you are going to war."

"Do you mind if I ask . . ." He hesitated. "How do the doctors know?"

She fell back onto the mattress and propped her head up on an elbow. "I was married, and I couldn't stay pregnant. I lost three babies, and then my husband died."

Luc tried to conceal his shock. "How long ago?"

"A year before I arrived here." She sighed heavily. "I was heartbroken—and tired of my family telling me that I had to remarry—so I shipped out first chance I had."

Luc exhaled and cupped her warm shoulder in his hand. "I'm sorry, Virginia."

She traced circles through his chest hair and planted a kiss on his lips. "Don't cry for me. At least we had a few good years. Sam was the love of my life," she added wistfully.

"How did you know?" he wondered aloud.

"When you experience that kind of loss, it crushes your soul. You need someone to help pull you out of the muck, remind you that life's still worth living, that you're still worth something, even if you can't bear children. Sam did that for me."

"He was a lucky man."

"I was the lucky one, but luck always runs out, kid." Her lips puckered as though she had just eaten a sour grape. "You see, I'm not easy. I just choose to remain unattached."

After the pair had shared a kiss and a tearless but emotional goodbye, Luc quietly slipped out the back door of Virginia's dormitory. As he strolled across the courtyard toward the soldiers' barracks, the moon painted a halo around the roofs and treetops and the breeze whistled through the leaves. When Luc thought of the evening he had passed, it wasn't the glory of Virginia's flesh beneath him that flashed through his mind—it was rather Ondine's disapproving pout.

Then, as if his thought had conjured her out of thin air, he saw her loitering in the shadow of a tall oak outside the men's barracks. She held a basket. Beneath the hazy glow of the street-lamp, her hair was spun gold. Her shoulders were a ridge of bone and meager flesh, hunched against the evening chill. Her dress was the same green as a starling's egg. When he caught her eye, she dropped her chin to stare at her clogs. Her fingers curled around the top of the basket.

"Ondine?"

———

Ondine's insides fluttered as Luc approached.

"Ondine? Why are you here?" he asked in a friendly, but bewildered tone.

"Was that your girl?" she asked. She tried to convince herself that she was merely protective of him, as a younger sister might be, but there was another niggling emotion she could not quite define, a combination of resentment and sadness.

"Virginia? No, she's just a friend."

Ondine remained silent. Friends did not wear silky robes to say goodbye.

"How did you get here?" he asked, shoving his hands in his pockets. "Grandmère will be frantic with worry."

"I drove."

"My motorcar?"

"It's not so hard, you know." She was gratified to see the flash of irritation in his eyes. Before he could chastise her, she held up the basket. "I brought you these."

Luc's eyebrows arched.

"Maxime and Richard. Our two finest."

"For?"

She leaned in and whispered, "If you learn anything about my father, please send word. *Le secret est sous la cage.*"

"You want me to smuggle our birds into the army and transport them to the front? Just so I can send you a message if I happen to find your father?"

"*Bien sûr.* You are our only hope. Otherwise, he may never find us."

"Ondine."

She would not allow his refusal. "Today is my birthday, did you know?" She hoped the roar of a passing truck concealed the desperation in her tone.

"You are eighteen today?"

She nodded. "*M'sieu,* you must do this for us." She thrust the basket of pigeons into his hands. "*Au revoir et bonne chance.* Michel and I will care for Monsieur and Madame Chevreau until you return."

She whirled around with the same, sudden, frenetic energy she had felt the evening she walked into the river's current with a lapful of stones. Luc caught her by the shoulder and gently turned her to face him. She wanted to melt into his chest again, to bury her face in his warmth. Instead, his tender lips brushed her cheeks, and his sweet perspiration floated around her, along with his paramour's perfume, a cheap, tawdry affair. She instinctively balked, but he held fast to her shoulders.

"*À bientôt, ma petite amie,*" he bid, the words hoarse with feeling.

He began to stroll away, the basket tucked under one arm. At five paces, he about-faced. Ondine stood, rooted. She could not take her eyes off him.

"Careful with that hand brake," he called, "it sticks like toffee." She sniffed and nodded. "And don't let our feathered friends become too fat and lazy to fly."

She laughed through her tears. With a mock salute and a wink, he hurried on, taking the corner before she could give in to the urge to run after him.

———————

NAPA, CALIFORNIA

"Is that the newsboy?" Marie asked, peering out of Sara's parlor window. She had arrived last evening, with Gemma and Rourke in tow, to see them off to New York and stay with Pippa for the weekend.

"Most likely." Sara pulled some coins from her pocket and greeted the boy at the door. Before the freckle-faced youngster could hand Sara her coupon, Marie had already coaxed the *Napa Register* from his grasp.

"What is so pressing?" Sara asked.

Marie scanned the front page, then snapped the paper open. "Matthew and Adeline both sent postcards. They departed New York on the *Leviathan* the third week in April, which means the ship should have arrived in Saint-Nazaire by now, even with a delay." After sifting through the entire contents, she folded the paper into a neat rectangle and sank back into the cushions of the settee. "Thank God. No U-boat attacks reported."

"They must be safe and sound. It has been over two weeks," Sara reassured her.

Sara and Philippe's former housekeeper, Rose, shuffled into the room with a pile of freshly laundered clothes. Sara unlatched the brass locks on one of three leather suitcases lying on the carpet. "Thank you, Rose. You're a godsend," she said, sorting her clothes and placing them in the case.

"And she still makes the best biscuits in the Bay Area," Marie added.

"The secret is fresh cream, ma'am," Rose replied cheerfully, clearly content to be relieved of her retirement for the next month. Though her shape had grown thinner and the creases of her face were deeper, she still had the spunk and work rate of a twenty-year-old. Sara could not have raised four children without her.

When Rose had departed for the kitchen, Marie said quietly, "For goodness sakes, Sara, Pippa is a grown woman. She is more than capable of feeding herself and doing the laundry and shopping. You're spoiling her."

Sara would not normally accept criticism from anyone about her parenting, but Marie was different. She had already raised Adeline into womanhood. "Perhaps, but with Johnny at the agricultural school and no one here at night, I want Pippa to have some protection. That's why I hired Rose for the five weeks we are away."

"Protection from what? Grizzly bears? Just give her Philippe's shotgun."

Sara grimaced. "To be honest, I'm concerned about the young man she works with."

"Billy? I haven't met him, but by all accounts, he seems to be a gentleman." Marie stood and approached the white plaster cast of Pippa's head on the half-moon table. "He created this, so he must be thoughtful and talented." Marie turned Billy's creation sideways so she could view Pippa's plaster profile. "It is an uncanny likeness."

Billy was an accomplished sculptor for his young age, and seemed trustworthy, but Sara still balked at the idea of Pippa's budding friendship with any man. "But Pippa is different," she blurted without thinking.

"How?"

"You know."

"No, I don't."

"Are you going to make me *say* it?" Sara whispered.

"Yes, because then you may hear how ridiculous you sound."

"Fine. I worry that she has some of her mother's . . . you know, tendencies."

"What?!" Marie's brow line scrunched in disbelief.

"Maybe it's in her blood."

"What's in her blood? *Whoring?* That's absurd! Pippa is the kindest, gentlest, most chaste young lady I know. She's the opposite of what you imagine."

"Shh! I don't want Rose to overhear."

"Sara, if we were to follow your logic, then Adeline and Luc would be lascivious scoundrels just like their father, Bastien."

Marie made an excellent point, but Sara could not help but feel that Pippa's situation was different.

"Sara, sit down." Marie clasped her friend's hands and guided her to sit on the chaise. "You and Philippe have brought Pippa up in the church and now she is twenty years old. By twenty, you and I were both raising toddlers and working alongside men, whom we eventually *married.*"

Sara sighed. Pippa had always needed her protection—from Linnette's indecent past, from the neighbors who said her cleft lip was the devil's mark and from the schoolchildren who ostracized her. "I did encourage her to take a job, independent of our vineyard, but she was accosted by our vile neighbor, Boone Sumter. He knew all about Linnette, and his gossip cut Pippa to the core."

"And yet, Pippa survived. Boone Sumter is angry that Jess is dead. He blames Adeline and, because of her association with your family, he'll do anything to hurt you."

"I suppose." Jess's death had been a tragic accident, but Sara had always been wary of him. In his presence, Adeline had slowly lost her light.

"Sara, listen to me. If I can stand by and watch my daughter go to war, then you can certainly encourage Pippa to pursue her passions and new friendships out here in the blissful countryside." Marie sounded exasperated. "You must trust her. You must give her the gift of confidence, no matter how much it pains you."

Marie's words splashed like ice water in Sara's face, but she was right.

———

Sara, Philippe, Lydia and Aurora arrived in New York five days later. When Sara had kissed Pippa goodbye, she refrained from reciting the diatribe rotating through her mind: *extinguish the fire in the cookstove after use, lock the doors at night, don't travel to and from the store alone in the darkness, don't invite Billy to call unless Rose is here to chaperone.* Recalling Marie's advice, Sara bit her tongue and silently offered up a Hail Mary as they departed for the station.

Lydia's enthusiasm for their adventure had distracted Sara from her worries about Pippa. Garbed in a blue gingham drop-waist dress and straw hat, she had chirped like a robin in springtime as they boarded their Pullman sleeper car and found their berths. During the daytime, Lydia had delighted in the cuisine of wrapped sandwiches and cold milk. She had whiled away the hours writing patriotic essays in the leather-bound journal Aurora had gifted her and playing endless card games with her father. The Southern Pacific train chugged across the small towns and expansive farmland of America, through Utah, Wyoming, Nebraska and Iowa, finally stopping in Chicago where the foursome changed trains for the final leg of their journey into Manhattan's beautiful Pennsylvania Station.

New York City had mobilized for war. Women mounted Liberty Loan posters on the street corners and children scavenged for scrap metal to aid the war effort. Sara was surprised to find a woman behind the wheel of their cab. With her husband called up to serve in France, she had taken over his business and now skillfully dodged the horses, motor cars and uniformed men and women that crammed the streets on the way to the hotel.

The morning after their arrival, Lydia linked arms with Sara and Aurora as they strolled with Philippe through the lobby and out into the May sunshine. Sara admired her daughter with fresh eyes. Lydia had sprouted another inch and was now a dark beauty, with dancing green eyes and long, dark chocolate curls fashionably swept up in an ivory silk ribbon. Though tall for her age, Lydia still possessed the innocent charm and ungainliness of a youngster. She was so enraptured by the vendors and street-cars that rushed by, Sara instinctively took her daughter's gloved hand lest she succumb to the distractions and be mowed down in the street.

It was a short walk to the Grand Central Terminal. As they approached, Lydia stopped abruptly and gaped. The soaring arches, gigantic windows and crowning sculptures of Mercury, Hercules and Minerva rendered her speechless.

"Quite grand, isn't it?" Sara exclaimed. Lydia nodded silently, tagging along as they entered the vast structure, carried on the wave of commuters streaming in with them.

From the towering windows, yellow beams of sunlight sliced through the station's shadows to illuminate the expansive, gleaming marble floor. Lydia craned to view the constellations of stars on the sky-blue ceiling. "Papa, how did they do it?"

Philippe leaned down, looping an arm around Lydia's waist. "I would imagine they constructed scaffolding just like

Michelangelo and the masters did when they painted the great cathedral domes."

"I have never seen anything so lovely. Pippa would marvel at such a sight!"

Philippe's expression changed profoundly in that moment. As he watched his daughter, his face brightened with a joy Sara rarely witnessed. He could be aloof, even maddeningly arrogant sometimes, but a well of tenderness ran deep within him, especially for his children. He cleared his throat, composing himself. "Now, Lydia, you are in for a treat. We are riding the new subway downtown."

Lydia's face registered confusion. Aurora explained, "It's an underground railroad, a magnificent feat of engineering modeled after the Métro in Paris."

"How did they build a railroad underground?" Lydia asked as they walked toward the platform, her feet dragging enough for Sara to have to coax her along.

"Using tunnels."

"Is it safe?"

"Quite. This line has been in operation for eight years." Sara gently nudged a reluctant Lydia toward the platform.

Lydia glanced up at Philippe, who wrapped an arm around her shoulders. "I'll stay right by your side, *chérie.*"

"Promise, Papa?" Lydia cringed as the train thundered into the station, brakes squealing as it stopped.

Philippe nodded, drawing her close and then into the train car. Sara and Aurora sat while Philippe and Lydia stood, clinging to a metal pole. Lydia squeezed her eyes shut as the train lurched, a metal barrel creaking and then careening toward Canal Street. New York had always been an assault on the senses, Sara reflected, but whereas she had lived here and quickly fell into step with the once-familiar chaos, Lydia was a country girl, accustomed to open fields, fresh air and fewer people. Her characteristically boisterous and brazen daughter had turned quiet and cowering overnight.

Five minutes into their ride, hurtling through the city's underbelly, Lydia opened one eye. "Almost there," Philippe reassured her with a squeeze. She tucked her face back into the crook of his arm.

"Think of it as a grand adventure, my dear Lydia!" Aurora exclaimed. "You are a pioneer, like Sacagawea or Susan Anthony—a young woman of the modern age." Aurora beamed beneath her wide-brimmed straw hat, lavishly decorated with gold silk taffeta flowers. It fit her personality perfectly.

The convent of the Sisters of Notre Dame was just as Sara had remembered: an imposing three-story edifice with wide flagstone steps and thickly painted double doors. The cool, dank stone walls of the interior, the soulful, lyrical hymns emanating from the chapel, the sunlit, blossoming courtyard garden were aching reminders of Sara's sister Lydia, who had died two decades ago while giving birth to Luc there. Lydie's soul had fled her body so quickly after Luc emerged from her womb, Sara had often wondered if her sister's energy had simply migrated to her newborn son in a final, heroic act of generosity. One thing was certain. During those sorrowful days, Sara had forged an unbreakable bond with Marie and all the nuns who had sheltered them there.

Once a shy young lady, Sister Paulette—now the Reverend Mother in charge of the entire convent—glided into the *salle d'attente* with open arms. She had the same sweet, round face, but now possessed an air of efficiency and confidence. Rosary beads dangled from the woolen belt that ran around her long, wide-sleeved black tunic and she wore the traditional wimple and black veil, but the white coif that framed her face was simpler than Sara had remembered.

"Welcome all!" She cupped Lydia's chin. "You must be the youngest of the Lemieux clan," she guessed.

"Yes, ma'am. I am Lydia." Lydia curtsied as if she were meeting a queen.

Paulette pressed her steepled palms to her lips to hide her smile. She cast a soft, sympathetic glance in Sara's direction. "What a lovely name for such an accomplished young lady."

After greeting Philippe and Aurora, Paulette announced, "We just had the pleasure of Adeline's visit in January."

Sara was heartened by this piece of news. "Matthew and Adeline have just arrived in France, so do keep them in your prayers."

"We pray for them every day—and Luc, too, of course."

Once they were all seated, Sara turned to her old friend. Could it have been twenty years ago when they first knelt beside each other, Sara wearing Paulette's straw hat, digging in the convent garden? Would her friend help them now?

"What do you think of our proposal?" Sara asked.

"I was astounded by your letter." She slipped her hands beneath her scapular. "What a novel idea! At first, I thought it too revolutionary for a small city convent like ours, but the more I pondered your plan, the more I began to see its merits." Her soft gaze sparkled with enthusiasm. "However, there are some details we must consider."

"Please, go on," Philippe encouraged.

"How much space would you need?"

"The basement of the convent and the adjoining apartment out back," Sara replied.

"We will acquire additional warehouse space near the railroad yard, but all we ask of you is to keep a small office open during weekdays, for taking orders," Philippe added. "We'll install a telephone so we can communicate, and we'll pay you a reasonable rent plus ten percent of the profits."

"Who will make the deliveries?" Paulette asked.

"We'll hire an independent company," Sara assured her.

"We thought it could be mutually beneficial," Philippe added. "You and the sisters could help take orders for the grapes and the sacramental wine, and we will provide you with a healthy addition to your income."

Paulette's gaze narrowed. "Mind you, I will not participate in any illegal operations."

Philippe feigned indignation. "Of course not. When the prohibition of alcohol begins, we will warn our buyers that if they allow their grape juice to sit for more than twenty-one days, it might ferment." Sara shot Philippe a warning glance.

"Well, we wouldn't want that, would we?" Paulette pursed her lips.

"What Philippe means to say is that we would take great care to insulate the convent from even a whiff of impropriety."

194

"Would you store the sacramental wine on these premises? I will not make this convent a target for thieves."

"Our intention is to take the orders here but distribute the wine to the parishes from the rail yard. The basement would be used for temporary storage, if at all."

"Still, your proposition is not without risk. We will therefore require an advance in the sum of five hundred dollars."

"Five hundred? For what?" Philippe asked.

"We need to repair the slate roof. And you need our space, our honesty and our network," she replied calmly.

"Your network?" Sara inquired. Apparently, little naive Paulette had become much more worldly and her nuns much less cloistered over the years.

"Of priests and rabbis. I'll need a copy of the letter from the San Francisco archdiocese endorsing the quality of your wine." Paulette glanced at the grandfather clock in the corner and rose to her feet.

"And the grapes?" Philippe asked.

"Will be purchased by the Italian and Jewish families throughout New York. I assume we will need permits for this endeavor once prohibition has passed."

"You'll have them," Philippe promised. Sara subtly pressed her knee into Philippe's thigh. "And the advance you requested."

"Splendid! We look forward to our new partnership with gusto!" They all huddled together, issuing *mercis* and *au revoirs*.

"Tell me, Reverend Mother, do you and the sisters ever leave the convent? For, say, spiritual outings?" Aurora asked.

"What did you have in mind?"

"Come along, ladies. That's it, single file, watch your step!" Aurora guided a line of ten nuns off the train, across the platform and into the gathering crowd of women outside of Hartford's Union Station.

Acting as the caboose, Lydia giggled at the sight before her. Sara shook her head in utter disbelief. Aurora had always made fast friends or enemies, but the speed with which she had secured the Reverend Mother's consent to bring ten of her nuns to a controversial march on Connecticut's capitol boggled the mind. Aurora sidled up to Sara. "The police wouldn't dare jail us while we are in the company of these veiled vigilantes," she whispered.

Sara eyed Aurora skeptically. *"Vigilantes?"*

"All right. Perhaps that's too strong a word, but you shouldn't underestimate the power of prayer! It's a formidable weapon!" She pumped a fist in the air.

Aurora had a point. The nuns, with black tunics and veils swaying gently in the spring breeze, cut through the white-clad crowd of women like a spoon through cream. Housewives, munition workers and march organizers alike greeted the cadre of nuns with cheers of enthusiasm. Their quiet, prayerful presence on the street seemed to embolden the demonstrators even further as they marched toward the capitol, banners held high.

Lydia tugged on Sara's coat sleeve. "Maman, why is voting so important to Tante Aurora?"

"Because if we live in this country, we should all have a say in how its laws are made and enforced."

Lydia read the picket signs. "Why do they call it suffrage?"

"It comes from the French interpretation of the Latin word *suffragium*, which means to pray or petition."

"Oh. Is that what the nuns are for?"

Sara chuckled. "That is most likely how your Tante Aurora enticed them to come, but remember, these nuns are women, too. In California and New York, women can already vote in local and state elections, but we want *all* women to have that right. That's why we're protesting in Connecticut today."

"I see." Lydia replied, her eyes widening at the spectacle before her. "But Papa says that when *all* women vote, they'll make wine be against the law and we'll go bankrupt."

Sara struggled to mask her ire. In a measured tone, she replied, "Your father exaggerates. We as women deserve the right to vote in all things even if we disagree sometimes."

On the capitol steps, hundreds of women gathered peacefully to raise their voices in support of the right for all citizens to vote. They chanted, and before long, a white-clad woman rose to speak through a megaphone behind a giant cloth banner that read *Connecticut Votes for Women*. She waved a piece of paper in the air. "We are sending this telegram to President Wilson today, urging him to take action and support national suffrage for women!" The crowd roared its approval, while picket signs bobbed and banners billowed.

"Who is that, Maman?" Lydia pointed.

"That's Aurora's friend, Minnie Hennessey. She was imprisoned for six months last year for picketing the White House for women's suffrage rights."

"Tanta Aurora traveled all this way to help a friend?"

Sara smiled, thinking about Aurora's brazenness and warmth and practicality. How lucky Sara was to have found her friendship all those years ago when she was new to this strange country. "Aurora is a unique spirit."

Lydia sighed softly. "People are her treasures."

When they walked into their hotel later that evening, Lydia frowned and kicked off a shoe. Squeezing Sara's wrist for balance, she reached down and began to massage her toes. "They call it 'suffrage' because of we have to suffer to win the vote!" Lydia cried.

"You are a warrior for women's rights, Lydia!" Aurora countered without sympathy. "Progress is always painful."

Just then, Philippe sprang up from a red leather chair in the corner of the vast lobby. He walked briskly toward them with a grave expression. Sara's heart skipped a beat.

"Pippa telephoned the hotel and left a message. A telegram arrived at the house. Luc is going to war."

NAPA, CALIFORNIA

With a promise to return home before supper, Pippa had convinced Rose that she could travel alone to St. Isidore's and return in one piece. When she arrived in Rutherford shortly before noon on Saturday, her mood brightened in anticipation of seeing her brother for the first time in several weeks. As she walked toward the cluster of tidy buildings and pens of chickens, pigs and cows, the smell of sun-warmed, freshly cut grass lingered on the breeze.

"Pippa!" a deep, unfamiliar voice called. She pivoted left to see Johnny waving to her from behind a wall of leafy vines. Just as she spied the tight bunches of green spheres growing between the leaves, a small line of heads appeared. The row of boys, ranging in age from five to twelve, if Pippa were to guess, gawked.

Johnny sprinted to greet her, wiping his hands on his dungarees as he approached. When he removed his straw hat, a sheaf of blond hair swept across his forehead. His hands were chafed, and his skin branded with sun, but he cut a robust figure in his work shirt and boots. Her little brother was no longer a boy, but a young man. He pecked Pippa on the cheek, a welcome change from the way he used to pinch her arm and tug her hair. She presented a basket of Rose's biscuits, a slice of ham, a jar of strawberry jam and two jars of lemonade wrapped in cloth.

"I never thought I would be so glad to see my sister!" he exclaimed with cheer.

"Your voice is so deep I thought you were Papa for a moment," she teased. Flicking her head in the direction of the water pump, she instructed, "Go on and clean up."

Johnny pumped the handle with ease, lathered his hands with the brick of soap and scrubbed them. "If I had known you were coming, I would've worn my Sunday best," he sassed.

She waved away his sarcasm and shifted her attention to the murmuring huddle of boys nearby. Johnny chuckled. "This is my sister, Pippa. Pippa, this is my crew today. We're thinning the leaves and trimming the shoots."

The boys doffed their caps and straw hats and greeted her. They stared in astonishment, as if she were as rare as a fairy.

Recalling that most of them were motherless, she graced them with her most pleasant, "Good day." Some continued to gaze in adoration, others muttered their replies.

"This is the trickiest vineyard work," Pippa announced. "The care you take to thin the vines will determine how much shade or sun the grapes receive and how the air circulates around the clusters to ripen them."

Johnny winked at Pippa. "This fine crew is very good at following my directions." The pealing of the chapel bell announced the noon hour. "All right, you hooligans, lunchtime. And please tell Father Crowley I'll be eating out here with my sister." Any fascination they had with Pippa was quickly replaced by their ravenous appetites. They crowded the pump, scrubbing and laughing. Within minutes, they scampered off to the mess hall.

Pippa and Johnny sat on a wooden bench beneath a leafy old maple. "Lord, have I missed these biscuits!" Johnny cried. After eating every morsel, he showed Pippa around the closest block of vineyard.

She expressed her amazement at the progress he was making.

"You really think so?" Johnny asked. "Luckily, the boys are about vine-height, with small hands." He rubbed his forehead. "It's a lot of work."

"Keeps you out of trouble," she remarked, her elbow jabbing his ribs.

"I don't miss my studies at the high school, but I do miss the girls. They don't even have dances here. I like baseball, but a man needs something to look at besides livestock, you know?"

Pippa laughed. "Well, your vineyard looks as tidy as Eagle's

Run," she replied. She reached into her satchel and pulled out a book. "Mac wanted me to give you this."

"*The Principles of Wine-Making* by Frederic Bioletti," he read aloud. "An Italian?"

"An expert Italian. Mac says this is your bible and you need to study it, especially parts two and three."

He cracked it open and scanned the pages. "Seems a bit boring."

"But necessary if you want those grapes to ripen in time to impress Papa."

"True enough."

Pippa stopped and touched her brother's arm. "Johnny, I also came to tell you that Luc has gone to war."

"Oh." He rubbed his forehead and squinted against the midday sun. He exhaled loudly. "It's hard to believe we haven't seen him in four years. Do you think he'll die?"

"I do worry, but he has joined the Pigeon Service, of all things."

Johnny snickered at the idea. "Who knew there was such a thing? Maman and Pop always said he would find a way to wheedle his way into the army."

"You two have that in common."

"What?"

"An aversion to the word 'no' that usually lands you in a heap of trouble."

"Think of us as adventurous."

"Or reckless."

"Perhaps, but Luc is a patriot. He's fighting for liberty, for the Allied cause. I'd do the same if I were eighteen."

Pippa rose and linked her arm in Johnny's. "You had better stay here. Keep your head down and keep busy."

A sad, faint smile crossed his lips. "Keeping busy won't keep Luc from dying."

When had Johnny become so intuitive? "I know," Pippa replied wistfully, recalling how, as a child, she would curl up against Luc's warm back as they slept. "But sometimes I feel like it might."

―――――

Pippa stepped down onto the Napa depot platform, still terrified for Luc, but astounded by the progress Johnny had made in the St. Isidore's vineyard. Papa would surely be proud when he returned in a few weeks. She would write Luc at once to tell him all the news, even if the chance was slim that her letters would find him.

Pippa walked along the silt road to the backside of the depot, only to find Billy feeding an apple to his horse. He was impeccably attired in his straw boater and crisp burgundy bow tie.

"What are you doing here?"

He bestowed a sheepish grin on her. "I stopped at the ranch. Rose told me you would be on this train, so I thought I'd take you home."

"That is kind."

He looked surprised. "Nothing more than any beau would do for his sweetheart." Her cheeks grew hot as his hands encircled her waist, lifting her up and into the saddle. The musky, spicy smell of him filled her senses.

They cantered in silence down the trail toward Eagle's Run. Motor cars and trucks passed occasionally, kicking up dirt in their wake, but Pippa was too focused on Billy's closeness to care. Seated behind her in the saddle, his sinewy thighs hugged hers and his long arms grazed hers as he worked the reins. When his body pressed against her backside, a pleasant, tingling sensation warmed her lower belly.

She was distracted by the notion that only a few layers of cloth separated their skin. His musculature had not been honed from farming the land, but rather from the sensual, exacting discipline of molding clay and chiseling rock.

After he helped her dismount, he pulled her close and kissed her lightly on the lips. "Pippa, I need to tell you something."

"Yes?" she asked, praying Rose would not appear at the door.

"You know how I applied to the École des Beaux-Arts in Paris?"

She nodded.

"They rejected me." His words dashed all her hopes. Reading her expression, he insisted, "It's for the best. With the war on, and my uncle needing me at the store, I can't think of going now. And there are other considerations."

"You mean me?"

"Of course," he whispered, bowing his forehead to touch hers.

Pippa stepped away. "No." She could not bear to be the reason he stayed here when there was a whole world waiting for him—for them. "You will apply again."

"Pippa, it's done. I'll continue to attend school in San Francisco and, perhaps one day soon, after I have some prospects, you and I may marry."

Anger bubbled deep within her. Certainly, they had been courting for several months now and she too had thought of marriage, but had Billy turned into a milksop overnight? "Do you want to study in Paris?"

"Yes."

"Then you will apply again in the fall." He started to object, but she lifted her palm. "Or I will not agree to marry you."

———

BREST AND TOURS, FRANCE

When the granite walls and hillocks of the Brittany coastline slid into view, Adeline elbowed her way to the railing on the upper deck. A briny breeze, a chorus of cawing gulls and blue-sand beaches greeted them as they sailed into the Bay of Biscay and eventually anchored in the Bay of Brest.

In the chaos that followed disembarkation, Base Hospital No. 30's head nurse, Arabella Lombard, gathered the group of nurses together. "We are going to be diverted to Vichy while the rest of the 30th moves on to Royat. It should only be for a few weeks."

"For what purpose?" Adeline asked, then instantly clapped her mouth shut, realizing she'd spoken out of order.

"To join up with Base Hospital No. 1 from New York. Many of their personnel have contracted the measles, a childhood pleasure evidently forgone in younger days."

Four nurses settled into each train compartment for what would be a two-day journey to Vichy. When the conversation waned, and they had eaten their rations of nuts and sandwiches, they took turns trading stories while poking their heads out of the small windows that opened into the corridor.

Seated next to the outside-facing window, Adeline was able to lean against the wall and doze off during the night. In the early morning hours, just as the four nurses ran out of the jam and tomato cans they had used to attend to nature's needs, the train lurched to a stop. A quick glance at the large sign affixed to the station house announced that they had arrived in Tours, not Vichy.

The head nurse unlocked their compartment and instructed them, "We're stopping to load up supplies. Be back in two hours, or you'll have to find your own ride to Vichy."

Adeline, still weary from lack of nutrition and sleep, lagged behind and was one of the last to descend onto the platform. With wisps of morning fog still clinging to the station and its iron railings, she did not see where her companions ventured. She strode across wooden planks toward the luscious fragrance of strong coffee, her thighs wincing in protest from hours of sitting. She pocketed her hands, but relished the cool morning breeze against her hot, train-flushed cheeks. A walk alone sounded like a superb idea.

Although it couldn't have been later than 0800 hours, corpsmen rushed up the platform to the rear of the train. As the fog dissipated, Adeline spied handsome young men loading sea bags, boxes stamped with red crosses, barrels of pickles and wine, and boxes of canned sardines, corned beef and hardtack. Although she appreciated the soldiers' quick glances and tips of their hats, she wished she had some running water to brush her teeth. Instead, she fingered the centimes in her pocket and made a beeline for the coffee stand in the corner.

While she waited her turn, she heard a familiar shout. *Her overactive imagination again.* The next time she heard the voice, it was deep and clear and right behind her.

"Addie?"

Her heart leapt with hope. She whirled around to find Luc, standing a head taller than her, striking in his army uniform, hat and brown leather boots. His chocolate eyes lit with warmth.

"It *is* you, isn't it?" His words rushed forth as he swept her up in his arms. "What are you doing here of all places?"

Breathless from the strength of his embrace, Adeline held her reply until her feet rested on the ground again. She explained that they had just landed and were on their way to Vichy. A group of corpsmen stopped to whistle and hoot.

Luc turned crimson. "She's my sister, you lugheads!"

Adeline gave an obligatory wave to the men as they dispersed, some disappointed, but others with a flicker of interest. "And you," she patted Luc's chest, "you've finally enlisted?" She regarded him intently, knowing Sara and Philippe would want a full report. He looked healthy and well fed, with clear eyes and skin and a strong constitution. In the nearly four years since she had seen him, a lantern jaw and pronounced cheekbones had replaced his round face. His hair, a smear of black ink beneath his hat, only accented his warm, penetrating, gaze. She wondered if Luc bore a striking resemblance to Bastien Lemieux, the father they shared but had never met.

He snapped to attention and saluted. "Private Luc Lemieux, at your service, *mademoiselle*," he announced.

Luc paid for their coffee and bought Adeline a demi-baguette and handful of fresh strawberries done up in a twist of newspaper.

He checked his watch. "I can spare a few minutes from loading supplies. The men will cover for me," he explained as he guided her to a nearby bench. "Where will you be stationed?"

"Vichy for a few weeks, but then Royat to prepare the base hospital there. My father is already en route. I am assigned to Surgical Team No. 50 and he to 51."

"How are Maman and Papa and your parents? The children?" He searched her face.

"All were well when I left them, although Tante Sara worries about you! Philippe will be pleased to know they accepted you into the army."

He blew on his scalding coffee and took a sip. "I'm headed to the front to meet up with the 23rd Infantry Regiment. The Huns have Paris in their sights."

Adeline had never pictured Luc on the front lines. As she contemplated this revelation, he continued calmly, "I have written Maman and Papa to tell them and I have instructed them regarding my wishes if the worst should happen." Acid crept up the back of her throat. She squeezed his hand. He was simply too young, too beautiful to die. He must live to have a wife and babies and a thriving vineyard. Their children, cousins, would play jacks and shoot marbles together one day.

"I have asked them to honor the terms of my will and give a share of my estate to you, along with my other siblings."

Panic compelled her to grab his wrists. "No! Don't say it—I won't have it! You must come back to us all," she pleaded like a petulant child.

"What right have I? No more than any other man in this war, Addie."

"Lemieux!" One of the corpsmen shouted and held up five fingers. The corpsmen shot furtive glances in the siblings' direction while they loitered in a huddle by the exit. Flustered by the hasty goodbye thrust upon them, she said, "You keep your head down and helmet on, promise?"

"I promise. And don't be dazzled by the Frenchmen you meet. They're all charm and accent and cheap wine. Chin up, smile bright, okay?"

A tear slipped down her cheek. "Oh, oh wait!" She fumbled in her leather bag and pulled out the comic book, folded into squares. "From Reverend Mother—er, Sister Paulette—at the convent in New York."

He opened it and laughed at the picture of Charlie Chaplin, pictured sporting a military uniform and sword. "No rosary or prayer books?" he teased.

"Apparently Reverend Mother thought it best to keep you grinning—the nuns will take care of the praying, as will I."

He drew her to him and brushed his lips against her forehead. "Thank you, Addie."

"I'll come see you in Saint Martin when you return home, yes?" she insisted in a tight, desperate tone.

He squeezed her hands and, with a beaming smile that would weaken any girl's knees, turned toward his comrades-in-arms.

She lifted her fingers to her lips. *"Bonne chance, mon frère."* Her words evaporated along with the morning fog.

Luc's words had traced an icy finger down Adeline's spine. Why did he seem so resigned to his fate?

Images flashed through her mind: Tante Sara, howling with grief, Uncle Philippe suffering a stroke of paralysis at the news,

Pippa and Lydia and Johnny huddled together over their brother's grave. How could she let him go? She wanted to run across the platform, drop to her knees and grab his calves to prevent him from walking off to war, but such theatrics would be foolish, embarrassing, futile. No, she would sip her coffee, as a proper twenty-six-year-old nurse should, and stuff all her spiny-edged fears deep down, where her work of cleaning wounds and sanitizing the surgery and comforting the boys would dull them—for a time.

NEAR CHÂTEAU-THIERRY, FRANCE

The Kaiser's 231st Division had shelled Château-Thierry and both banks of the Marne River, successfully seizing the strategic hill to the west that overlooked the entire town. Today, the army had advanced as far as the stone ruins of the castle for which the town was named. They halted there, thwarted by a storm of French and Senegalese machine-gun fire from the south bank of the river, only seventy meters wide at this point.

Heinrich was kneeling on the dirt floor inside the ancient castle's keep and bandaging the bullet wounds of an infantryman when the *Oberstleutnant* burst in.

"When night fell, the Americans were lined up on the south bank. Expect more casualties imminently, Leutnant Sommer."

"What's our objective?" Heinrich asked.

The *Oberstleutnant* recoiled, as if Heinrich had no right to ask. But surprisingly, he answered, "To establish a bridgehead, invade the southern half of the town and gain control of the railroad."

"Do you want us medics closer to the fighting?"

"Too dangerous. Stay here for now and await orders."

Heinrich finished patching up the soldier's arm and washed his hands with a mixture of two parts sand, one part soap, and water. He lit a cigarette and peered out into the inky darkness from beneath the castle's stone archway. An occasional burst of gunfire or shouting erupted, but nothing out of the ordinary. Heinrich ducked his head back in to suck a drag, careful to keep his hand and the orange glow of his cigarette hidden, lest he be caught in a sniper's crosshairs.

He did not particularly relish the bitter taste of tobacco, but the smoke soothed his nerves before each battle and the subsequent endless stream of injured men.

Had the residents of this sleepy French town all evacuated? By the time the 231st had approached at dusk, the ivory and terracotta houses that speckled the slopes of Château-Thierry were vacant, windows gaping as if stunned by the abrupt arrival of the enemy.

Somewhere behind Heinrich in the gloom, a soldier called for water. Just as he was about to extinguish his smoke, a giant flash of light burst, illuminating the town's buildings and bridge below. Three dark lumps—bodies, Heinrich guessed—flew twenty meters into the air and landed out of sight. A clatter of dirt and rocks rained into the river and onto the street.

Shrieks assailed Heinrich's ears, snapping him out of his bystander's trance. He yelled *"Hilfe! Hilfe!"* into the castle tunnel, grabbed his helmet and a stretcher, and ran to the stairs, stumbling down the steps and into the street. He ducked and ran toward the Marne, gripping the stretcher above his head, flimsy protection against the bullets that whizzed past, deafening or slaying all in their path.

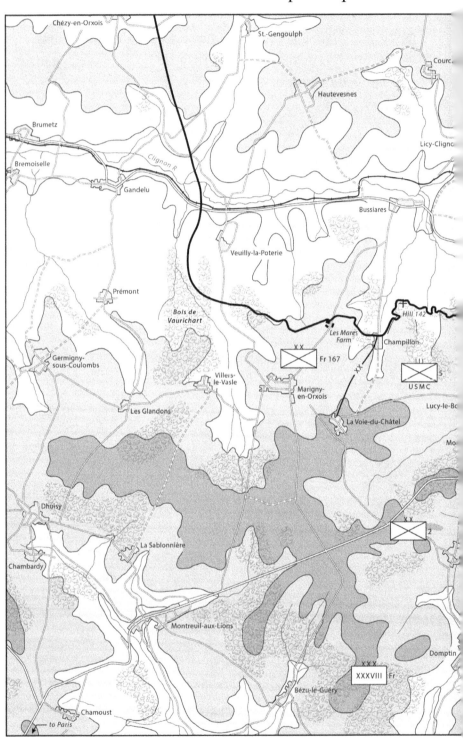

Chézy-en-Orxois

St-Gengoulph

Hautevesnes

Courc.

Brumetz

Licy-Clign

Bremoiselle

Clignon R.

Gandelu

Bussiares

Veuilly-la-Poterie

Prémont

Bois de
Vaurichart

Hill 142

Les Mares
Farm

Champillon

X X

Fr 167

X X

Germigny-
sous-Coulombs

Villers-
le-Vasle

Marigny-
en-Orxois

X X

S

USMC

Les Glandons

Lucy-le-Bo

La Voie-du-Châtel

Mo

Dhuisy

La Sablonnière

X X

2

Chambardy

La Sablonnière

Montreuil-aux-Lions

Domptin

XXX

XXXVIII

Fr

Bézu-le-Guéry

Chamoust

to Paris

at Chateau Thierry and Belleau Wood

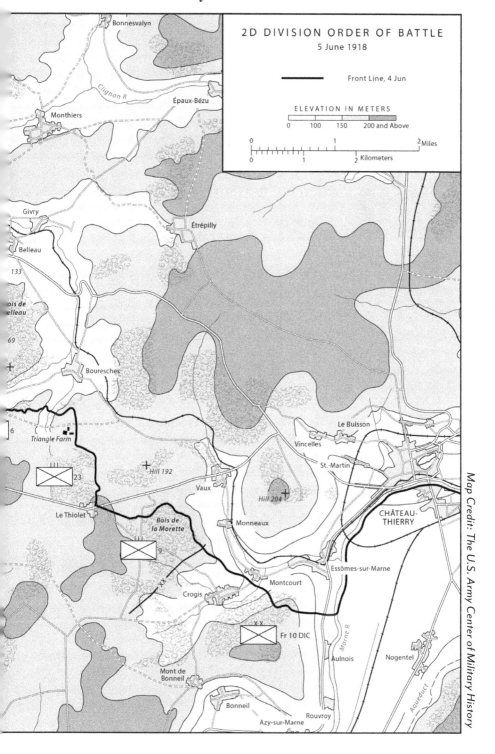

2D DIVISION ORDER OF BATTLE
5 June 1918

——————— Front Line, 4 Jun

ELEVATION IN METERS

| 0 | 100 | 150 | 200 and Above |

0   1   2 Miles

0   1   2 Kilometers

Bonnesvalyn

Clignon R

Monthiers

Épaux-Bézu

Givry

Étrépilly

Belleau

133

Bois de Belleau

69

Bouresches

Triangle Farm

23

Hill 192

Le Buisson

Vincelles

St.-Martin

Vaux

Hill 204

Le Thiolet

Bois de la Morette

Monneaux

CHÂTEAU-THIERRY

9

Essômes-sur-Marne

Crogis

Montcourt

Marne R

Fr 10 DIC

Aulnois

Nogentel

Mont de Bonneil

Aqueduct

Bonneil

Rouvroy

Azy-sur-Marne

Map Credit: The U.S. Army Center of Military History

CHAPTER 8

First Days of June 1918

EN ROUTE TO CHÂTEAU-THIERRY, FRANCE

The small band of Signal Corps pigeoneers were ordered to strike out with their single mobile loft of carrier pigeons on the northern road from Paris to join up with the 23rd Infantry, under the command of Colonel Paul Malone. The 23rd was en route from Chaumont-en-Vexin, just northwest of Paris, to the Château-Thierry sector.

Just before midday, Luc and his fellow pigeoneers encountered the 23rd and the 2nd Engineers along the Paris–Château-Thierry road. Gray dust covered the thousands of trucks that snaked eastward to meet the Huns, who had burst through the lines at Soissons and now occupied Bouresches, ninety kilometers east of Paris. The U.S. army regulars, dubbed "doughboys," and the Signal Corps drove through quaint villages where French citizens lined the road, throwing flowers, pressing their hands together in gratitude and blowing kisses.

As they neared the front, they encountered the westbound refugees: hay wagons, wheelbarrows, screaming babies, hunched old men leading cows, sagging old women clutching baskets, and young girls shuffling along, occasionally waving with interest at the foreign band of soldiers, bare-chested in shimmering heat, but still animated, their songs and joking often muffled by the roar of engines. On the road with his new comrades, marching against a common enemy, Luc was certain America and its Allies would prevail.

In the passenger seat of the mobile loft's cab, with tight hamstrings and an aching *derrière*, Luc ate the last of the nuts and raisins he had purchased in Paris, one by one, to savor what might be his last meal for a while. The rolling kitchens did not seem to be part of their caravan, and he silently hoped they had rushed on ahead to greet the soldiers with a hot meal.

Peering out the window, he admired the countryside. The sprawling farmland was untouched by war, blanketed with half-grown wheat and studded with an occasional stone farmhouse or stable to divide the properties. One of the odd, yet appealing, things he had discovered about French farm life was that, except for some vineyards like Saint Martin, most farmers lived in town, while their crops and vineyards were located just on the outskirts. He had felt so isolated at Saint Martin with just his grandparents for company, but Michel and Ondine had breathed new life into his days.

As he gazed through the windshield, where streaks of mud from the wipers' action still obstructed part of his view, he spied a girl of no more than nine, with a scrawny kitten hoisted over her shoulder and a tawny froth of curls that bounced as she trudged down the road with her family. She looked a smidge like his sister Lydia, who had been eight when he had left Napa. Grandmère kept the intricately woven Amboise lace they had planned to send on her twelfth birthday in the kitchen cupboard, for they were not able to post anything for overseas delivery these days. Lydia had been born on the same day the flames engulfed San Francisco in 1906. She was a phoenix, unlike Pippa, who was a veritable sphinx, and most unlike Johnny, who was a rough-and-tumble rabble-rouser with scraped knees, gapped teeth and a sprinkling of freckles across his nose. Luc sighed with relief, grateful that his brother at sixteen was still free to revel in the pleasures of adolescence and that his family members were all tucked safely in America, far from the gaping mouth of hell.

The trucks charged past Meaux and finally stopped by the roadside near Montreuil-aux-Lions, southwest of Belleau Wood in the heart of the Château-Thierry sector, seventy kilometers from Paris. The men tumbled to the ground and bivouacked by the roadside. Dinner consisted of emergency rations of bacon and hardtack—a saltless, flatter version of Maman's biscuits on which he'd nearly broken a tooth—while they waited for the food and rolling kitchens to arrive.

Orange flames spiraled above the horizon, all that was left of the burning villages to their east. Flashes of white light appeared as the cannons fired, but the booming noise was too far off to reach Luc's ears. Using his sixty-pound pack as a pillow, and a flimsy poncho and blanket to cover himself, he rested on the fresh-smelling, untrodden grass. Tiny pebbles jabbed his side.

217

He rolled onto his back, stretched his legs and flexed his feet and fingers, to ease the stiffness of so many hours on the road.

The purr of plane engines grew louder. Nearby, artillery fire erupted so intensely, Luc's heart punched his ribcage with alarming speed. The noise persisted, assaulting his senses like a never-ending drumroll. He wished he could burrow deep into the soil and hide. He turned on his stomach, inhaling the nutty scent of the earth. It trembled beneath him like a stricken child.

The soldiers around him slept so soundly they did not seem to notice. One slid his helmet over his face, as if that would add a layer of protection. Another turned on his side, away from the blasts. During the few gaps between bomb blasts, all Luc could hear was the oddly comforting trill of crickets' wings and the coughing and log-sawing snores of his fellow soldiers.

Luc signed the cross and whispered an Our Father. His notion of heaven was admittedly juvenile—since he was a child, he had always pictured a white-bearded Holy Father, a handsome Jesus, a blue-veiled Blessed Mother, and all the angels and saints floating on a cloud above Mount Tamalpais back home. Funny how such images lingered into adulthood. Luc had learned his prayers by rote, never giving much thought to the words he recited every evening, but rather trying to summon a general attitude of reverence as he spoke them. Tonight was different. His mind hung on one line and he repeated it as he signed the cross again and again: "Deliver us from evil." This cup of suffering would not pass by any of them. Christians, Jews, Muslims or atheists as they might be, they were all in communion with Christ now—as sacrificial lambs being sent to the slaughter.

JUNE 4, 1918

The American and French artillery barraged Belleau Wood, where the Germans had retreated into their foxholes over the past few days. *Le Bois de Belleau*, as it was known in French, was a tangle of trees on the edge of a historic French hunting ground and the primary objective of the doughboys and marines of the U.S. 2nd Division. In a crude sketch of the sector, which Sergeant Rivers shared with his men, the wood itself looked like a long rectangle, stretching two kilometers from north to south and one kilometer wide. A large chunk was bitten out of its southwest side where an expanse of wheat fields swept northeast from the village of Lucy-le-Bocage to the waist of the wood.

The roar of heavy cannon fire and exploding shells reverberated in Luc's eardrums day and night. As the sun rose, Luc and the band of pigeoneers strapped on their gear and followed on foot the string of telephone operators, runners, linemen, scouts, riflemen and machine gunners of the 23rd Infantry. They marched east, carrying the pigeon cages, feed, watering buckets and equipment to a spot just south of Lucy-le-Bocage and the southwestern tip of Belleau Wood. Fatigue clutched Luc's stomach and pinched his eyeballs. He was too miserable to be afraid.

Corporal Houle, another pigeoneer, patted his midsection. "I'm officially starving. Look, my stomach is concave. How long does it take one of those rolling kitchens to drive here? For Chrissakes, what's the damn holdup?"

219

"The Germans are shelling the Gobert ravine and the trucks can't make it through to us or the marines," Marty said.

"Gob Gully is under attack? Sheez. Still, they should walk that beef stew over to the troops. We'll be fine, but those men—" He pointed to the infantrymen ahead of them, carrying only their rifles and bayonets. "You can't send them to their deaths on an empty stomach. That ain't right."

"We should have trapped and skinned one of those trench rats. Probably tastes like chicken if you roast it. You see those things? Big as cats, ugly as sin." The sergeant's expression contorted with disgust.

Luc shuddered at the memory of the trench rats' claws scampering over his oilcloth blanket during the night. He lamented, "One of those suckers gnawed through my pack and ate my last ration of bacon."

The infantryman eavesdropping ahead of them chuckled and turned. "LeRoy over there brought an ant-bear with him. It chases and eats all the rats during the night!"

"An ant-bear?" Luc asked incredulously.

"A sort of raccoon or something. From Haiti."

"No kidding?" And Luc had thought himself bold to sneak his two pigeons from Vouvray into the mobile loft.

As the brilliant yellow halo of sunrise painted the horizon, the retreating stream of French *poilus* and their commanding officers parted to make way for the advancing Americans. Regiments of Senegalese riflemen and French chasseurs, who had occupied the northerly Les Mares Farm until this point, staggered away from the advancing Germans with haunted eyes, bloodied bandages hastily tied, shoulders slumping.

"La guerre est finie!" one wept. An older man with a bushy beard and a bulging stare cautioned, *"Beaucoup d'Allemands!"* He uttered a string of warnings in French as he fumbled with a brass lighter while an unlit cigarette dangled from his blood-crusted lips. Luc rested the birdcages on the ground and gently lifted the trench lighter from his hands. With the flick of his thumb, he produced a flame. The *poilu's* cigarette burned as he sucked deeply.

"Merci, monsieur, pour votre courage," was all Luc could think to say, he was so shocked by the *poilu's* grisly descriptions of the battle.

The old *poilu* turned a soft blue gaze on him and patted his cheek. *"Retournez-vous, vite, vite!"*

Sergeant Rivers, who walked ahead, bending the ear of Major Elliott, the 3rd Battalion commander, turned around and shouted, "Lemieux, back in line!"

As Luc fell into step, now bringing up the rear, Major Elliott dropped back and sidled up to him. "You spoke French to that soldier, son?"

Luc's spine straightened. Was this a reprimand? He was still adjusting to army life. Best to shorten his replies. "Yes, sir."

"Are you fluent?"

"Français est ma langue maternelle. French is my first language, English, my second, sir."

"What did he say?"

"He said that the war is over and that we should turn back because there are too many Germans to fight. Then he described the beheadings and butchery he had witnessed. And he warned us about the deadly precision of the Hun machine gunners and riflemen."

The major stared straight ahead. "Thank you, private. March on."

Pity for the French swelled in Luc's heart, but dread made it stumble a beat. Could the marines and doughboys truly stop the Huns and succeed where the French had failed? Or was this a suicide mission?

By midday, the French counterattack had collapsed, and the Germans had pushed through to advance into the northern edge of Belleau Wood and to the outskirts of Les Mares Farm. However, by the end of the day on June 4, Luc and his comrades had learned that the Americans had helped repulse the Germans from Les Mares Farm by spraying them with heavy rifle fire, sending them running back to their dugouts in Belleau Wood.

———

JUNE 5, 1918

Luc and his comrades finished their sidestep to the east and assumed their position with the 23rd Infantry. With the pigeon-eers entrenched directly behind them, the 23rd took control of the line closest to the marines from Triangle Farm south to Le Thiolet, facing due east. The 9th Infantry continued that same line, running south but curving east from Le Thiolet through Bourbetin and around Bois de la Morette, where they faced due north toward Belleau Wood. There, at the eastern edge of Bois de la Morette, the 9th Infantry linked the 2nd Division's right flank to a French division. Altogether, the Franco-American line stretched seven kilometers south to the Paris–Metz road.

The soldiers of the 23rd dug two-meter long trenches, less than a meter wide and a meter deep, which they dubbed their "graves." The gunners positioned their Chauchat and Hotchkiss machine guns behind boulders and atop ravines, while the telescopic riflemen trained their rifles on the fields to the north and east, presumably to provide cover fire for the marines who would engage with the Germans as soon as the attack order was given.

Behind them, Luc, Marty, Houle and Rivers dug a long trench to house two men and twelve pigeon cages, fitted with respirators and a covering to protect the birds against gas attacks. They had brought twenty-four of the forty birds that had survived the trek from Paris—eight that would home to Tours, fourteen that would home to Paris and two that would home to Vouvray, per Ondine's instructions. The remaining pigeons had been left safe in their loft with Private O'Malley to oversee their care.

Luc gave the birds the last half gallon of water, fed them and examined each one's feathers. Several birds had dry, sunken eyes and seemed listless. The pigeoneers would need to find a water source soon. He wished he could allow the birds to exercise in their large wire cage, but they had been forced to leave it behind with O'Malley and the mobile loft.

Before his company could discuss where to go for water, a runner appeared with an order from Colonel Malone, the 23rd Infantry commander. "Sir," he announced to the sergeant, "We have runners and telephones, but German shells have shredded some of the lines, and they've been stealing most of the messages we do send. We'll need the pigeons to relay messages to Paris and Tours in case our traditional methods fail."

"Stealing messages? How?"

"They have powerful induction coils, sir. Man and bird are our best options at this point."

Sergeant Rivers flicked his head in Luc's direction. "Give your message to Lemieux. He'll send it toot-sweet." Luc arranged the metal message holders and blank rice paper and scribbled duplicate dates, times and messages: *23rd in position south of BW near Triangle.* Since there was extra space, he repeated the message in French. He folded and slipped the notes into the metal bands and secured them to the two cocks' legs. With two hands, just as Ondine had taught him, Luc released the birds while muttering a Hail Mary.

When he rejoined his company to ask for further orders, the sergeant was smoking his straight-stem pipe, digging another trench and holding court. Houle and Marty huddled, kneeling close to the sergeant so they could hear his instructions over the screech of the artillery. "Most of the French are moving out," he shouted. "That will leave us on the front line against the Germans. I need a volunteer to run for water. There's a creek a mile to our south." The sergeant jerked a thumb over his shoulder to vaguely indicate a road behind them.

"I'll go, sir," Luc offered, before his mind presented any doubts. At least he would be able to help the troops and birds while slaking his own thirst. The birds had grown unusually quiet. He surmised that to wait any longer could be disastrous.

No one offered to accompany him. Sweat trickled down his comrades' foreheads, arms and bare chests as they lifted the dirt with their spades, carving out a massive line of trenches. Luc struck out with his rifle and bayonet, twenty canteens roped around his neck and an empty bucket. Before he reached the road, Marty called out, "Hey, knucklehead, you forgot something!" He waved Luc's gas mask and respirator bag in the air. "Krauts are spraying mustard gas. If the wind kicks up and you see a yellow cloud drifting toward you, put it on!" Luc cheeks flamed at his naivety, but he gratefully grabbed the satchel and headed southwest along the dirt road. As he walked, his eyes darted in every direction and his ears pricked at each foreign sound.

Over a kilometer down the road, with no sign of any water, Luc came to a break in the stone wall where a ditch led away from the road. He dropped down and followed it. *Always head downhill if you're looking for water*, Papa had taught him. There was no sign of man or animal nearby, save for the buzzing of the French Spads overhead, floating above the tree line and dipping down to get a closer look at the battlefield. A hawk circled, leaving Luc to wonder if it was an animal's carcass or, heaven forbid, a soldier's that had caught the predator's attention.

As the ditch deepened into a ravine, Luc scanned it for dark vegetation, or moss on the rocks—anything that might indicate that a stream might be near. Between the oaks and pines, the sun glinted on a glasslike surface somewhere in the distance. Luc tugged the rim of his helmet down to shield his eyes as the yellow orb rose in the sky. Quickening his pace, he followed the bottom of the ravine and eventually discovered the mouth of a stream.

White-capped, clear water rushed over a line of smooth stones. Exhilaration swept over Luc. He dropped the canteens to the ground and splashed cool water on his cheeks and arms and combed it through his hair. The follicles on his sweaty head sang with relief. Luc scooped the water into his helmet and guzzled it down, rivulets trickling down his chin and neck and cooling the exposed triangle of flesh at his open collar. The canteens gurgled with joy until they brimmed with the life-sustaining liquid.

It was nearly midday when Luc returned to the front. He was greeted with waves and buoyant cries of delight from his comrades. While he was gone, the men had organized the birds by place of origin and stacked sandbags against the eastern edges of their trenches to protect from mortar attacks.

Once he had distributed water to the men and the birds, Luc sat down next to Marty and Houle, who had already busied themselves with lunch. The rolling kitchens had never appeared, despite assurances they were coming. The emergency rations— two pounds of bread and one and a half pounds of bacon—were dwindling. Over a fire of kindling, lumps of dough hissed and popped in a kettle filled with a thick sludge of golden oil. Luc leaned over and sniffed.

"Heavenly. What is that, fellas?"

Marty replied, "Soldier's trick."

Houle stabbed at the fried ball of dough with his tin fork. "You fry up the bread in the bacon fat. *Voilà*, a trench doughnut." He held up the dough and blew on it. The crust sizzled as the scent of pig grease wafted over the firepit. He tore off the corner of a paper packet with his teeth and sprinkled sugar crystals all over his creation. "Just like Mom used to make," he said with delight, devouring the morsel in two bites.

"You have to try one, Froggie." Marty sat back and chewed, a grin stretching across his face. Luc still bristled a bit at his nickname but decided to view it as a compliment. He followed Marty's example, smushing the bread into a ball and dipping it into the pot of bubbling oil.

He pulled out the golf-ball-sized nugget when it turned a deep amber. The tantalizing smell of bacon and the warmth of the afternoon sun on his shoulders relaxed his muscles. If he closed his eyes, he could imagine himself seated at the kitchen table at his family's Napa ranch, sunlight filtering through the windows as Rose and Maman, hip to hip at the cook stove, rustled up bacon, eggs and flapjacks on a Sunday morning. Once Luc's doughnut shimmered with sugar crystals, he bit in, relishing the sweet and savory taste.

He gathered another twenty empty canteens from the machine gunners and riflemen in front of them. They were drilling with the weapons they had just inherited from their French counterparts. From the frustration on the soldiers' faces, he guessed the assembly was not going to plan. A hothead named Vito hurled profanities, wadded the instructions into a ball and chucked the paper.

"Need help?" Luc ventured.

Vito's lip curled, revealing twisted front teeth and a hole where a left incisor should have been. "I doubt a pigeoneer would have better luck assembling this piece of French crap," he scoffed.

"This one might," Luc replied, ignoring the slight. He squatted and flattened out the wrinkled paper, securing it with the toe of his hobnailed boot. "Are you having trouble with that half-moon clip?"

Vito rubbed his day-old beard and glanced at Luc suspiciously. "It's too flimsy." He handed the weapon to Luc, who was surprised by the lightweight design of the beastly automatic rifle. He scanned the directions until he discovered how to secure the clip that held the magazine of fifty-millimeter brass bullets. With two swift movements, Luc completed the task.

"You know your way around weapons, kid. Nice work."

"Not really," Luc replied, pleased that he could do something useful. "I just know how to read French. I'll leave the cover fire to you." He handed back the Chauchat, slapped his comrade on the back and set out for the creek again.

The trip was faster this time, and Luc returned with two hours of daylight left. After distributing the water, he squatted on the ground, his glands salivating at the thought of those bacon-fat trench doughnuts. A spade crunched the dirt near his boot. The sergeant, still smoking his pipe, growled, "Get digging, private, or you won't have any place to sleep tonight."

Luc's spade split the earth. He hoisted a dozen stones as big as melons, but beyond that, the soil was springy and soft and dark with nutrients—too fine for growing grapes, which required less irrigation and more stress on the vines to produce a minerally chenin blanc like the grapes he cultivated at Saint Martin. God, what he wouldn't give for a decent glass of cellar-chilled wine! Hell, he'd settle for warm *pinard* at this point.

Some Americans liked to joke that the French couldn't finish off the Germans because they were too drunk on wine to lift their rifles. In this case, American bravado obscured the truth. Based on what he'd learned from the *poilus* who had visited Saint Martin, the French command was to blame. They herded the *poilus* and threw them to the Germans without a care for the cost. The weary French soldiers they had met on the road had planned their retreat. They had repelled the Germans for days and had earned a rest.

Mercifully, as the sun set, a breeze cooled the soldiers. For his third trip to the creek that day, Luc learned he would have a companion.

"No moon again," he observed to the sallow-faced runner from the 23rd who accompanied him. Benson was his name—a college man from Princeton.

"How the heck are we supposed to find this elusive stream?" Benson whispered. "They'll wring my neck if I show up empty-handed. Might as well surrender to the Germans as go back."

"Stay close. I'll guide you."

"How? We can't see a blessed thing!"

Luc stopped. Benson stumbled into him. "Look closely. See the contrast between the light pebbles on the road, the deep black of the trees and foliage, and the midnight navy of the sky? It's subtle, but it's there if you look closely."

"I suppose so."

Luc shrugged. That sounded like a definite *no*. "Where'd you grow up, Benson?"

Benson drew in a deep breath. "Manhattan. Why?"

A city boy, just as Luc suspected. It was a relief to discover one kid who was even more wet behind the ears than he was.

"Just curious," he replied nonchalantly. "Hold out your hand and run it along this stone wall to your right. Now follow it around this curve and when it breaks, you turn right and drop down into the ditch—but don't let your ankles wobble, or you'll end up with a sprain faster than a streak of greased lightning." Luc amused himself by using his Tante Aurora's favorite phrase. He guided Benson's fingers to the side of the wall, for the top edge, he had noticed earlier in the day, was serrated with sharp stones and glass. "Don't move your hand any higher. Just feel the stone beneath your fingers. Concentrate."

Benson winced. "Ow!"

"Keep your hand where I showed you!" Luc hissed. "The jagged top edge is designed to keep deer and urchins with quick fingers from jumping the boundary and pilfering fruit and livestock."

Benson laughed. "That seems rather futile now that the Germans are running roughshod all over the countryside."

"How would you feel if the Germans bombed your carefully constructed skyscrapers?"

"Isn't that why we're all here? To make sure the Fritzies never reach our shores?"

Luc lowered his voice. "Quiet—observe your surroundings. Here's the ditch. Drop down and follow the slope into the ravine."

Benson did as Luc instructed, and the pair zigzagged until the rocks and dirt turned to a soft carpet of grass underfoot. The stridulating of crickets' wings and the croaking of bullfrogs— between distant artillery blasts—led them deeper into the crevice lined with scrubby pines. The earth squished and moss bounced beneath their boots. When there was another momentary break in the distant shelling, Luc stopped abruptly. Benson lurched into him again. The glorious sound of lapping water filled Luc's ears. "Just a few minutes now," he announced cheerfully.

Benson's breath was steady behind him. As they walked deeper into the wood, the underbrush snagged their canvas pants, the twigs crackled beneath their treads and the summer flora tantalized, filling Luc's nostrils with the tangy scent of greenery—a delicious respite from the oniony sweat of his fellow soldiers or the artillery smoke that stung his nostrils and sank like a dagger into his lungs.

When they reached the midpoint of the fizzing stream, he squatted down and cupped the water in his hand. "Tastes clean. This is the spot."

"Just a minute, Lemieux. I gotta take a shit."

Benson's belt clinked and Luc gripped his arm. "Not here you don't. You'll contaminate the entire water source!"

"All right, okay. Shoot! I didn't know."

"You can go when we leave—up by the road." They dunked the canteens and jugs they carried until they overflowed with fresh water. They reached the upward slope of the ravine in ten minutes or so. Gripping the narrow tree trunks, they used them like pegs in a board to hoist their bodies and heavy cargo up the hill. The trees bowed beneath their grasp, their crowns swaying and rustling together as the men approached the stone wall at the top of the ravine.

"Now?" Benson begged.

"Sure," Luc agreed. Taking pity on his charge, he added, "Take the big oak leaves to wipe your arse, not the poison ivy," he advised, recalling the fiery rash he had acquired on his arms and face after unknowingly ripping a large tangle of the plant from the perimeter of Tante Aurora's garden when he was twelve.

"Right-o," Benson called as he disappeared through the gap in the stone wall. A few moments later he sounded off with relief.

Luc leaned against one of the trees. If he sat down, he might never get up again. He must be carrying close to fifty pounds of extra weight, the same as his army pack, but much more cumbersome with the swinging canteens and the jugs he tried to hold steady so the contents wouldn't slosh.

Despite his best efforts, his knees buckled with fatigue and he sank down, squatting on the ground. Suddenly shots whizzed by in rapid succession, shredding the tree trunk above his head. He instinctively dropped, lying prone against the earth. He took a quick inventory: helmet and chin strap in place, limbs all moving, no pain detected, shots flying from across the road, beyond the wall.

"Benson?" he hissed.

No reply.

Luc peeled off all but one canteen and dug his elbows into the ground, one in front of the other, propelling himself upslope on his belly for ten meters to Benson's last location. Panting, he poked his head around the wall. The sight of Benson's dark, hunched figure sent a trickle of panic down Luc's backbone. "Benson?"

Benson's breath shot forward in rapid bursts, as if he were hyperventilating.

Luc waved his hand until he found Benson's meaty shoulder. "You hit?"

The air crackled with rifle fire and another spray of bullets flew over their heads. A barrage of metal thudded against the trunk of the trees, tattering bark and shooting splinters everywhere. One lodged in Luc's hand, but he quickly pulled it out.

Benson's voice warbled. "In the calf. Doesn't hurt too bad. What are the fucking Germans doing over here, behind our line? Are we surrounded? Christ!"

A few days ago, the fighting had raged just a couple of kilometers west of where they were now. It was possible that the Germans were driving southeast from Marigny-en-Orxois toward their exact location. But Luc did not want to panic Benson with this notion. "Could be our guys conducting target practice with those Chauchat rifles. They tend to jam, I hear. Let me feel the wound." Benson's blood was hot and thick under Luc's fingers. The bullet had struck the flesh of his calf. The tibia and fibula bones appeared to be intact. "Feels like it sailed clean through. There's an entry and exit wound." Luc unfastened the canteen strap and cautioned Benson to hold still while he tightened it above the wound, fashioning a tourniquet. He took off his shirt, wrapped it around Benson's wound and tied it securely.

"Six hundred yards," Benson announced between clenched teeth.

"What?"

"That's how close they are."

"How do you know?"

"If the sniper was closer than six hundred yards, the force of the bullet would have torn a piece out of me. If the bullet was more than six hundred yards away, it would still be stuck in my leg. Six hundred yards is the shooting distance of a bullet that runs clean through."

Maybe Benson did know a thing or two about warfare.

"Drink." Benson gulped water from the container Luc held to his lips. Luc had hoped to listen for approaching footsteps but could hear nothing over the artillery blasts in the distance, which meant their assailants could not have heard them either. *Shit.* They had stirred the crowns of the trees hiking down and up the slope to the river. The shooters must have somehow seen the treetops wobble in the darkness.

"How do you feel?" Luc asked Benson, whose breathing had steadied.

"Like I've been shot."

Luc felt around the makeshift bandage. It was soaked but the bleeding was beginning to ebb. "We'll patch you up, don't worry."

Luc abandoned the jugs of water and threw Benson's arm over his shoulders. "Don't try to walk on it, just hop on your good leg." The pair limped the kilometer and a half to the 23rd silently. Luc prayed to God they would make it back alive, because he sure as hell wasn't about to die collecting water.

When they found the medic, he injected Benson with anti-tetanus serum, cleaned his wounds with iodine and bandaged his leg properly. Benson retired to his trench to rest.

Luc found Marty near the empty firepit, with no trench doughnuts in sight. Instead, Marty handed him one of the twelve cans of monkey meat he had bartered from the 43rd French Infantry in exchange for cigarettes. Threads of meat lodged between Luc's teeth. His stomach, despite its hunger groans, revolted at the gristly texture and bland taste. Luc grimaced, but before he could comment, Sergeant Rivers approached, still puffing on his pipe. "What the heck happened?" he demanded.

"Not sure. Benson thinks the shots came from about six hundred yards to our west, on the other side of the stone wall that runs beside the road at the top of the ravine. Do you think it's the Germans? They were awfully close only two days ago. They could have advanced southeast, attempting to surround us . . ." Luc's mind muddled with fatigue.

The sergeant ignored Luc's theory. "We'd best entrench deeply tonight, because come morning, the marines are going to unleash hell on the Germans."

After he thanked Marty for the substandard meal and checked in on Benson, Luc curled up beneath his oilskin blanket. His thighs tightened against his chest with every blast. The fat farm rats scuttled over his body all night. If his helmet slipped so much as an inch, their long, soft tails would slide across his cheek, causing him to shiver with disgust. Thank God they had the canvas gas tents to cover the birds so the rats could not detect them in their cages. He would have sold his eye-teeth for an ant-bear that night.

———

June 1, 1918, Royat-les-Bains

Chèrs Maman, Gemma and Rourke,
After a side trip to Vichy, we are now reunited with Papa and
the physicians and corpsmen of the 30th in Royat-les-Bains.

Would you believe that I encountered Luc in the flesh when our train made an unexpected stop in Tours? He is in good health, but I am sad to say our dear boy was headed to the front and most certainly has arrived by now. I pray the rosary every week for him.

Royat is a beautiful resort town, untouched by battle. It is tucked into the Auvergne mountains and boasts natural hot springs that have existed since the Romans occupied Gaul. We now have the challenge of converting eight glamorous hotels into a modern hospital fit to care for thousands of soldiers.

I share a room with three other nurses: Millie from San Jose, Rosemary from the San Francisco Dogpatch and Julia from Sacramento. We are all up at dawn to scrub the Metropole Hotel from ceiling to floor until nightfall. We scrubbed so hard, we removed three coats of paint before the doctors deemed the spaces sanitized enough for our boys!

The fresh air, sunlight and clean water are abundant. The cesspools, however, overflow regularly into the newly restored kitchens! The local honey wagon (as we call the horse-drawn pump and wagon that empties them) requires several weeks' notice when they overflow within seven days of the last service. We must solve the problem before the troops arrive, any day now.

Maman, you will be pleased to hear that Papa has organized the surgery with his usual precision. We have a folding surgical table, all the necessary instruments and an X-ray machine. We have been instructed on how to use

236

nitrous oxide for anesthesia and the Carrel-Dakin method for disinfecting open wounds. I have enclosed the specific percentages of the sodium hypochlorite solution for use in your surgery. It stings like the dickens, but it kills infection and often prevents amputation.

Water and electricity are intermittent luxuries. On any given day, the enlisted corpsmen must haul buckets of water up and down the stairs to us for drinking, cleaning and attending to nature's needs.

We enjoyed a short respite from our labors last night, when we attended the Decoration Day festivities at the Red Cross headquarters in nearby Clermont. After an afternoon of sports, games and dinner, the sun set between the mountains and we danced until nine. Papa and I revived our version of the fox-trot, and our comrades cheered us on!

I do not know when I will be able to write again, but I send all my love. Tell Gemma and Rourke to behave and tend to their studies, for Papa and I will be working tirelessly. As for you, Maman, please, do not worry! The only true hardship is the food's lack of flavor, but I still have the Ghirardelli chocolates you packed me—I ration one square per day. They are bites of heaven. Send more when the weather cools!

Your devoted daughter,
Adeline

Just as Adeline finished the flourish on the *e* in her name, Sally Dunn appeared, beckoning her to Lieutenant Colonel Kilgore's office. When she arrived, the other members of Surgical Team No. 50 were huddled around his desk. He stood with his fingers steepled, a grim expression darkening his face.

"The 2nd and 3rd Divisions of Marines have been sent into Belleau Wood," Lieutenant Colonel Kilgore announced. "The French Sixth Army's losses were great during the spring offensive. They have notified us that they will be unable to fulfill their promise of hospitalization for Americans. The AEF HQ telegraphed today, asking for help. The army has requisitioned the collège at Juilly and we're sending Surgical Team Number Fifty." The stack of orders cut the air with a sharp snap as Kilgore handed them over to Major Weeks, whose sinking left eyelid lent him an air of relaxed indifference, in stark contrast to the broad shoulders and tight musculature of the Wolverine quarterback he once was. Too many hits to the head, Adeline guessed.

———

By the time they arrived a few days later in Juilly, Seine-et-Marne, the army had relocated the two hundred fifty boys who had once boarded at the collège and sent medical supplies, equipment and personnel from the American Red Cross in Paris. The boys'-school-turned-evacuation-hospital had expanded its bed space to eight hundred.

The eight members of Surgical Team No. 50—two surgeons, three nurses, including Adeline and Sally, and three corpsmen, trudged up the narrow, cobbled walkways from the train station to reach the old city just after two in the afternoon. The ancient pile of structures included a cathedral and a grand edifice to their right. An American flag flew high above its white stone gateway and the Virgin, perched on the peak of the nearest building, held out the Christ Child, his arms extended in the posture of the cross. At the corner of the great building, a pile of bloody bandages and surgical debris reached as high as Adeline's chin and attracted a frenzy of flies the size of hummingbirds.

The team zigzagged through an open-air courtyard, taking care not to snag or crush the grasping, outstretched palms of the men who lay on stretchers across the thick, green grass.

"Water," one gassed soldier hissed, as another croaked, "My eyes sting! Switch off the light!" Nurses on their knees irrigated eyes and clipped blisters, disinfected them and packed them in Vaseline-coated gauze. The sightless trudged single-file to the lavatory, linked in a hand-to-shoulder chain.

By three o'clock, after having hastily eaten sandwiches, the surgical team was escorted up the stone stairs and into the long, narrow Ward B, which was lined with beds fitted with wooden Balkan frames used to elevate limbs. At the other end of the long ward, the team was ushered into the anteroom to the operating rooms, where they dressed in white gowns, caps and masks. Men on litters crowded the floor, awaiting surgery. The doctors and nurses inspected their first surgical case: a marine from the 2nd Division who was one of the first men to fall near Belleau Wood.

Surgeries to extract bullets, knife blades and pellets were common at the University Hospital back home, but this was something much more sinister. Machine-gun bullets had sprayed across the legs of Private First Class James Book, who appeared to be fresh out of school with a smattering of blemishes across his cheeks and a fine fuzz of dark hair upon his upper lip. Sweat matted his short black hair, and he had lost consciousness, presumably from blood loss. Someone had scrawled the letter *M* on his head in iodine, indicating he had already received a dose of morphine. The boy was lucky, not only because he was still alive, but because the Germans hadn't riddled his abdomen and head with bullets as his body crumpled to the ground.

Adeline prepared him for transport to surgery by cutting off his puttees, muddy shoes and blood-sopped breeches. Sally Dunn cut off his shirt and underwear and wrapped him in a hospital gown. Stretcher-bearers emerged from the operating room after depositing a patient inside and cried, "Next!" They lifted Private Book and carried him into a five-meter-square room of brilliant white with one door and two high windows. White-cotton-clad teams surrounded two surgical tables, murmuring and clinking surgical tools against metal trays. The third table was empty, but Adeline and her team had to wait for the orderly to finish scouring it free of blood. The scrape-scrape-scrape of the abrasive sponge set Adeline's teeth on edge. The sharp odors of rust and soap and antiseptic swirled in the air.

Once the stretcher-bearers deposited Private Book on the table, the surgical team scrubbed in at the lavatories against the right wall. The supply nurse opened two square packages containing sterilized gowns wrapped in muslin. She tied the strings behind the necks of Major Alanson Weeks and Captain John Woolsey, the two surgeons on the team. The men rinsed their hands in alcohol then snapped on their black rubber gloves.

A cookstove sat against the left wall. In a huge copper pot, water boiled, steaming and sterilizing all the metal instruments. The space between the two impressive windows was spanned by a wooden table, clothed in a sheet, on which rested the tools of their trade, shining and sharp, lifesaving or potentially lethal.

They turned back to the soldier in their care. Major Weeks gently peeled back the rudimentary dressings applied in the field and identified the three entry and exit points: two cleanly through the thighs, just missing the femoral arteries, but the last through the calf, shattering the boy's tibia. God's exquisite handiwork desecrated by man's crude killing machine. Adeline sucked air between her front teeth, stuffing down the anguish that threatened to break her composure.

"Let's wash the holes again with Dakin solution," he instructed Sally. "Nurse Donnelly, administer the ether and prep for amputation of the right leg just below the knee."

———

HILL 204, WEST OF CHÂTEAU-THIERRY

When the French blew up the stone bridge that crossed the Marne on June 1, four men of the 231st had flown sky-high. Nine others had sustained shrapnel injuries but survived. After four days of house-to-house combat in the streets of Château-Thierry, the Kaiser's 231st Division was now on the defensive, precariously dug into position atop Hill 204.

Hauptmann Wilhemy had ordered Heinrich and a handful of medical officers into the slit trenches at the hill's summit. There, as the cool night air swept across his dugout and a soft rain danced across his face and hands, Heinrich prayed.

He slipped his hand into his pocket and fingered the wooden rosary beads his mother had given him before she died. With a Hail Mary, he begged the Blessed Mother to protect his son, to end the barbarous killing. Before Heinrich could finish the decade, Leutnant Weber, a fellow medical officer, slithered on his belly and elbows to the rim of the dugout and dropped in.

"Comrade," Leutnant Weber said and offered Heinrich a soil-covered potato. By this point in the war, Germany lacked flour, sugar and milk. Heinrich could feel his hipbones and his ribs beneath his tunic. His mass had always been equally spread over his six-foot-two frame, but a few more weeks of near-starvation rations might just whittle him down to a pile of bones. A few gulps of water each day were a victory.

Weber chomped on his own potato. "*Hauptmann* says if we hold this hill and Belleau Wood to the north, nothing will stand between us and Paris." Weber beamed with anticipation. Of defeating the Allies? What would a victory even mean at this point?

Heinrich tried to clean the potato with the corner of his tunic and bit in. It crunched between his teeth and tasted like dirt. "This war is a swindle."

"You just miss the *Heimat*. We all do."

Yes, Heinrich missed his homeland, but he was more desperate for this bloody mess to be over, even if it meant abandoning the Fatherland to become French.

Weber rambled on. "The *poilus* have slid southeast and taken the village directly west of us."

"Monneaux?" Heinrich's stomach sank. The French would not retreat now the Americans had arrived. Wilhemy and the German commanders had to be mad to press on and invite even more casualties.

"Yes, that's the spot." Weber wiped his mouth with his sleeve.

Heinrich sank back against the trench wall, batting away a scrawny rat that landed on his shoulder, but not before its claws, like tiny knives, shredded a piece of his tunic. Tired of idle talk, he pulled his helmet down over his eyes and slept fitfully until awakened by a barrage of machine-gun fire. Soldiers shrieked like animals in pain; others shouted for help.

Weber grabbed Heinrich's arm. "Stay down." The bitter smell of smoke and singed flesh wafted over the trench.

"What's happening?" Heinrich wondered aloud.

"The French and Americans have dug in with machine-gun nests on the southern side of the hill. We must have sent some men to try to clear them."

"We must retrieve the wounded."

Weber's grip tightened. "Not yet," he hissed.

"But they'll die out there."

"We must wait until dawn or we'll die too."

———

During the night, the French and American gunners infiltrated the hillside and fired mercilessly on Heinrich's comrades, attempting to rout them. At dawn, when the sun cast its pale glow over the fissured southern slope of the hill, indifferent to its atrocities, the French shouted, *"Cherchez les blessés!"*

Heinrich and Weber waved their Red Cross flag high above their trench before hoisting themselves out and crawling on hands and knees toward the victims. Further downhill, the French and American medics trudged up toward the battle terrain.

The smoke was still dissipating. Cadavers—clad mostly in German field gray, but some wearing U.S. olive green and French mustard khaki of the colonial troops—dotted the abysmal landscape. The rats had already set about their work, but the crows had not yet dared to approach the savage, unnatural scene.

Heinrich hurried toward the first gray uniform he saw. Nausea threatened to overtake him when he realized the boy was riddled with bullet holes. He must have bled out in less than five minutes. Heinrich dropped to his elbows, holding his head.

"Désolé. Il est mort," a Frenchman lying on the ground five meters away uttered hoarsely. Heinrich checked the German's pulse, confirming this was so.

"C'est la guerre, non?" Heinrich responded bitterly. The Frenchman's gaze locked on Heinrich's face. His helmet had been shot off and he had sustained a nasty gash at his temple. Blood matted his dark blond hair against his forehead and drenched his khaki jacket at the elbow. Based on the crispness of his clothing, his smooth, even-textured skin and groomed mustache, Heinrich guessed he was an officer. A white handkerchief was tied to his rifle. After careful inspection, Heinrich could see that the Frenchman at least knew enough to use his belt for a tourniquet. It was strapped above the joint.

He handed the Frenchman his canteen. Glancing at him with surprise, the enemy soldier guzzled it. *"Merci, camarade."*

Heinrich wrapped the soldier's bullet wound with a square of gauze and a bandage. He injected him with a syringe of anti-tetanus serum.

"S'il vous plaît, le mouchoir." The soldier motioned weakly to the white square of cloth tied to his rifle. The ache in his voice told Heinrich it must be of sentimental value. He untied it and was about to pass it to the soldier when he spied a flock of black birds flying against the blue sky overhead.

"Grenade!" the Frenchman screamed. Instinct propelled Heinrich as he curled his torso over the soldier's bare head.

The last things Heinrich remembered the Frenchman's hot breath and spittle against his cheek and then a blinding white light.

CHAPTER 9

June 6–8, 1918

NORTHWEST OF CHÂTEAU-THIERRY, FRANCE

A t 0345, the artillery barrage of Belleau Wood began, just north of the 23rd Regiment's entrenchment. Luc tightened his blanket around his throbbing temples. Lying in his "grave," his thoughts drifted to Ondine and the hopeful glint in her eyes when she had handed him the basket of birds before he left. The scent of hay and sweet perspiration had swirled around her. She had whispered something which he only now recalled: *"Le secret est sous la cage."* He had assumed she had fastened more "secret" instructions for the birds' care beneath the cage but had forgotten to look during the chaos of deployment that followed. What if there were another secret hidden there?

He would wait until sunrise to examine the cage. Waiting was the worst part of military duty so far. Waiting meant contemplating death.

As they filtered back to the rear, the French soldiers had warned—even taunted—the U.S. 2nd Division, describing the atrocities they had experienced at the hands of the Germans. The French had the pallor and sunken cheeks of walking corpses. Luc banished these startling images from his mind and began to count blasts, straining to distinguish between the squeal of the high velocity shell and the rumble of the trench mortar. He longed to fight. Action meant the absence of thought. It meant relying on pure instinct: kill the enemy to save yourself and your brothers.

As the cacophony reached its peak and the sky lightened, Luc peered out of the trench. A glorious sunrise bathed the northern wheat field in golden light. Puffs of morning mist and gray smoke floated eerily across the farmland that stretched east from Lucy-le-Bocage, just north of them, where the marines waited, to Belleau Wood, where German machine gunners hid, according to the latest intelligence.

While the 23rd Regiment gunners prepared their automatic rifles and directed them toward the southern tip of Belleau Wood, Luc added gentian to the birds' water as a tonic to ward off any illness. The sergeant instructed him not to feed the birds until later that morning—after the initial battle had been fought and the messages delivered. Maxime and Richard, exempt from military operations, received both water and food. The birds perked up considerably and hardly flinched at the noise, to Luc's surprise.

He swiped a hand beneath their cage. A small square of oilskin secured with string was wedged there. He wiped the package on his pants to dry the drops of moisture that had settled on its surface. When he opened it, a piece of photographic paper fluttered to the ground. Luc picked it up and read: *Capitaine Pierre Marchand, La Dixième Troupe Coloniale.* On its other side, smaller versions of Michel and Ondine beamed. Ondine wore a light-colored summer dress and straw hat, Michel his school smock. A middle-aged man, presumably their father, Pierre, towered above them in a pale uniform and kepi. His hair was trimmed and pomaded and, although his face was rather long and narrow, his cheeks plumped with amusement above his tidy mustache. He had the striking looks of an aristocrat, and Luc could understand, just from this small glimpse, why his children held him in such high esteem.

This was most likely Ondine's only photograph of her father, and she had entrusted it to Luc's care. He tucked it in his jacket pocket for safekeeping.

Throughout the morning, the sergeant passed Luc messages from Colonel Malone, which had come to the colonel by runner from the troops positioned outside of Lucy. Luc transcribed each one and sent them off to Paris and Tours, using only the healthiest birds to do so.

At 0730, *Turrill's 1/5th marines have reached Hill 142.*

At 0830, *Turrill's 1/5th marines have taken Hill 142.*

At 1030, *Turrill's casualties heavy, all officers gone, calling urgently for medical care.*

The first attack against the Germans in Belleau Wood had gone off, but with considerable bloodshed.

At 1430 hours, Major Elliott, the commander of the 3rd Battalion, whom Luc had met on the road there, approached the company of birdmen. They snapped to attention and saluted the compact, stern-faced major. "At ease, Sergeant Rivers," he ordered as he waved away their formality. "One of your men saved Benson's life yesterday." His gaze moved across their line and landed on Luc.

"Privates Lemieux and Benson were collecting water when they were shot. As I informed your command, we're not sure if it was friendly or enemy fire," Sergeant Rivers replied.

"Probably enemy fire, but just scattered nests of gunners. Most of the German army is hiding throughout Belleau Wood and north of Les Mares Farm." The major turned and addressed Luc. "Well done saving Private Benson's bacon, son. He's recovering, but we need to fill his shoes with another runner, to go between the Sixth Marines and the Twenty-third." With narrow eyes, he inspected their small company. "Sergeant, which of your men will serve?" He pointed to a cluster of boulders and scrub brush about 450 meters across a piece of pristine farmland. A runner would have to cross the field with no shelter, but only tall shafts of wheat for protection. Marty took one long stride forward.

The sergeant shook his head. "With respect, sir, I can't spare Private Martin. He's my best birdman."

The major's head snapped back as he looked up. "And he's too tall. Kraut snipers would pick off that son of a gun as soon as he started to run. What about you, soldier?" The major clasped Luc's shoulder. "Benson tells me you have a keen sense of direction in the pitch black."

"Yes, sir."

"How is that?"

Luc shrugged. "I'm a country boy with eyes like a cat, sir."

"And we know you can speak French."

"Yes, sir."

"Do you read it and write it, too?"

"Yes, sir."

"You'll need to keep your helmet on, head low and run like the dickens. It's not for the jumpy or faint of heart. Will you help us, son?"

Acidic bile surged up Luc's throat. He stared at the grizzled, silver-sideburned old-timer, weighing the risks and benefits of what the men called a "suicide squad" job. Luc had barely been in the army a month. Sure, he was a sharpshooter and a hunter, and he knew how to fasten a gas mask, but to elude the Huns who seemed to be lying in wait everywhere he turned? That would require not only skill, but a hell of a lot of luck.

"Yes, sir," he croaked.

"Follow me, son."

The major spread out a map of the sector on a nearby boulder. "Colonel Malone has given me orders to advance in this direction at seventeen hundred." His finger traced a line from their current position—south of Triangle Farm—around the edge of Bois des Clerembauts toward Hill 192. If they succeeded, that would place the army a kilometer west of Vaux. "We will flank the marines on the right while they lead the attack into the southern portion of Belleau Wood and drive toward the town of Bouresches. Waddill's First Battalion will follow suit, protecting our flank."

"And what exactly do you expect me to do, sir?"

The major glanced at him warily from beneath the brim of his metal helmet. "To stay in the rear while we advance. You'll deliver messages between me and the Sixth Marines and Brigade Command. It's an important but dangerous job. You'll need your gas mask."

"What about my rifle?"

"Runners don't carry weapons—too heavy and not your job. Wear this around your arm, so we can identify you in battle." He pulled Benson's red armband from his pocket. Not exactly suitable protection from a barrage of enemy bullets. Besides, wouldn't a strip of red serve more as a bullseye than a deterrent to enemy fire?

"We attack at seventeen hundred hours, son. Find anything you can to eat, then run up to Lucy and deliver this message to Major Sibley." He handed him a folded square of paper. "Memorize it and leave it here. And shake a leg, understand?"

Luc did as he was told, munching on some hardtack and bacon and organizing what little gear he could carry: his gas mask and bolo knife, which he sharpened and slipped into his belt. He tidied his uniform, secured the chinstrap of his helmet and set out immediately. Luc covered the kilometer to Lucy in eight minutes, taking time to note clusters of rocks, scrub brush and any dips or cuts in the landscape that would make for good hiding places.

As he approached the town, the scope of the destruction startled him. Lucy-le-Bocage, once inhabited by a thousand or so villagers, had been gutted like a pig on Christmas Eve. Splintered wood, some pieces nearly two meters in length, twisted metal and limestone rubble covered the space where the town's buildings once rose. A baby pram, a rocking horse, papers, a cookstove, pots and pans and clocks littered the streets, all vestiges of a life—a civilization—decimated.

Although Luc had witnessed fire and mass destruction in the earthquake of 1906, nothing had prepared him for this. He scooped up a handful of shrapnel bullets the size of marbles on the edge of the street, remnants of the previous week's shelling by the Germans. The enemy must have interrupted the lesson in the village schoolhouse, too, for on the blackboard someone had scrawled *"Un jour du grand vent."* A day of big wind, indeed, Luc thought bitterly. Luckily, it looked as though students and teachers had abandoned the room, along with their textbooks and chalk, before the Germans had hit it.

Luc neared the cemetery adjacent to the skeletal remains of the parish church. To his surprise, the iron gate remained intact, though further down the metal fence had curled from the force of an explosion. Most of the graves were marked by stones, but the bodies beneath the mounds of fresh dirt, with grass as scant as hair in leprosy, had been given a French *poilu* burial. A wooden cross rose at the head of each grave and an empty wine bottle, filled with a scrap of paper detailing the deceased's name, date and cause of death, had been corked and stuffed neck-first into the ground. Luc was seized with an irrational urge to examine every bottle. What if Michel and Ondine's father were here, hurriedly buried hundreds of kilometers away from his home to the north and from his children to the south? What if they never learned his whereabouts?

There was no time. Luc's attention flashed to the church. The blasting had concussed and shattered the stained glass. Half of the bell tower's fieldstone visage had crumbled, exposing the scaffolding of timber beneath. Luc entered the church from the side, where a shell had blown a hole the height of two men, and encountered a few marines loitering in the rubble. Just as he resolved to ask them the whereabouts of the elusive Major Sibley, he was struck by their piety. They signed the cross and muttered prayers with a rare reverence. The huddle of marines was staring up at a wooden crucifix supported by a single beam that extended across the bottom of the sanctuary's archway. The smooth marble figure of the Christ—his fragile face, arms, legs and torso—was unscathed by German artillery. In fact, the only damage Luc observed to the Christ's body was that originally perpetrated by mankind: dark spikes pierced his hands and feet, and a painted trickle of blood flowed from the spear wound in his side. The Christ's head bent low under the weight of his crown of thorns. With eyes closed, his face held an expression of supreme serenity. Behind the cross, four more structural arches supported the walls and ceiling from caving in on the Savior and the sanctuary.

No doubt every soldier there believed he was witnessing a miracle—confirmation that God was on the Allies' side. Luc's heart suddenly lurched with a deep shame. This was indeed a miracle, but it was also a challenge. If Jesus sacrificed himself so that all mankind could be saved, how could mankind now justify annihilating itself?

———————

Major Sibley was short but athletically built, with a glint of mischief in his eye and an air of quiet confidence that impressed

254

Luc. He listened to the message and gave Luc another to convey verbally to Major Elliott before dismissing him. "My lad, make sure you visit the spring and refill your canteen before you return."

One of Sibley's aides directed Luc to an underground spring, which babbled and glistened beneath a concrete rectangular opening. "It's the only safe drinking water in this area. Germans have poisoned almost all the others." That would have been helpful information to have a few days ago, Luc thought wryly. Luckily, no one had perished from the water he had discovered south of their position, but he would be better off drinking at Lucy from now on. He dunked his canteen, quaffed a third of its contents, refilled and headed south back to Elliott's position.

On his path back to the 23rd, Luc passed Sibley's five hundred men. They waited in shelter trenches south of Lucy, ready to lunge forward toward Belleau Wood when the order was given. The marines, or leathernecks as they were called, wore their khaki uniforms with shiny belt buckles. They had stripped off their heavy gear and carried only what was necessary for light-marching order: small rations of food, rifles, bayonets and hand grenades. The machine gunners of the 6th had taken up their positions just shy of the front line.

At sixteen hundred, once Luc had returned to the 23rd, Major Elliott instructed him to synchronize his watch with the commanding officers' timepieces.

At sixteen hundred thirty, the American and French artillery fired for half an hour, shelling Belleau Wood and all the Germans hiding in the pockets of rough terrain inside. At seventeen hundred, the clamor of the guns abruptly stopped. Silence floated across the fields, encircled the trees, slid over boulders and nestled into the foxholes and ravines along the edges of the poppy-flecked wheat fields that extended toward the wood. Luc crept up on all fours, just behind the gunners of the 23rd, barely able to breathe. Their joking had ceased, and their bootheels crushed cigarette butts into the soil. The teams dropped to their bellies and elbows in their dugouts, peering through the sights of their rifles. Something like an electrical charge coursed through the corps—an invisible yet powerful force that would propel them straight into the dragon's lair.

As the hands of Luc's wristwatch touched the zero hour, a single shout pierced the silence. Major Berry's marines, located the furthest north, leapt up and simultaneously drove forward, in lines of twelve, a meter and a half apart, across the 360 meters of still-green winter wheat. Other than the breeze-bent wheat, the flat country offered no protection. The Germans polluted the air with sizzling bullets and the regiment of marines furthest from Lucy dropped to the ground. They did not rise again during daylight.

Just to the north of Luc and the 23rd Infantry, Sibley and Holcomb's leathernecks jumped forth from the earth and swept like broom straw across the southernmost portion of the fields toward Belleau Wood. The companies marched in four waves, with men placed roughly four meters apart. Luc's hands clenched; his muscles grew taut with fear. "Why aren't they charging?" he murmured. Their pace was steady, deliberate, but lacked speed and verve. *Shouldn't they charge before the Germans slaughter them?*

The gunner in front of him stirred slightly but didn't turn around. "They're saving their breath for the bayoneting."

256

The marine brigade marched quietly and deliberately, with gas respirators secured, toward the gentle slope at the base of the wood. The woods obscured Luc and the 23rd's view, so they watched and listened with bated breath. Luc's stomach roiled witnessing such courage. Would he possess the necessary valor when the time came?

A few seconds after the first row of men vanished from view, a clattering of guns erupted. The harrowing shrieks that followed scorched Luc's ears and set his heart grinding in triple time. As Luc would later discover, the Huns had opened fire on the marines at a range of forty-five meters, mowing them down as they persisted in advancing in waves up the hill.

Every sinew in his body screamed "Run!" Yet, as he watched and listened to the marines descend into hell and sacrifice their lives to save France, he was moved to tears. The next waves of leathernecks never hesitated but moved onward, a single sweeping menace, rattling their rifles and bayonets until the entire brigade disappeared beyond the slope into the jaws of the enemy. Above the howl of artillery and the *brat-tat-tat* of the guns, the blood-curdling war cries of the marines gushed forth as one mighty roar. Luc had never heard such a demonic howl, enough to strike terror into the heart of the most wretched enemy.

Fifteen minutes later, as the marines continued to disappear over the crest, Major Elliott gave the order to attack. With enthusiastic yelps, the 3rd Battalion of the 23rd, led by the K and M Companies, advanced across 275 meters of open wheat fields toward the small wood south of Belleau Wood that hid Hill 192.

Without warning, an infantryman in front of Luc dropped

his rifle and about-faced. He darted past Luc to the rear of the formation. Panting and gripping his head between his hands, the would-be deserter cried, "I can't do it, I can't! I've only been in the army a month! You can't make me go!" He ran aimlessly, like a chicken searching for its head, and finally dropped into one of the dugouts. Had he noticed the scowls on his comrades' faces, the private probably would have withered beneath their blatant disgust for his antics.

Every man here knew fear—they just chose to ignore it. Why should this man's plea—or panic—be indulged? Luc grabbed the soldier's rifle and bayonet off the ground and ran over to the trench where he cowered. He pointed the bayonet at his quivering backside and yelled, "Get your cowardly ass out of that hole now!" When the soldier didn't move, Luc nicked his right buttock with the tip of the bayonet. "Now!" he barked.

The young man rose, crying and shaking, but he had ceased to beg. He scurried out and stood upright. Luc shoved the rifle into his grip. "Just rely on your training, soldier. Now go protect your brothers! They're counting on you!"

The stunned soldier bolted toward the advancing companies, seemingly more afraid of Luc than the Germans. Luc rushed to follow him. His mind flashed to the long ribbons of Ondine's yellow hair floating on the surface of the Loire River like an oil slick and how Michel had trembled when he had recounted how the miserable Huns had violated her. "Courage, men!" he raged. "Kill the Krauts!"

The companies of the 23rd marched in columns. Major Elliott dropped closer to the rear and sent his company lieutenants

charging forward toward Hill 192. Gunfire crackled, punctur-
ing the soldiers in both forward companies with bullets. Elliott
had ordered them in with no artillery support—no cover fire.
Gunfire spewed from at least three different directions where
German machine gunners hid, nesting in ravines, behind rocks,
up in the trees. Sour smoke thickened the air. Frightened soldiers
instinctively streamed back toward the rear.

At eighteen hundred, Elliott grabbed Luc's shirtsleeve.
"Where the hell is Waddill? He's supposed to be covering our
flank! Go tell him to move forward—rapidly!" Elliott yelled.

Luc ran a half a kilometer through the Bois des Clerembauts.
This was no wilderness. The foresters had cleared out the underbrush and cared for the timber so that none of the trees' trunks
were more than fifteen centimeters in diameter and all were
densely packed. When his American comrades who held the wood
at various posts along his route called out, "Halt!," Luc responded
by waving his red-banded arm and shouting, "American runner
for Major Elliott!" The men directed him through the maze of
trees to the other side of the forest where Major Waddill waited—
for what, Luc could not fathom. Had his men not witnessed the
butchery right next to them?

Luc scanned the battalion until he spied him. "Major Waddill,
sir. Major Elliott requests you launch your attack immediately
to cover his flank. The 3rd Battalion is taking fire from all directions, sir, with heavy casualties," he shouted. Luc bent over, hands
planted on his knees, trying to catch his breath.

Waddill recoiled. "My orders are to stay put until Malone
orders us to advance. Did Malone order the advance?"

"No, sir, but Major Elliott expects you to cover our flank right now, sir!"

Flustered but spurred into action, Waddill organized his troops immediately and sent Luc back to Elliott. When Luc relayed that Waddill would soon advance, Elliott ordered him up to the front. "Keep your head low until you reach our men up on Hill 192. By then, Waddill's men should have reached the hill as well. Find one of the lieutenants and report back."

Luc swallowed his fear and focused solely on the task at hand, using his senses to guide him from danger. He zigzagged through the Bois de Clerembauts and toward the violent cacophony that rose from the smaller, adjacent wood, where the 23rd and the Germans battled for control of Hill 192 contained therein. Within six minutes, he spied a clearing: a small expanse of wheat that he would have to cross without protection. He reckoned that one unarmed man running toward a battle was less of a target than a cluster of men armed to the hilt. He strapped his red band to his right arm, to be certain the infantries directly to his south did not mistake him for the enemy. He fastened his gas mask in case he ran into the deadly yellow mist. He signed the cross, ducked and dashed through the wheat and brilliant red poppies that streaked the fields like stains of blood.

His gaze darted from right to left. Sun glinted off the bayonets of fallen soldiers—soulless bodies now, slumped in sickening, twisted positions. He hurdled a meter length of marine khaki. Only after he had surged forward twenty paces did his consciousness register that he had just leapt over a man's severed leg. Nausea gripped his stomach. He muscled the horrific image from his mind and ran on.

In the wood where the survivors now battled for control of the hill, grenades exploded, launching dirt and small shards of metal everywhere. As the German mortars hit, they sliced the bark and flesh of the trees into toothpicks. Machine guns clattered, and olive drab and field gray uniforms clashed, wrestling to the death with rifles at the ready and bayonets unsheathed. Beneath his cumbersome gas mask, moisture poured down Luc's forehead and cheeks and fogged his eye cups as he feverishly dodged gunfire to reach one of the lieutenants at the base of the hill. He leapt over bodies strewn like ragdolls—some lifeless, others pleading for help—until he reached a trio of officers firing from behind an outcropping of rocks. Judging from the insignia on his collar, this was the second lieutenant crouching before him.

"Lieutenant? I am to report back to Major Elliott on your progress."

The officer shifted position and shouted to the grenadiers to his left. "Launch!" They ran uphill and threw their metal eggs into the German machine-gun nests. As he gave the order, the drumming of machine guns sounded behind them. A bullet ricocheted off Luc's helmet. He wrapped his arms around his head and prostrated his body and face in the dirt.

"What's our objective?" the lieutenant shrieked. "Tell Elliott that Lieutenant Ricks needs a clear directive!" He turned abruptly, searching for the source of the latest attack. He ranted on, spewing garbled words from behind his mask. Luc was able to gather the gist of his meaning: they were doomed.

When the gunfire temporarily ceased, Luc sprinted from the foxhole. He dashed from tree to tree, narrowly missing bullets, winding through the tall oaks and out of the forest. Miraculously, he did not suffer a scratch, but time was still his enemy. When he reached Major Elliott fifteen minutes later, he ripped off his gas mask and drew a deep breath before speaking. "The lieutenant says his objective was never given. The troops are being fired upon by our own machine guns!"

The major peered through his field glasses. "Where is the fire coming from?" Just as Luc opened his mouth to speculate, Elliott exclaimed, "Oh, Jesus, no! It's the Germans! They're circling around their rear and firing from behind!"

"The whole M Company is wiped out, sir, and most of Company K," Luc choked out.

Major Elliott scanned the fields and woods around them. "The Ninth and French Tenth are supposed to be advancing on our right flank," he announced.

"The French Tenth Colonial Division, sir?"

The major glanced at him with a furrowed brow. "Yes, why?"

Luc shook his head. "Nothing, sir. What should I tell Lieutenant Ricks?"

"Tell the lieutenant to take Hill 192 and drive the Germans back as far as he can. Reinforcements are coming," he added unconvincingly.

Luc reached Lieutenant Ricks in the heat of battle and relayed the message. Ricks handed Luc a rifle and bayonet and ordered him to start shooting.

A half hour later, Luc reported back to Major Elliott that the Boches continued to blitz the companies of the 23rd from the right and rear, and many of Elliott's doughboys had fled to the east. Luc would later learn that the Germans had captured them all.

Major Elliott ordered Luc to make one last run that evening—into Belleau Wood. His assignment was to find Major Sibley of the 6th Marines, give him the status of the 23rd and report back on the progress made by the marines.

Luc doubted he had the strength to do it. The blisters on his feet pulsated. On his almost two-kilometer hike north, he intersected a shallow creek to the west of Triangle Farm. He sniffed the water, which smelled clean, and filled his canteen. Guessing the Germans had not come through this area and poisoned the water, he still offered up a quick prayer, then splashed some of the heavenly liquid on his face, chest and arms. A sudden breeze kicked up, cooling his hot skin, salving his open scrapes and bolstering his resolve.

Luc trudged on toward the heavy artillery fire until his legs started to wobble. Halfway to Belleau Wood, he ducked into a small orchard. He chose a spot where three apple trees leaned in, their leaves and flowers providing a canopy of cover. He climbed into the low boughs of the center tree and leaned against its knobby branches, hooking his limbs around them so he wouldn't fall. He noted lacerations on his arms and legs and a stinging sensation that persisted from his cheek to his temple. He touched his fingers to the spot, but he felt only the flakes of dried blood and the thin line of a scab forming.

Luc's eyes closed. The whispering wind ruffling his hair and the sweet fragrance of the blossoms swirled around him, overpowering the acrid scent of smoke that hung in the air near the battlefields. A deep longing stirred in Luc. He recalled hiding in the apple trees at Eagle's Run with Pippa, laughing and running around the farm, splashing each other at the pump until Maman inevitably scolded them for wasting water. His cheeks puckered as he remembered the crispness and sour taste of his family's apples, the best he had ever eaten.

After ten minutes with his feet up to restore the blood flow, Luc headed further north toward the ravine that ran from Lucy to Bouresches. Less than five hundred meters out, wounded and dead marines lined both sides of the ditch near the road. To the left, at the entrance to Gob Gully, Luc spied the dressing station where the medics rushed to patch up or evacuate the wounded. It seemed that the Germans might respect the Red Cross, for they hadn't fired upon the stretcher-bearers, medics and pharmacists—yet.

Luc cautiously approached a medic who was bandaging a soldier's head and asked for Major Sibley. The medic scrutinized Luc for a moment and then flicked his head up the gully. About a hundred meters away, Sibley marched up and down, fists balled and arms swinging. Luc moved in closer. Sibley had misplaced his hat and jacket, and a red rage spread over his face and neck. He spat curses faster than the enemy could shoot bullets.

The attack had not gone to plan. The major had lacked the munitions he needed to take the section of Belleau Wood where German gunners hid behind boulders the size of small motor cars and riddled his men with metal. Now, Sibley's other companies continued the fight in the southern and eastern portions of Belleau Wood, but only occasional flashes of yellow lit the sky.

Reports filtered in that twenty-one of Holcomb's marines had made it into the village of Bouresches, to the east. They mowed down some of the withdrawing Germans and sought reinforcements to hold the village. Sibley directed Luc and a handful of his men to don their gas masks and follow him back into the eastern edge of Belleau Wood.

The forest belched smoke. It was an imposing dark labyrinth, with twisted jungle undergrowth on its edges and splintered trunks and shredded branches throughout. More than once, Luc used his trusty bolo knife to cut back the brush that encircled his ankles and threatened to trip him.

Lifeless marines lay sprawled across the prickly landscape, some of their faces serene, with blank, staring eyes, and others contorted in such ghastly pantomimes that Luc understood all too clearly the horror they had endured during their final moments. The odor of rotting flesh, putrefying in the heat, overwhelmed the forest, making it necessary for the surviving men to tie sacks of camphor under their noses to ward off the scent—and the fat, venomous flies. Medics darted from one body to the next, kneeling beside the stricken, checking for a pulse and then, finding none, removing the soldiers' gas masks for further use.

Luc felt as if he alone were watching a catastrophic picture show, while the emboldened recruits around him blathered on about their conquests.

"The Huns are afraid of the steel blade. We jumped from nest to nest, bayoneting them and driving them out like chickens."

"And as soon as we saw the edge of their helmets, we dropped to the ground and started firing."

265

"Must've potted ten Fritzies, right, Mackin?"

"Yes, sir. They're piled up three and four high in their graves now!"

The lance corporal placed a steel *Stahlhelm* on his head. "The prisoners we took couldn't wait to throw up their hands and yell, '*Kamerad! Kamerad!* Mercy!'" He lifted a pair of German wool trench coats. "These will keep us warm tonight, *ja?*"

Although he loathed to admit it, Luc had felt it, too: the savage thrill of killing. It had swelled in his chest when he had shot the German grenadiers who had killed five of Lieutenant Ricks's men, scattering shreds of their skin and bone over a forty-meter range. He was uneasy with their gloating, but he could not bring himself to condemn their plundering. When killing becomes a holy duty, stealing trophies from the enemy is only a petty crime.

As they reached the edge of Bellcau Wood, an engine back-fired and stirred Luc from his musings.

One of the marines cried, "Lizzie's back, God bless her old, tired bones!"

"Lizzie?" Luc asked.

A battered Ford truck pulled up to the edge of the woods, spewing a cloud of exhaust. "Yeah." The lieutenant's round face glowed. "Our fearless Ford, here. She's a bee-yoot, ain't she?"

The lieutenant sidled up next to the parked truck as her drivers started to unload water, food rations and explosives. He caressed her side. "I count at least seven holes over here."

The lance corporal placed his hand over his heart. "Our Joan of Arc!" he proclaimed.

266

"Another five on this side, Frank."

"Twelve bullet holes in all and she's still running. Lizzie is as unstoppable as our marines, lad." The lieutenant clapped Luc on the back. "Stick around for some coffee and a meal before you shove off."

At twilight, a runner appeared with an update for Sibley: his companies now held the entire eastern edge of Belleau Wood.

JUNE 7, 1918

Before the morning sun crested the horizon, Luc caught up to Major Elliott and what remained of the 23rd Regiment as they retreated to Le Thiolet, a town just southeast of Hill 192. The major had aged ten years in a day, with deep creases across his forehead and purple smudges beneath his eyes. The 23rd had left an estimated twenty-seven dead and 225 wounded or missing soldiers scattered across the dark battlefield near Hill 192. They had no water and no comfort, save for the hand of God—or the itchy trigger finger of a German who would shred them with bullets if they so much as sneezed.

As he collapsed on the dirt behind a wall of sandbags in Le Thiolet, Luc could not banish the stink of roasting flesh and cries of the crippled from his memory. He squeezed his eyes shut, tucked his knees to his chest and shuddered uncontrollably. With balled fists and curled toes, he struggled to purge the black grief that surged from his lower belly, seeped into his lungs and clotted his airway.

Colonel Malone had ordered the 1st and 3rd Battalions of the 23rd Regiment to keep the enemy engaged while the marines tried to capture the primary objective: Belleau Wood. However, unclear orders, lack of coordination and the complete absence of cover fire had left Elliott's 3rd Battalion in shambles. The men of the battalion had served their purpose admirably—as sacrificial lambs. Luc was heartsick for them all. No one would walk away the victor from this battle.

<hr />

Hands the size of baseball mitts gripped Luc and shook him ferociously. "Chow's on!" a shadow announced. "Hot beef stew and coffee!" the soldier gushed with the giddiness of a man who had cheated death.

Luc hoisted his beleaguered body off the ground and stumbled toward the ring of men who huddled around the mobile kitchen. The men of the 23rd were unrecognizable: faces smeared with mud, purple bruises and pink lacerations peeking through their shredded uniforms.

Luc clasped the warm tin bowl. His hand trembled as he brought the thick, brown liquid to his mouth, the salt stinging the cuts on his lips. Somewhere beyond the tree line, where the artillery blasts began anew, God flicked a switch and the light came on. Luc feared the sun more than anything now. For with it came the undeniable knowledge of the destruction wrought by both sides. And in the sunlight, he could not hide his movements from the snipers.

When he had finished slurping his soup, Luc glanced up. Where were his fellow pigeoneers—Marty, Houle and Sergeant

Rivers? Had they not trailed the 23rd as they fought at Hill 192? Had they not rejoined the infantry as they all retreated to Le Thiolet?

Luc searched the faces of his fellow Americans. None of them would meet Luc's gaze. When he saw Vito, he jumped to his feet and confronted him. "Where are the pigeoneers?" Panic tinged his inquiry.

Vito, his rifle arm now in a sling, pulled Luc to the side of the chow wagon. "They were supposed to track us and hide in the woods while we fought, but no one has seen them since we advanced."

"Has anyone gone to look for them?"

"We've been a little busy."

"Where were they last?"

"Just south of Triangle Farm."

"Near the woods?"

Vito shrugged. "North of the woods."

As if propelled by an invisible hand, and without the permission of his superiors, Luc walked north toward Triangle Farm. When he reached the southern edge of the Bois des Clerembauts, he sprinted into the forest.

With any luck, they had taken shelter in the woods. Panting from exhaustion but determined to search the three kilometers north of Le Thiolet to Triangle Farm, Luc pushed on. He twined through the looming pines, around clusters of boulders and over crags jutting from the forest floor, all the time scanning the shadows, hoping for a glimmer of life.

Thrice along the route the American infantry halted him. He quickly identified himself, tapped the red band on his arm, stated his destination and ran on. As he neared the familiar northern edge of the wood, just south of Triangle Farm, he spotted something: three lifeless figures huddled over a smoldering fire with a pot at its center.

Fallen leaves and twigs crunched beneath Luc's boots. The vivid shapes and colors of the wood blurred, and his movements slowed as if he were in a dream.

The shell had detonated within meters of the threesome and their empty trench, gouging the earth and spraying shards of metal. Pigeon feathers rose on the breeze and fluttered back to earth around the tiny, winged corpses that dotted the landscape.

Sergeant Rivers's face was hidden in his lap. From his neck to his waist, a line of metal shark teeth protruded from his back, gleaming in the morning light.

Houle had landed at the root of a scrub oak. His mouth and eyes were frozen open in surprise.

Marty's skin was an eggshell blue. His fingers still gripped a slender tree branch. On its tip, a golden trench doughnut sagged. Where Marty's head had once dwelled, petals of red blood had bloomed and dried.

Luc collapsed, retching until he could only spit green bile. *What should he do?* Their bodies had been so mutilated, he hesitated to touch them, and yet, he would not want his own corpse to be left unattended. He clutched at the curling green oak leaves that blanketed the woodland floor, gasping for breath. When his heartbeat normalized, he wiped his mouth with his handkerchief and tied it around his mouth and nose.

He could not find Marty's dog tags but slid one each of Houle's and the sergeant's into his pocket. The duplicate tags he left hanging around each man's neck. He half carried, half dragged his comrades to their trench, where he stacked them like firewood next to the mangled birdcages.

He located the severed blade of their trench spade and used it to shovel dirt over their communal grave. With his knife, he carved his friends' surnames and *U.S. Signal Corps* into the detached shaft of the spade and laid it atop the mound of dirt. With the sign of the cross and a prayer that God commend their souls to heaven, Luc trudged back into the gloom of the forest.

———————

JUILLY, FRANCE

As the 6th Marines had stormed the wheat fields at Belleau Wood the evening of June 6, shells had sent shrapnel flying into the leg of Corporal Shepherd Holmes.

"They're supposed to clean the wounds out, debride them and remove the dead tissue before sending them to us. This poor bastard has been on a train for half the night with this infection festering." Dr. Weeks pressed on the massive blister that covered the entry wound and grimaced. "What the hell is this? Potts?"

A man of average height, wearing spectacles and a blood-stained gown, shuffled over from another operating table, hands raised.

"Can you educate us on this one, Fred?"

Potts peered at the croissant-like layers of skin that had closed over the murky gash below. "Bottle wound," he replied. "Fragments of metal shell casings make deep, jagged lacerations that carry pieces of cloth, chips of bone, you name it." He pointed

271

to two lines of silver nitrate on the thigh. "The X-ray surgeon has marked the shrapnel location—right at the intersection of these lines." He shook his head. "A ghastly business. Make sure you give him the anti-tetanus serum."

"And the bubbles?"

"Gas bacillus. These boys are entrenched in farmland, battling it out. The mortars hit the fertilized fields, the shells burst and their fragments, laced with bacteria, rip through and contaminate flesh."

"Damn," Dr. Woolsey replied.

"Just like fermentation, you mean?" Adeline asked. "When the skin closes over the wound, the oxygen breaks down the sugar in the tissue and produces carbon dioxide, right?"

Heads snapped and everyone stared. As Adeline's cheeks flushed behind her surgical mask, she explained, "Our friends own a winery. As a youngster, I helped them crush the grapes, ferment the wine, you know . . . it's the same kind of thing."

"Your expertise may really come in handy around here," Weeks chuckled as he laid four sterilized towels around the wound. Adeline wasn't sure if his comment was sarcasm directed at her or bitterness directed at the situation, for as they stood in this operating room only 150 kilometers west of Champagne, the French, Belgian, English, American and German soldiers battled, trampling the farms and vineyards of the region. They had swapped scythes for Springfields, wine for blood.

Adeline's mind drifted to the sun-scented hills and leafy grapevines of Napa. After the harvest celebration Sara and Philippe held every year, Adeline would tour the winery, inhaling the wafting fragrance of the freshly crushed fruit, the oaky, damp cool of the cellar room.

The stomach-churning scent of rotting cabbage jolted her back to the present. Weeks had made the incision with the scalpel and Corporal Holmes's skin sprang apart, revealing the fatty layer beneath and the red muscle below that. Blood gushed like the juice from a cherry pie. The corpsman, now a sterilized assistant, mopped it up with gauze, and Woolsey clamped the small blood vessels off with hemostats. With the scalpel and scissors, Weeks carved out shards of shrapnel. Each one clinked and reverberated as it hit the metal dish in Sally Dunn's hands.

In the early morning hours of June 7, Adeline stumbled into Ward D, drunk with fatigue. Her toes cramped, her calves burned, and her back knotted. Perspiring profusely, she unbuttoned her collar.

Prostrate patients in cots were bundled in white linen and gray army blankets. The tang of chlorine, gangrene and excrement floated on the air. Many of the men were still in an ether-induced dream, cursing, wailing or stringing gibberish together. Those of sound mind cracked jokes and shared stories. They were all young men—most no older than Luc—with the same softness of cheek and athletic physique untouched by gluttony or disease, but rather marred by the atrocities of war. Violence had drained the color from what was left of their bullet- and shrapnel-torn faces, and their eyes glistened in an otherworldly fashion—with relief or terror or resignation, Adeline did not know.

273

After double-checking the tag affixed to the head of his iron bed, she greeted Private Book, whose leg they had amputated a few days before.

He groaned and stared at her, licking and smacking his lips. "Where am I?" he croaked.

"You're at the American Red Cross Hospital at Juilly, thirty miles west of Belleau Wood."

"I made it?" he asked between cracked lips.

She touched his shoulder and wedged her scant hips between the cots to sit on a stool. "Yes, but I'm sorry to say we had to amputate your right leg."

He observed the loose bandages where his leg used to rest. "Feels like it's still there. You're not playing tricks on me, are you, ma'am?" Panic permeated every word.

She lifted a cup of water to his chapped lips, wondering if he were still in shock. "Unfortunately, soldier, I'm not a magician. Drink and then lie back. I need to soak the wound."

Private Book whimpered, tears trailing down his cheeks. "How long?"

"For ten minutes every two hours for nine days or so, to make sure you are free of infection, then we'll close the wound if the bacterial counts are negative."

"How long before I go home?" he clarified.

"Oh, hopefully just a few weeks."

Book stared at his fresh stump. "Will I be able to use it at all?"

"Indeed. Once we've made sure the wound is clean and there's no trace of infection, we'll close it up and send you to Paris, where you'll be fitted for a prosthetic leg."

274

The boy winced as Adeline peeled back the bandages and then grew silent as she soaked his stump in a pan of Dakin solution. He raised himself up to meet her gaze. "Us leathernecks, we're going to win the war. That ain't magic, neither. That's good ol' fashion grit, ma'am. We ain't afraid of nothin'. The Frenchies, they told us to retreat, but we said, 'Hell no, we just got here!'"

"The French have been fighting for four long years. I'm sure they were relieved to catch sight of you. Now get some rest and keep drinking water."

"You won't hear a peep from me, ma'am. I suppose I'm happy to be alive."

"Oui, vous êtes pardonné, monsieur." Adeline smiled, hoping to cheer him, but she may have overreached her mark.

"Maybe when I get out of here, I'll put on my left dancing shoe and my wooden leg and take you for a night on the town. Whadya say?" Slackening muscles slurred his words.

"I'd say the morphine they gave you has started to work, soldier." She cradled his neck as she adjusted his position and plumped up his flat pillow.

Adeline allowed herself to keep a five-minute vigil by the amputee's bedside, dozing as she sat next to him, her elbow propped on the sill of the window that stretched to the ceiling, her head in her hand.

A dull snort roused her. She wasn't sure if the noise had come from her or the patient, but a quick glance at the clock, the only decoration on a wall of bleached horizontal planks, confirmed that she had best seek out her other patients before heading to her tent.

Corporal Holmes, the bottle-wound patient, slept in fits, his cot the fifth in a row of twelve. Moisture streamed down his face, drenching his pillowcase. Adeline lifted the sheet and scratchy wool blanket that draped warmth over his elevated legs. She pulled back the bandages and steeled herself against the stench. The debridement had come too late—the pus still smelled like decaying cabbage. Given his fever and the bluish cast of his face and extremities, Adeline suspected wound shock.

She called to the attending surgeon, who was scribbling notes at a school desk in the center of the ward. His shiny boots gleamed. Leather crunched as he neared. His expression soured when he examined the wound. The soldier's eyes followed the pair of them.

"I'm dying, aren't I?" Corporal Holmes asked.

Adeline raised her gaze to the surgeon.

"Yes, corporal, I am afraid that you've lost a lot of blood and the infection has spread, despite all our efforts." He sighed and squeezed the boy's shoulder. "You'll have maybe a few days. We'll give you some more morphine to ease the pain. I'm so sorry. . ." his voice trailed as he turned to go—to return to his stack of paperwork.

Such a feeble, trite explanation to a man in his prime, who had fought and would now die for his country. Adeline didn't know what to say, but she sure as hell couldn't leave the young man to die alone. He was only a year or two younger than Adeline herself. *All the good men, sons, brothers, sweethearts, husbands were dying—but for what?*

The soldier studied Adeline's face. "I understand," he muttered.

She racked her mind for something to say—anything that might bring comfort. "Rumor is that the marines have captured part of Belleau Wood. You are part of that victory, soldier."

His Adam's apple bobbed beneath skin speckled with a few days' stubble. "Call me Shep." The ward nurse lingered nearby, no doubt eavesdropping on their conversation to determine if she should intervene. She gingerly approached with a basin of warm water and a washcloth. This was Adeline's chance to escape. She should hand this case off to the nurse on duty right now. After all, Adeline was a surgical nurse and needed rest for her upcoming shift that evening. Yet something in Shep's gaze—a silent plea for companionship—captured her.

Adeline took the basin from the ward nurse, whose hair sprang loose and frizzy from beneath her cap. Her skin was clammy and pale; she obviously needed rest. Adeline guessed she looked similar. With a flick of her head, Adeline dismissed the other nurse. She dipped a finger in the small jar of Vaseline and dabbed it on his cracked lips. She poured water into his glass and cradled his neck, raising his head to drink. His eyes danced, revealing a glimmer of the warring spirit now resigned to its fate.

"You remind me of my girl back home," he rasped.

"I get that a lot." She instantly regretted her clumsiness and forced a smile.

"No, truly. Bernadette has curly, dark hair like yours, with threads of copper running through it. So soft—" He groaned and bit his already bloody lip. The blanket crimped between his fingers. She reached for his hand. His large palm relaxed as she

277

moved the soapy cloth between his fingers and beneath his nails, carefully teasing out all the blood and dirt. She had cared for many men during her five years as a nurse, but these men were a different breed. His sinewy, capable, brave hands surrendered to her care, and his trust seeded in her an acute despair.

"Let me give you more morphine so you can sleep," she whispered.

He laughed and winced simultaneously. "Ma'am, I may be dead tomorrow. Plenty of time to sleep then." He swallowed as if to punctuate this revelation. "Do you sing?"

"I'm afraid not."

"Bernadette is a songbird. She sings while she's feeding the animals or washing the dishes, and she performs a solo in the choir at church."

"She sounds lovely." Adeline swept the picture of the pair out of her mind. If she allowed herself to contemplate the injustice of their earthly separation, she might never recover. She emptied the basin in a nearby sink and placed the now contaminated washcloth in the bag of unsanitary items tied to the foot of Shep's bed.

"Ma'am?" She sat down by his side. "May I?" His rough, rifle-calloused fingers, now pink and clean of the soil of the trenches, curled around hers. His eyelids dropped, and he said, "This is what I miss. Holding Bernadette's hand when we would walk out to the cinema. She loved those Mary Pickford films, you know. I didn't care much for them, but I would bring her just to hear her giggle or to offer her my handkerchief when she would cry. I was so proud to escort a girl like Bernadette."

A pebble of grief lodged in Adeline's throat and she tightened her grasp. His hand grew moist with fever. "Would you like to write Bernadette and perhaps your parents in these last hours?"

"I've never been good with words, ma'am."

"Call me Adeline."

"French?"

Adeline nodded.

"Bernadette's mother is French. Named her after Bernadette of Lourdes."

"And your parents?" Adeline ventured.

Tears glistened. "I don't want my death to bow their heads. I want them to know I died a man of honor, to liberate France from the Boches. And please, don't tell them how much pain I suffered. Tell them I slipped into sleep and never woke up."

"Do you have a sister, a brother?"

He gnashed his teeth and grunted. Adeline administered a dose of morphine. The creases on Shep's forehead softened. "Two younger brothers—Michael and Daniel—working on the farm, not here, thank God."

He grabbed her wrist. "My noggin's gettin' cloudy. The medicine . . . Ma'am? Nurse?" His head nodded and he reached for her. He blurted, "I'll need the Catholic rites, and prayers. Promise? It'll bring some peace to my mother to know a priest attended me."

"Of course. The chaplain will—"

"And what will they do with my body?"

"There's a cemetery here."

"Just make sure that I'm buried with the men from the 2nd Division—marines, not doughboys, understand?"

As if such distinctions truly mattered now. "I promise to do my very best, Shep."

She retrieved ivory stationery and a pen from the surgeon's desk, stacked there neatly for this express purpose. As if stocking the writing desks and hospital cabinets were more important than stopping the stacks of bodies that rolled in each day.

Shep's words reverberated in Adeline's head like a wailing gong. She jotted down his name, rank and burial wishes and attached them to with a wire to his white gown. She scribbled down a few notes about his family and set out to retrieve the chaplain.

At midday, after five hours of sleep, Adeline sat on the lawn, cradling the meal of ratatouille prepared by the collège's Soeurs de Saint Louis as if she expected someone to snatch it from her hands. The nuns' kindheartedness reminded Adeline of the Sisters of Notre Dame back in Manhattan. The bees that buzzed around her as she lifted her fork to lips were also oddly reassuring. They hummed and dipped, busy with the mundane tasks of life, oblivious to the massacre of men taking place only fifty kilometers from this very spot. If Adeline were to lie back on the bouncy, green grass and close her eyes, she might be able to imagine herself in the backyard of her parents' Nob Hill home, if not for the growl of the Howitzers in the distance, the General Motors ambulances idling nearby and the motorcycles revving as they sped back to the front. Her next shift would begin at 1300 hours.

That afternoon, over five hundred wounded were evacuated from the hospital in Juilly to Paris as the guns thudded, rattling her internal organs against her ribs with every blast. On the road from Château-Thierry, an interminable stream of gas and burn victims, chest wounds and head wounds arrived at the hospital in a long, brown line of muddy ambulances pelted with artillery holes. They rumbled through the archway and unloaded four to six men per vehicle. Adeline examined their tags and sent them to the operating rooms.

Most memorable was Captain John Neville. A hail of machine-gun bullets had sheared his nose off his face. The rest of his body was unharmed, in pristine condition for a thirty-year-old.

On her short break that evening, Adeline found Captain Neville in the isolation ward, adjacent to the ward that held Shep. She looked straight at his bandaged face, knowing that he was reading her reaction. Adeline smiled gently.

"I'm one of the nurses who operated on you," she said, resting a comforting hand on his arm. "Do you remember what happened?"

He turned his head toward the wall. "I'm sorry. It must have been hideous," his voice trailed off. "When I was hit, it sounded like someone shattered a glass on a floor of porcelain tile."

As he spoke, she casually stashed the metal bowls and bedpan beneath the cot, so the captain would not inadvertently catch a glimpse of his face when they checked his bandages. "I'm sorry to disappoint, but you aren't the worst case I've seen. And you're lucky the bullets didn't knock an eye out."

"Lucky? They tell me I have no nose."

"Before you return home, we're sending you to Paris."

"Why?"

Adeline slipped him a card with a name and address on it. "There's a studio where they make portrait masks for the facially

281

wounded. It's run by a sculptress and highly recommended by the staff here."

"They'll make me a mask? For my comfort, or for the comfort of those who have to look at this horror of a man?" His voice caught on the last word and tears slipped from his eyes.

"Both, I suppose," Adeline said practically, against every instinct she possessed. She could not allow herself to feel these patients' profound loss. She could drown in sorrow later—after her job was finished.

―――

When Adeline passed through the hallway on her way back to the operating room, two stretcher-bearers squatted, unceremoniously toppling their cargo onto the floor outside the operating room. The patient groaned between clenched teeth.

"German?" Adeline guessed from the field-gray uniform.

"Yeah, a sauerkraut for sure, but he's a medic." The patient's white arm patch, stamped with a red cross, was partially torn—or blown—off. Thick blood drenched the mélange of fabric on his left shoulder, just beneath the epaulette. "He was tending to a French Tenth when he was hit with flying debris."

"Where were they? When did the shell hit?"

"Not a mortar, a grenade. Hill 204, south of Belleau Wood near Château-Thierry sometime yesterday."

"What was a German doing so far from his comrades?"

The litter-bearer shrugged. "Chasing butterflies?" he chuckled. When Adeline did not crack a smile, he bolted to attention. "Don't know, ma'am. Most likely rounding up the wounded. All's I know is there was blast and he protected the Frenchman with his body. Took the brunt of the blast himself. Saved the man's life, and that's the truth of it, God as my witness."

A spray of small metal chips tangled in the threads of the German's bloodied collar. Adeline carefully lifted the medical satchel from around him, examining the lacerations on his neck. Just a few millimeters more and his carotid would have been severed. She unfastened the buttons of his coat and peeled back his clothing. Shards of metal poked from his pale skin like tiny shark fins lurking in a red sea.

The ward surgeon on duty, Lieutenant Colonel Jenkins, drew near, gazing over Adeline's shoulder. "His fever is rising," she asserted after touching his perspiring forehead and the nape of his smoldering neck.

"There are others in line before him," the lieutenant colonel remarked. He flicked his head in dismissal.

"He's a medic, like us."

"Allies will be treated first."

"You would delay his care—even when he saved one of our allies? The entire army of wounded will be here in a matter of hours, and he'll surely die then," she grumbled, then realized complaining was futile. "These men have all been triaged . . . we could save him if we act now."

"I'm appalled that you'd even suggest such a thing. It borders on treason."

"Not treason, sir. Human decency. And, with respect sir, if you refuse to provide this man care, then I will." Adeline whirled around, tied on a fresh apron, snapped on gloves and removed his coat.

"You're a nurse!" he blustered.

"I may be a just a nurse, but my parents are both surgeons and I've witnessed thousands of operations in my lifetime." She changed tack. "At least let me try if you won't." Eager to get to work, she blurted, "He saved one of our allies, sir. I'd like to return the favor."

She turned on her heel before the flummoxed lieutenant colonel had time to form a response. With the operating tables occupied by American and French soldiers, Adeline laid the German on a blanket on the floor. His brown eyes narrowed. She leaned in. "Hold still, soldier." He stared blankly. *"Ne bougez pas,"* she commanded.

"Oui, je comprends," he replied in thickly accented French. She lowered the mask to cover his nose and mouth, but he grabbed her wrist. *"Merci, 'moiselle."* She nodded, administered the ether, then scrubbed in and gathered the operating instruments herself, under the stares of five surgeons and ten or so of her fellow nurses.

Just as she sanitized the skin around the wound, Sally Dunn crouched down beside her. "You're going to get us both court-martialed, or worse," she warned out of the side of her mouth, taking up the tray of sterilized instruments.

"We pledged our 'devoted service to human welfare.' Not just American welfare, *human* welfare," Adeline finished with a sidelong glance. "You and I both know he can be saved, as long as there's no infection."

"You're a troublemaker, Addie," Sally whispered and handed her the scalpel. "Count me in," she murmured.

After what they had witnessed the night before, this surgery was rather simple. Adeline started from the outside of the wound, picking out the metal, dirt and cloth pieces with her scalpel and cutting the wound back with scissors until healthy muscle was exposed in all directions. By the end of the surgery, the wound was roughly six centimeters wide by four deep. She rinsed it with Dakin solution and inserted a small rubber tube at its edge. She bandaged the wound loosely and clipped a safety pin to the end of the tube so they would be able to administer the Dakin solution every two hours to keep the wound drenched with antiseptic.

Within moments, Lieutenant Colonel Jenkins's breath blew hot on Adeline's neck as he knelt beside her to inspect the patient. Adeline's scalpel and scissors clamored on the metal tray. Sally gave her a long stare and then stepped over to the lavatory to clean the pile of instruments.

Remembering her mother's cautionary observation that Adeline's remarks could sometimes be as sharp as a splinter in a lion's paw, she asked, "What would you recommend next, doctor?"

"Keep him separated from our boys in the ward, for they just might rip out your pretty handiwork." Adeline straightened her shoulders. "Let me know when the wound is clear of infection and I'll suture it up," he offered with surprising chivalry.

Adeline bowed her head. "Very good, sir. Forgive me, sir, I'm often headstrong. Too . . . morally inflexible."

"That can be admirable trait, but in war, and in the O.R. when our soldiers' lives hang in the balance, you must choose sides," he insisted, his fingers squeezing her waistline. Adeline jumped to her feet as if scalded. The lieutenant colonel rose to his full height, which was nearly two heads taller than her small frame. He rested a hand on her shoulder. "Whose side will you take?" He winked and walked to the lavatory to scrub in for his next surgery.

———

JUNE 8, 1918

"How is he?" Adeline asked the ward nurse as she stood over the bed of a recent gas victim.

The nurse felt for a pulse. "How kind of you to ask, but Private William Wilkes here is dead, Nurse Donnelly." Her expression soured. "While you and Dunn were patching up the German last night, he was drowning in the fluid that collected in his lungs."

Had word traveled so quickly? Or had this nurse also been in the operating room?

"I did what my conscience bade me, and though I grieve for this boy, you and I both know there is nothing that can be done for pneumonia patients, save for making them comfortable."

With a scathing glance, the nurse began to shuffle down the center of the ward, checking the charts of some of the other patients her team had operated on that day. Adeline waited until the ward nurse was tending to a boy at the far end of the ward before she searched for the German.

———

Heinrich lay at one end of a gigantic room of beds, cloistered behind heavy green velvet curtains and elevated on a stage of some sort. He slept on a child's cot and his feet poked out from beneath the sheet to dangle over the end of the mattress, beneath the iron rail to which his ankle was shackled. He wiggled his toes, relishing the cool freedom.

His shoulders spanned the width of the mattress, one wrapped with a snowy mound of bandages. The wound beneath hurt like hell, but it was the kind of pain to reassure a man he was still alive. Heinrich was out of danger, content for now to sleep and heal and perhaps send a letter to his son.

A pale, petite hand drew back the curtain. Yellow sunlight spilled across the lower half of Heinrich's cot. The woman, a nurse he presumed, was dressed in all white, save for practical brown boots. Loose curls of chocolate brown flowed from beneath her cap to her jawline, where they had been fetchingly trimmed. Her nails were naked of color, her hands scrubbed pink. Her skin was as pale and clear as a bowl of cream, but fatigue darkened the delicate skin beneath her eyes. Heinrich had not gazed at a woman in over eighteen months, and her close physical proximity stirred him deeply.

Her dark lashes fluttered as she examined his chart and the bag of personal items tied to the end of his bed. He could guess what was contained therein: his rosary and the photograph he carried of Anna and Werner. Perhaps the handkerchief he had clasped in his hand when they had found him, or Anna's note, which he kept in his pocket. They would have seized the syringes and bandages he carried for their own use.

The white-uniformed nurse sat on the stool next to the bed, unclipped the rubber tube that protruded from his bandages and squirted solution into Heinrich's wound with a bulb syringe. The prickly, cooling sensation caused him to twitch. She pressed his left arm into the mattress with her free hand, presumably to guard against his interference. His mouth twitched with amusement, for he could have easily thwarted her grip if needed.

"La Blanchette," he muttered with a lazy half grin. She frowned, for she must have guessed she looked like a puff of meringue.

She replied in French. "You may call me Nurse Donnelly. And your name?" He was surprised they had not gleaned this information from his dog tags, but then again, they clearly had their hands full.

Heinrich grunted while adjusting his position. "Sommer . . . Heinrich Sommer."

Shrieks erupted from the main floor. A team of orderlies rushed over and gently subdued one of the blinded gas victims. He had escaped his cot and begun fumbling around, tripping over bedpans and crying out, so unbearable was the sting from his burns. Nurse Donnelly winced at the sight.

"Mustard gas," the German confirmed in a husky voice. "Terrible, terrible invention." Her dark eyes met his.

"How are you feeling?" she asked.

"Tired. It's not easy to sleep here." He scratched his itchy neck.

The nurse slipped a thermometer under his tongue and checked her watch. "Just be thankful you didn't fall victim to your own chemical weapons," she quipped.

A patient in a cot nearby began to cough and clamor for air, his arms flailing helplessly. His paroxysms subsided somewhat after he drank greedily from a cup the orderly handed him.

Five minutes later, Nurse Donnelly pulled the thermometer from Heinrich's mouth. "No fever, which means no infection so far."

As Heinrich continued to observe the coughing soldier, he became more agitated. "I did not create mustard gas, nor do I condone its use," he replied. "What are they doing to help him?" he asked, as if the ward nurses were to blame.

"The normal protocol. Gas victims are stripped of their clothes, bathed and given new clothing before they are transported here. Blistered skin is clipped away, and the skin is cleaned with antiseptic. Sodium hypochlorite and Vaseline gauze are used to treat the burns. Menthol is typically used for cough."

"Do you have a pen and paper?" he asked.

"Why?"

"They need to put that man in a croup tent and heat a kettle with camphor, menthol, and oils of eucalyptus and thyme," he insisted.

"And you know this because . . . ?"

"I am a medical officer, trained to help gas victims." She scrutinized his face. Had she guessed that he was trained to ease the suffering of Germans who might accidentally inhale the gas they planned to use on their enemies?

"The perils of war," she replied darkly.

She rose, but he caught her wrist. When panic flashed in her eyes, he let go. "Tell them," he ordered softly. "It may not save him, but it will at least bring him some comfort and allow him to sleep."

Her cheeks flared pink.

"Merci, Blanchette." He guessed she would be headed back into surgery soon and did not want to add to her duties. "Leave the solution and syringe in reach. I will clean my own wound."

CHAPTER 10

June 13–15, 1918

ON THE OUTSKIRTS OF BOURESCHES, FRANCE

During the week that followed his first day as a runner, Luc estimated he ran over ten kilometers each day and dodged just as many Mauser-wielding snipers. On the morning of June 13, Luc savored his first cup of hot coffee in days. Beneath his comrades' two-week-old beards were dark creases, and the delicate capillaries of their eyes flared red. Many men of the 23rd were plagued with diarrhea and fever. Even worse, it seemed like nothing the 2nd Division did to advance the line north in Belleau Wood had succeeded, despite the crushing loss of life. The German army still crawled through the trees like a spider, regenerating legs and catching Allies in a web of destruction.

The Germans rained shellfire on the marines and the dough-boys for days. The doughboys of the 23rd hid behind rocks and in the trenches they dug, which protected them from shell fragments but not direct hits. The relentless shells screeched and smashed into the ground so quickly that the noise and vibrations froze Luc's senses, stifling all instincts, leaving with him the terrifying sensation that his mind, perhaps even his soul, was no longer tethered to his flesh.

Some of the men had begun to tremble involuntarily—their faces twitched and their torsos convulsed wildly, like fish writhing on dry land. When the Americans attacked with heavy artillery on June 9, turning Belleau Wood to mincemeat, this only weakened them more.

The Germans had repulsed Sibley's line back to the southern edge of Belleau Wood earlier in the week and, the day after the U.S. artillery barrage, the 5th Marines failed to secure the northern woods during a two-pronged attack. Another 225 souls had perished, but the Allies had not gained an inch of forest.

When the shelling paused on the afternoon of June 13, Luc ran south to Le Loge Farm, less than three hundred meters north of the Paris–Metz highway, to report to Brigadier General James Harbord, commander of the 2nd Division Marine Brigade, that Colonel Malone's 23rd had moved into position next to the 9th Infantry and now occupied a line from the woods north of Le Thiolet to Bouresches, facing east. The general had commandeered the small peasant farmhouse at Le Loge—built from field stones and tightly shuttered—for his headquarters. He sat behind a small table in a narrow room where rows of worn, dusty volumes filled rickety bookshelves. The general cut a formidable figure in uniform, with a long stern nose, thin lips drawn into a slight frown, and crepe-paper eyelids that drooped in the corners just enough to soften his visage and lend an air of compassion to his tall, imposing physique. The luster of his russet leather boots and the sweep of his neatly combed hair made Luc uneasy about his own appearance: muddy boots with a blood- and sweat-stained uniform, shredded in parts. Luc jutted his chest out, standing as straight as a steel bayonet.

Adjacent to Harbord's office was a room filled with black, mostly useless army telephones. The lines had been cut so often, and were so unreliable, that the runners had become even more vital. Luc stood in the half-light of the foyer and waited at attention for the general and commander of the marine brigade to see him. High-ranking officers filled the dark rooms, their heads grazing the ceiling beams, and Luc wondered what kind of mettle and experience it required to organize and coordinate these attacks. He waited and listened.

Within moments, General Harbord's assistant waved him into the office. Luc saluted and relayed Colonel Malone's message, along with what he knew of the 9th Infantry's position.

"Thank you, lad." He handed Luc a note for Malone. "Safe journey back to Bouresches."

Just as Luc stiffened and saluted again, another red-banded runner burst through the door. His unblemished ebony skin perspired, and his eyes sparked with excitement above his sculpted cheekbones. *"Excusez-moi, messieurs!"* he said breathlessly. The khaki uniform—so different from the French army regulars' horizon-blue uniform—piqued Luc's curiosity.

The young soldier relayed his message and General Harbord asked the Frenchman to wait while he crafted his response. The

French runner stepped out into the foyer, where Luc lingered. He extended a hand. "Luc Lemieux."

"Jean-Daniel Lacroix." His grip was sleek and muscular. He could not have been more than eighteen.

"*Vous êtes de quelle division?*" Luc inquired. Rapid French would be best for the conversation he had in mind.

"*La Dixième Troupe Coloniale, et vous?*"

Hope filled Luc's chest. The French 10th Colonial was Pierre Marchand's division. "*Le vingt-troisième. Connaissez-vous Pierre Marchand?*"

"*Capitaine Marchand de Lille? Mais oui.*"

Lacroix's gaze did not waver as he confirmed that he did indeed know Ondine and Michel's father. Luc took this as a good sign. "*Est-il . . . ?*" He could not bring himself to say the word.

"*Il survit,*" Lacroix responded.

Luc grinned widely. Marchand was among the living. Luc must get a message to him at once. "*C'est fantastique! Pouvez-vous lui donner un message de ses enfants?*"

"*Ses enfants? Les dames et les enfants des Lille ont été évacués, n'est-ce pas?*"

If they knew the women and children of Lille had been relocated by the Germans, had Capitaine Marchand also received word that his wife was dead? Most likely not. Luc hesitated for a moment, trying to read Lacroix's expression. The young man's inky brows rose in expectation.

Luc pulled the photograph from his pocket. "*Voilà, Ondine et Michel. S'il vous plaît, dites à Capitaine Marchand que ses enfants habitent à Vouvray avec moi—Luc Lemieux—près de Tours dans la Loire."* He slowed to emphasize the location of the children. *"Luc Lemieux de Vouvray, vous comprenez?"*

"Oui, je vais lui dire." Despite Lacroix's assurances, Luc preferred to write this all down to avoid any inaccuracies. He scanned the square room for a piece of paper but found none. He could rip one of the pages from a book, but that would not be neighborly, and they would probably reprimand him. The Americans seemed to be much more careful with French property than his own countrymen, Luc had observed. Luc patted his pants pocket, recalling the rice paper he had tucked away just before Elliott had recruited him to be a runner.

He snatched a pencil from a nearby table and wrote the details on the rice paper for Lacroix. *"Voilà. S'il vous plaît, donnez ceci à Capitaine Marchand aujourd'hui. C'est très important."*

"Bien sûr, mon ami," Lacroix replied, tucking the paper in his satchel before Harbord's assistant interrupted them with a curious glance. Luc saluted, thanked them both and exited into the bright courtyard. He stopped for a cup of thick, bitter coffee at an outbuilding with smoke spiraling from its chimney, to quietly celebrate his good fortune and pray that his note would reach Marchand.

———

JUNE 14, 1918

The doughboys of the 23rd slept in the fields outside of Bouresches. The marines held the town, but the Germans still controlled the rail station to the north, and therefore the flow of goods and soldiers in and out of Bouresches.

Mortar shells whistled and whizzed over the half-meter-wide dugout where Luc Lemieux cowered. They landed far too close, rutting the earth and spraying dirt.

Luc dozed in snatches until a wet sensation, like a sprinkle of morning rain, woke him. The sweet and spicy scent of lilacs mixed with horseradish settled in his foxhole. Then his nostrils began to burn as if someone were singeing the tender flesh inside with a lit match.

Tin mess pans clattered. "Wake up! Gas! Gas!"

Luc clamped his eyes and mouth shut. Holding his breath, he scrambled to his feet and reached for his canteen in the gloom. He swigged water, gargled, swished and spit. He splashed more water on his face, then tipped his head back, the liquid streaming into his nostrils. Blowing hard, he tried to expel the poison from his nose. Luc pulled his gas mask from its satchel, fastened it over his face and secured his helmet. He sprang from the dugout and charged back down the Gobert ravine with only the silvery haze of moonlight to guide him.

Luc's tongue poked a painful boil inside his right cheek. Had he stopped breathing and donned his mask fast enough to prevent the gas particles from blistering his lungs? He recalled his basic training: gas was heavier than air and settled in low-lying areas. In the dark, the glass eye cups of his mask obscured his vision, so he navigated by touch up the rocky slope of the ravine to higher ground. He clawed his way to the top in a few minutes and sprinted across the flat, grassy farmland.

When he reached a tight cluster of trees, Luc slumped to the ground. Beneath his mask, hot and dank with perspiration, he battled to breathe through the respirator. Panic crept up his throat, demanding fresh air. His hands flew to the mask, but the gnawing voice of his sergeant stopped him: *Never remove your mask until you are certain the gas is gone.* Luc concentrated instead on breathing threads of oxygen through the respirator. Threads eventually expanded to ribbons of air, and Luc's heart settled back into a semi-normal rhythm.

What else should he do? He swallowed hard to push it back down. He must survive, for Maman, for Papa, for all of them. He must return—for Ondine.

There was only one thing left to do. Luc signed the cross. *In the name of the Father, and of the Son and of the Holy Ghost. Amen.* He toppled over on his side. He had no choice but to wait until dawn.

———

A beam of morning light pierced Luc's glass eye cups, scorching the delicate skin of his already sore eyelids. After wiping the exterior of the cups with his sleeve, he examined his surroundings. The trees were familiar, with white blossoms and gnarled trunks that leaned in toward each other, creating a canopy of sorts. He recognized the orchard where he had taken refuge only a week ago. He did not detect any yellow powder or liquid on the tree branches. The grass was a soft, green carpet, seemingly untouched by the poison.

Suddenly, Luc's arms and legs and inner thighs began to prickle with undeniable heat and a hundred tiny shards of glass chafed his throat. He threw off the gas mask and peeled off his puttees, tunic and breeches to discover large, red welts all over his body. It felt like a thousand tiny legs scampered across his skin, and he could not resist the urge to scratch them away but scraping his nails against his skin only exacerbated the inflammation. Blisters started to form on his inner thighs. Standing in his olive drab wool underdrawers, with his boots still fastened, Luc dropped beneath the apple trees and rolled in the cool blades of dewy grass.

The relief was only temporary. Luc glanced at his discarded uniform. A pale-yellow substance, reminiscent of dried talcum powder, covered it. He couldn't risk placing the fabric against his skin again. He washed his hands with the water left in his canteen and used the apple tree leaves to wipe the corners of his swollen eyes, just in case any poison lingered. He guessed not, for it would probably have blinded him overnight.

Just as Luc had resolved to return to Gob Gully to help the rest of the men who did not reach higher ground, a stab of pain in his abdomen stopped him. He doubled over and voided the contents of his bowels and stomach into an obliging bush. Beneath his itchy, blistering skin, a deep ache set into his bones. A childhood memory tugged at his consciousness. Yes, he remembered this excruciating ache from when he was twelve years old and had contracted a fever during which he suffered through a day of vomiting and diarrhea. After half a day in the water closet, he had ached the same way. Dehydration had been the culprit.

Luc fantasized about the sparkling, underground spring he had drunk from at Lucy-le-Bocage. He did not have the strength to make it that far, but he could see a swarm of soldiers and ambulances less than a half a kilometer away. They must have relocated the Red Cross dressing station atop the northern slope of the ravine, near the southern tip of Belleau Wood. This way they could avoid the yellowish-green vapor clouds floating like ghosts at the bottom of the Gobert ravine, stalking their prey.

Luc stumbled several hundred meters and then crawled the rest of the way to the first aid station. He willed his arms and knees forward by mouthing the numbers: *one-two-one-two.* When he was close enough to distinguish the medics from the wounded soldiers, his belly hit the ground.

JUILLY, FRANCE

Adeline carried two amputated legs down to the incinerator. Less than two weeks ago, the sheer horror of the act had moved her to tears, but today, she simply completed her assigned task, grateful to still have the use of her own limbs.

As she approached the bed where she had last visited Shep Holmes, a white sheet snapped and billowed in the air, then cascaded over the thin mattress. An orderly smoothed the fabric over the length of the bed and added a gray army blanket and freshly cased pillow. Adeline's throat constricted and she clenched her fists, digging her nails into the flesh of her palm. "Has he died?" she rasped.

The orderly checked his clipboard. "Shepherd Holmes, time of death nine thirty-five this morning."

That was only an hour ago. "Where is he?"

"Morgue, most likely," was the curt reply.

The cemetery detail consisted of six enlisted soldiers who dug the regulation graves, three feet wide by six-and-a-half feet long by six feet deep, in a wheat field afire with crimson poppies. For the burial service at 1700 hours, a burly workhorse towed five bare wooden caskets in a cart. An American flag draped the ends of the coffins as the procession lumbered toward the cemetery, led by a French urchin bobbing along and holding a crucifix, followed by the chaplain, the local parish *curé*, a bugler and a band of mourners, one of whom held the portable font of holy water.

The bugler held every mournful note of "Taps" to an excruciating degree. The hymn lingered, and Adeline's lips trembled as she sang the sorrowful words: "All is well, safely rest, God is nigh." She had to believe God was nigh, that Jesus had been with Shep during his last hours of suffering, and that the angels had swept down and borne his soul to the heavens. For what was the alternative?

By the time the wooden crosses were mounted, and the graves covered with soil, the crowd had dispersed. The soldiers of the grave detail fell in line behind the cart, spades resting on their shoulders, and marched back to the hospital in silence.

Standing near the graves, overcome by the scents of earth and rust, Adeline collapsed. Stems of wheat swallowed her tiny frame as she sank to the ground and rested her head among the brilliant red poppies. From the church spire, the Angelus rang out, three strokes of the bell, a pause, and then nine strokes . . .

"Hail Mary, full of grace," Adeline uttered before drifting into oblivion.

"What troubles you, *Blanchette*? The light has vanished from your face." *How could the German sense her moods so easily?*

"A soldier I was caring for died today." As Adeline examined his shoulder, she marveled at the cords of muscles, so pronounced in his arms and back. One did not develop sinews so thick without manual labor. She wondered if he had been a farmer before he became a medic.

She marked his chart with her findings.

"You cannot grieve over each one, *Blanchette*. It will tear you up inside, and then how will you do your job?" he asked.

She knew she shouldn't confide in him, and yet his expression was so open, so caring, she faltered only a moment before explaining. "It's not that. We both knew he was dying, but I wanted to be there, you know, so he would not be alone or afraid."

"I see." Heinrich searched her face. "When you write his parents, tell him about your time with their son, what you spoke about, what concerns he had. Enclose something in the envelope as a keepsake for them."

"Like what?"

"Did he have a crucifix or a snuffbox or some small treasure?"

"I don't know."

The German sighed and closed his eyes. "You will think of something, *Blanchette*."

"You may call me 'Nurse Donnelly,'" she said with a hint of irritation.

"When you call me Heinrich, *Blanchette*."

———

JUNE 14, 1918

My dear Mr. and Mrs. Holmes,

If I were seated in your living room, I could explain so much better about your son's battle wounds and all the things that mean so much to parents who miss their boy.

Your son was brought here to Evacuation Hospital #107 in Juilly, France, in the early morning hours of the 7th of June. The day before, at Belleau Wood, he was wounded in the right leg by fragments of a mortar that had exploded near him. We removed the shrapnel and cleaned and disinfected the wound, but despite our best efforts, the infection spread to his blood.

The infection weakened him, and he ate only a few spoonfuls of soup in between hours of rest. Before he fell into eternal sleep, he spoke of his devotion to you and his brothers, Michael and Daniel, and his love for his sweetheart, Bernadette. He asked me to tell you that he did not suffer, that he was a man of honor who proudly fought to liberate France. It was his greatest wish that his death would not bow your heads.

The chaplain attended him several times, blessing him, hearing his confession and administering the last rites. Shepherd drew his last breath at 9:35 this morning. The chaplain was by his side and wishes me to say, "Have no fear, for your son died in the comfort of Jesus's embrace."

Shepherd was laid to rest in the American cemetery here next to his comrades, the Marines of the 2nd Division. His grave number is 617. His name, rank and serial number are carved into the simple, white wooden cross. A similar tag rests around his neck bearing the same serial number, 2467339.

As the chaplain read Psalm 23, the psalm for which you named your son, the sun's beautiful yellow glow set like a halo behind the big hill that overshadows the place. We prayed that you all would have great strength for the battle ahead. We, the hospital staff, offer our deepest sympathy in your hour of sorrow.

Be assured, the villagers visit the cemetery every week to care for it with loving hands and make sure it is fresh and clean. I have enclosed Shep's identification tag and a remembrance from the oak tree that stretches its arms to shade the very spot where he now rests.

This country will always honor your boy, and the sacrifice both he and you have made in the defense of liberty. This sacrifice is not in vain but will make the world a far better place.
Sincerely,
Adeline Donnelly

Adeline slipped two green oak leaves into the envelope and placed her letter in the outgoing mail. Before it reached Shep's parents, the government would send them a terse telegram notifying them of their son's death. *Were her words true? Would his sacrifice make the world a better place?*

Propped up on two pillows, Heinrich opened his eyes to see Blanchette standing over him holding a small white ceramic bowl. She lowered it toward him, and he clasped it in his palms. Inside rested a mound of shiny, dark red cherries.

"*Qu'est-ce que c'est?*" he asked.

"With appreciation for your counsel yesterday—from the *fruiterie*."

He didn't know if she thanked him for his advice about the croup tent or the dead soldier's parents, but he didn't care. Her care and this gesture were the only kindness he had known in the last eighteen months.

"*Asseyez-vous, Blanchette.*" With his right arm, the German slid the stool closer to where she stood. "You are exhausted."

She was as limp as a wet *spaetzle*. He lifted the bowl of fruit. "You need the sugar." She bit into a cherry with closed eyes. Her plump lips sucked its flesh. He popped a whole one into his mouth, nearly moaning at the glorious burst of flavor. "You and I are the same, *Blanchette*. We are innocents. We do not wage this war. We clean up the mess."

Her expression hardened. "We are not the same. You Germans entered the war to gain power. We Americans entered the war because you sank our passenger ships with your U-boats."

"It was also reported that we Germans cut the fat off dead British and French soldiers to make soap for our troops."

Blanchette recoiled in revulsion.

Heinrich clarified, "Of course this is a lie. You shouldn't believe everything you read." Still, from her point of view, Germans had shredded the American soldiers piling up in the hallway outside her operating room. He wanted to make her understand. "*Blanchette*, those passenger ships were stocked with weapons and munitions for the Allies, although I do believe the passengers were innocent of that knowledge. But let's not talk politics. Millions of men, women and children on both sides are dying or suffering because of the action of a handful of spiteful leaders."

"German greed started this, this . . . murderous rampage."

"German greed, or Germany's fear of its enemies? Germany entered the war to protect its alliances. The Kaiser also tried to end it, but the Allies refused his peace offering."

"And now American soldiers must pay the price. Will it ever end?" she asked, cradling her forehead with her palm.

"I believe it is ending," he asserted.

Her head lifted. "How did you end up so close to our line? Close enough to save the French soldier?"

"Perils of war, as you said. I was looking for wounded. An *Eierhandgranate* hit the dirt about ten meters from where I knelt. I covered the Frenchman as it detonated and that's the last I remember." He began to scratch absentmindedly behind his left ear as he told the story.

Blanchette caught his arm with her hand. "Heinrich, stop scratching!" It was the first time she had used his Christian name. Exhilaration coursed through his veins. "Do you know what happened to him? The Frenchman?"

"No."

Blanchette's forehead scrunched in contemplation. "Are you sure it was a hand grenade? I have only seen concussion and hearing loss, not fragments, from grenades."

Heinrich glanced at the ceiling and sighed before closing his eyes. "They fitted them with a *splinterring*, or a sleeve, so they would fragment and cause more damage to the advancing troops." Heat burned his cheeks. He could no longer hold back his tears. So much senseless death. So much misery. He ached for Werner. He missed his son's cheer, his playfulness, his sweetness. "This hellish war," he croaked.

She leaned in and whispered, "How long have you been a soldier?"

"A year and a half. Despite what you read in the papers, or what you have been led to believe, our men are sick of the war and want peace. We are all tired of the killing."

"Do you now expect me to become sympathetic to the German plight?"

"Of course not, but perhaps to my cause?" The corner of his mouth shrugged into a sad half smile.

"And what exactly is your aim?"

He could not tell her about his son, his faithless wife. The emotion was too raw, too tender. Fortunately, footsteps on the hardwood floor interrupted their exchange.

"Fraternizing with the enemy, Nurse Donnelly?" a reedy physician remarked as he sidled up to Heinrich's bed.

"Setting him straight, for his perspective on the war is not quite accurate, lieutenant colonel."

Heinrich struggled to sit upright. "Careful," Blanchette cautioned, holding his bent arm steady so he would not disturb the bandages.

The newcomer stopped at the other side of the cot, where Blanchette sat. He bent over and inspected Heinrch's shoulder wound, which the surgeons had closed in the operating room several days earlier. "Should be completely healed by tomorrow. Well done, Nurse Donnelly." Blanchette edged away from her superior and rounded the foot of the bed. There, she made a fuss about checking Heinrich's chart. She put on a good show, scribbling with her pencil, but something was amiss.

The doctor grumbled unintelligibly and sauntered down the narrow gap between the cot and table toward her. He hooked his arm around Blanchette's waist and squeezed. Heinrich instinctively snapped his large foot sideways, catching the surgeon's calf and toppling him to the floor.

"Dammit, man!" he yelped, rubbing his knee as he rose to his feet.

"Pardonnez-moi, docteur," Heinrich replied without remorse. The corners of Blanchette's mouth twitched with laughter. It was certainly not the smartest idea to infuriate a surgeon, but Heinrich couldn't help himself. Leveling that boor was the highlight of his day.

CHAPTER 11

June 14–15, 1918

ON THE OUTSKIRTS OF BOURESCHES, FRANCE

He felt dreadful, lying in the dirt in only his skivvies, dog tags and boots. The yellow-and-scarlet pustules on his skin reminded him of a cheese *roux* left to boil, burn and pop on the stovetop.

Luc shielded his face from the shiny, persistent pinprick of sun in the sky that punctured his eyes. He released a harrowing whimper. The pain was impossible to bear. It was as though the Germans had doused him in gasoline, flicked a match and set him on fire.

Voices suddenly surrounded him: one with the clarity of a bell and another with a muddled baritone. When Luc opened his mouth to speak, his dry lips fissured, and his throat grated his speech.

"He's been gassed," the bell-peal voice announced. Cool, thin fingers rested on his forehead while someone lifted his jingling dog tags from his chest. "Luc, I'm going to open your eyelids with my fingers and administer drops. I need you to hold still, all right?"

Luc tried to croak out the word "yes," but instead he resigned himself to a nod. The drops soothed his aching, burning eyes instantly and he was grateful for the relief. He sensed a flurry of movement about him. Strong hands gripped his ankles and another pair encircled his wrists, lifting him up and placing him back down on a delightfully scratchy wool blanket. The woman with the bell-peal voice made hasty work of wrapping his arms and legs in wet gauze and stuffing rolls of the soaked cloth between his blazing legs and in his blistering armpits. If he had not been so miserable, he might have blushed.

"Put him in the empty berth of that ambulance over there— the one to Juilly. And make sure he has water with him." She was an angel—an angel with the no-nonsense grit of a general.

Once they slid him into the dark ambulance, Luc peeked at his surroundings. Though he was still sensitive to light, he could discern fuzzy shapes—he was not blind yet. The ambulance held four berths, stacked two by two. A large, burly soldier squirmed in the upper bunk across from him. "It's hot enough to hatch chickens in here," he complained with a thick southern drawl.

Luc struggled to reach the canteen by his side. His bunkmate obligingly cradled both of Luc's hands around it. "Want a little help there?" he asked. Luc nodded and the soldier cradled his head in his meaty hand, lifting Luc so he could take a swig. "That's it, nice and slow like, just one small sip at a time."

"Thank you," Luc rasped, once his palate was wet again. He rolled his tongue over his cracked lips.

"Chuck's the name. Gas bit you, eh? Nasty stuff. Me? I took some shrapnel in the leg. A German shell shrieked like a hawk, flying over my dugout—could have sheared my head right off. I sure am lucky to be a lame duck instead of a headless horseman."

Luc turned his face away from his chatty bunkmate. He shivered at the memory of Marty.

"They'll patch me up just fine at the hospital," Chuck said.

The medic climbed on board, taking his seat between the bunks. He knocked twice on the cab in front of him and the ambulance lurched into gear.

"How long's the trip, friend?" Chuck asked the medic.

"To Juilly? It's about fifty kilometers, but it may take two hours—depends on the route."

The cabin of the ambulance jostled the men as it motored down the uneven dirt roads. One of the patients in the lower bunks yelped when they hit a bump. The medic sprang to his feet and tightened the man's arm splint. Luc's mind churned over the sights and smells of the battlefield, and he could not wrestle the image of his mutilated friends from his consciousness. His stomach rolled hard, and he began to vomit.

————

JUNE 15, 1918

Adeline tried to eat more and bathe in sudsy water at least once a day to wash the oniony smell of perspiration from her skin.

Today, with renewed spirit, she planned to complete a long over-due task. As she approached Heinrich's cot, she was shocked to see his entire face, without his disheveled beard. The recently shaved skin was fairer, and his sturdy jawline and supple lips were now visible. In his clean hospital gown, he cut a striking, lanky figure. He was eating oatmeal and reading his chart. Although the notations were in English, he apparently understood enough to cobble together the facts.

"You did not tell me *you* removed the metal from my shoulder."

"Give me that!" She snatched the papers from his hands. "You didn't ask."

"Why didn't one of the surgeons do it?"

"Why, aren't you happy with the result?"

"Indeed. I'm just curious."

"Why do you think? They weren't about to operate on a German before an American."

"But you did?"

"I took an oath that I honored, just like you," she said curtly.

Heinrich pointed to the thick red line on his shoulder. "Your doctor friend sutured me up nicely, despite how disagreeable he may have found the task."

"He is not my friend." Adeline was perturbed to discover that Heinrich had removed his own stitches.

"Lovers' quarrel?" he persisted.

"No!" she huffed. "His attentions are not encouraged, nor are they desired." Heinrich must certainly be bored if he was interested in her non-existent love life.

312

"Has he made unwanted advances?"

She bit the inside of her cheek.

"He has, hasn't he?"

"I don't know why I confide in you."

"You didn't. I guessed."

She grimaced and dropped her voice to a whisper. "I never encouraged him. He snuck into my tent while I was sleeping," she admitted. "When I awoke, he was—trying to take liberties."

Heinrich's eyes widened.

"He didn't get very far. Sister Thérèse clocked him on the head with an iron ladle."

Heinrich laughed. "She is a sphinx, that one! Nothing gets past her. When she brought my soup yesterday, she insisted the orderly shave me for she felt I had been neglected. So, our good doctor has been rebuffed twice in a week—first by a little old nun and then by a big-footed German. How humiliating!"

Adeline pursed her lips. Sensing the eyes of the ward nurse on her, she supposed she had better return to the business at hand.

"You do know you are beautiful, yes?" Heinrich's words startled her.

"I know no such thing." *How was she supposed to respond to such flattery from the enemy? She thought she was attractive, with a lean shape, decent gams, loose brown curls and smooth skin, but no one aside from Jess and now Jenkins had ever desired her.*

"I can say this—without expectation of course—since I am married." She recalled the photo of the woman and boy she had seen in the bag of personal items still tied to the bed. Something in his eyes betrayed a deep-seated sorrow. A moment of silence passed between them. His voice faltered slightly before he continued. "When a man is so far from women for so long, even the presence of *La Blanchette* stirs in him a longing."

"You can't say such things," she bristled.

"Why? Can we not be honest? Our paths will never cross again."

She looked away. Of course they would never see each other again. Why did the idea of his absence grieve her so?

He closed his eyes and pressed the back of his head against the wall. "I just mean that you, *Blanchette*, are formidable."

"Which is why I have come to escort you to the Cootie Shack." She lifted a pair of new American boots.

He raised a questioning eyebrow, but she ignored him and instead guided him to stand. She linked arms with him, to prevent a possible fall from dizziness. She had to tighten her abdominal and thigh muscles to support his weight, for he relied on her bolstering more than she expected.

He hobbled down the stage stairs, gripping the iron railing, his legs seemingly still as weak as a newborn kitten's. Despite his numerous requests to be unshackled and walk about the ward after his surgery, the commanding officer had not allowed any such freedom until today. She led him out of the ward and onto the sprawling lawn of the collège. Shadows crawled across the thick grass, but despite the late hour, Heinrich squeezed his eyes shut when they stepped into the sharp, low-dipping sunlight.

"You must think me a feeble specimen, *oui, Blanchette*?"

"I'll petition the commanding officer to allow you to walk about some more—for your health."

"He'll probably object. After all, he wouldn't want a German POW to regain his strength before he is relocated."

She led him to a long shack with steam pouring from its single chimney. The sign bolted to its side read *Disinfecting Plant, Loaned and Erected by the American Red Cross.*

"*Qu'est-ce que c'est?*"

"Delousing station."

He groaned. "I must be clean of vermin before they ship me off to God knows where?" Adeline ignored his repeated musings that he would soon leave them. She had no idea what would happen to him.

She turned him over to the sergeant in charge and lied in English, "I have strict orders that Mr. Sommer is to be unaccompanied, no other soldiers in the station with him, understand? I will collect him at the exit."

After eyeballing the German with a flash of disgust, the young, trim sergeant nodded and yelled, "Turn on the water again, Jimmy!"

The patter of water began inside as the water heated up. The sergeant's gaze drifted from the top of Heinrich's head down the considerable length of his body—the German measured well over six feet tall. The sergeant shrugged before handing Adeline a pile of freshly boiled and dried civilian clothes and a new suit of men's underwear. His German uniform had been burned on her orders, along with the colonies of lice crawling in its seams.

"Get in and strip," the sergeant ordered. Heinrich glanced furtively at Adeline. She opened the door, stuck her hand under the nearest end of the long shower and, upon confirming its warmth, explained in French, "Strip inside. Place your gown, underwear and socks inside the big bag and give it to the sergeant. Then wash all your hair, all your parts, with this cresol oil." She handed him a small bottle and ushered him inside.

Heinrich flashed her a wary look before stepping into the shower. She latched the door behind him and crossed over the lawn to the other side of the shack to await his exit. A line of ten American soldiers trudged toward the shack. "Hold up," the sergeant raised his hand. "Y'all gotta wait for the German."

A flurry of cuss words and insults rippled through the line of soldiers. They scratched their heads and necks and limbs with a vengeance. Red streaks appeared on their soiled skin and blood crusted under their nails, from scratching or killing, Adeline could not say. She instinctively moved closer to the men. Perhaps knowing a nurse was present would subdue them or, at the very least, clean up their language for the time being.

"Ma'am," some of them mumbled and nodded their bare heads, for they could not offer the customary tip of the hat.

She fidgeted outside the opposite end of the shack, waiting for some sign from Heinrich that he was ready to return to the ward. In a few minutes, Heinrich poked his head out, hair dripping and an impish grin lighting his face. He was wrapped only in a large Turkish towel. He could be any American young man—until he opened his mouth. The bones of his feet and hands were long and elegant, like the monture and ribs of a folding fan. A tawny down spread across his chest and down to his navel. His belly was pale but flat, and the wound on his shoulder had healed much faster than Adeline had expected. Her heart pinched as she considered the damage wielded by his own army's weapon and then again by her scalpel. She had to admit that Jenkins's stitches had smoothed over her less than artful carving. She hurried over to dry the patch of skin.

Heinrich pointed inside the shack. "Too hot."

"The water?"

He nodded and waved her closer. She handed him the stack of clean clothes.

Adeline shooed him back inside and sat on a tree stump conveniently located nearby. Bright green leaves fluttered and rustled above her, and gauzy white clouds scuttled across the summer sky. Adeline reached down to pick a handful of long stalks from the wild lavender plant by her feet. She folded them in half and slipped them into her surgical apron, planning on drying and crushing the flowers with the hope they would remain fragrant through the fall months.

"What's the holdup?" the sergeant called. The line of soldiers behind him clawed at their scalps and necks, clung to their crutches, and grumbled amongst themselves. Compassion's warmth spread across Adeline's chest. Their shirts, unbuttoned to aid in the absorption of sunlight, flapped around their atrophied torsos. Some of them were no doubt still recuperating from the bouts of dizziness, headaches and shooting shin pains of trench fever.

Adeline had seen the Cootie Shack work miracles on the crankiest and most despondent of soldiers. When they finally emerged, their skin would be squeaky clean and critter-free. They would whistle and sing and possess a renewed sense of vigor. Hopefully, Heinrich would experience the same relief.

She knocked on the door and called to him. He did not respond. She couldn't possibly go inside the dressing room, even if Heinrich was her patient. There were certain boundaries of propriety, even in wartime, which one simply could not cross.

Adeline approached the sergeant. "Why don't you check on him?"

The sergeant hopped up the ramp and disappeared into the shack. He reappeared in moments. "Ma'am!"

Adeline rushed in to find Heinrich sitting on the bench, slumped over in his new suit of underwear. She felt for his pulse, which was faint but strengthened beneath her touch. The sergeant attempted to lift him up, but she redirected him. "Water, he needs fresh water," she insisted.

"Breathe deeply through your nose," Adeline urged Heinrich, holding a hand against his back. He leaned forward on his long arms, the elegant, sinewy fingers of a pianist fanned out across his thighs. Adeline's cheeks burned and her stomach fluttered. She sucked in a stream of breath.

When he finally lifted his head, his drowsy eyes rolled open and he squinted at her. *"La Blanchette, La Blanchette,"* he muttered, clearly lightheaded but smiling drowsily.

The sergeant returned with water. She could hear the rumbling of the crowd that had formed outside the entrance to the shack. After he had a few sips, Adeline and the sergeant hoisted Heinrich up from the bench and dressed him in the shirt and pants that were too short for his limbs. His new boots rose to cover the inadequacy of his dungarees. A length of rope served as a makeshift belt.

Heinrich trudged down the sloping ramp on his own but draped his weaker arm around Adeline's neck for support. Upon seeing the pair, one of the soldiers shouted, "If it weren't for the Boches and the cooties, it would be a mighty fine world!" Adeline's throat thickened with fear. Heinrich's head bobbed from side to side with fatigue—he had not understood.

The sergeant tried to usher the band of ten or so men into the showers, but they stood rooted in place, staring her down. The loudmouth suddenly bolted, charging straight at them. He punched Heinrich in the stomach, but as he went to knee the German in the groin, Adeline swung her leg and kicked him with her boot-clad foot. The young man doubled over. Beneath the force of his momentum, Adeline's knee crunched, and a bolt of pain shot up her thigh. She crumpled to the ground on all fours as the mob closed in around Heinrich.

Gritting her teeth, Adeline stood on her rickety knee. Sweat beaded on her forehead and her pulse raced with a kind of fury she had never known. She hurled words like bullets. "Stop! Stop! When will it end? When will you stop?" she screamed, battering their backs with her fists. When the searing pain in her knee was too much to bear, she crouched down and shouldered her way between their legs like a dog. Crawling through the dirt, she elbowed away the grubby hands that grabbed her waist and tried to pull her back. Heinrich, on his back, had thrown his arms up to shield his face. Using her good knee, Adeline launched her torso over Heinrich's chest and bloodied head. *Courage, camarade,* " she yelped as the kicking subsided, but the chanting grew louder. A small stone, probably intended for the German, ricocheted off Adeline's temple. Her stomach somersaulted and the world faded to a blackened silence, with only the lingering scent of trampled lavender.

———

"Addie." Sally Dunn's freckled nose and bright smile came into focus. She clapped her hands above Adeline's face. "Addie!"

"How long have I been here?" Adeline strained to ask. She discovered a soft wad of bandages adhered to her temple. The pain beneath felt like the sear of a branding iron. When she tried to sit up, the tent began to spin. Her knee, now propped on a mountain of pillows, throbbed beneath the sheet.

"Only a few hours. It's nearly chow time, not that you'll be partaking this evening." Sally wiped Adeline's mouth, handed her a glass of port and bid her to rinse and spit. The alcohol stung her cut lip, swollen to the size of a marble. She knew she must look a terrible fright.

Tears streamed down her cheeks as she remembered the taunting, twisted faces of the soldiers. "Where is . . . where is the German?" she rasped, fearing the worst.

Sally lowered her voice. "Back in the ward. He suffered a concussion, like you, and some bruised ribs, but he'll recover in time."

"And our assailants? Who stopped them? Will they be punished?"

"Sergeant Constas called for reinforcements and the orderlies broke it up."

"No officers? No surgeons or nurses saw what happened?"

"I'm afraid not. We were all in surgery." She paused as one of the newly arrived nurses entered their quarters.

"How is she doing?" she inquired.

"Just fine. She's come to and is talking coherently, so that's a good sign." Sally patted Adeline's thigh.

The nurse plopped on her cot, removed a boot and began to massage her toes. "Good, because we have a new batch of gassed soldiers on their way from Belleau Wood and we'll need all hands on deck tonight. Sleep while you can, girls."

Adeline closed her eyes, for the fading afternoon sunlight was still too much to bear. "Where are the men who attacked me?" she asked. Her hand reached for her crucifix, but her neck was bare.

Sally sighed. "Most likely eating dinner in the mess tent."

Adeline's eyelids flew open, but the sting of sunlight forced her to shade her face. "But they attacked me, an army nurse!"

"From what I understand, they attacked the German and you fell in their way."

"Yes, but they pelted me with rocks. Does the army not punish men for assaulting one of their own?"

"Not when the nurse is defending a—well, defending the enemy," she replied.

"He isn't one of them—he's a medic. He saved one of our boys."

"Your German is not human to them. He's a Hun, a Boche—and our enemy. Period."

"*Our* enemy? You too, Sally?"

"Listen, I helped you save his arm, but I will not stand by and watch you jeopardize the trust of our fellow army men for some Kraut who patched up German soldiers only so they could continue killing our American boys."

Adeline's face prickled with shame, but the longing to see Heinrich again, to make sure he had recovered, constricted her breathing.

Sally sprang to her feet. "Get some rest. You won't be good to anyone until tomorrow." She collapsed on her own bed and stared at the trio of moths floating near the canvas above them. "He's on the wrong side, Addie, and you simply cannot defend that."

———

Heinrich lay in a fetal curl upon his cot. Pain flared between his ribs with every breath. His ankle was no longer shackled, for he was too dizzy to stand. He had already vomited the contents of his stomach into the piss pot the nurse had placed nearby. His eyes clenched shut, cringing at the mere thought of light and its splintering pain.

Murky images swirled in his memory: Werner in his blue sailor suit and matching army-style peaked cap, running through the green grass. Blanchette's pillowy breasts and sharp hip bones pressed to his chest. *"Courage, camarade."*

CHAPTER 12

June 16, 1918

JUILLY, FRANCE

L uc's lungs burned and the tender flesh of his underarms and groin felt as though it had been seared by a hot iron. "Nurse!" A familiar southern drawl called. "Our boy here is awake and he needs tendin' to."

Luc glanced to his right to see Chuck's big mug gazing over at him from the neighboring cot. A wood contraption elevated his foot as he casually perused a magazine. "Welcome back to the land of the living, my friend."

Luc tried to sit up, but a nurse, reminiscent of a nun in her white gown and veil, hustled over. She gently propped him up on pillows and poured a glass of water. He instinctively sniffed it before taking a sip. The rush of cool liquid soothed his throat and temporarily quelled his cough.

Luc observed his surroundings. They were outside, but sheltered, in some sort of courtyard. Beds were arranged beneath a colonnade around a square lawn covered with wounded men. His stomach clenched as he remembered the sickly yellow mist. "How long have we been here?"

"Long enough for these kind folks to remove the shrapnel from my leg and stitch me up right fine." Chuck chuckled. "Day and a half."

The nurse pulled back Luc's sheet so abruptly a chill rushed over him, reminding him of the cool, dewy grass that had saved him near Bouresches. She efficiently donned gloves, removed the yellow and pink-stained gauze from his suffering crevices and replaced them with freshly dipped bandages. Luc's relief was sublime.

"Thank you," Luc said. She was a plain woman, perhaps his mother's age, but her touch was so kind, he could have wept with gratitude.

"Where you from, Luc? I hail from Alabama myself," Chuck persisted.

"California for me, but I've lived here in France for a few years."

"Huh, you're practically a native. That was a hell of a fight back there, wasn't it? I was as jittery as a long-tail cat in a room full of rocking chairs."

Luc smiled at Chuck's colorful language. "Do you think we can win?"

"The battle or the war?"

"Either."

Chuck was uncharacteristically silent for a moment. "Germans like to hide behind their rifles and machine guns, but if you run at them with a bayonet, they throw their hands up to surrender as soon as they see the glint of cold steel."

"So, you think the Allies have a chance?"

Chuck scratched his whiskers. Just the sound made Luc crave the feel of a sharp, steel razor blade against his cheek. "Nobody wins, my friend." He leaned over and whispered, "Besides, how can we expect to win when some of our own nurses sympathize with the enemy?"

"What?"

"Rumor is our boys here at the hospital got outta hand, attacked a German outside the Cootie Shack. One of our nurses tried to shield him."

"No."

"A surgical nurse," Chuck rambled on, flipping a page. "Even patched up the German when the surgeons refused."

"She should be arrested," Luc groaned, his head throbbing.

"I second that." Chuck stretched his mitts toward the ceiling and released a giant yawn. "I have got me a hankering for some catfish. That's what I miss! Waking up early, wadding up a few balls of stale bread and sitting on the water, all quiet like. Cooking 'em up in a skillet with some butter and a little salt and pepper . . ." He smacked his lips together. "Mmm, mmm! They are slap-yo'-mama good."

Luc's mouth watered just thinking about white fish flesh sizzling in butter.

"What do you miss?" Chuck asked.

"About home?" His mind flashed to Ondine, delicate and almost angelic in her green dress, with blond waves of hair to her shoulders. Would his note reach her father? Had he even survived the last battle?

Luc glanced at Chuck, who still waited for his answer. "Picking and roasting chestnuts. You have to be quick to beat the squirrels."

Adeline's knee ached like the dickens—and had swelled to the size and color of a pink grapefruit overnight—but she would not give Sally or Jenkins or anyone else the satisfaction of seeing her wince in pain. Still, it was hard to hide the wobble in her step.

She walked through the sunny court, past the wide cloisters that ran in front of the children's dormitories—now Wards F and G—and shaded hundreds of gas victims that had filtered in over the last two days. The collège that once had only 250 beds now swelled at the seams as an army hospital, with over two thousand soldiers admitted since June 4 and at least five hundred new gas cases in the last four days.

Adeline supported herself with her hand against the cool, smooth marble of the thick colonnades that supported the roof of the open arcade. As she strolled past the line of beds, she felt the weight of the soldiers' gazes. Beneath their blisters and scabs and open sores, youth still lingered in their curving cheeks and smooth hands. Their participation in the war—their hunting and killing of the enemy—was an abuse perpetrated by their conniving commanders, not a duty they relished. Sorrow swept over Adeline. *What was the point of all this suffering?*

Many of the gas victims existed in a hazy delirium. Others cried, moaned or squirmed in their cots. Some fought for breath, though Adeline had instructed the ward nurses and orderlies to use the herb croup kettle that Heinrich had recommended. All they could do was give the worst cases oxygen and frequently change the wet dressings to relieve the sting of the chemical burns.

Adeline smiled and greeted the boys, shifting her thoughts to their recovery. What harm was there in offering a kind word, a compliment or even a cigarette? Hers could be the last friendly face they ever looked upon. After Shep and Heinrich, and countless other patients she had encountered, she knew these men needed more than just bandages and morphine to heal them. Yet today, instead of returning her greeting, some folded their arms and diverted their gazes; others even scowled. The news had filtered out. They thought her a sympathizer. *Was she to be shamed now?*

Though she felt the urge to flee the arcade, she stopped in her tracks when she spied a long, lean boy lying on his side. Sweat matted his midnight hair to his forehead. The cut of his jaw beneath his strong beard traced a cold finger down Adeline's spine. She wedged herself between the cots and leaned over him to listen. His breath was shallow, but even. His pulse beneath her fingertips was normal. A string of blisters wound like freshwater pearls around his neck, but the upturned side of his face was unmarred, save for a few thin scratches. Her hand trembled with anticipation as she wrapped her hand around his. She would know those fingers anywhere. They were hers, just longer and larger.

"Luc? *C'est toi?*" she whispered.

327

The lashes peeled back to expose the dark chocolate irises. He squinted, then gripped her wrist. "Addie?" he croaked.

"Yes, yes! It's me." She squatted down. "What happened?"

"I thought you were in Royat!"

"For less than a month. They transferred me here with one of the surgical teams."

"And Matthew?"

"He's closer to the front lines. I haven't received any word yet."

Luc tried to sit up, but Adeline halted him. "You look well," she fibbed, as she returned to the foot of his bed to read his chart. No signs of breathing difficulty. Apparently, the gas had not reached his lungs, and he must have stripped immediately after the attack, for he had blisters only on his exposed skin and near his sweat glands, which was the most common spot.

He corners of his mouth curled. "That's a barefaced lie."

The coughing and shrieking from the other patients in the cloister mounted a crescendo. Adeline returned to the head of his cot and crouched down to continue their conversation.

"How long have you been here?" she asked.

"Couple days."

"And I'm just finding out now?"

"I didn't know you were here," he reminded her. Shaking his dog tags, he added, "And since we don't share a last name, how would anyone guess we were related?"

Sally soon appeared. "Whom do we have here?" she inquired brightly.

"My brother!" Adeline answered with delight. "Luc Lemieux, meet Nurse Sally Dunn."

"I see the resemblance," Sally replied, extending her hand to Luc. Winking, she joked, "The other nurses will be relieved to hear you're siblings and not sweethearts.

"I am afraid you have me at an extreme disadvantage, Nurse Dunn." Always the flirt, Luc ignored Adeline's protests and sat up.

"Not at all. We'll have you fixed up and heading home within the week." Sally placed a hand on her shoulder. "They need us in surgery now, Addie. O.R. one."

"Of course. I'll be back as soon as I can, Luc."

"I'm not going anywhere."

"Good, because you owe me a story."

The light in his face dimmed. As Adeline turned to go, he blurted, "Any news from Belleau Wood?"

"Last I heard, we're still holding the lower portion of the wood," she replied, her mind flipping back to her last moments with Shep. Her throat thickened with a mixture of melancholy and gratitude. Thank God Luc was not the one lying under that big oak in the graveyard.

—————

Adeline assisted in another amputation and consulted with her fellow nurses on several respiratory cases that had cropped up and were unrelated to gas. The symptoms—fever, aches and fatigue—clearly indicated influenza, an illness that had been present in pockets among the troops since April. The men were quarantined to stem the spread of the disease.

After washing her hands with soap and water and donning a fresh apron, Adeline stepped out into the balmy June air scented with sweet lilac. She hobbled up to a large, blooming bush and tilted her nose to inhale its glorious, flowery aroma. How she wished she could bring Heinrich out for a walk, but he was recuperating and she, of course, was forbidden to go near him. She clipped off three blooms with her pocket shears.

She returned to Luc and cheerfully slid the vase of flowers on the floor at his bedside.

He brushed her arm away. "How could you?" he seethed.

"I'm only paid thirty dollars a month and hothouses are hard to come by here," she joked unsuccessfully.

Luc's expression hardened. Adeline's pulse raced. *He knew.*

"The Germans are bombing our hospitals. They mutilated my friends—pigeon handlers, not warriors—at Belleau Wood. And you have the nerve to save one of them?"

"You must not listen to gossip, Luc."

"Is it gossip?" Luc shot back. "Or is it truth?" He started to hack uncontrollably. Adeline poured more water and offered it to her brother. She slid her arm beneath him and sat him up. His gown was damp with perspiration. He sipped until the cough subsided.

"I simply upheld my oath and did what any decent nurse would do for a wounded man."

Luc watched her intently. "I have no desire to involve myself in your personal affairs, Adeline." Her cheeks flamed under his scrutiny, despite her best effort to remain composed. "But I am your brother and your only blood relation here. I'm certain I speak for Matthew and Marie when I say you must protect your reputation. You are in a position of trust here—you cannot be seen consorting with the enemy."

330

She could not deny the strength of his argument. Did the soldiers who flashed her those withering looks now fear her? Despise her? "I was not consorting; I was caring for him, nursing him back to health." Adeline struggled to explain. "He is not the enemy. He's a German medic who saved one of our allies on the battlefield. That's what the stretcher-bearer told me."

Luc said quietly, "He *is* the enemy, Addie, and you are a fool."

She tried to pull away, but his fingers dug into her arm. The older sister in her wanted to slap him, but the nurse in her was relieved his strength had returned. Exasperated, she fired back, "Not everything is black and white, Luc. Not everyone is *all* good or *all* evil."

"Listen to what you're saying, Addie!" She recoiled but he tugged harder, his eyes wild with rage. "This is not kindergarten and you are not a simpleton. Look around you! Bed after bed, men maimed and gassed by that Kraut's countrymen! Have you no heart? Are you not a patriot? He *is* the enemy and any relationship with him is not only improper, it's treason!"

"*Treason?*" she practically shrieked. The soldiers' gazes darted in their direction and held fast. Amazingly, upon sensing a little drama, they had perked right up. Adeline lowered her voice. "I was his nurse."

"And you became his friend?"

"Perhaps, but only because he was too weak to defend himself from the soldiers who kicked and beat him."

"I heard what happened," he said with disgust. "You threw yourself on top of the German to stop the men from hurting him. That's not exactly ladylike or befitting of your station here, is it?" he snarled.

"This may be a regimental aid station, but it's just another kind of war. We operate for sixteen hours straight, on some boys who are barely old enough to shave. I've had to tell a boy of eighteen that we amputated his leg! I've buried a young man and then written to his parents with hollow words of comfort! Day in and day out, we have to clean up after this butchery, and you have the nerve to call me a *traitor*?" Shaking with rage, she wrenched her arm from his grasp. "I took an oath, and I will honor it, whether it requires me to care for a fellow American, a German or a damn extraterrestrial!"

Sally appeared from nowhere and with a feathery touch steered Adeline away from Luc's bedside. Adeline clenched her fists. She had made a spectacle. Had everyone in the ward witnessed it?

"They do not pay us to scream at the patients, dear, even if they happen to be our annoying little brothers."

"Half brother," Adeline clarified.

"Regardless, you need to calm down." Sally steered her back to their shared tent and poured a shallow cup of whiskey out of the flask she kept hidden beneath her cot. "Toss it back."

The warm, soothing sensation of the alcohol flowed from Adeline's mouth to her toes. Her strained muscles loosened within a matter of minutes. Sally returned with a cool washcloth for her face.

"I'm sorry. I have never had such a heated discussion with my brother."

"Half brother. And discussion? That was more like a brawl, but without the fists."

Adeline buried her face in her hands. "Was it that bad? Do you think I'll be reprimanded?"

"Most likely, but that's not what concerns me." Sally knelt and gathered Adeline's hands in hers.

"I was just trying to be decent, Sally. What should I have done? Watched them kick him—stone him?"

"You should have run for help."

Adeline's chin dropped. She stared at Sally's white apron, streaked with the blood of Americans. Her defense of Heinrich had revealed too much about her feelings for him. She had not been honest with herself, when everyone else could see what she tried to deny.

Sally, however, put words to it. "You do not love him, Addie. You had a connection with him—you were both tasked with saving lives. Maybe he is the first man you have ever felt for—or physically desired—and that can be intoxicating, but you don't love him. You will find an American or a suave Frenchman to sweep you off your feet. Let him go and get on with your job. There's a war, and there's no time for sentimentality, understand?"

———

Heinrich couldn't recall what day it was. Through the slit in the rail-car door, he had observed sunlight, then darkness, then sunlight again, but the dull ache around his skull and the fog in his mind prevented him from ascertaining the date or time.

The train stopped and the doors squealed open, revealing a wall of field gray on the platform—German soldiers with shaved heads, shackled and stripped of their helmets and weaponry.

French citizens surrounded them, spitting, hurling rocks and flinging insults. There was a savagery in their eyes that Heinrich had not seen before, even on the battlefield. Blue-uniformed Frenchmen prodded the prisoners into the cars with sharp, shiny bayonets and rifle butts. *"À Gièvres, cochons!"*

They were packed like vegetables in a tin. Heinrich was pressed into a black corner of the car, far from the cool, clean stream of air that had flowed through the slit in the door on the first leg of his journey. The air was thick with the smell of urine and feces, causing him to gag. Beads of sweat trickled down his forehead. Panic seized his throat, strangling his breath.

Heinrich slid his hand into his pocket and squeezed the soft, balled handkerchief he had saved from the Frenchman, a reminder of a life saved. He closed his eyes and retreated deep inside himself.

Over and over, her words sounded in his head: *Courage, camarade.*

CHAPTER 13

June 22, 1918

Adeline had disappointed Luc, but he was grateful that she had agreed to visit him one last time. Now that the German had been dealt with, their relationship could mend.

"I've been honorably discharged, and I leave for Saint Martin this afternoon," he announced as she approached.

"You have served the army well and helped them win Belleau Wood," she replied flatly.

Was she still angry or just fatigued? "I'm sorry, Addie, but I do care about you," he said.

She scanned the pages of his chart. Adeline's head wound had healed to a scab, but she still faltered on her left knee. The youthful glow had vanished, but she was still a dark beauty. "You may still have some breathing difficulty from time to time, so don't tire yourself; hire locals to help with the August harvest," she suggested.

His breath was shallower than before and he did still feel twinges of extreme pain, but he was lucky to be alive and returning home, he reminded himself. A part of him felt a duty to stay, to help his comrades, but the army disagreed. The searing memory of his fellow pigeoneers, and especially Marty, guillotined without warning, invaded his dreams each night. He awoke trembling, crying, heart racing.

"Luc?"

He mustered a smile. "I hope you'll come to Saint Martin when you have your next leave. My grandmother and your great-uncle Jacques will serve you roasted pigeon and chenin blanc, and you'll sleep until you can sleep no more. I promise we will spoil you." If the family connection did not tempt her, perhaps this morsel would. "Besides, you must meet my new charges."

"Charges?"

"A temporary situation. A motherless pair from Lille who escaped the German work camp by stowing away on a train outside of Paris, and then my wagon in Tours."

Adeline smiled slightly. "They sound resourceful."

He rolled his eyes to the heavens. "You have no idea."

"That would be nice," she capitulated.

He extended his palm. *"Au revoir, ma chère soeur."*

Adeline squeezed his hand. *"À bientôt, Luc."*

Adeline limped the full length of Ward B between the rows of cots and up to the stage edge, which met her at eye level. No sign of Heinrich. Another man rested in his bed, but his feet did not dangle, nor were they shackled. The new tenant was short and stout and snoring.

Her gaze swept across the stage floor, where the boys of the collège must have performed plays and chorales and gloried in their commencement exercises before the army had requisitioned their school and scattered them in homes across the countryside. She scanned the planks of the dusty floor until she spied a small packet tucked between the wall and a leg of the cot.

Adeline hopped up the five stairs to the stage, her left leg suspended slightly. A few cots had been added to the stage, but they were bare of sheets and soldiers. She checked the enormous ward to see if anyone watched her. Through the sea of lame, hacking soldiers, Lieutenant Colonel Jenkins strode the length of the ward toward Adeline. She squatted near the new patient's bed, pretending to lace her boot while slipping the small cloth bag into her apron pocket before he reached her.

"I'm relieved to see you have recovered, Nurse Donnelly."

"Thank you." She made a move to pass him, but he held her arm. "Leave me alone." She had hoped to hurl the words with more force, but she still felt weak and unsteady on her feet and only wished for an escape from his leering, fake manners.

He released her arm and stepped back. As she hobbled toward the stairs and grabbed hold of the cool black iron railing to support her swollen knee, he asked, "Don't you want to know where Leutnant Sommer has gone?"

"No." She would not give him that satisfaction. "I lost my crucifix and thought it might have fallen to the floor when I was last here," she lied.

"Gièvres, Nurse Donnelly. He has been sent to Gièvres, where all the prisoners of war first go when they are well enough to travel. Your brother and I thought it best he be removed."

To think she had tried to reconcile with her brother, and he with her. She would never forgive Luc's betrayal.

"Surprised?" Jenkins clucked.

"But he had a concussion and contusions—or so I'm told."

"He was deemed well enough to travel."

By Jenkins himself, she guessed. "May I see his chart?"

"I'm sure it was transferred with him." *Of course.* The blow to her head had muddled her thinking, undermined her good sense and sapped her of energy.

"When I last examined him and signed off on his transfer, he asked for you by name, first in German, then in French, which the nurse was able to translate for me. He wanted to know if you had recovered. He wanted to thank you before he left. Knowing you would need adequate time to heal, I refused his request," he sneered.

She turned back toward the stairs, struggling to breathe. "Allow me," Jenkins offered, looping his arm around her, just below her breasts. When her elbow jabbed his ribs, he released her.

She fumbled down the stairs and trudged down the length of the ward. Aware of the men and nurses and doctors who observed her now, Adeline clenched her jaw and gulped air, trying to stem the despair that pooled in the corners of her eyes. When she opened the door to the outside, the air rushed in along with the stinging odor of the fires burning uniforms infected with vermin and viruses and bacteria and all manner of human filth.

She scanned the green lawn and impenetrable foliage and headed toward the delousing station. No steam blew from its tin chimney. No line of men awaited its hot showers. Adeline wandered closer, to the spot where she had rushed to cover Heinrich with her body just days ago. Rocks littered the grass, along with a sprinkling of crushed lavender. There was no sign of the crucifix or the chain that had secured it around her neck.

The wind shifted and the soil swirled and suddenly she smelled it all again: balmy perspiration, sharp rust, syrupy-sweet herb. His chest was a hard plank beneath her before the stone smacked her head. Her lungs had compressed beneath his weight. *Beneath his weight?* His large palm pressed against her cheek, his warm breath in her ear, *"Ma Blanchette, ma Blanchette!"*

"Nurse Donnelly?" The callow sergeant approached, ringing his cap between his hands. "Are you well, ma'am?" he asked bashfully, as if he would rather forget the episode.

She edged a step closer. "I've lost some of my memory about that day, sergeant, and I was hoping you could tell me what happened after—after I was hit and lost consciousness." He shuffled uncomfortably. "I heard you called for help and saved us," she encouraged.

"Yes, ma'am. I had trouble breaking through the mob of soldiers, but when I spied the German roll over on top of you, I started screaming for help and the orderlies who had come out to grab a smoke came rushing over."

Adeline trembled. "He rolled on top of *me?*"

"Yes, ma'am. Them soldiers wouldn't stop, ma'am, even when you tried. As soon as that stone hit your head, the German stopped the bleeding with his hand and rolled you over, protecting you from another attack." He reached out, as if to steady her. "Ma'am, you look as pale as a bread roll. Do you want me to get a nurse or doctor?"

She waved away his concern. "How badly was the German injured?" she persisted.

"Bruised ribs, a concussion, a lot of blood, but some of it was yours, ma'am. I hear they shipped him out to a POW camp west of here."

She swooned and the sergeant threaded his arm through hers. "Thank you," she said breathlessly. "Did you happen to find a dark wooden crucifix, about this long, in the dirt, or anywhere near here?"

"No, ma'am. Sorry, ma'am."

When she had regained equilibrium, she walked back to her vacant tent. Mosquitoes danced and flies buzzed and flitted aimlessly in the humid midday air. She opened the small cloth bag that had been attached to the foot rail of Heinrich's cot that she had just retrieved from the floor. The photograph of the woman and young boy was gone, as was Heinrich's rosary. In their place was a letter, folded to fit neatly in the packet, dated back to December. It was from Heinrich's wife. Wrapped around it was Adeline's crucifix and chain.

Adeline scanned the brief letter. The scrawl was hurried, almost frantic. Though she understood very little German, she was able to translate a few key words. Heinrich's wife had left him and given away their son? He had received this six months before he came to Juilly, yet he had never uttered a word.

Had he grasped his wife's meaning, or had he dismissed her words of abandonment as the ranting of a woman at her wit's end? Why had he left this lone letter for Adeline?

Outside her sweltering tent, the church bells tolled for a full minute. Ambulances rolled and clattered to a stop with the distinct clicking sound of brakes. Feet pounded like galloping horse hooves against the dusty pathway beside her tent and the clamor of voices shouting directions began. Adeline closed her eyes and sighed. More wounded. *Would it ever end?*

———

TOURS, FRANCE

After a short stay in Gièvres, where he was subjected to a physical examination and his paperwork was completed, the U.S. Army saw fit to redeploy Heinrich into its massive civilian workforce. When he and twenty other prisoners disembarked from the train at Tours, the American supply garrison, he assumed they would be put to work hauling crates or some such thing. He was wholly unprepared when the sergeant in charge escorted them through a door with a sign that read *Sabotier*.

The pungent smell of freshly milled oak hung in the air. Sawdust covered the expansive workshop floor, reminding Heinrich of his parents' workshop. A scented, summery breeze flowed through two tall windows that opened to the street. Wooden *klompen,* or clogs, were stacked in a herringbone pattern three meters high, carved and fitted for every size foot. Compared to the battlefield, this workshop tucked away in the middle of the American army supply hub was a little corner of heaven.

The master *sabotier,* a cheerful, balding, fit middle-aged man, showed the prisoners how to measure and chop wood into blocks, work the machinery and utilize the finishing tools to fashion clogs. He examined each prisoner's hands before declaring that Heinrich would be the one to wield the *rouanne* to smooth the bumps on the footbed of the *klompen.*

The *sabotier* treated Heinrich fairly, perhaps because of Heinrich's unassuming manner, or his French, or the fact that he towered above the little man. The *sabotier's* instructional encouragement was unnerving after the hatred Heinrich had experienced on the way to Gièvres.

Day after day, Heinrich scraped the *klompen* and watched the wood shavings curl and fall gently onto the table below. The repetition soothed him. Every evening, Heinrich wrote letters, first to Anna, then to Father Gunther at the cathedral, then finally to the only two orphan asylums he knew of in Köln, pleading for their help in locating Werner.

CHAPTER 14

July 1918

Ondine had filled the days since Luc had gone to war with cleaning, feeding and exercising the pigeons, laundering clothes and linens, walking to the market, and assisting with the trimming and fertilizing the ten hectares of vines in preparation for the growing season at Saint Martin, now in full swing. Before twilight, she always meandered through the waist-high vines. The chenin blanc grapes had progressed from flowers to bunches of petite orbs and were now green and packed together in heavy clusters. The vineyard hummed with insects, skylarks and hummingbirds. Ondine was careful to watch where she stepped for fear of disturbing the snakes.

She strolled along, sweeping her outstretched palm over the thick, wide, green leaves of the vines. With a quick glance up the road to town, she spied a single traveler lumbering toward her. His movements were awkward, as if he might be limping or nursing an illness. At the end of the vine row, she squinted, trying to discern his identity. He stopped and waved and then she knew. Relief weakened her knees and she gripped a rough, gnarly vine for support.

She inhaled and exhaled several times until she regained her composure. Then she sprinted into the road and up to meet him. "Luc!" Realizing he would not be home so soon if he had not been injured, she cried, "Are you hurt? What happened?"

"Ondine," he said, breathlessly. Though his presumably new uniform looked as crisp as the day she had left him in Tours, his neck was wrapped in gauze and he gritted his teeth every time his legs moved. She slipped the large bag off his shoulder onto hers and welcomed him home.

He draped an arm over her shoulders. "It's good to be here," he replied.

"You are hurt?"

"I'm recovering," he explained. "I was gassed."

Ondine gaped. "What's that on your neck?"

"A bandage to hide the blisters."

She did not know what to say. Truth was, he looked tired and beaten, but his kind brown eyes still softened when he looked at her. She cracked a smile. "We'll tend to it all, don't you worry," she said with an extra dose of cheer.

———

Luc stayed confined to his room. Ondine had not seen him in two days. Madame tried to coax him down to the dinner table with wine and pastries, but Jacques simply said, "Let him be. A man needs time to adjust when he returns from war." Michel whittled unidentifiable creatures from fallen branches and placed them on Luc's dinner tray with small, square notes of encouragement.

Ondine could bear it no longer. She rapped twice at his bedroom door. He did not answer, so she stole inside.

He glanced at her blankly.

"It's time for your walk."

"I don't take walks."

"You do now."

"I can't go out like this." He motioned to the pink welts on his neck.

"Of course you can. Besides, Jacques needs your help in the vineyard," she fibbed.

Outside, they walked twenty paces before he begged to sit down on a nearby stump. "I'm sorry," he muttered. "I can't." Ondine stood motionless, arms dangling helplessly.

After a few moments of silence, she squatted down and clasped his hands. It was the first time their skin had touched since the night before he left for the front. "Look at me."

He shuddered and began to weep, quietly at first, and then with convulsive catches of breath. She instinctively placed a hand on his knee. She could guess what plagued him. There was no escape for the soul when one experienced such extreme violence. She had tried to banish her memories in the frigid, flowing waters of the Loire, but he had stopped her. After that, she had had no choice but to wade through the mire of rage and despair she carried inside her. She had nearly lost her mind, but they had all urged her on, and now every day held a glimmer of hope—that she might be reunited with her father.

"You must trust me," she said softly. "You know what the Huns did to me."

His red-rimmed, cloudy eyes met hers. "I am so sorry. They are monsters," he whispered, more tears pooling and slipping down his cheeks.

"And yet, I survive."

His gaze held a question.

"And so will you," she insisted. "Do you want to know how I healed?" She did not wait for his reply. What she was about to say, as a woman to a man, was indelicate, perhaps indecent, but necessary. The brutality of three men had made it so. She forged on, for Luc's sake.

"I pictured my insides," she whispered forcefully. "The flesh they violated, the sores and scrapes they inflicted." The back of her hand gently brushed the blisters on his neck. Luc squeezed her fingers, lending her the courage to continue. "And then I breathed deep lungfuls of this country air and imagined those wounds healing. The more I breathed, the more I healed," she rasped.

"You will never forget, Ondine."

She bristled at the truth in his words. *How could she explain?* "No, but every day, since you saved me from drowning, I endure. Some days are easier than others."

He sighed. "I am useless, Ondine."

She cupped her palm around the nape of his neck and pressed her forehead to his. "Not to me." She glanced over at Michel, who knelt at the edge of the vineyard, pretending to inspect the fruit. "Not to us."

NAPA, CALIFORNIA

By mid-July, Napa and neighboring Sonoma were a hive of activity. Sara and Philippe had spent the last month turning the soil between the vines and, most recently, racking, blending and re-barreling the wines in the cellar. Johnny had rejoined them at Eagle's Run but still made the trip every other week up to St. Isidore's in Rutherford to tend to the ten acres of grapes he had cultivated there in anticipation of the harvest. He and his crew were constructing lug boxes in preparation for their first shipment of *Alicante Bouschet* grapes to the Manhattan distribution office at the convent.

Since their return to California in mid-June, Billy Hudson had become a regular caller at Eagle's Run, a development that delighted Pippa but irritated Sara. She knew his disability prevented him from serving in the army, but his mere presence reminded her of Luc and left a bitter taste of jealousy. Her gut clenched and her heart raced every time she imagined Luc fighting the Germans, with their flamethrowers and massive artillery barrages and expert marksmen riddling American flesh with their bullets. She awoke breathless at night, wondering why, all those years ago, God had led her and Luc to safety after her sister died giving birth to him, only to plunge him into war. *What right did Luc, or Billy for that matter, have to survive above others?*

Late one afternoon, Philippe appeared just as Sara and Lydia were scrubbing and rinsing out the last of the barrels. He looked stricken. "Sara," he said gently. She stiffened. She handed the hose to Lydia and walked toward her husband. He rested a large, warm palm on her shoulder. "Luc was gassed at Belleau Wood. He's suffering from some minor respiratory problems and is weak

347

from the ordeal but should make a full recovery," he said in a quivering voice.

Lydia, who had apparently overheard him, rushed to her father and wrapped her arms around his waist, burying her head in his chest. "Don't worry, Papa," she said in her sweet, singsongy voice. "Luc is the strongest boy I know."

Sara squeezed Philippe's arm. Her mind flashed to Luc teetering as he braved his first steps on the path outside, his first day of school at the Las Amigas schoolhouse, how he and Pippa would climb into the boughs of the apple trees and remain quiet as church mice so they wouldn't have to finish their chores. It had been four years since she had seen his beautiful face and dark, dancing eyes, or stood on her toes to embrace him. She gulped down the stinging bile climbing up her throat. "Was he blinded?"

"No, I don't believe so. He doesn't say." He handed her the letter and stroked Lydia's hair. "Your brother is alive, that's the most important thing," he said, as if trying to convince himself.

Sara read Luc's letter, startled by his shaky handwriting. "We must go to him."

Philippe shook his head. "Not yet."

"But this war could go on for months more!"

"We can't risk it, not when we have other children to care for."

Of course, Philippe was right, but what could they do for Luc here—half a world away from their boy?

———

Pippa slipped Marie's invitation into her satchel. The note had been cryptic at best, but Pippa was thrilled to have an excuse to leave Eagle's Run, if only for a Saturday. The fact that Billy had agreed to accompany her made the prospect of traveling into San Francisco even more exciting.

It had not taken much convincing for Maman and Papa to allow Johnny to drive Pippa to the station early that morning. Johnny was always eager to take Papa's motor car for a spin at top speed down the dirt road to the junction.

Maman and Papa were preoccupied and bone weary from preparing for the upcoming harvest and worrying about Luc. When Pippa tiptoed out of the room she shared with Lydia, her sister was still curled up, clutching her two favorite dolls, the bedsheets twined around her long, filly-like legs. At twelve, she was already taller than Pippa and a restless but deep sleeper.

The 6:30 train arrived two minutes late. Standing on the Napa Junction platform, Pippa surveyed her surroundings and frowned. As the train rumbled to a standstill, spitting black smoke, Billy sprinted up the stairs at one end of the platform, clutching a paper bag and an umbrella.

An umbrella? There wasn't a cloud in the sky. He slowed to a walk, winking when he spied her. The compression in her chest eased as he approached, wearing his dark suit, boater and a patriotic red, white and blue bow tie. He looked rather dashing. The few artists she had met in the Bay area were all geniuses, but generally scatterbrained and disheveled in their appearance. Billy, on the other hand, took great care with his toilette.

"You didn't think I'd forgotten, did you?" Her annoyance at his lateness evaporated as he gallantly handed her up the step into the rail car.

"No, but it's so unlike you to be tardy, I thought you might have suffered an accident," she retorted.

As they took their seats on the train, Pippa reveled in her newly claimed independence. Though she felt a pang of guilt for not divulging to Papa and Maman that Billy would be joining her for the day, she knew they would find out soon enough from Marie.

"So, what exactly is the purpose of this clandestine meeting?" Billy opened his bag, pulled out two hot rolls wrapped in paper and handed one to Pippa.

After biting into its soft, buttery insides and thanking him for his thoughtfulness, she explained. "Marie says in her note here that she's inviting some artists—specifically painters and sculptors—to her surgery to discuss how we can help with the war effort."

"Sounds intriguing."

"Marie and her husband, Matthew—who is serving in France now—have run the surgery for years and they see hundreds of patients each month."

"A medical family? Impressive." He unfolded the letter and, as he read, his eyes widened. "What does she suppose we can do?"

Pippa shrugged. "I have no idea, but knowing Tante Marie, it will be an unconventional, herculean endeavor that requires skill and daring."

Billy sat back, closed his eyes and grinned. "I like her already."

The train chugged its way from Napa Junction through Vallejo, Richmond and Oakland and arrived at San Francisco's Market Street station in two hours and thirteen minutes. From her window seat, Pippa admired the leafy vineyards, blooming orchards and undulating mountains of the bayside towns. Every station stop filled her with a renewed sense of possibilities. One day, she promised herself, she would journey far away, like Addie had, where no one knew her background or set her limitations. One day soon.

Marie, Gemma and Rourke met them at the station. After the necessary introductions, Marie shook Billy's hand while scrutinizing his visage. "Is that Tom Dannel's work?" she asked bluntly, her gaze trained on Billy's artificial eye. Confused, Pippa looked to Billy for his reaction.

He chuckled as if he were asked the question every day. "How did you know?"

"Exquisite. I thought so," Marie replied, obviously pleased with her powers of observation. When she stood on her tiptoes for a closer look, Pippa thought she might die right there in front of the Ferry Building. "Dannel is the best ocularist in the city, worth every penny."

Marie loaded them into the back seat of the Cadillac. Pippa mouthed an apology to Billy, but he waved off her concern. "I admire her frankness," he whispered.

"Thank you two for coming out on a Saturday. I think you'll find the trip worthwhile. I have a few more artists meeting us at the new surgery at noon for lunch and a discussion."

"About what?" Pippa asked, pinching the brim of her hat as Marie accelerated and they zoomed up California Street toward Nob Hill.

"All in good time!" Marie shouted from the driver's seat, her words devoured by a rush of wind and the squeal of tires against the asphalt road.

The Donnellys' medical boarding house was larger than the one they'd had before the earthquake, but simpler in style. In 1910, Marie and Matthew had purchased a row of homes adjacent to theirs and constructed a three-story, Mission Revival–style hospital, complete with overhanging eaves, arched doorways and windows, a gabled tile roof and simple stucco walls.

Marie toured Pippa and Billy past the two operating rooms and ten patient rooms, each of which featured six to eight beds and a fireplace or a wood-burning stove. Nurses in crisp white uniforms and pinned hats whipped in and out of the linoleum-tiled wards with an efficiency Pippa admired. She attributed their lack of idleness to her aunt's tireless work ethic and penchant for order.

Pippa had only a vague recollection of the one time she had visited the old surgery to repair her cleft lip when she was young. She remembered Tante Marie's quiet, kind demeanor, the bright lights affixed to the ceiling, and her short-lived fear of the ether mask. When Pippa was twelve, Maman and Marie had shown her a photograph of herself before the surgery. The image of a little blond pixie with a sharp, ghastly slit in her upper lip had shocked her to the bones. There was no arguing she had looked monstrous. What had her birth mother thought of her? Was her cleft lip the result of the sin between her parents?

She would never know, but Marie and Matthew had found a surgeon to sew the two halves of the lip together. The procedure, though it left Pippa self-conscious about her thin scar, gave her a chance to be just like any other girl. Forever grateful, Pippa would do anything to help her aunt.

Glancing around this modern medical boarding house, she could tell Matthew and Marie had spared no expense. With the tasteful, soothing wallpaper, the sturdy iron beds, starched linens, toilets, telephone and its very own laundry, it had earned a reputation as one of the best small hospitals in the city.

The operating rooms reeked of ammonia, and the metal instruments that lined the shelves gleamed like mirrors. They even had their own X-ray tube. Marie smilcd and explained, "A man may have invented these, but it took Marie Curie, a French woman, to figure out how to transport them to the front lines."

"Is that so?" Billy marveled, admiring the splendor of the hallway and its decor, complete with landscape paintings.

"Indeed, Madame Curie has her 'Little Curies,' or mobile units, driving all over the Western Front as we speak." She waved a finger in the air. "And, naturally, she has trained an army of women to use them."

"Incredible," Billy replied, clearly as awestruck by her aunt as the rest of Pippa's family was.

Marie stopped abruptly to check the timepiece attached to her belt with a gold chain. "Gemma and Rourke, our other guests will arrive in an hour. Could you please go downstairs and set the table?" Her bubbly adolescents raced down the carpeted stairway. The promise of lunch seemed a much more alluring enticement than talk of radiology.

"Have you received a letter recently from Addie?" Marie asked as she guided Pippa and Billy down the hallway.

"Addie is my cousin, the one who's a nurse at the front," she explained for Billy's benefit. "I did receive one in June, from the hospital in Juilly. It was quite heartbreaking to hear what they must endure. She sounded tired."

"Did she mention one of her patients? A special case?" Marie asked.

"No."

"Ah, that's why she asked me to relay the details of this letter to you." Marie pulled a piece of ivory paper from the pocket of her surgeon's coat.

"Oh, really?"

"Indeed. Follow me." Marie led them into her office, a snug room off the upstairs hallway with a frosted glass pane door that read *Matthew Donnelly, MD, DO*, and beneath, *Marie Donnelly, MD*. Photos of her children and Matthew lined a shelf behind two dueling desks inlaid with burgundy and gold leather and stacked with patient files, Pippa guessed.

With spectacles teetering from her nose, Marie read a few lines of Addie's letter aloud. When she finished, she looked up expectantly. "What do you think?"

Billy leaned forward. "Interesting. May I read it over?" he asked, his expression contemplative. Marie handed him the letter. Pippa remained silent, flabbergasted at the possibilities of such an innovation.

Billy rubbed his chin thoughtfully. "We'll need a more complete set of instructions. And how will we procure the copper?"

Marie and Pippa exchanged a knowing glance.

"What am I missing?" he asked warily.

"Marie's husband Matthew is Matthew *Donnelly*."

Billy sat back, crossing his arms. "Of the iron Donnellys?"

"Precisely. Their foundry is in the Dogpatch. Matthew's brother Jimmy has connections with all the foundries down there and can find us the cheapest copper."

Billy grinned widely. "Well, then, count me in!" His enthusiasm was the most endearing trait about him.

———

By two o'clock, Marie had served Billy, Pippa and five other painters and sculptors a small luncheon of sandwiches, cakes and bottled Moxie cream sodas, no mean feat for a wartime meal. Many of the artists lived and worked south of Market Street. They all seemed eager to be of assistance, even though the project was daunting.

Marie disappeared from the room with Gemma and Rourke and returned by herself. She closed the door and lowered her voice. "I would like to introduce our guest of honor today, but before I escort him in, I must warn you. His appearance is disquieting, some might even say grotesque. Children fear him; adults are repulsed by him." The room grew silent. Marie continued with gusto. "But this man is a brave soldier who survived an explosion that sent shrapnel flying into his left side. He returned home to us a hero, but one who has been rejected by his community because of his appearance. He has been under my care since his return last month and I'm holding this meeting with his consent. Please, listen to him and open your artists' minds to the opportunity here."

Marie opened the door. "Sir, if you please. Ladies and gentlemen, Rex Gardner."

The patient shuffled in, wearing a burlap hood with slits for eyes. Marie closed the door and nodded in his direction. He lifted the burlap. A sharp intake of breath resounded in Pippa's ears and her heart began to race.

Rex Gardner's body was lean and athletic, but his face was inhuman. Vivid blue irises glistened from atop a gaping hole where his nose and left jaw should have been. What barbarous villains would create a weapon that maimed so viciously? While the others stayed rooted in shock and despair, Billy instantly rose and approached the newcomer.

"Welcome, Mr. Gardner. I'm Billy Hudson. Please, take my seat." Billy motioned to the empty chair. The rest of the artists followed suit, approaching him as they would any other, shaken from their astonishment by Billy's unfailing civility.

After clasping Mr. Gardner's hand in hers, Pippa wanted to weep. His diction was intelligible but slurred, and his features registered no emotion, frozen in this gruesome expression by the enemy's weaponry and the surgeon's blade. Yet, those striking blue eyes twinkled with vitality. Sadness threatened to overwhelm her.

Billy caught Pippa's gaze and, with an imperceptible shake of his head, warned her to keep those sentiments in check. He was right: to shed tears would be unprofessional.

Rex Gardner addressed the group. "Thank you, Dr. Donnelly, for your care and for putting me in touch with these fine people." He sighed deeply. "I know I'm disgusting. My sweetheart finds me repulsive now. I broke off our engagement. It's only fitting that I set her free, you see." He slid a photograph from his shirt pocket and pushed across the table to Billy, who had taken a seat across from him. "This is me before the war."

The cadre of artists leaned in. A tousle of dark hair spilled across Gardner's youthful forehead beneath his army cap and a small smile reached the apples of his beardless, high-boned cheeks. He had been undoubtedly handsome. "The mortar shell exploded, and the fragments of hot iron sliced through my skin and bone, shearing my nose right off." He raised a fist to his mouth and choked up a bit before continuing. "I'm not a monster, and I don't want to look like one. I want to be able to walk down the street without hearing the shrieks of frightened children."

Marie placed a hand on Gardner's shoulder. "Thank you, Rex." She lifted a file in the air for all to see. "Rex is not the only veteran of this great war who suffers. They are coming to us in droves. I invited you all here today to enlist your help. My daughter Adeline, a nurse on the front, has written of what they call the Studio for Portrait Masks in Paris, where sculptor Anna Ladd and her staff design metal masks for these *mutilés*.

"I have written to Mrs. Ladd to request more explicit details on the process, but in the meantime, I think we can figure something out. I suggest we open two similar workshops—one in Napa and one here in the city. We will see patients on the weekends, if you are willing, but keep it hush-hush until we have perfected the process. We will accept referrals only from physicians and surgeons who can attest that the patients' wounds are fully healed before we make the masks."

A thin man with paint clinging to his fingernails asked, "And who will supply us with the materials?"

"I will," Marie responded, "until I can persuade the Red Cross to donate funds."

"What will we charge per mask?"

"That depends on the degree of difficulty, the time it requires and the soldier's ability to pay. We will work out the details, but we need to help these men now. Who is willing?"

———

Pippa had concluded it was best to tell her parents she had to help Mr. Hudson with the store inventory on the weekends. Billy had sworn his parents to secrecy once they agreed to let them see patients in the small barn he used for his workshop. The Copper Chop Shop, as it was dubbed by their first patient, who was missing part of his jaw, was in its first month. Even Tante Marie refused to announce its existence. She wanted to guard the patients' privacy and spread the word through the medical community rather than the general public.

When Pippa arrived Saturday morning at the shop, she announced her arrival with one knock followed by three more raps in quick succession. Billy peered through the crack in the door and then flung it wide. He motioned to their first patient of the day, already seated in the brown leather and metal reclining chair they had purchased from the Napa barbershop for twenty dollars of Marie's money. The single seat, complete with a metal footrest and leather headrest, took up nearly a quarter of the room but gave the modest, cramped space the air of professionalism they desperately needed. White plaster casts of the *mutilés'* faces hung like gargoyles across the back wall.

Pippa introduced herself to the patient. Mr. Wells shook her hand. His chin, left ear and cheek had been torn asunder by hot shrapnel at the battle of the Lys, he confided. While Billy mixed the plaster of Paris, Pippa tacked two photographs of Wells before his injury to the corkboard.

She then draped the patient's shoulders and torso with an old bed sheet Billy's mother had loaned them. "Lean back, please, Mr. Wells."

"You sure are a pretty thing, miss. Do you mind if I ask how you got your scar?"

"You're very observant, sir." Pippa smiled. For the first time, she felt grateful for her scar, if only because it helped her build trust with the patients. "I was born with a cleft lip."

The patient winced. "That must have been rough for a little girl."

"My father used to say it was as if God had nicked my lip with a paring knife." She cranked the chair back. "Close your eyes and rest."

Wells chuckled. "A creative way to explain it to a youngster. When did they repair it?"

"When I was four." She used a brush to carefully apply oil to his mutilated face.

"The surgeon sure did a fine job." He pointed to the cavern that ran along his jawline and engulfed what used to be his chin. "This is the best an army surgeon could do for me! I suppose it was too tall an order."

Pippa replied gently, "We will certainly do our best for you here, Mr. Wells. Keep your eyes closed for me." She rested two squares of tissue paper over his eyelids and smeared Vaseline over his brows to keep the plaster from sticking.

"You have a lamb's touch, my dear," he said with a sigh.

Billy drew near with the bucket of warm plaster and a brush. "You may find the next step a bit unpleasant, Mr. Wells, but just keep your eyes closed and your breathing steady." Billy quickly spread a thin film of plaster over the patient's face, leaving nostril holes for breathing. He topped the first layer with thick dollops of the stuff until it looked like a rich lather.

Thirty minutes later, Billy and Pippa lifted the dried plaster from his face. "Now what?" Wells asked as Pippa sponged the remaining flakes of white from his skin.

Billy ran his fingers along the interior of the freshly made mask. "The inner surface is now a negative replica of your face."

Wells's forehead creased in confusion. Pippa interjected, "From that we will eventually create what we call a 'squeeze' of plasticine—a mask of how your face looks today. Then Billy will use the photographs you gave us to shape his best version of your God-given face."

"No kidding?"

Pippa nodded. The more she pretended to be confident, the more she felt so. "After that, we will mold very thin copper around the plaster and the result is a copper mask that resembles, well, you."

"How long will it take?"

"A couple weeks. Then I will paint it to match your skin."

"We have another patient coming in for a mask fitting right after you. If he agrees, would you like to stay and watch?" Billy suggested.

Wells sat up, and his eyes danced with a smile that didn't reach his mouth. "I'd be most obliged."

⸻

Pippa gingerly presented the mask to Jamie Riley. She had attached a mustache made of human hair to his mask with spirit-gum. As she lifted the mask to Riley's marred face, the effect was stunning—even better than she had envisioned. As Billy held it against the patient's skin, Pippa coiled wires around Riley's ears to attach it.

"Astonishing!" Wells slapped his knee.

"Truly?" Riley cried, his tone charged with hope. "May I see?"

Pippa held up a mirror. "This is only the first step. I still have to paint it to match your skin tone."

A tear slipped down Riley's cheek, disappearing behind the card-thin mask. He raised his open palm and his fingers caressed the sliver of metal that shrouded his face.

"Thank you," he croaked.

As Pippa suspected, the flesh-colored base coat of the mask did not quite match his skin. She moved him to a seat by the window, then grabbed her palette of paints and a stool. This was the most frustrating part for Pippa—blending the color so precisely that it matched a patient's actual skin color at night and during daylight. She mixed sienna with white and shades of pink and dabbed the color on the cheek. Then she moved him outdoors.

Sunlight flooded the tiny garden and picnic table where the soldiers often waited. A wide hedge of aromatic sweet bay hid their disfigurements from the neighbors as they drank coffee and shared war stories. Neither Pippa nor Billy had anticipated how much they craved the camaraderie and delighted in each other's company.

As Pippa rotated around Riley in a semi-circle fashion, concentrating on selecting the right color mix for his new face, she heard the clatter of boot heels on the cobbles leading to the workshop. "Pippa!" a voice hissed.

She whirled around. "Maman? What are you doing here?" Pippa asked, flustered. "Excuse me," she muttered to Riley.

Maman's hand hovered against her open mouth. Pippa raced to her and ushered her down the path into the front yard of the Hudsons' home.

"What is this?" Maman squawked. Pippa thought she might have to call for smelling salts. She had never seen Maman so discombobulated.

"Maman, stop," she pleaded between clenched teeth.

Maman pulled her arm free of Pippa's grasp. "You said you were working extra hours in the store, but all this time you have been . . . lying to us?"

Pippa wanted to die of embarrassment.

In her peripheral view, she saw Billy reassuring the patients. He turned and walked toward them. "Maman, please ..." Her mother was perspiring heavily, clutching the fabric at the waist of her dress, struggling to catch her breath.

"Mrs. Lemieux," Billy called. "Please, allow us to explain."

Pippa grabbed her mother's wrists. "Maman, look at me." Her green eyes were bloodshot, and she was almost panting. "You are unwell."

Maman doubled over. Pippa held her upright until Billy could grab a chair from the workshop.

"Could you get a glass of water?" Pippa asked him. She stroked her mother's hair until he returned a few moments later.

After Maman had finished her water, Pippa touched her cheek. It nearly scorched her hand. "Maman, you're feverish."

———

Papa burst through the kitchen door as Pippa and Maman arrived at Eagle's Run in the Hudsons' carriage. "What on earth? Sara, where have you been?" He looked to Pippa for answers.

"She just showed up at Billy's, spouting nonsense." Pippa stepped down and helped her father lift Sara from the seat.

"What were you doing at Billy's?" He cradled Maman in his arms.

"Working on a secret project. I think we should call the doctor, Papa. She fainted on the way here."

"I'm fine," Sara insisted. "Put me down, I can walk."

"You're burning up," Papa pressed his cheek to Maman's flushed skin. "Pippa, find Aurora."

Tante Aurora returned with Pippa carrying her satchel of potions: eucalyptus oil, various tree barks, homemade teas and honey. She announced that Maman had most likely contracted a mild case of influenza and prescribed rest, soup, tea and quarantine.

The next morning, Pippa found Lydia lingering in the doorway to their parents' bedroom. She gripped a lilac branch. "Lydia, you cannot sit with Maman."

"I brought her these. I'll read to her until she is better." Lydia pointed to a stack of books on the floor and the newspaper she had tucked beneath her arm.

"Dearest, you are sweet, but Papa needs your help in the winery."

"Maman needs me more."

Pippa squeezed her little sister's shoulders.

"Will she die?" Lydia whispered.

Maman slept fitfully, shivering beneath heaps of blankets during the second-warmest month of the year. "No, she should recover within the week," Pippa reassured her.

"When we traveled East, I saw the convent where she lived all those years ago, where Luc was born. The city was loud—and crowded."

"She was young to travel so far away from home."

"She was brave."

Pippa kissed the nest of springy curls on the crown of Lydia's head. "She *is* brave. When you were in her belly, she traveled by scow to San Francisco as it burned. She was determined to find Papa and Luc."

"And she did."

"And you were born on the way home—on the deck of the U.S.S. *Preble!*"

Lydia beamed. "I didn't want to miss all the excitement."

Pippa sat down cross-legged on the floor by Maman's bedroom door. She pulled Lydia down beside her, for she was too long-legged now to sit in her lap. Lydia's navy blue skirt billowed as she sat, sparking Pippa's first memory of Maman, when she had buried her three-year-old face between the folds of her soft, dark skirt.

CHAPTER 15

August–October 1918

VOUVRAY, FRANCE

On Luc's twenty-second birthday, influenza struck Saint Martin. This was more than the three-day fever Luc had seen on the battlefield. Vouvray's old, rheumatic doctor, who had come out of retirement to help the village while its younger doctors and nurses were serving at the front, confirmed that *la grippe* was spreading throughout the Touraine region. Villages like Vouvray had shuttered their markets, town halls and churches. Socializing was forbidden. Masks were mandatory.

After a day of a racking cough and spitting up blood, Luc's honorary uncle and mentor Jacques turned a lurid shade of blue. As Grandmère kept vigil by his bedside, a rosary twined around her fingers, he suffocated in his sleep. His decline was so rapid, Luc did not even have time to say farewell, to tell Jacques what his steady presence and patient instruction had meant to him over the past four years. Nausea curled Luc's insides. *Would the dying ever end?*

The speed and ruthlessness of this new influenza was startling. Luc now feared for Ondine and Michel, who had both taken to bed that morning with chills and a fever.

Though Grandmère had lost her second husband the previous evening, she bottled her grief to prepare hot bone broth for Ondine and Michel and tent their beds with sheets to contain the spread of the sickness. When she called Luc to the kitchen and clutched his shoulders, anguish flickered in her eyes. He had an important duty to fulfill, she explained.

Afraid to use his wagon for fear of contaminating it, Luc choked back tears as he placed Jacques's shrouded body on a blanket and dragged it across the lawn of the estate to the western edge of the vineyard, where the tall oaks had stood sentry over his grandfather and namesake's grave for nearly twenty-three years. Two hours later, with his feet planted two meters below the surface of the earth, Luc finished shoveling the dirt, tree roots, fist-sized stones and curling earthworms to carve out Jacques's final resting place. He paused to lean against the wall of soil and catch his breath. In between sobs, he raised his chin to the clouds above.

No priest had answered Grandmère's call to attend Jacques and administer the customary sacrament of last rites. Jacques had tilled Saint Martin for over half his life, first as Luc's grandfather's cellar man in the years after the best friends fought in the Prussian War together, then as foreman when Maman and Papa had entrusted Saint Martin into his care twenty years ago. Had

Jacques not aided Maman and her pregnant sister, Lydia, Luc's birth mother, to flee France, Sara might have met a tragic fate and Luc's family would have been forever altered. All these years, Jacques had been a quiet source of strength for the children and grandchildren of Luc and Marguerite Thibault, whom he'd loved as if they'd been his own.

Luc lay Jacques's corpse in its grave and piled the soil to the top. He placed an oval ring of stones around the grave, intending to replace them with a proper headstone when one could be made. Jacques was laid to rest next his best friend, Luc Thibault, on August 22, 1918.

Luc burned the blanket he had used to transport Jacques and scrubbed his hands with soap and water at the pump. He retreated to the shed, feeling once again as though God had sucked the wind from his lungs and sapped all hope from his body. He could not bear to face Grandmère yet. Instead, he rummaged around the outbuilding and used old grape crates, a hammer and nails to fashion two signs. He staked one at the entrance to the caves and one at the front door of the house: *Pas de logement. La grippe.* French soldiers had most likely brought the influenza to Saint Martin, and he could not risk more infection, no matter how desperate the men might be for food or lodging.

Grandmère sat near the fire, staring into a cup of coffee. Luc reached for her hand, cradling her warmed, knobby fingers in his. He swallowed hard and answered her silent question. "It is done." Her lips tightened to a thread and her shoulders shuddered with fresh agony.

———

Ondine floated in and out of sleep. Ribbons of cool air streamed through the open window and across her skin, leaving a trail of gooseflesh on her bare arms. A familiar voice penetrated the quiet room, uninterrupted in its soliloquy, steady in its timbre and pace. *"Chaque fleur s'évapore ainsi qu'un encensoir; Le violon frémit comme un coeur qu'on afflige . . ."*

Luc was speaking someone else's words. Her eyes flew open. "What are you reading?"

He sprang to his feet just outside the doorway. "Ondine!" he cried, rushing to her side.

His relief was so palpable, she wondered how long she had been ill. Behind a splitting headache, she observed the dingy book in his hand.

He turned it over to read from its spine. "Baudelaire."

"'The violin quivers like a tormented heart?' More like a tormented ear." She sat up on her elbows. "Have you always read morbid poetry?" she teased.

"No, but it was all I could find. My grandfather's, I think, from last century." His tender expression set Ondine's heart thrumming. Adrenaline coursed through her veins and her mind reeled. She craned her neck, searching the room and finding only an empty bed where her brother once lay. She panicked. "Where's Michel?"

"Grandmère insisted he take a bath as soon as his fever broke."

She collapsed back onto the pillow and exhaled loudly, her breath catching. "He will live?"

"Yes, and so will you." She detected some hesitation, or a thought that had not yet reached his lips.

"What is it? Tell me," she urged.

"Jacques. He passed away three days ago."

"Oh." Her face crumbled. "I remember now. I am so sorry, Luc."

Luc replied hoarsely, "He was the best of men." Ondine ached for Madame Chevreau. She knew how excruciating the abrupt, senseless loss of a loved one could be.

"I dreamt of Père while I was sick," she confided.

"You miss him."

"He's all we have."

"Ondine, I didn't tell you this because I didn't want to raise your hopes. When I was near Belleau Wood, I learned that your father was still alive and fighting nearby. I sent word to him, about you and Michel, through the Tenth Colonial messenger, but I don't know if he ever received it."

She gulped. "Or if he survived?"

"There were many battles after that day, many French and American lives lost." He swept a loose strand of hair from her face. "Don't give up hope. Know that I'll care for you and Michel if . . . if . . ."

Luc's kindness was a balm for her weary soul, and yet her words batted away his trite assurances with unintentional force. "My father will return, Luc." She could not bear to think of the alternative.

———

NAPA, CALIFORNIA

When the harvest began in mid-September, grape growers spoke in hushed tones of shipping their grapes east in 1919, but this

369

season the demand for wine soared sky-high, along with prices, in anticipation of the prohibition. Sara and Philippe were determined to take advantage of this boom and relieved they had decided not to replant their grapes with other crops before the 1918 harvest.

Grape quality was good, as expected following a cool month with plenty of rain. Pickers, wary of the influenza but enticed by the high wages, tied on masks and wielded their secateurs on bended knee deep into the night, trying to bring the grapes in early.

Sara's recovery from her bout with the sickness in July had been slow but steady. Nearly two months later, she had regained her stamina and worked shoulder to shoulder with Aurora, Philippe, Lydia, Pippa, Johnny and the laborers to slice the chardonnay grape clusters from the vines and drop them gently into her basket.

"Maman," Lydia whined, bending and stretching her fingers in dramatic fashion. "May I please go to bed?"

"You're going to have to buck up and endure some discomfort if you're going to be a successful *vigneron,* my love." Sara's passion for picking grapes had started when she was ten, learning how to measure the sugars and pick the fruit. Her small, lithe hands had been a blessing then. She feared Lydia had not acquired any particular interests yet but flitted like a butterfly from one brilliantly colored flower to another.

"What if I want to be an actress instead?" Lydia ventured.

Sara's mouth twisted disapprovingly. "We'll ask your father when the time comes. Now, scoot. Take some bread and cheese from the larder if you're hungry but wash your hands with soap first!"

Lydia drooped with fatigue as she neared the water pump.

Aurora glanced at Sara. "Don't let your worries swarm like bees."

"You think I was too harsh?" Sara asked, wiping her brow with her sleeve.

"No, but don't let your worries block out the ray of sunshine that girl is. Just because Lydia possesses a lightness of spirit, that doesn't mean she is a flibbertigibbet."

Sara's laugh was muffled behind her mask. "No?"

"All I'm saying is that Luc and Johnny seem to have a knack for the family business, but perhaps Lydia does not."

"I only ask that she take some sort of interest in the business. After all, Philippe and I have built it for them."

Aurora released an exasperated sigh. "Perhaps Lydia will seek another sort of treasure."

———

When Sara traipsed upstairs in the early morning hours, Lydia tossed in her bed, groaning and complaining of a deep ache in her limbs. Her thin body shivered, and her teeth chattered beneath two layers of quilts. Sara immediately instructed Pippa to sleep on the settee downstairs. Sara claimed a spot on the pine floor, atop a nest of pillows and blankets, to be as close as possible to Lydia's bedside. She did not want to disturb Philippe; he had just crept into bed after a grueling day of picking.

A cloth dipped in icy water cooled Lydia's hot forehead, but before long she erupted in a coughing jag. When frothy blood rose from her throat and leaked from her petite nostrils, Sara propped up Lydia's head and torso on a mountain of pillows to try to ease her breathing. She wiped her face clean with the cool cloth. Lydia quieted, and before drifting off to sleep, she murmured, "Thank you, Maman." Her tender tone dissolved Sara's heart.

She sank to the floor and pulled her knees to her chest. *What else should she do for her daughter?* The post had delivered a letter from Marie yesterday, but it offered little advice on treating the symptoms. Marie and Rourke had just recovered from influenza, but Gemma was still sick, now battling pneumonia. Even Marie, an accomplished physician and surgeon, felt powerless to help her own children in the throes of this disease.

The city of San Francisco and the entire county of Napa were paralyzed with illness, and fresh air seemed to be the only deterrent to the spread of the disease. Church services and even court hearings were moved out of doors, into the open fall air of the city's parks. Remembering this, Sara opened the windows a few inches, hoping the cool air would ease Lydia's breathing. Once that task was completed, there was nothing left to do except pray. After losing count of how many rosaries she had uttered, Sara slipped into sleep.

She awoke with a lurch, startled by a shift in the room. Hazy sunlight sundered the darkness, and dust motes spiraled like tiny resurrected souls in its path. She sat up and, in that first moment, hardly recognized her child. Small mahogany bruises spotted Lydia's cheekbones like muddy boot prints across a snowy yard. Her purple lips gaped as she rasped. Sara scrambled to the kitchen to find the jar of eucalyptus salve and returned to slather

Aurora's potion all over Lydia's chest. As her fingers slid across her daughter's gossamer flesh and shuddering ribs, terror pierced Sara.

Philippe hovered in the doorway, rubbing his eyes. *"La grippe?"* he asked, his face also half shielded by a handkerchief. Sara shook her head. This was not the ordinary grippe. She sat as poised as a statue, if only to conceal her rioting emotions.

Sara had uttered hundreds of Hail Marys and Our Fathers and kissed the cold metal of her rosary crucifix, begging the Lord to take her life instead. Hollow, idle prayers. Sara knew. She felt it in the marrow of her bones, as only a mother could.

Lydia had been born while San Francisco's great fire raged. Sara had believed this child could and would survive anything. In those first dreamlike moments of her daughter's life, after Marie had cleaned and swaddled her, Lydia had tipped back her tiny head to gaze wondrously at Sara's face. When she had first gurgled with laughter, when she had scraped her knees, Sara had been by her side. A daughter's fears and delights are a mother's trials and triumphs. Despite all these indelible impressions on a mother's heart, one never knew when God might snatch a child away—on the battlefield or as she slept.

Philippe knelt to cradle Lydia's hand, rubbing his thumb in soothing circles across her chalky skin. Sara choked back a sob when she spied the sickly bluish tinge that now capped Lydia's fingertips. Her lashes fluttered, a crescent of feathers. Philippe gently jiggled her shoulder, encouraging her to rally. "Lydia! That's it, my darling girl, open your eyes," he coaxed.

Sara remained silent. She did not have the heart to stop him. Instead, she slid her body beneath Lydia's, gathering her daughter into her arms, cradling her head against the soft curve of her chest. Lydia had always been tall for her age, but her lankiness was now a bittersweet reminder of how close she was to becoming a woman—of the future this illness would steal from all of them.

Sara crooked her head to kiss Lydia's perspiring temple. She pressed a hand to Lydia's scalding forehead. Her little girl's chest heaved. As she struggled, Lydia's gaze widened with fright. Sara steeled herself, palming her daughter's forehead. Now was not the time for the hysterical sob rising in Sara's throat.

She shifted her body to face her daughter and held Lydia's sweet face between her hands. They locked eyes. "Gentle, small breaths, darling, there you go." Lydia stared back at her mother, searching for the truth, panting with desperation.

Sara pressed her wet cheek against Lydia's. She wanted to crawl inside her child and rip the disease from the recesses of her thin, ravaged body.

Philippe sputtered, "We love you so much, Lydia. Please don't leave us." He squeezed and kissed Lydia's cyanotic hands as she drifted in and out of consciousness, chest rattling as she labored for each breath.

Sara's competing emotions circled like two lions in a cage. *Should she help her daughter die or insist she fight?*

Sara recalled how compliant Lydia had been as a child. As a toddler, she would not eat without permission. She would not even nap without her Maman's say-so. Sara whispered, "Do not be afraid, Lydie. Do not be afraid to go with the angels when they come for you, my love." Philippe shuddered and bowed his forehead to Lydia's chest. He broke into violent sobs.

374

Lydia nestled into the cocoon of her mother's arms until her last exhalation. Sara had learned long ago, through the death of her infant daughter, that the greatest blessing God bestowed on a mother was the power to comfort her child, to hold her hand, to guide her—even in death.

Maman's muffled grief seeped out beneath her bedroom door and into the hallway, clinging to the walls of the house. Papa had just peeled her away from Lydia's body, parting her from her youngest—her only once-living, once-breathing blood daughter.

He lingered outside the room Pippa had shared with Lydia and inhaled loudly. He turned the knob and creaked the door open. Pippa's heart thudded as she looked past his shoulder to Lydia's empty bed, beneath the gaping window dressed in yellow calico, as if sunshine itself had once slept there, leaving a rumple of quilts, a dimpled feather pillow and a jumble of cloth dolls strewn helter-skelter near the footboard. Papa's tormented expression made Pippa fear for his sanity.

"Go to Maman," Pippa insisted. "I'll sit with Lydia downstairs."

Pippa entered the kitchen, cut a fresh piece of cheesecloth and wrapped it around her nose and mouth. She sat in silence beside Lydia, rolling a glass rosary bead between her thumb and forefinger. The repetition allowed her to sit calmly while her insides twisted, rebelling against the sheer horror of her sister's lifeless, empty husk.

When she felt the weight of warm hands alight on her shoulders, Pippa glanced up. Johnny had not yet returned from Aurora's. The room was empty, save for an invisible, benevolent presence of some sort. A sensation of intense bliss surrounded and then penetrated Pippa to her core, lifting the weight of her despair and enveloping her in unspeakable joy. She did not want to fight it—she could not fight it—so she closed her eyes and allowed the peace to drift through her like a slow-moving cloud.

Minutes later, the kitchen door swung open and a warm breeze, scented with grape pulp, swept through the house. Johnny charged into the parlor and the presence withdrew.

"Pippa." Johnny bent over, clinging to the doorjamb. He was pea-green and huffing as if he'd sprinted a mile.

"What is it? Are you ill?" Terror shot down her spine. Would she lose Johnny, too?

He tamped at the overflow of tears with the heel of his hand. "Tante Aurora."

"Oh no," Pippa exclaimed. Johnny, unable to steal even a look at Lydia's body lying there, knelt beside Pippa.

"Yes," he squeaked. Pippa hugged her younger brother, halfway between a boy and a man. Their parents appeared as if summoned. They must have heard the door or felt the air surge through the house.

How much sorrow could one family endure in a day? "Maman, Papa. Johnny has just come from Aurora's." She strained to speak the words that would shatter her parents all over again. "Aurora . . . she . . . she is with Lydie now."

———

Pippa could not bear to sit idle while Maman and Papa fretted over what to do. The morticians and gravediggers were ill themselves, and they were still searching for caskets to give Lydia and Aurora a dignified burial. Pippa could not even fathom the thought of her sister sleeping below ground.

She lifted her pad and pencils from her satchel and began to sketch. With long, short, thick and thin strokes of her pencil, she brought Lydia back to life on the page. Pippa knelt beside her sister's body and studied the length of her nose and the curve of her earlobes. The peachy hue of Lydia's skin, the ebullience of her smile and the glint in her dark eyes Pippa would have to recall from memory.

"Pippa!" Johnny hissed from the hallway. "What are you doing?"

"I'm creating a series of portraits," she replied calmly, alternately observing the curve of Lydia's cheek and then recreating it on the page.

Johnny stepped closer. "Now?" he demanded, in an uncharacteristically shrill voice.

A fist of grief punched her gut. "I know it may seem strange, but I believe I can help Maman and Papa."

"Strange? That's the creepiest thing I've ever heard." Johnny was nearly hysterical.

Pippa certainly doubted her own sanity at that moment. "Listen, I just want to make a set of drawings. I thought that if I could show Lydia in different poses, with different emotions and then add color and dimension, it would help Maman and Papa remember her as she was in life."

Johnny gawped in disgust, shredding Pippa's composure. "I'm so afraid I'll forget her laugh, her voice, her smile, Johnny. Where will they go? I can't just let her go!" Her tears fell, blurring the lead marks.

He squeezed her shoulders. "Pippa," he half choked out the words, "what if the best thing is for them to forget? For all of us to eventually forget?"

"How can you say such a thing?"

"I didn't mean forget Lydia. I meant remember her life but forget her death."

Pippa clung to her conviction. She knew what it was like to lose someone you loved and to not have any physical token of their beauty—or their spirit. This was her way of trying to honor Lydia, as backward as it might seem to her brother.

Pippa murmured, "Listen, Johnny. Close your eyes and listen. She's here, watching us. Can't you feel her, Johnny?"

The front door smashed open and the wind blew, rattling the kitchen crockery and fanning the gold threads of Pippa's hair across her face. When the gust settled, the same sensation of unfettered joy Pippa had felt earlier surrounded the siblings. Johnny lifted his head, a look of astonishment spreading across his features. *Lydia.*

———

JUILLY, FRANCE

By Friday, September 20, Adeline had worked sixteen-hour shifts seven days a week for fourteen of the weeks since her arrival at the hospital in Juilly. The only week she had been excused from duty

378

was when she had fallen ill with influenza in August and remained in bed for six days. The wounded—victims of gunshots, shrapnel, high-explosive shock, mustard gas and bayonet wounds—had flowed through their operating rooms at such an alarming pace in the last month that Adeline wondered if she would ever sleep uninterrupted again.

The news spread around the operating table as the nurses and surgeons locked shoulders around a neurological patient with a piece of artillery shrapnel lodged in his skull. Base Hospital No. 30 was ordering Surgical Team No. 50 to take three weeks of rest and relaxation in Paris before returning to Royat. They would depart via train on Monday morning.

Adeline had other plans. After her shift, she marched into Major Weeks's office. "Sir, my family has encountered some hardships. My great-uncle died last month of the influenza, and my brother was gassed at Bouresches and has returned to the family farm in the Loire. It's nearly harvest time. I would like to request to spend my furlough with them."

Weeks gave his permission and promised to arrange the necessary paperwork if Adeline provided him with her address in Vouvray and a few bottles of *vin blanc* when she returned. She thanked him, hesitating only slightly before asking, "Has there been any word regarding the location of Surgical Team Number Fifty-one?"

"Matthew Donnelly's outfit? He's your father, yes?"

"Stepfather," she blurted. *Now why would she bother to make that distinction?* "I'd like to send any news to our family back home."

Weeks scratched his head, then shuffled through a stack of papers. "I did see something." Upon finding the document in question, he peered over his spectacles and replied, "The Fifty-first arrived at the evacuation hospital in Toul, near Nancy, on September tenth. We shan't see them for a while—they're supporting the St. Mihiel offensive."

"Thank you, sir." She would update Maman at once.

She turned to leave, but Weeks tented his fingers and cleared his throat. "You have performed your duties and served your country well, Nurse Donnelly, despite any previous missteps you may have made with the German prisoner. I assume you don't have any contact with him now?"

"Of course not, sir!" she answered with feigned indignation. In July, Adeline had sneaked into the records office at Juilly hunting for information on Leutnant Heinrich Sommer's whereabouts, but had turned up nothing useful, save for confirmation that he had been transported by train to the prisoner-of-war camp at Gièvres on June 17. They had probably moved him to a work camp soon after. She wondered if Heinrich had ever heard from his wife or child again.

"Good," Weeks said, interrupting her train of thought. "Then go visit your family and rest up. God knows we've all earned it."

———

Adeline's first full day at Saint Martin was a whirlwind of activity and conversation that somehow proved more tiring than her last sixteen hours of surgery. To her surprise, Luc had gushed with relief upon her arrival. Madame Chevreau had embraced her as she might a long-lost daughter, and their wards, Ondine and Michel, crowded around her, eager to hear of her war work. Although Adeline still had a bone to pick with Luc over his role in Heinrich's premature transfer, she was willing to overlook it for now and cherish her time with family and the joy that came with leading a normal life, if only for a few weeks.

Over a lunch of roasted pigeon, chèvre and ripe blackberries that exploded with sweetness in her mouth and reminded her of the cherries she had shared with Heinrich, Adeline collected all the news. "Have you been into town lately? Have you seen Pip and Mim?" she asked, sipping the prior year's vintage of chenin blanc, so crisp and tangy on her tongue. She had not realized how the foul and rusty smells of the operating room had dulled her sense of taste until she had returned to the clean country air.

"I haven't seen them since New Year's Eve. When I returned from Juilly, the tavern was closed because of the influenza. I did write to tell them of Jacques, and they sent their condolences, along with promises to visit when the influenza had passed."

Adeline could only pray that her mother's parents had lived through the epidemic themselves. "I am so sorry for your loss. This flu is killing more of our men than the war itself, I am afraid."

Madame placed a tray of small tarts on the table and patted Michel's shoulders. "We were lucky that Michel and Ondine survived it."

Ondine, a bright but cautious girl with spun-gold hair nearly the same shade as Pippa's, watched Adeline intently, her blue eyes blazing. "Did you operate on any French soldiers, *mademoiselle*?"

"Their father, Capitaine Pierre Marchand, was stationed in the Château-Thierry sector with the French Tenth Colonial at the same time I was," Luc explained. He still had a trail of red scars on his neck from the gas blisters. He also became easily winded when gesturing or walking, but otherwise he seemed to be recovering from the scourge of the mustard gas.

She turned to Ondine. "No, I'm sorry. I don't believe I did. Have you had any word?" she asked hopefully.

Ondine rose and began to stack and clear the crockery. "No, not yet." Luc's dark eyes tracked her across the room. Her movements were quick and quiet, deliberate but never disruptive. Adeline could not discern if Luc's mien was one of worry or longing, but a cord of understanding certainly stretched between them.

Gravel crunched on the driveway outside. Madame stared out the window. Her brow puckered with disapproval. "A friend of yours, Luc?" she inquired.

Through the glass-paned aperture, Adeline saw only a flash of blond curls beneath an army-issued cap. Luc sprang to his feet. "Oh, it's one of the Hello Girls. Virginia is her name." He swerved and headed out the front door.

Too curious to resist, Adeline hovered in the foyer, peeking out the half-open door as Luc approached the jeep to greet Virginia with a peck on each cheek. Even in an army-issued Signal Corps uniform, she had the gams of a dancer, the scarlet pout of a geisha and the chest of a pinup girl. *Where was her mask? Didn't she know there was an epidemic afoot?*

"She's one of the signal operators in Tours. His girlfriend before he left for the front," Ondine whispered, violently wringing a dishtowel between her hands.

Adeline was startled by her frankness. "And now?"

382

Ondine shrugged. "I don't know."

There was something about Ondine's honesty and stark beauty that immediately won Adeline over. "I'm about to find out." She swung open the door, strolled up to her brother and exclaimed, "Virginia! So nice to meet you. I'm Luc's sister, Adeline."

With one glance at her younger brother, who cleared his throat and pawed the nape of his neck under her scrutiny, Adeline surmised the exact nature of their liaison. She casually eyed Virginia's midsection. *Thank goodness!* She didn't appear to be with child. Then again, she looked far too worldly to make such an error.

"Enchantée," Virginia replied in flawless French, puffing on a cigarette, then tilting her head to release a plume of smoke. "You're an army nurse?"

Adeline confirmed she was. Virginia explained that she had heard Luc was back from the war, so she decided to visit on her day off. "They could use a set of spare hands at the S.O.S. in Tours," she said to Adeline. "Our poor boys are dropping like flies—and the prisoners, too."

"Adeline has just spent over three months in surgery. She's earned her rest," Luc countered with a gentle smile.

"Why of course she has!" Virginia trilled, resting her hand on Luc's arm as if laying claim to him. Adeline wanted to ask Virginia about the prisoners but changed her mind. She did not want to stir Luc's suspicions.

Virginia rambled on. "I'll leave you two to catch up, but before I go, may I buy a case of your *vin blanc*? The girls and I have missed it so!"

383

"Consider it a gift!" Luc exclaimed, enthusiastically leading Virginia toward the caves. Adeline crossed her arms and rooted herself in place until they returned, nearly fifteen minutes later. His cheeks flushed red and he wore a smudge of lipstick on his collar. Adeline glanced back at the house but saw no sign of Ondine, thankfully.

When the half siblings had wished a hearty *"Adieu"* to Virginia and watched her jeep diminish to a speck on the road, Adeline linked arms with Luc and leaned in. "What are you doing?"

"What do you mean?"

The sly devil. Did he really think, after he meddled in her personal affairs, that she would stay silent about his? "What is Virginia to you?"

He drilled the toe of his boot into the pebbles. "Just a flirtation, is all."

"Be careful. You don't want a flirtation to turn into entrapment—especially if you don't love her."

Luc stepped back as if wounded. "It's not like that between us."

Adeline's tone lightened. "Well, there is flirtation and then there is *devotion*. The first is always obvious to men, the other usually isn't."

"What are you saying?"

She glanced toward the kitchen, where her aunt and Ondine huddled over the sink, their faces visible through the recently opened window. "Learn to recognize the difference, little brother."

———

After two days of rest and eating her fill at Saint Martin, Adeline was refreshed and eager to explore Tours. Under the pretext of visiting her grandparents at their tavern, which she did plan to do as well, she convinced Luc to loan her the motor car for the day. This suited her brother just fine. He had to clean the barrels and fermenting tanks for the October chenin blanc harvest. The grapes' sugars were climbing, and he estimated they would begin picking in one or two weeks' time, at which point Adeline would help pick and crush the grapes.

After breakfast, Adeline raced off in Luc's car, exhilarated at the prospect of being alone and unreachable, if only for the twenty-minute jaunt along the river and across the bridge to Tours. She donned a mask, wore her uniform and flashed her American Expeditionary Forces identity card at the gate to the base. The guards let her pass without incident after directing her to the infirmary—for prisoners of war.

Her hastily formed plan was admittedly preposterous, and yet some inane instinct urged her on. As she entered the plain, single-story barracks that housed the prisoners' infirmary, her heart punched her ribcage and her stomach churned. *How on earth was she going to pull this off?*

She turned in at the poky office near the entrance and extended her hand to a scowling fortress of a nurse with a clipboard. "May I help you?" the woman muttered from behind her surgical mask.

"I came to help you," Adeline responded, scanning her name tag. "Nurse Loring, I am a surgical nurse. I served at Juilly and I'm currently on leave," she explained, careful not to give too many details. "I heard you're in the throes of the influenza epidemic and came to offer my assistance."

The nurse raised a skeptical brow and asked for Adeline's identification card. After examining the card—and Adeline from head to toe—the nurse about-faced. "Follow me, Nurse Donnelly." Adeline searched the room before ducking out. Three tall, metal file cabinets flanked the wall. Prisoner records, Adeline guessed.

Nurse Loring waddled down a narrow aisle with two lines of cots on each side. Between the cots, nurses had strung sheets to protect the patients from spreading the virus, making it impossible for Adeline to examine their faces as she passed. There must have been hundreds, coughing, sneezing, wheezing and moaning in German. The air was rank with the musky odor of men.

When they reached the far wall, Nurse Loring smirked. "Don't worry, there's more." She pushed open the door to the outside. A gust of fresh air greeted them. Before her, on the vast field behind the building, a white-tented village spanned acres, framed by fencing topped with the shiny, sharp spears of barbed wire.

"Are they all sick with influenza?" Adeline asked, thunderstruck.

Nurse Loring pointed to the largest tent. "That's the overflow for the morgue." She swiveled and motioned to a tent half the size. "That's the overflow of sick POWs."

"All Germans?" Adeline asked, watching stretcher-bearers shuffle their cargo between tents.

"And a few Austrians sprinkled in." She chuckled. "Your choice."

Adeline was momentarily baffled. "Oh, I'd prefer to work with the living, since that is my expertise."

"You're immune?"

"I have been infected and recovered."

"Good enough." Nurse Loring flicked her head in the direction of the POW tent. "Nurse Callaway is in charge right now. She'll show you the ropes." She retreated toward the infirmary building.

Adeline ducked beneath an open flap. She paused to examine the face of every patient she passed. Of course, she did not expect to find Heinrich Sommer among them, but she hoped to uncover some clue about his whereabouts. To ask the patients would only raise suspicions, and besides, she didn't speak German. Adeline would bide her time, build trust with the staff and wheedle her way into the office to search those file cabinets. After all, this was one of the AEF's hubs, where they kept military records of countless prisoners throughout France. Their cache of intelligence was second only to the files housed at Gièvres.

Adeline fingered Heinrich's letter, tucked away in her skirt pocket. She told herself she simply wanted to make sure he was alive, so that he might eventually reunite with his son. She had an inexplicable need to preserve this piece of her humanity, to see this through. She refused to make an enemy of an entire race of people because they were on the opposite side of a senseless war. *But did this unpopular sentiment make her a traitor to her own people?*

By October 3, Heinrich had recovered from the influenza and begun serving as a litter-bearer. The abundance of *sabots* underscored the dwindling number of feet in need of the clogs and the shop had closed. Heinrich now spent his days transporting his fellow prisoners from their barracks to the infirmary tent when they fell ill, and from the infirmary tent to the morgue after they regrettably gave up the ghost.

What was this strange plague that killed ruthlessly and indiscriminately, suffocating its victims over hours or days? The weak perished, but so did the strong—men and women in the prime of their lives. *Why had he survived its grip?*

God was merciful. Father Gunther's letter had found its way to Heinrich in Tours. Werner was safe in the orphan asylum run by the nuns at the cathedral convent in Köln. By all accounts, Anna had vanished. Heinrich had written at once to thank the priest and ask him to tell Werner his father was alive and assure him that as soon as he was released, he would return to Köln to claim him. Every day, Heinrich allowed himself to imagine how it would feel to hug Werner, to swing him around, small feet dangling, his delicate shoulder blades vibrating with laughter beneath Heinrich's fingers. Every morning before he left the barracks, he made sure to carry his four most precious possessions with him: his oval dog tags, his wedding ring, which he had hung on the same chain, the priest's letter with Werner's location and the French soldier's handkerchief, folded into a neat square.

Heinrich still wheezed and coughed occasionally, but he had regained his strength quickly. After lunch, he and his *Kamerad,* Walter Schlichter, had been instructed to retrieve a body from the newly fitted operating tent. Heinrich was so tall, he had to bend at the waist to clear the tent opening.

Despite his medical training, he recoiled at the sight before him. A German soldier, marked with dark bruises, a hallmark of advanced influenza, lay dead and bundled on a sheet. On the operating table, an American surgeon in white gown, mask, cap and gloves hovered over another, living patient holding a large needle over the man's chest, poised to strike.

"*Nein!* No!" Heinrich called, dropping his end of the stretcher and waving his hands frantically. "Please, no!" he shouted in halting English, his gauze mask vacillating from the force of his breath. *How could he explain? They would surely kill the man.* He tried in German, but when their faces blanked, he switched to French. *"Pas une aiguille!"*

The surgeon cried, "Get him out of here!" Schlichter and one of the nurses grabbed Heinrich's arms.

As he wriggled to free himself, a clear, high-pitched voice cried behind him, "The German is right. You'll kill that man if you use a needle to extract the fluid from his lungs." It was not the words she spoke, but rather the lilt of her speech that arrested his attention.

She was certainly an incarnation of his imagination. His mind had often played tricks on him since the concussion. The relaxing of the skin around her eyes and the flicker of recognition in her dark gaze convinced him otherwise. *Blanchette.* She was close enough to touch, her cascade of mahogany curls a little longer, but just as springy.

She rounded the operating table and pointed to the patient's heaving chest. "When I was working as a nurse at Rockefeller Hospital in New York, we treated many cases of influenza. Whenever we found fluid in the chest, we would draw it out with a needle. In nearly every case, the patient was dead by morning.

Do not remove the fluid unless you are certain it's frank pus, do you understand?"

Heinrich could understand enough English to know she was communicating the same concerns he had stated only moments ago. But he exhaled only when the surgeon lowered the large syringe. Blanchette glared at Heinrich and Schlichter. "What are you waiting for? *Portez cet homme à la morgue.*" She motioned to the cadaver on the floor and the two men snapped into action, hope sticking like a stone in Heinrich's gullet.

Heinrich carried the rear of the stretcher as he and Schlichter trudged out of the stale, confined operating tent. A few paces away, he glanced back over his shoulder to see Blanchette's diminutive frame, now standing outside the tent. She yanked the mask down off her face and her tiny nostrils flared, drinking in the fresh air. Heinrich's lips tweaked into a half smile. Blanchette's face beamed with relief, dissolving any doubts he had.

He had to see her—alone. He wanted to do more than just thank her, but of course that was impossible. A quick exchange would have to suffice, if he could orchestrate it. As a prisoner in the *sabotier's* shop, he had been watched constantly, but out here as a litter-bearer in the midst of an influenza crisis, the physicians and nurses hardly glanced at him, unless it was to issue orders to cart another one of his poor countrymen to the morgue.

Heinrich was sitting on the grass eating a ham sandwich when Blanchette approached him. Her hard stare flashed a warning. He clamped his mouth shut and finished chewing.

"You look sick, soldier."

Heinrich hesitated. *What was she up to?*

"Parlez-vous français?" she persisted.

"Oui, Bl—mademoiselle."

"Come with me," she commanded.

He followed her dutifully into a nearby tent, behind a cloth examination partition.

"We don't have much time. Listen carefully," she continued in French.

"I won't let you risk any more for me."

"Have you located Werner?"

Upon hearing his son's name spoken aloud in this godforsaken place, where no one cared whether they lived or died, Heinrich choked up. "Yes."

She glanced left and right and, once certain no one was listening, she whispered, "I know what it's like to live without a father. No child should bear it, especially if it can be prevented. Trust me." Sensing his reluctance, she insisted, "You don't have another choice, do you?"

Bewildered, but exhilarated at the mere thought of seeing Werner again, Heinrich acquiesced. When he had wedged his wife's letter and Blanchette's crucifix between the wall and his cot at Juilly in June, he had intended for Blanchette to find it, but simply so she would understand that his wife had abandoned him and that the affection he had shown for Blanchette at Juilly was sincere. Never in his wildest imaginings did he think she would interpret the letter as a summons to reunite him with his son.

He must have gaped like a fish, for Blanchette tugged his arm and said, "Follow me and start coughing—loudly."

She led him outside and back to the infirmary tent for POWs, to an empty cot in a corner close to the entrance. She strung up a fresh sheet between Heinrich's cot and his neighbor's, inhabited by a bearish man in the final throes of the dreadful disease.

"You have been ill already?" she whispered.

"Yes."

"Then act like you are sick again." She hiked a blanket to his chin, stuck a thermometer in his mouth and began to scrawl on his chart.

When she was finished, she pressed a hand to his shoulder. "I will return for you on Monday. Be ready, shoes on beneath the sheets." Before he could object, she pivoted and rushed out.

CHAPTER 16

October 1918

VOUVRAY, FRANCE

Without Jacques's guidance, Luc struggled to estimate how many pickers he would need to hire. He
sat at the old davenport in the parlor, rubbing his
forehead and tapping a pencil against his pad of paper. Ondine
placed a cup of *café au lait* by his elbow and hovered over his
shoulder. "What are you figuring?" she asked.

"How many women and children I need to employ as pickers."

Ondine, balancing her mug, hooked her foot around the
nearby hassock and dragged it over to the desk. She sat down and
blew on the coffee, her lips poised in a pretty pink bow. "How
long did it take you to finish picking last year?" she asked.

"A fortnight." He grinned, amused at the crinkle in her brow
and the seriousness of her tone. She was rather gutsy to attempt
to help him with a dilemma she knew nothing about.

"How many hectares?"

"Ten," he answered.

"And how many tons did that yield?" She pinched the corner of his tablet between her thumb and forefinger and glanced at the numbers he had scrawled.

"Why does that matter?"

"Trust me. Answer the question."

"One hundred twenty-seven." He didn't know where she was headed with her inquiry, but her expression was one of such determination, he felt duty bound to follow her.

"And each vine yields how much fruit?"

"On average, three kilograms."

"How many hours did the pickers work each day last year, not including the lunch hour or Sundays?"

"We usually picked from five in the morning to one in the afternoon, then broke for lunch, then worked the assembly line to pick the debris and bugs out of the grapes from two until five. But I worked until seven myself." Luc secretly doubted he would be able to maintain such grueling hours this year.

"And how many pickers did you employ last year?"

He shrugged. "Ten or so."

She placed her mug on the windowsill. "May I?" she asked, while taking the pencil from Luc's grasp. She multiplied some numbers on the page. "So, if we assume that twelve men, including you and Jacques, each worked an average of eleven hours per day for twelve days, that means the harvest took a total of approximately fifteen hundred man hours."

"That sounds about right."

"But, since you are employing women and children this year—not men—let's assume they work eight hours a day, not including lunch. Is that reasonable?"

"I suppose so," he replied, leaning in. Ondine jotted some more calculations on the paper. As her intensity increased, she bit her lip. Her flaxen hair, cinched in a chignon, looked so silky and enticing, Luc briefly fantasized about slipping the pins out to watch it fall. When a stream of air flowed through the window, ruffling the gold strands at the nape of her neck, his breath caught in his throat.

A triumphant smile lit Ondine's heart-shaped face. "I recommend you hire ten women and five boys, Michel's age or older, for a period of two weeks. With you, Michel and I picking, too, that should be enough if you think it's fair to assume we can each clean twenty-five vines of fruit each hour."

Luc was astounded. "How did you figure that out so quickly?"

"I just divided the total man hours required by the hours your new laborers would work each day to figure how many pickers you would need. Then I converted the one hundred thirty tons to kilograms and calculated how many vines—at three kilograms of grapes each—we would need to pick in an hour and divided that by our eighteen laborers."

Luc examined her calculations and found them to be entirely accurate. "You are a wizard."

She edged closer, glinting like a newly minted penny. "I just love numbers."

"My savior!" he cried, stretching his arms wide. "Thank you!" He instinctively clasped her shoulders and drew her near, pecking one cheek and then the other.

She stiffened. He dropped his hands to his thighs. "I'm sorry, I didn't mean to—"

Ondine's head tilted and her soft, moist lips grazed his mouth. "You're welcome," she whispered before stealing from the room.

Ondine's touch had been so feathery, he wondered whether she had truly kissed him. What he did not question was the spark of lust her closeness had kindled in him. There was something about her—that unlikely blend of courage and vulnerability, half woman, half fairy—that captivated him. She was so different from the overtly coquettish Virginia. The mere thought of those depraved German soldiers defiling Ondine triggered Luc's urge to kill.

He steadied his breath, trying to calm the pulsing adrenaline in his neck. Ondine was a mystery. She possessed layers of complexity that Virginia never would—and he suddenly had the desire to cautiously peel back each one.

———

With the local papers reporting record-breaking death tolls from influenza, Luc decided to telephone rather than visit the newspaper's offices to place an advertisement. He dictated the notice of intention to employ ten able-bodied women and five young men between the ages of fourteen and seventeen to harvest the grapes at Clos du Saint Martin. He specified that all candidates must have contracted and survived the influenza and visit the vineyard the morning of Friday, October 4. Of the thirty that showed, Luc selected a hearty sixteen and instructed them to return the following Monday.

"When will the harvest start?" Adeline asked, in French for the benefit of the rest of the household seated around the table.

"Within four days is my best estimate." Luc sipped his brandy, wondering if he would be able to pull it off without Jacques. He sighed at the sheer enormity of the task: picking, de-stemming and pressing the grapes, fermenting the wines, moving them from one tank to another, and hopefully producing three hundred barrels of premium chenin blanc, or swill if he mistimed the harvest. After investing all this time and energy, there was still no certainty that demand or prices would rebound. The only hope for Saint Martin was an end to the war, the free movement of French exports across the seas and, sadly, an American prohibition that might cripple his family's California wine business but boost demand for European wines. He hardly knew what to hope for.

"Do you need me to give up my troglodyte paradise for the pickers?" Adeline asked. "It is rather exotic and cozy," she added.

"No, these will be day laborers. We'll serve them dinner here, but they'll sup at home in the evenings."

"And how much will I need to cook for these pickers each day?" Grandmère grumbled. Although she had singlehandedly prepared the luncheon for every harvest for the last twenty years, her patience had thinned since Jacques's death.

Luc balked. He had not planned that far ahead. Ondine perked up. "Nineteen *fouaces* stuffed with chèvre, nineteen roasted pigeons, nineteen liters of wine and perhaps an apple for everyone?" she suggested.

"Someone's on the ball," Adeline said admiringly. She seemed enthusiastic about everything since she had started volunteering at the infirmary.

"Ondine is my secret weapon," Luc announced.

Michel frowned.

"And you, too, Michel. I wouldn't be able to harvest this year without the two of you," he was quick to add. Michel glowed at the compliment.

"How is it working out at the hospital?" Grandmère dabbed her mouth with her napkin. "What will they do when you leave?"

"I plan to help with the harvest, so we shall see. The infirmary and the morgue are overwhelmed," Adeline explained, pouring another glass of chenin blanc for herself and Grandmère.

"That reminds me, what time do you need me to drop you at your grandparents' in the morning?" Luc bit into the warm crust of bread, relishing the saltiness of the fresh, creamy butter.

"Eight o'clock would be perfect, thank you. They'll drive me back Sunday evening." Adeline hesitated for a moment before asking, "Would you mind if I borrowed the car on Monday? We have some paperwork we need to finish up and it could go late."

"Sounds fine to me," Luc agreed. "Please give Pip and Mim our regards." His cheeks warmed, remembering Adeline's grandfather's *"Mon Dieu!"* when he'd spied Luc and Virginia locking lips in the tavern storeroom last New Year's Eve. It seemed like a lifetime ago. Luc could only hope Pip possessed the class not to divulge Luc's indiscretion to Adeline over supper. His sister clearly did not approve of Virginia.

"I expect to be home around ten Monday night, so don't wait up."

"I'll hang a lantern by the caves if I remember." Horse hooves thundered outside, interrupting Luc's train of thought. He reached the door just as a single postal rider dismounted. Luc felt a clench of alarm. Messengers at suppertime never delivered good tidings.

The telegram was from his father in California. The words on the page knocked the wind clean out of him.

Tears cloaked Luc's eyes. Adeline rushed to his side, asking, "What is it?" He handed her the telegram and glanced at Grandmère.

Adeline, upon reading it, began to sob. Fingers trembling, she moved toward his grandmother, squatted down beside her and took her hand. She stammered, "Tante Marguerite, I am . . . so sorry to tell you that little Lydia . . . and our family friend Aurora have both died of the influenza."

————

On Saturday, after insisting Adeline continue with her plan to visit her grandparents, Ondine assumed all of Madame's household chores while Michel helped Luc prepare for the upcoming harvest. Madame languished beneath the weight of her sorrows; Luc drove himself too hard, as if scrubbing barrels, swabbing floors and fine-tuning the bottling equipment fifteen hours a day might dull the spear of loss that gouged him once again. He kept to himself, except when ordering Ondine and Michel about.

Ondine raised Luc's soft work shirt and inhaled its earthy aroma before dropping it into the washer. His scent was so soothing, nothing like the leathery, wet-wool smell of the German soldiers with their beer breath. She still gagged at the memory.

Once the machine was running, she hitched the basket of damp, clean clothing to her hip and strolled out to the clothesline. The air was thick with the sweet scent of ripening grape flesh and chalky laundry soap. She and Mère used to sing the old French standards and the "Marseillaise" as they plunged and scrubbed the laundry by hand, an exhausting chore that had often ended in a war of splashes on hot summer days. Mère could be silly like that sometimes. A familiar ache flared beneath Ondine's ribcage.

She slipped clothespins off her apron string to hang a sheet. A streak of scarlet had sullied its corner. There was a bead of blood on her fingertip. She sucked it until the blood began to clot.

The wind gusted and the sheet fluttered up. Luc suddenly passed into view, raking back the lock of dark hair that had fallen over his forehead. Ondine's gaze followed the curve of his bronzed bicep down the length of his forearm to the tips of his sinewy fingers. She blushed, recalling the honeydew taste of his lips. He marched toward the entrance to Saint Martin, urgency clouding his features. Ondine craned her neck to see what trouble had come to call.

Behind the safety of his gauze mask, Luc conversed animatedly with a French soldier dressed in the standard horizon-blue uniform and kepi. Ondine's hand rested on her hip. *Hadn't the soldier read the sign staked by the entrance? Was he illiterate? They could not risk more infection!*

The interloper gestured wildly, apparently refusing to leave. *Should she fetch one of the hunting rifles from the gun cabinet?* She knew where Luc kept the key. She decided against such hasty action when Luc, rather than escorting the soldier off the property, clasped the man's hand and shook it robustly. The pair then turned toward Michel, who ran up and bounded into the soldier's arms at full speed, causing him to stagger backwards.

400

Hope beat frantically in Ondine's chest. She held fast to the clothesline pole as her knees weakened. In her daze, she fleetingly wondered why Père was not wearing the mustard-khaki uniform of the colonials.

"Ondine! Ondine!" Michel shouted. The breeze muffled his cries and his waving arms slowed to a snail's pace. Ondine stood between the billowing white bed linens, her gaze fixed on the three men she loved most in the world. *Had he truly returned for them?*

Ondine would never recall the speed with which her father closed the distance between them or how his voice trembled as he spoke to her for the first time in nearly four years. She would only remember how his chest and arms curled around her, swallowing her whole.

———

NAPA, CALIFORNIA

Sara ran her hand across the redwood staves of the giant fermenting tanks as she wandered the length of the Eagle's Run winery, her mind still fogged with the unfathomable shock of Lydia and Aurora's deaths. She did not know how many bottles would be sold from this year's vintage—possibly their last—nor did she care. She did not even know what day it was.

The door to the winery creaked open. A halo of yellow light appeared and then retreated into the damp gloom again. Philippe walked toward her. Anguish furrowed his brow and webbed the skin near the corners of his eyes.

"Any news from Marie? How is Gemma?" Sara asked.

"Still fighting, according to Marie's last letter."

Sara pressed steepled fingers to her lips in a silent prayer.

"I sent word to Luc," Philippe continued, pulling her into his arms, his chin nuzzling the top of her head. "I don't know which is worse"—he choked on a sob before collecting himself— "living now that Lydia is gone, or watching her siblings struggle with such a loss, knowing I can never ease their pain."

"Because we know what it is to lose a brother, a sister." She gazed up at him through a veil of tears. "We should never have sent Luc to France. We shouldn't have separated the family."

"That was always our plan."

She brushed at her eyes. "All I ever wanted after my sister died was to give her boy a home, and eventually Saint Martin. I wanted to preserve the vineyard my grandparents started. Instead, I sent him straight into a war. He's alone with Maman now."

"He would have gone to war either way. And his presence here wouldn't have prevented any of these horrible things from happening."

Sara buried her face in Philippe's shoulder. Her stomach somersaulted, revolting at the reality of it all. In truth, she did not understand how her heart was still beating, or how her lungs were still breathing. She was sinking and could not muster the will to fight.

"When this blasted war is over, we will set sail for France. To rejoin our family and to retrench." He twined his fingers in her hair and kissed her softly, mingling his salty tears with hers. She squeezed him tightly, trying to stem her violent shivering.

He must have understood the depths of her despair, for he had just thrown her a lifeline. "Promise me, Philippe," she whispered.

"I promise, my love."

———

If it hadn't been for the all-engrossing harvest, and Johnny's company, Pippa was certain she would have lost her mind. Billy and his family remained quarantined in their home as the threat of influenza lurked on every street and around every corner of Napa. The Copper Chop Shop was closed, and Hudson's Dry Goods had been shuttered for a month with no hope of reopening anytime soon.

Pippa did not understand why she and her father had not contracted the disease. Johnny had caught it shortly after Maman but recovered quickly. *La grippe* had caused him minor troubles—a runny nose and a cough—when it had ruthlessly sapped the life from Lydia and Aurora.

On the heels of Lydia's death, suffering through the excruciating void that her sister's bubbling laughter and sweet smile used to fill, Pippa decided there was no rhyme or reason to life. The worst thing she could imagine had happened. Her little sister, her friend, her soul twin, had been ripped from their arms without warning.

What else could she possibly fear now? She was determined to do what she wanted, when she wanted, with whomever she wanted. She would no longer hide or doubt her ambition.

She climbed the steps of Tante Aurora's front porch, remembering the evening when her honorary aunt had ushered her in, comforted her on the settee and made her toss back an entire bourbon-spiked hot toddy. Pippa had licked the residue of honey and ground cloves from the side of the mug and her heart had swelled with gratitude for Aurora's grandmotherly friendship. Now Papa's wagon waited outside, hitched to their horse, ready to cart away a lifetime of Aurora's personal belongings. Barney lounged on the porch, chin on paws, and released a soulful whine when Pippa scratched him behind the ears.

Maman's greeting jerked Pippa from her reverie. The silver strands of her mother's hair were brighter, the lines on her face deeper, and the shadows beneath her eyes darker. "You needed me, Maman?"

Maman glanced at Papa, who finished piling papers into a crate.

"We have something important to discuss with you, Pippa." He motioned to the parlor, where they all sat. It had been only a few weeks since Aurora's death, but already the air inside was thick with dust. Pippa could no longer detect the familiar scents of lemon, vinegar and oil soap.

Papa clasped a few sheets of paper in his hand. "When we were packing Aurora's things, we found her will." He cleared his throat. "She left this house, all the land and the money in her savings account to you and Lydia."

"But why?"

Maman smiled, a gesture that lifted Pippa's spirits considerably. "You girls were like granddaughters to her, and she knew that Luc had inherited Saint Martin and that Johnny will take over Eagle's Run one day. Knowing Aurora, she wanted to give you girls the gift of independence."

"Wait. What does that mean?" Pippa asked stupidly. She could not wrap her mind around the implications. She could not dare to.

Papa grinned. "It means that once we visit Aurora's attorney and complete the paperwork, you will own this house and this land free and clear, and you will have an additional nine thousand dollars and an ongoing stream of royalty payments from Aurora's publishers."

Moisture streaked down Pippa's cheeks. "I would give it all back in a second." Her throat constricted, silencing her.

Papa squeezed her tight. "We know you would, we all would, but we can't. So, take this gift and do some good in Aurora's name."

Maman offered Pippa her handkerchief. "Or else you'll have hell to pay, young lady, when you arrive in the afterlife." Her lips twitched with amusement.

Pippa laughed softly, picturing Aurora's bramble of fiery red hair, streaked with white, her plump, dimpled cheeks and twinkling, mischievous eyes. For some reason, God had spared Pippa's life, which, in contrast to Aurora's and Lydia's, seemed so small and pale. But Aurora's unexpected gift gave her a shot of confidence. Pippa filled her lungs with air, bolstering her resolve.

———

She had been so dazed by Papa's revelation that she had entirely forgotten to share her own news. Regardless, she now knew what she had to do, as difficult as it might be.

Pippa rode her bike to the Hudsons' home near midday. The doorbell rang with an irritating buzzing sound. Pippa much preferred the simple door knocker at Eagle's Run.

She wistfully peered around the back, remembering her excitement at the novelty of sharing her talents with the *mutilés* and creating art with Billy. If she was going to recapture that feeling and follow her heart's desire, she would have to act now. She could not give in to Billy's flirtatious smile or hangdog expression.

The door cracked open. Mrs. Hudson's hair was surprisingly unkempt, her skin sallow. Pippa instinctively stepped back.

"Pippa? We were so worried, dear! How are your parents holding up?"

"It's hard for all of us, as you can imagine. Lydia was a bright light."

"Of course she was!" Mrs. Hudson exclaimed. "Do give them our condolences, my dear. You'll be wanting to speak with Billy?"

"Is he here? Is he well?" Pippa inquired.

"Indeed, he's recovering. I'm sure the sight of you will cheer him to no end. But I am afraid I can't invite you in. Mr. Hudson has quite a bad case of pneumonia," she explained.

"I hope he heals quickly," Pippa said, suddenly remembering the basket in her arms. "Oh, and I brought these for you. Fresh apples from our orchard."

"Aren't you an angel! I'll take them with thanks, especially now the market's been closed these three long weeks. I told my Billy what a gem you are." She winked. "He didn't need convincing from me, mind you!" she whispered. Pippa heard Billy's voice booming behind his mother. In an instant, Mrs. Hudson retreated, and her son appeared.

Billy had combed his brunette hair back stylishly and sported trousers, suspenders, and a striped collarless shirt. His bare feet indicated he hadn't expected any visitors. He looked as dashing as one could behind a white gauze mask. "Aren't we a handsome pair of bandits?" he joked. His fingers caressed the sleeve of her white cotton blouse. "I wish I could hold you, kiss you."

"Me too," Pippa said wistfully. "I received your note. Thank you."

He shrugged and plunged his hands into his pockets. He pulled out a handkerchief, turned and hacked for a minute or more. Spasms racked his chest. "I'm so sorry. Perhaps I should go inside and call on you when I'm better."

"No, it's quite all right." She shifted uncomfortably. "Billy, I have to say something. It's not easy, so I need you to listen and not speak until I'm finished, okay?" she asked gently.

"Sounds ominous, Pippa."

She pressed her gloved hands together. "I love you. You will always be my first love, but I find . . . I find that I cannot think about marriage right now. I need to live on my own. I want to travel and pursue a college degree in art before I marry."

Pippa could have knocked Billy over with a feather, so stunned was his expression. "Do you just need more time? Will you ever consent to marry me?"

"I can't say right now, Billy. With the war and so many dying, I don't even know what tomorrow will bring. I can't speak for our future right now."

Billy exhaled loudly and stared at the cumulus clouds, floating like tufts of cotton. "I promised God that if he spared my life, I would dedicate the rest of my days to making you happy."

Pippa ignored a pang of guilt. "That's just it, Billy. I can't rely on you to make me happy. I won't." *How could she explain?* "I need to do this on my own."

He clutched the door handle. "I can't promise I'll wait for you, Pippa," he warned icily.

She swallowed several times, trying to quell the uncertainty she still felt. He offered the security of a home, a friend for life—and yet, she wanted more. "I understand."

"Good luck to you then." The door clicked shut behind him.

Her hand pressed against the black lacquered door, Pippa murmured, "Goodbye, Billy."

———

VOUVRAY, FRANCE

Although everyone rejoiced over the return of Capitaine Pierre Marchand, the earlier news of Lydia and Aurora's deaths, along with Luc and Marguerite's anguish, had frayed Adeline's nerves. Such devastating loss for the entire Lemieux family. *And dearest Pippa!* How would she endure such heartache? The frustration of living a world away from her family and cousins, of not being able to comfort or help them, was too much for Adeline to bear.

If the influenza had spread to Napa, it was likely running roughshod all over San Francisco, especially in her parents' medical boarding house. Had Maman closed it down? Had her little brother and sister succumbed to the deadly disease? The uncertainty of their fates would slowly kill Adeline if she gave in to its unrelenting assault on her psyche.

She circled the craggy floor of her troglodyte dwelling the Monday morning after Ondine's father had returned. Adeline had been elated to witness the reunion of two long-suffering children with their father. However, Ondine and Michel's joy—and sorrow as they mourned their mother all over again—left Adeline feeling like a wrung-out mop.

She plopped down on the edge of her cot, smoothing her hand over its soft quilted coverlet. *What should she do?* After all, lives were at stake. Whether they were German lives, or French lives, or American lives, did it matter? If Adeline did not try to reunite a good man like Heinrich with his son, shielding them from the loss she had felt so acutely as a child without a father, then what good was she? Heinrich Sommer had committed no crime; he had saved lives. And yet, if she aided him, she would be committing treason—and if she were caught, she would hang.

Images of blinded and blistered men, severed limbs and wasting corpses flickered through her mind. Her gut clenched. No matter how hard or how long she worked, she could never dam the tidal waves of death and disease. She dug her nails into her fists and pounded the mattress, wanting to scream at the sheer stupidity, the futility of it all.

While she calmed herself with deep breaths, her fingertips instinctively grazed the crucifix around her neck, which Jacques had carved for her mother so many years ago. She thought of the millions of young men, like Corporal Shepherd Holmes, who would never be husbands and fathers. She thought of all the children who would never be born. She thought of all the children, like Lydia, who had died of influenza. If she did not act, she would never forgive herself.

Adeline would set things in motion tonight and prayed Heinrich would be ready. She had formed only half a plan. For the final and trickiest part, she would have to rely on Heinrich's keen wits and, as a last resort, her presumably uncooperative brother. She couldn't worry about that now; she would have to rely on her instincts.

After promising she would stay home to help with the harvest tomorrow, she set off in Luc's motor car for Tours.

————

Adeline parked next to two ambulances in the field adjacent to the bustling infirmaries. She strolled into the prisoners' tent with renewed determination. When Nurse Loring had assigned her the task of reconciling the morgue's records with the patient records two days ago, Adeline had seen an opportunity. She had searched the prison records for the file of Heinrich Rolff Sommer from Köln, Germany, assigned to the *sabotier* shop.

By eight o'clock, Adeline had worked eleven hours and darkness had descended on Tours. She sat at a large wooden desk, working by the light of a kerosene lamp. Perched in the upper left-hand corner of the leather blotter was a pile of death certificates. Adeline lifted the form on top and studied the coroner's signature. She placed the tip of a black fountain pen on the signature line of a blank death certificate and forged his name. She placed the blank certificate against the platen of the Corona portable, rolled it into position and punched the keys. The typebars struck the characters of Heinrich Sommer's name on the white page. Sadly, but not coincidentally, Leutnant Sommer died of the measles on that very evening of October 7.

Once Adeline slid the fake form into Heinrich's file, there was no turning back. Her heart jumped into her throat when Nurse

Loring waddled into the infirmary office at half past eight. "Why are you still here?" she asked sourly. The woman refused to show a smidge of gratitude.

Adeline rose and smoothed her skirt. "We've had a death in the family, so I'm afraid this is the last day I am able to volunteer. I'm due to report back to duty with my surgical team in a few days. I thought I would stay late to finish this paperwork."

Loring shifted uncomfortably. "Sorry for your loss," she blurted unconvincingly. "One of the other head nurses—Roland, I think—will be on in five. Make sure you check in with her before you leave, understand?"

"Yes, ma'am. Pleasure working with you," Adeline added in a syrupy-sweet voice.

Loring slid her trench coat off the rack and onto her arm. "Yes, well, good luck to you, Donnelly."

―――――

Adeline navigated the shift change with a twinge of trepidation. She left Nurse Roland on the night shift with another stack of morgue records to be reconciled and filed, a freshly brewed pot of coffee and her assurances that she would make her rounds in the tent before she left for the evening. She wanted to make sure Roland would have no reason to wander out of the office for a good half hour or more.

Adeline swept up and down the aisles of the infirmary and the overflow tent outside, checking in with the ward nurses, and soon arrived at the corner cot where she had left Heinrich. He slept on his side, facing the wall of canvas. He was raw-boned, but finely built, with a long physique, roman nose, high

411

cheekbones and a two-day-old, sun-bleached beard against his smooth, bronzed skin. He snored softly until Adeline touched his cheek and pressed her palm against his arm. He flinched in alarm, but his mouth hitched into a smile when he recognized her.

She adjusted the sheet the nurses used as a partition between patients to hide nearly the entire length of Heinrich's cot from curious eyes. She lifted a finger to her lips, pointed at the spot where the tent wall met the ground and flashed five fingers for five minutes. Heinrich nodded his understanding. Adeline detached his mock medical chart from the metal footrail of the cot and slid it into her satchel.

She walked out of the tent and meandered towards the morgue, loitering until a few American soldiers passed, then doubled back to the spot where Heinrich would be waiting on the other side of the tent's canvas wall. When the coast was clear, she ducked beneath the tunnel of guy ropes. *"Maintenant!"* she whispered, sliding her hand beneath the tent canvas.

Heinrich appeared instantly, headfirst, lying on his belly. He wriggled out into the shin-high grass. Adeline helped him up and draped a blanket around his shoulders. She had forgotten he was nearly two heads taller than she. *Would the guards believe her story? Would she be able to stop her galloping heart and lie?* Adeline dug into her apron pocket and pulled out her mask. After fastening it and issuing Heinrich his instructions in French, Adeline marched her German prisoner toward the field where she had parked Luc's runabout.

"Where are you going, miss? May we see your identification?"

Adeline flashed her credentials for two seconds—long enough so they could identify her face and see that it was in fact an army-issued card, but short enough she hoped they wouldn't remember her name.

"Forgive me, gentlemen, but I simply cannot dawdle. This man must be quarantined immediately. Measles," she added gravely. "High fever, dry cough, horribly painful spots in the mouth."

Heinrich curled over and exploded into a coughing jag. The two guards stepped back, swinging in unison like a door on its hinge. "Shouldn't we call the ambulance, ma'am?"

"Do you want to be held responsible for contaminating the ambulance crew and starting another epidemic? I don't. Luckily, I am immune to the measles and my automobile is right over there. I'll transport this man to the infirmary for infectious diseases before I depart for the evening."

"There's another infirmary?"

She tapped her foot to show her impatience. "Of course. A much smaller one for the non-influenza cases. Right near the *sabotier*'s workshop," she lied confidently.

One of the soldiers eyed Heinrich skeptically. "Would you like one of us to escort you, ma'am? For your safety?" he asked.

"Pish posh, gentlemen!" She waved away their concerns. "I may be petite, but this Hun couldn't hurt a flea. He's as wobbly as a drunk!" They laughed, relief flooding their features. "It's only a two-minute drive and, I promise, I'll shout for help if I run into any difficulty."

Just then, a line of army jeeps barreled toward the hospital, distracting the guards, who bolted to attention to receive their visitors. Adeline guided Heinrich through the teeming soldiers and slipped into the driver's seat of Luc's motor car, while

413

Heinrich, covered with an army blanket, huddled in the back. They sped out of the gate toward Saint Martin.

———

Lying on his side, knees tucked to chest in the bed of Blanchette's motor car, Heinrich's bones and teeth rattled. As they bumped along the back roads of Touraine, fumes of petrol mingled with the crisp night air.

There were moments when Heinrich could have wept at her kindness and daring, and others when he doubted everything. *Why would she help him?* He was a fellow medic, but still the enemy. Yet, he could not deny the bond they had forged in Juilly, although he could not define it.

When the car slowed and abruptly turned, Heinrich poked his head up. Rising from the inky darkness was the outline of a modest stone house, its rectangular windows lit in vivid bronze. Behind the home, in the distance, a single lantern swayed as if suspended in midair. He ducked down again and listened. The wind rustled through leaves above him and around him—was it a farm or orchard of some sort? The sweet aroma of fruit danced on the breeze.

Blanchette cut the motor. A man's voice sliced through the deep country thrum of bullfrogs and crickets' wings. "Adeline?" Footsteps crunched. Heinrich sank as low as possible, his cheek pressed against the cool lacquered bed of the runabout.

"Yes, Luc, it's me. Thank you for the lamp and the use of the car." He strained to listen to their conversation as Blanchette walked toward the man.

"Sure thing. Are you hungry? There's stew and bread." His tone was youthful but melancholy.

"Yes, I'll be in shortly. Thank you," she replied tenderly. "How'd the first day go?"

They spoke American English. Heinrich's stomach somersaulted. *Was this Blanchette's husband? Fiancé?* She didn't wear a ring, but then no surgical nurse could. *Had he misjudged her situation?*

"Fine. It may be a record crop. I'm going to bed. Early start tomorrow." Heinrich could not decipher every exchange, but their tone was both affectionate and somber.

"What time do the pickers arrive tomorrow?"

"Six."

"I'll join you soon after. Don't tax yourself. Your lungs are still recovering."

The man said something inaudible, and his treads wandered away from Heinrich and Blanchette. Within moments, she whispered, *"Suivez-moi! Vite!"*

Heinrich sprang from the car and followed Blanchette into what looked like a multiple-storied fortress of rock. With the lantern held high, she guided him through a tunnel of limestone and up a set of narrow stairs carved from the creamy-colored rock. He shivered as his hands pressed against the rough, dank walls. The place was eerily like the cave where he had billeted with the German army in Champagne.

She unlocked a thickly painted door and they stepped inside a womb-like cavern entirely hewn from rock. A large hearth spanned the left side of the room, its chimney presumably rising one or two levels higher and thrusting up between the rough patches of vegetation. The space was the shape of a backwards *L*, with a narrow living area that spanned left from the entrance to the hearth and then hooked left into a sleeping nook, hidden from the entrance but close enough to the fireplace to benefit from its warmth.

Blanchette placed the lantern on a table. "Would you please start the fire?"

Heinrich knelt before the mouth of the vast fireplace. He stacked the wood and arranged the kindling. Blanchette lit candles in the nooks of the cave walls and disappeared after issuing a warning. "No one can know you are here."

Heinrich stoked the small flames until the fire surged and began to devour the scaffold of logs. The cave was well furnished, with three straw pallets covered in bed linens, the table, four chairs and a wardrobe. A small portmanteau stood next to an austere mahogany chiffonier. Heinrich opened the wardrobe doors and fingered the clothing therein. A white nurse's uniform, like the one Blanchette wore now, a lacy shirtwaist, a navy skirt, trousers, a dainty chemise, a petticoat and a soft, flesh-toned brassiere all hung in a stately row. Heinrich quickly closed the doors, ashamed that he had trespassed into Blanchette's inner sanctum without her consent. Still, it had been a valuable thirty-second adventure, for he had learned her visit was temporary.

Blanchette pushed the door open with her shoulder and entered carrying two large metal buckets of water and other sundry items tucked under her arm. Heinrich rushed to assist.

She poured the water into the kettle hanging in the fireplace and they remained silent for a few moments while the flames danced and licked the copper basin. Blanchette handed Heinrich two towels and a brick of soap. "For washing, once the water is heated. I'm sorry I don't have a bathtub here. I usually bathe in the main house, you see."

She ducked out again and returned ten minutes later with two bowls of hot stew, thick with carrots, potatoes and some sort of fowl, he guessed. As he sat across from her at the table, he dunked a wide cut of chewy baguette into the hearty soup.

"You're hungry." She smiled.

He lowered his head bashfully. "I'm always hungry. May I ask where we are?"

"My brother's vineyard, a few kilometers from Tours. I had three weeks of leave, so I came here to visit rather than going to Paris with my colleagues."

"And that's when you discovered me and decided to break me out?" he asked incredulously.

"Yes," she answered softly.

An awkward silence drifted between them. Blanchette, though paler than he remembered, still possessed a feminine grace and beauty that captivated him. He studied her closely. "Something has happened since I last saw you. There is a fresh sadness, no?"

Her dark chocolate eyes widened. She dabbed her mouth with a cloth napkin. "My twelve-year-old cousin and a dear friend of the family died of the influenza back home in California," she confided tearily.

Heinrich reached for her hand, so dainty beneath his. "I'm so sorry." His words were inadequate but steeped in sympathy. Her vulnerability at this moment was palpable. "Are you sure you want to take this risk—to help me?"

She slid her arm off the table and rested her hands in her lap. "My brother, the man outside tonight, was a patient at Juilly when you were there. He heard about how I protected you—of my behavior," she added bitterly, "and he conspired with Lieutenant Colonel Jenkins to have you transferred immediately."

Heinrich crossed his arms, leaned back and considered this revelation. "He was right to do that."

"How can you say that?"

"Long ago it might have been acceptable for a German soldier to . . . to begin a friendship with a Franco-American nurse, but not now. It had to end."

She stood abruptly, her eyes narrowing. "You don't believe that! You left that letter behind for me to find."

He had, but he regretted it now. "I confess I did."

"Why?"

"To show my gratitude," he fibbed.

"No." She shook her head. "It was more than that."

"To show I cared. We were never supposed to meet again."

"Is that so?" Her tone soured. She began to stack the soiled bowls and utensils in her arms, her eyes darting to the kettle. "You'd best bathe. The water is nearly boiling."

"Thank you," he replied placidly. *Had he angered her with his honesty?* He silently cursed his inability to adequately express himself in her language. He had unwittingly driven a wedge between them.

"I'll leave you in privacy." She backed toward the door.

He stood to his full height and threaded his thumbs through his rope belt. "You needn't leave," he ventured.

Her dark lashes fluttered as she elbowed the door open and tightened her shawl around her shoulders. "Of course I must."

When she was gone, Heinrich disrobed, dropping his filthy prisoner garb in a pile. He dunked the small towel in the water and squeezed out the excess. He rubbed the soap brick against the fabric until he worked up a robust lather and then scrubbed every square centimeter of his body—even between his toes. His long legs were leaner, the sinews more defined than before the war. He could now see the outline of his ribs poking out beneath his skin, not a surprising result of having to replace his prewar *Biergarten* luncheon with canned military rations.

Heinrich was used to bathing, bunking in and eating with a multitude of prisoners each day. The simple luxury of being left completely alone to bathe cheered him more than he expected.

He rinsed off and toweled dry, leaving a sizable puddle near the hearth. Upon hearing the metal lock click, he about-faced, bare-chested and suddenly shy about the scar on his shoulder. As if she had read his thoughts, her gaze fluttered over the flaw, down the planes of his chest and lingered at his navel, beneath which Heinrich had wrapped a light blanket, for the towel had proved too small. Blanchette's sharp intake of breath told Heinrich everything he needed to know.

He crossed the room in three long strides, hooked his arm around her waist and lifted her chin. When he began to kiss her, she momentarily resisted, her hands flattened against his chest. Then, as her warring heart and mind reconciled, she slid her palm around the nape of his neck and melted into him. His tongue gently probed until her lips parted, inviting him to explore the ripe, peachy flesh of her mouth. He hadn't realized how he had craved this—the pleasure of her moist, tantalizing tongue, her petite fingers as they caressed his bare skin, her heart pulsing against his lower ribs.

When they had no choice but to break for air, she asserted, "The letter. You wanted me to read it so I would know you are free—free to love?"

"Free in that sense, not in others," he said wryly, glancing around the interior of the cave. "But so close," he whispered as he lowered his face to hers and stole another kiss.

"Heinrich?"

He caressed her neck with his lips. "Mmm?"

"We must keep you hidden."

"For how long?" he asked lazily, hoping to prolong this moment for eternity.

"A day, maybe two. Until we figure out the details."

He pulled away, disappointed at her reluctance to linger with him in the moment. "Details?"

"Of your escape. Obviously, we will depart at night. Switzerland is our only hope, for we can't cross directly into Germany." She made a beeline for her satchel, dug through its contents and returned to spread a map of Europe on the table. Her finger traced the proposed route. "It's just under five hundred kilometers, as the crow flies, to the Swiss border near Geneva." Blanchette's face crinkled with consternation when she glanced at Heinrich. "I estimate it will take two days with a stopover south of Nevers."

He shivered next to her. She ran a warm hand up his arm. "Gooseflesh. You're cold." She retrieved a stack of men's clothing from a basket, folded in neat squares and smelling freshly laundered. *Luc's things?* She angled her body toward the roaring fire, allowing him some privacy, though he would have welcomed the novelty of her burnished gaze roving over his anatomy.

He tugged on the wide, short denim dungarees and blue work shirt and frowned. Beggars could not be choosers, he recalled.

He admired Blanchette's audacity, but could they make it to the border undetected? Would they even be allowed through the checkpoints? He yearned to rejoin Werner as soon as possible, but not if he had to risk Blanchette's life to do it.

When he indicated that she could turn around, she gave his ensemble the once-over and started to giggle. He struck a pose and batted his eyelashes. Blanchette's laugh was a delightful arabesque. He had never heard it before.

"I'm sorry. I'll find something more suitable for you to wear tomorrow."

He rested his hands on her slender waist. "Why don't we stay here and keep me hidden until the war is over? It cannot last for more than a few weeks, maybe months, but the German army is gutted—the French, too. There will be no more men left to kill," he added macabrely, slinking his fingers through hers.

Her face fell. "I have to report back to Royat on the fourteenth."

He swept her into his embrace and nestled his chin into her dark, springy nest of hair. "Then we will go, but we will make the most of the hours we have left."

———

They whispered for the next few hours, but at eleven that evening, Heinrich had to insist that Blanchette retire. She had changed into a simple white nightdress while he perused the map. She looked angelic, but there was something in the way her sweet toes wriggled beneath her hem that left his throat parched. He could have ravished her right then. The knowledge that they would probably never see each other again would justify it but could just as easily prove an argument for remaining celibate.

Aware of her growing fatigue, he tucked her into her straw bed, stroked her hair and kissed her softly. Her delicate fingers coiled around his wrist as she drifted to sleep, the trace of his name like a secret stretching between them. "Heinrich."

There was no greater cure-all than a woman's touch. Lying in the cot adjacent to Blanchette, listening to the ebb and flow of her breath, soothed his fears. His chest nearly burst with happiness at the thought that he had earned her trust, enough to sleep alone in a bedroom with her an arm's length away.

Heinrich sank into a surprisingly dreamless sleep until the late morning hours—and awoke to an empty cave, dark save for a sliver of light that flowed through a crack between two broken shutter slats on the single window. He vaguely remembered the cock crowing earlier in the darkness and the sweep of Blanchette's fingers against his cheek, but that was all.

She had left him a thick slice of salty ham, two bread rolls, a pot of jam and a now-cold cup of black coffee. After availing himself of the chamber pot, he spread strawberry jam on a roll and then savored its fluffiness and the explosion of sweetness on his tongue. He could not love a woman more.

The eruption of gleeful shouts from the vineyard outside distracted him from the inevitable truth—that he would have to leave her in a few days' time. How he would love to run through the vineyard with Blanchette! But for now, his only entertainment was to sleep or peek through the fissure in the shutter. He chose the latter.

He could see a small block of the vineyard from his vantage point at the window. Blanchette, dressed in clogs, straw hat, pants rolled at the ankles and a man's collarless work shirt coiled at the elbows, bent before a vine, snipped it with her shears and placed the grapes gently in a large, cone-shaped metal container. Heinrich examined the laborers' faces, wondering which was Blanchette's meddling brother or perhaps another relation, but with their masks on, it was hard to discern.

Then his gaze alighted on a tall, dark blond. The man had doffed his cap and was singing a tune. When he walked, Heinrich noticed that the elegant man's left arm did not move as adroitly as his right. There was a niggling familiarity about him, but then again, Heinrich had encountered so many soldiers during the war, he could not be expected to remember all of them. He unconsciously scrunched the white cotton cloth in his pocket, a habit he had developed since Château-Thierry, one that comforted him when he felt anxious. He touched the clusters of yellow thread, the tiny flowers someone had artfully embroidered at each corner. He chuckled at his childishness. Most soldiers kept souvenirs from the men they had slain, whereas he had unintentionally claimed a souvenir from the man he had saved.

The minutes passed like honey poured cold. He kept occupied, sitting for a while on the top step outside the door, still fully hidden, and inhaling the fruity aroma that wafted from the sunlit rows of vines a level below. By the time Blanchette arrived with supper at five, Heinrich had worked out the rough sketch of an even better plan to sneak across the border. He had also developed a wolfish hunger.

The door flew open and Blanchette stopped short at the threshold, a large basket made of grapevines dangling from her arm. She giggled upon seeing Heinrich, hunched over, sweeping the cave floor with her little besom. Her skin boasted the pink, healthy glow of exertion. "I snuck into the kitchen and the larder and took these before Marguerite rang us for supper." As soon as the words crossed Blanchette's lips, the bell pealed five times. "I must go, or they'll grow suspicious."

"Can't you complain of an affliction of some sort?" he begged, taking the basket and catching her hand in his. She closed the door behind her.

"I suppose," she teased, dawdling.

"Go on, then!" He waved her away with a wink.

———

After complaining of a headache and bidding goodnight to her family, Blanchette returned with a large plate of roasted fowl, cheese, pastry and a jug of wine. They ate from the basket and the single plate, Blanchette with the utensils—Heinrich had insisted—and he with his hands. Succulent roasted pigeon flesh washed down with a cup of crisp chenin blanc was the most delicious supper Heinrich could ever remember tasting.

Blanchette ate heartily, too, and they conversed in hushed tones about the details of the harvest, the heartwarming reunion of Capitaine Marchand with his children, Blanchette's concern for her mother and siblings back home and, of course, their plan to smuggle Heinrich out of France. Heinrich relayed his plan to Blanchette: they would drive to a rail yard close to the Swiss border and he would stow away on a freight train.

Blanchette fluttered her fingers excitedly. She confided that she hadn't considered the trains. All this time, she had worried that Heinrich would have to cross on foot, which would be nearly impossible with the heightened security and documentation required to gain entrance into Switzerland as a political refugee.

"The hospital trains run from Lyon."

"How do you know this?" he queried.

"I came across the records in Tours—lists of the *grands blessés*—prisoners missing limbs or afflicted with tuberculosis or paralysis—who cannot fight or work. They are sent to Lyon and then into Switzerland for the fresh air. Two hospital trains run daily from Lyon to Geneva."

"I must be on one of them."

Blanchette nodded. "We will leave tomorrow night after everyone has gone to bed. It will take twelve hours with a few stops."

"Your brother will think his automobile was stolen and call the *gendarmes*."

"I'll explain that I need it to visit my grandparents, an emergency of some sort at the tavern. I'll figure something out." Her expression darkened. "What if you are captured, or worse?"

"I'll surrender before they shoot me. It is a chance I must take for Werner."

Having cleaned her plate of every morsel, Blanchette stood and began to pace. "You'll need more than luck," she insisted, opening the wardrobe and digging deep into a pair of civilian boots. She pulled out a roll of currency and began to peel notes off. She handed him a stack of francs and dollars. "You'll need bribe money."

"American dollars?"

"A franc is only worth twenty American cents. Dollars are far more valuable right now, and I believe the mark is worthless."

"How did you—?"

"My mother gave it to me in case of emergency."

"I cannot accept." He dropped his napkin on the table.

"You must, Heinrich. This is a grave emergency. You must return to Germany to claim Werner. A child needs his father," she snapped, ending any further protestations on his part.

The fierceness of her conviction startled him. "Thank you," he replied.

Blanchette edged toward the crackling fire, one hand pressed against the wall over the mantel, the other massaging her neck. With her arm lifted, the fabric of her work shirt strained against her round breast. My God, he would give almost anything to have her. He was contemplating his options when three quick knocks struck at the door.

They both froze.

"Adeline?" a young woman's voice inquired.

"Coming," she replied, pulling Heinrich into the corner nook where the beds were located. Even with the door open, the visitor would not be able to see him unless she stepped into the room.

426

Blanchette greeted the woman. They exchanged pleasantries and the young lady continued, "Madame swears by the mustard oil, to soothe aching muscles, and of course, here is water to heat for bathing and some fresh towels."

"Un grand merci, Ondine." Blanchette set the buckets, a small covered pot and towels on the floor where Heinrich could view them, then leaned against the doorjamb, arm extended, barring the girl from entering. "How are your father's spirits?"

"As well as can be expected. His left arm is still weak."

"How did he take the news—of your mother?"

The woman paused before answering, "He grieves her absence so deeply. But we have all suffered, *non*?"

"Yes, indeed. At least you have each other now."

There was a moment of silence and then the young woman asked, "Yours?"

Blanchette's head turned and Heinrich followed her sight line to the white tepee of cotton cloth beneath the table. *His handkerchief.*

"Yes," Blanchette answered. "I was collecting the laundry for tomorrow and it must have fallen from my pocket."

"Exquisite needlework. Where did you get it?"

"I can't recall," Blanchette lied. "I received many little gifts from the soldiers I attended." Silence again. "Ondine?"

In a flustered tone, Ondine uttered, "Yes, of course. Good night, Adeline."

"Bonsoir, Ondine."

Blanchette closed the door and, while she poured the water into the cauldron, she explained. "Ondine is the *capitaine*'s daughter. The runaway." Her gaze flicked toward him, narrowing ever so slightly. "Her mother was killed by German soldiers in their family home in Lille."

Heinrich's heart dropped. "I am . . . so sorry."

"My brother and Marguerite and Jacques, when he was alive, have cared for Ondine and her brother, Michel, since Christmas of last year. Luc is a good man."

"He must be, if he's your brother."

"I don't wish to deceive him, but he will not tolerate—"

"A Hun in his home." He picked up the pot of mustard oil and sat down on the straw bed. He plopped a feather pillow on the floor, planting his feet on either side of it. "Come sit."

She paused for a moment, as if deliberating, then quietly sank down between his knees, leaning her back against the straw mattress. He dipped his fingers into the small jar of dark, golden oil and began to rub her neck. She released a small sigh. He tried to ease his fingers in the direction of her shoulders, but her shirt restricted his movements.

"Undo the top buttons," he coaxed.

She momentarily tensed. After one deep breath, she relented and did as instructed. His palms glided across her shoulders and his thumbs gently teased the braided muscles along her spine and below her blades until they unraveled. Her head drooped forward in utter relaxation as he moved to caress the delicate muscles of her lower scalp. He threaded his fingers through the silky tendrils of her hair and closed his eyes, relishing the heat of her flesh and the tangy aromatic mixture of the oil, perspiration, and fruit pulp rising off her skin.

She rose to her knees and pivoted toward him, her tiny waist wedged between his long thighs. She circled her thumb around his oily palm, kneading the abductor, creating a tingling sensation. "Did you know that mustard oil improves the circulation of blood?" he whispered clumsily.

She cocked her head ever so slightly and contemplated his lips. "It most certainly does," she muttered before kissing him with unbridled fervor.

When she broke away, it was only to unfasten the rest of her shirt buttons.

Heinrich stopped her, resting his forehead against hers, still trying to catch his breath. "You are certain, *Blanchette*? Because once we start, I will not stop."

She responded with an alarmed expression. "I should bathe first," she said. He caught her hands as she tried to stand and slid her onto his thigh.

"No," he replied, slipping his hand beneath her cottony brassiere. "No," he repeated as his mouth sought hers.

———

After they had made love, Heinrich spread a blanket for Blanchette at the hearth and bathed her with the same reverence a master painter might offer his burgeoning fresco. Most men, including himself, desired full-bodied women with ample breasts and fleshy buttocks, but Heinrich found the sharpness of Blanchette's hipbones and the toned muscles of her legs endlessly arousing. The pleasure he had taken in her lush tightness was indescribable.

They lay for hours, limbs tangled and faces close in confidence. Heinrich's instincts were heightened, the colors and shapes surrounding him more vivid. "What are these?" he asked, reaching over her shoulder to run his fingers over a pattern of shells on the tawny-streaked tufa wall.

"Oyster shells and other fossilized sea life."

"Truly?"

"Millions of years ago, all of this was part of the ocean floor," she divulged with a flourish of her hand.

"Fascinating." He kissed her deeply, then moved his lips down the delicate skin of her neck, eventually freeing his tongue to roam the length of her exquisite body. It took half the night and two more couplings before they sated their appetite for each other and finally slipped into a deep sleep.

———

Heinrich rose at five-thirty with Blanchette. He was determined to see her off to the vineyard, to savor their last moments before they made their run for the border later that night.

Just as Heinrich cinched the rope belt around his waist, metal clanked against metal and a dark-haired, vigorous young man stormed into the room holding a hunting rifle. A young woman—most likely Ondine—followed him. She appeared mildly inquisitive, while he seethed with rage.

"Goddammit, Adeline, what are you thinking?" he shouted in English, then, glancing at his companion, switched to French. "You were harboring this German? For how long? How could you be so cold, so thoughtless?"

Of course. Germans had killed Ondine's mother and gassed Luc. God knows what other atrocities had been committed by both sides in the name of righteousness. Blanchette stepped toward Heinrich. "Oh, I see. You're his whore," Luc said bitterly.

Blanchette launched forward. The crack of her palm against Luc's cheek echoed throughout the small space.

"Enough," Ondine said, touching Luc's arm. She flicked her head at Heinrich, but her eyes rose to meet Luc's. "*Le mouchoir.* Ask him."

"Give us the white handkerchief."

"What?" Blanchette asked.

"*Le mouchoir!* The one that I saw on your floor last night." The vaguely familiar command rang in Heinrich's head like a wailing gong: *S'il vous plaît, le mouchoir.*

Still confused, but eager to thwart trouble, Heinrich pulled it from his pocket and gave it to Ondine. She turned the fabric over in her hands. Tears spilled down her cheeks.

"You shot my father! You thought you had killed him, but he's alive—he lives to spite you, you German devil!" Rabid, the pink-faced blonde rushed him. Heinrich staggered back into the wall, palms raised in surrender while she scratched his face and beat his ribcage with her fists.

He would never forget the flash of horror in Blanchette's eyes as she watched. Before he could make sense of the situation, Luc cocked his rifle, walked around Ondine to Heinrich's side and aimed it at Heinrich's head.

"Luc, no!" Blanchette cried as Ondine backed away.

"I want him gone. Now! Or so help me God, Addie."

Luc nudged Heinrich with the tip of the rifle, ushering him to the door and down the steps. The sun had just crested the horizon, bathing the vineyard in ethereal light. Others had gathered outside, curious about the commotion. Among them were the stately dark blond man and an adolescent boy.

"Père," Ondine's voice quivered. "This is the German who shot you, Père." Her glare could have seared steak.

Heinrich's mind churned. *A white* mouchoir *attached to the rifle, whipping in the breeze. The bloody gash on the man's head. The belt tourniquet strapped to his left arm. Metal birds falling from the azure sky.* He tensed.

The Frenchman smiled crookedly. *"Camarade?"* he inquired, his words hanging on hope, his gaze alighting on Heinrich's shoulder.

The air rushed from Heinrich's lungs. His throat tightened with emotion. *"Oui, Kamerad,"* he answered, half weeping.

The Frenchman kissed Heinrich's cheeks and pumped his hand. *"Marchand. Capitaine Pierre Marchand à votre service."*

"Sommer. Leutnant Heinrich Sommer," he croaked, sagging with relief.

"Père?" Ondine trilled.

"Capitaine?" Luc lowered his rifle, dumbstruck.

"Leutnant Sommer is the medic who saved me," Marchand explained, his face beaming with gratitude. "I was injured—shot atop Hill 204 near Château-Thierry—and he gave me water from his canteen. He shielded me from a grenade attack and took shrapnel in his shoulder for it." Blanchette twined her arm around Heinrich's and squeezed.

"But how—why did he have the hanky Mère embroidered for you?"

"I had tied it to my bayonet, as a sign of surrender, and had asked the *Leutnant* to untie it for me. Before he could hand it to me, the hailstorm of grenades hit the ground near us." He turned to Heinrich again. "You kept it all this time?"

Heinrich shrugged. "It was my way of keeping you alive, in my mind."

Marchand wiped his eyes. "Sommer, these are my children, Ondine and Michel." He drew Ondine forward and pivoted. "Michel? Where did he go?" Marchand asked no one in particular.

Fifty meters away, Michel charged out the back door of the house and stalked toward them, with another shotgun pointed directly at Heinrich. He had never been the object of such brazen hatred from one so young. Every fiber of the boy's body seemed to pulse with pain.

"Non, Michel," his father cautioned calmly, gliding toward Michel, palm extended, trying to ease the tension.

Michel flashed him a mutinous look and screamed, "You killed my mother! You ruined my sister! Die, you Boche bastard!"

The boy's maniacal tirade struck terror in Heinrich's heart. The air crackled and the world around him decelerated. Everyone remained rooted in place except for Blanchette, who sidestepped in front of Heinrich with widespread arms, and Luc, who had suddenly appeared behind Michel to wrench the gun from his grasp—but not before it discharged.

A woman's voice screamed, "No!"

Blanchette crumpled to the ground at Heinrich's feet.

"Oh God, no!" Luc cried. He teetered, then dropped to his knees, his hands clawing his head. "Addie!" he pleaded.

Heinrich scrambled to help, relying on the adrenaline coursing through his body and his medical training. Blanchette's face clenched in pain, her fingers instinctively pressed to the wound on her arm. He motioned to Marchand. *"Le mouchoir, vite!"* He coiled it around her bicep and squeezed. There was so much blood, he could not determine with a quick glance if the bullet was still lodged in her arm, or if it had just grazed the skin as it whizzed by.

"Blanchette, Blanchette," he begged. "Tell me, were you hit anywhere besides the arm?"

She winced and bit her lip. "No, I don't think so," she replied, struggling for breath.

He raised her arm and asked Marchand to continue apply pressure while he inspected Blanchette for other wounds. After a cursory examination, he found none.

By then, a snowy-haired woman had appeared with bandages, towels and iodine. Heinrich nodded in gratitude and set to work, fashioning a tourniquet from a towel and bandaging the wound.

"Heinrich," Blanchette said. "Were you shot?"

"No," he grumbled, wishing he had taken the bullet instead of her.

Blanchette's lips twitched in pain. "Werner," she said breathlessly. "For Werner."

Once Blanchette's arm was stabilized and Heinrich had guided her into the house to Ondine's bed, he inspected the gash.

Luckily, the bullet had sped by and torn the flesh from her bicep without any damage to the bone. Luc, Ondine and Marchand all hovered over patient and medic as Heinrich cleaned the wound and rebandaged it.

Though pale and weak, Blanchette still managed to issue commands from her bed. "Luc, we must get Heinrich to the border."

"I'm not leaving you now," Heinrich said.

"You must. We can't draw any more attention to my family."

"But—"

She patted his cheek. "I can care for myself." She choked back tears. "And your son needs you." Sniffling, she turned to Luc. "You must drive Heinrich to Lyon. There he can hop one of the hospital trains to Geneva. It's our only hope."

Luc bristled. "Addie, no."

Marchand curled his palm around Luc's shoulder. "I am duty-bound to help Leutnant Sommer," Marchand chided. "That is what I intend to do."

Ondine glanced expectantly at Luc. Even at a few paces, Heinrich could feel the electricity pulsating between them. Luc finally acquiesced. "I will leave the decision to your father."

"An eye for an eye?" Ondine gazed at her father expectantly.

"A tooth for a tooth." Her father smiled gently.

"A life for a life," she said earnestly, stepping forward. She pressed a cool hand to Heinrich's cheek. "A life for a life," she repeated fervently.

CHAPTER 17

November–December 1918

VOUVRAY, FRANCE

Since July, the Allies had steadily pushed the Germans back, expelling them from most of France and Belgium. British troops had pierced the Hindenburg Line, and the Allied forces had contained the U-boat threat in the Atlantic. From July through November, Germany suffered close to a million casualties, but the Americans had increased their boots on the ground to nearly two million, or so the newspapers claimed.

Papa's letter from Napa had confirmed the details of Lydia and Aurora's deaths from the influenza, along with Pippa and Johnny's good health. Marie, Rourke and Gemma had lived through a terrible bout of *la grippe*, but Gemma's lungs were still asthmatic.

In Vouvray, hundreds of kilometers from the front, and having evaded the influenza himself, Luc had every reason to be optimistic, but his grief was crippling at times. He inhaled the cool afternoon air until he felt its familiar sting. He followed Ondine's advice every day: he envisioned his lungs breathing more steadily, filling more expansively, healing every shred of damage perpetrated by the sickly yellow gas. The results taught him to hope that one day he might feel as vigorous as he had the day he had enlisted.

Luc surveyed the ten hectares of vines at Saint Martin. Over the last week, the leaves had changed from shades of vibrant green to brilliant gold with strokes of crimson. The harvest had ended with two hundred eighty barrels of chenin blanc aging in the cellar. Capitaine Marchand had delivered the German to the Swiss border with only minor difficulty, and Adeline's wound had healed enough for her to return to Royat to continue her nursing duties. Luc had anticipated that the *gendarmes* would come looking for Adeline and her German, but they never did. He could not understand why.

Capitaine Marchand walked toward him, between the vines, and upon catching Luc's eye, doffed his cap and waved it in the air. He was tall, elegant and impeccably mannered, even in the sack coat and dungarees Luc had loaned him. Still, Luc's heart began to beat in triple time and his palms grew clammy. *Should he just blurt out his question, or ease into it? Did Marchand already suspect?*

"We just received the news! The Kaiser has abdicated. It will only be a matter of time now before France and Germany stop fighting." This announcement, on the heels of German general Ludendorff's forced resignation the week before, meant that peace was truly within reach.

438

The men clapped each other on the back. During the month since Marchand had arrived at Saint Martin—with an honorable discharge from his division—the two men had formed a strong bond. Although Luc had disagreed vehemently with Marchand's insistence on helping Sommer escape across the Swiss border, he had come to respect the man's sense of duty and honor.

Watching Ondine and Michel reconnect with their father these past few weeks had reminded Luc how important family ties were, especially amid such gut-wrenching loss. He had swallowed his pride and made peace with Adeline, but he had only begrudgingly given Sommer his favorite trousers and some food for the journey.

"*Capitaine*, I wish you and Michel and Ondine to stay on with us—here, at Saint Martin."

"That is a very kind offer, son, but we must establish our own life, find our own way without Brigitte. We will return to Lille when the war is officially over."

Luc had never heard Madame Marchand's Christian name. "Brigitte," he repeated under his breath.

"Yes. Her loss is sometimes too much to bear," Marchand confided, grief welling in his eyes.

"Of course, sir." Luc wrung his felt hat between his hands and inhaled. "Sir, do you think that your Brigitte would approve of me?"

"Of course. You and your grandparents saved our children. She would be—she is—eternally grateful, as am I."

Luc nodded, squinting into the sun. "I mean"—he paused, gathering courage—"I mean, would she approve of me for her daughter?"

Marchand's expression was caught somewhere between bewilderment and suspicion. "You care for Ondine in that way?"

"Yes, sir. I love her."

Marchand scratched his half-day beard and began to walk. Luc fell into step beside him. "Does she return your . . . affection?"

"I believe so."

"She has endured the unimaginable." He shook his balled fist and his voice thinned, as taut as a high wire. "Such violence. I have never experienced its equal, not even on the battlefield."

"I know," Luc agreed hoarsely, diverting his gaze to allow Marchand a moment of privacy. "I promise, I will protect her."

Marchand stopped abruptly. "She may never recover completely."

Luc knew this, but he could no more quash his need for Ondine than he could stop breathing. "I understand."

"Tell me, Lemieux, when you found Leutnant Sommer and had him at gunpoint, what did you intend to do? Before I intervened?"

Luc debated whether he should tell Marchand the truth. "Kill him," he said with conviction. "For what the Germans did to Ondine—to your family."

"You would not have delivered him back to the army?"

"No, sir."

"Ondine convinced you to let him go."

"Yes."

"How?"

Luc kicked the clay loam beneath his boot and mulled the question. Truth be told, he would have done anything to gain

Ondine's approval, to prove his worthiness. "If Ondine saw fit to discern between the Huns who hurt her, who killed her mother, and the man who saved her father, then it was not my place to interfere with such an act of generosity."

After a few moments of contemplation, Marchand extended his hand. Luc grasped it, a strange sort of exhilaration—or maybe it was hope—surging through his veins.

Marchand raised his gaze to the heavens, then lowered it to meet Luc's expectant smile. "You have our blessing, son." He chuckled. "But that's the easy part."

———

In the early morning hours of November 11 in the Compiègne Forest, in France, the Allies and Germany signed the armistice agreement. At the eleventh hour of the eleventh day of the eleventh month, the armies ceased their fire. When the Vouvray church bells finally stopped tolling an hour later, Luc quietly led Ondine away from the vineyard celebrations to the *pigeonnier* in the woods—and offered his hand in marriage.

Ondine blinked hard. Kneeling on the grass, his fingers threaded through hers, Luc waited patiently. His warm mahogany eyes, muscular shoulders, high cheekbones and silky tousle of dark hair made him physically irresistible to her, but she had not anticipated this. Since their first kiss a few weeks ago, they had stolen others, but he had made no declaration of love until now. She could not imagine her life without him—the mere thought of his absence raised a knot of despair in her throat.

"Ondine?" he rose and kissed her hands.

Since the attack nearly a year ago, she had retreated to the darkest corners of her mind, replaying the sights and smells and horror of that night over and over. When Luc had rescued her from the river, the unexpected force of his embrace had anchored her spirit to her body once again. Four months later, when he had comforted her in the *pigeonnier*, she had felt the first flicker of desire. Now, as she felt his warm skin against hers, she feared she might burst into flames. Ondine wanted to lie beside him, to run her hands over his bare chest, to be as close as a man and woman could be, but did Luc truly feel the same? Heat rushed to her cheeks. *What if her body betrayed her?* She gulped before blurting, "What about Virginia?"

He recoiled. "What about her? That ended months ago."

"Why?" she asked innocently.

He hesitated for a moment. "Because I was injured in the war, and I didn't feel the same about her anymore."

"Or she didn't feel the same about you?" Ondine probed.

"It wasn't like that! You are the woman I love, the one I need. I know that now."

Desperate to escape his scrutiny for a moment, she tugged on the *pigeonnier* doors. The paint had begun to peel. Pigeons darted past her and swirled over their heads, eager to fly and feed. The aroma of bird dung and sun-drenched hay wafted from the entrance.

Ondine whirled around to face him. "I see. You and I are both damaged, so we would make a good pair," she said bitterly.

"Why are you doing this? Why are you dredging up the past?" He eased toward her, looking confused and forlorn.

She glanced up at him, moisture spilling from the corners of her eyes. "What if I can't give you what *she* gave you?"

His knuckles grazed her cheek. "Oh, Ondine, you have already given me so much more."

She averted his gaze. "But I am not a virgin."

He lifted her chin. "You are to me," he said solemnly.

"What if I am scarred . . . forever?" she whispered. "What if I can't—?"

"Do you love me? Do you trust me?"

"Yes," she replied hoarsely.

He tucked a flyaway strand of yellow hair behind her ear. "Then we will come to know each other over time. Slowly, carefully."

The notion was tantalizing, almost too pleasurable to bear. She beat back her embarrassment long enough to pose one final question. "*Alors*, you do intend . . . that is to say . . . you do desire me?" She held her breath, waiting for his answer, each second an eternity.

He leaned toward her, his mouth hovering near her ear. "I think my intentions would make you blush," he said, gently biting her earlobe. Their hips melded and his moist lips parted hers, stealing every doubt, rendering her speechless. "Did you ever consider that I've been holding back all these weeks because I didn't want to overwhelm you or . . . threaten you in any way?"

She slid her arms around his neck. "A marriage of polite friendship would never satisfy me."

"What would?" he asked playfully.

"I think my answer would make *you* blush."

"I doubt that." He placed his arms on her waist, lifted and twirled her around until she was dizzy with happiness.

"Say yes," he commanded.

"*Bien sûr,* yes!"

———

NAPA, CALIFORNIA

On November 21, ten days after the armistice was signed, Congress passed a full statutory wartime prohibition that would take effect on July 1, 1919 and render the sale of all alcoholic beverages illegal. Sara questioned the logic of passing a wartime prohibition when the war was clearly over, but Philippe reminded her that Congress rarely acted logically and that the war would not technically end until the peace treaty was signed.

The grape quality that harvest had been excellent, but the demand for wine had skyrocketed in anticipation of the prohibition to come. They had more orders than they could fill, especially now that new prune trees had replaced acres upon acres of grape vines in the neighboring farms across Napa.

Sara scanned the *Napa Register.* Her finger slid down the impossibly long list: *Victims of the Influenza.* Her macabre ritual had started the week after Lydia's burial. In some backwards way, it gave her comfort to know which souls—which friends and neighbors—now kept company with Lydia and Aurora in the heavens. When she discovered Boone Sumter's name, she grieved for his wife, who had now lost both husband and son, but felt certain that God had reserved a special closet in purgatory for gossipmongers.

She heard Philippe's springy footsteps approach the parlor. In his work boots, dungarees and sack coat, he was thinner, but his penetrating azure eyes and fair, rugged good looks still gave her a jolt every time he walked into a room.

"Any news?" she inquired, shame-faced that he'd caught her lolling around reading the paper when she should be in the winery helping to rack the wines.

"I've ordered more wooden shook to make lug boxes for shipping next harvest. That ought to keep us occupied this winter." He waved a small piece of paper in the air. "And we just received a telegram from France."

Sara steeled herself. "Good news, I hope?"

"Luc is to be married." He reread the lines. "To a Miss Ondine Marchand of Lille, on Christmas Eve." He gave it to Sara.

"Lille? By the Belgian border?"

"Apparently."

Sara's heart leapt with joy for their adopted son, their nephew. How Lydia her sister and Lydia her daughter would have given anything to stand by Luc's side on such a momentous occasion. Sara stared down at the newspaper resting on her lap. Her daughter's sudden death had nearly killed her. She had wanted to die with Lydia, to sleep between her daughter and Aurora in the graves by the edge of the orchard. But now the road split like a snake's tongue and she must decide.

"Sara?" Philippe sat beside her. How many times had she asked him not to sit on the settee in his work clothes so as not to spoil the fabric? *What did any of that pettiness matter now?*

When he squeezed her hand, she inhaled deeply. "How soon can we book passage?"

"Ha, ha! Yes!" He cradled her head in his palms and kissed her hard on the lips. "That's my girl," he whispered, bursting with hope. "That's my intrepid girl."

———————

The next day, Philippe and Johnny disappeared with promises to return by suppertime. Coincidentally, Marie appeared at Sara's door an hour after they left. She had left a convalescing Gemma and a mischievous Rourke at home. Though the influenza epidemic was waning, Marie kept her children quarantined with their nanny and a nurse to tend them. She had been forced to shutter the medical boarding house and had seen a limited number of surgical cases since the epidemic had spread.

Sara eyed her friend suspiciously. "Philippe asked you to come?"

"He worries about you."

"I worry about him, so stoic. And you. Any word?"

"Nothing from Matthew in over a month, I'm afraid. Adeline wrote. She's back in Royat after a visit to Saint Martin. She must have met this Ondine, although she didn't mention her."

"Perhaps she didn't like her?" Sara speculated, although the thought had never occurred to her that they would not love the woman Luc chose to marry.

Marie shrugged. "I just think she's preoccupied, with her duties and Matthew's whereabouts. What about Pippa? How is she adjusting to her new life as an independent woman of means?"

"She plans to continue on at Hudson's and making masks once the epidemic is over."

"Even after she broke it off with Billy? That could be awkward, don't you think?"

Sara's gaze narrowed. The innocent expression on Marie's pretty, round face was all too familiar. "What are you hinting at?"

Marie covered Sara's hand with her own. "Just that her plans may be quite different than you suppose, my dear."

———

Later that evening, Pippa, who had spent the last two weeks cleaning Aurora's former home and lovingly organizing the photos and keepsakes she had salvaged, gathered with the rest of the family and Marie at Eagle's Run for supper. Philippe rushed to share the news: they would all depart for France on December 1, with a stop in New York City. He had booked their passage this very morning. Marie, regrettably, could not join them. She still feared for Gemma's health and would leave it to Sara and Philippe to report back on Adeline and Matthew's well-being.

Pippa bubbled with excitement. "Might we journey to Paris while we are there?" she asked.

"Perhaps in the days following the wedding, if there's time." Philippe seemed surprised by his daughter's sudden interest in travel.

Sara knew better. "How long will we be in New York?" she asked.

"Our ship sails on the eighth. We'll be there just long enough to check in on the Reverend Mother and give her this." He slid an envelope across the table to Sara.

"They finally did it?" Sara asked hopefully as the note crinkled in her hands.

"Read."

By virtue of appointment of his Grace, the Archbishop of San Francisco, my colleagues and I have continuously supervised the making and distributing of the Altar Wine made at the Eagle's Run cellars in Napa County, California. The Vineyard belongs to Mr. and Mrs. Philippe Lemieux. From my personal supervision of the making of these Altar Wines, and as an agent for his Grace, the Archbishop of San Francisco, I hereby testify to the purity of all the Altar Wines manufactured at the Eagle's Run cellars.

It was signed by Monsignor O'Brien. "Our good friend had to nudge the good archbishop to agree," Philippe pointed out.

Johnny interjected between bites of roasted chicken, "And Pop sweetened the deal by—"

"Let's not bore Maman with all the details," Philippe said. The boy's mouth clamped shut. "We have our license to sell sacramental wine for the duration of prohibition. We just need to convince the Reverend Mother to act as our broker with the eastern archdioceses."

"You just leave that to us," Sara replied, with a quick wink at Marie.

Billy had not telephoned, nor had he come to call in the weeks after Pippa had ended their courtship. She had followed up with a note to say that she was leaving California, but no reply came.

He had made her feel beautiful and cherished. She missed him terribly, but she could no longer ignore the gnawing truth: she did not love Billy Hudson, just the notion of him.

Pippa scanned the crowd as she stood on the Napa Depot platform, just moments before she and her family would board the train bound for San Francisco, where they would change to another for New York. Billy was absent. Perhaps he did not love her either, or she had wounded him too deeply.

As mild mannered as Pippa normally was, frustration percolated inside her. She was angry with Billy, with God, with Maman. This ire now fueled Pippa and had driven her to make her decision—independent of what anyone else thought.

It had all been arranged: the trip to Europe with her family, Marie's letter of introduction to Anna Coleman Ladd and the artists at the Studio for Portrait Masks in Paris, Pippa's reservation at a reputable women's *auberge* nearby for the month of January, until she could find more long-term lodgings. She had rented out Aurora's house to a teacher and his family, who would take up the lease on January 1. She would open a bank account in Paris with some of the money Aurora had left her. That money, along with the rental income and royalty payments, would support Pippa for at least two years in the City of Lights. She dreaded telling her parents.

Pippa, Johnny, Maman and Papa settled into their compartment. No one said a word. The atmosphere was stale without Lydia—her bouncing curls, her effervescent chortle. Maman was thinner, paler, quieter. Dark smudges beneath her eyes told of sleepless nights. Jagged fingernails and unpolished boots told of a woman who could barely rise from bed, never mind tend to her toilette.

Pippa feared that Maman might die from heartbreak. She watched her like a bomb that could detonate at any moment. Pippa could no longer endure the strain, nor could she allow her mother's grief to guilt her into staying.

Papa, who constantly endeavored to act as Maman's cheerful foil, sat next to her and across from Pippa and Johnny, reading the newspaper and popping handfuls of nuts into his mouth.

"Papa?" she ventured.

He offered her the bag of peanuts, which she refused before announcing, "Papa, I need to tell you and Maman something." He lowered his paper, and Maman even lifted her head from his shoulder, her senses still heightened, still fearing and anticipating the worst.

"This oughtta be good," Johnny teased, nudging Pippa with his elbow. "What's up, sis?" he asked as he shuffled a deck of cards.

After an obligatory eye roll, Pippa launched in. "I won't be returning to America with you. I have made plans to stay in Paris."

Maman and Papa exchanged a glance. Papa spoke first. "What kind of plans?"

The words *I am independent now* perched on Pippa's tongue, ready for deployment, when she realized she might not need them. She smoothed her skirt, trying to anticipate her father's next reaction. "At my request, Marie has kindly written a letter of introduction to Anna Coleman Ladd, the American sculptor who runs the Studio for Portrait Masks in Paris, on which we based our studio."

"Really? Will you be working with her, then?" Papa asked nonchalantly. Johnny's jaw hung in disbelief.

"Yes, and living in an *auberge* close by until I can make another arrangement."

"Just make sure that you write us every week and call your brother Luc every Sunday."

"That seems fair," Pippa agreed, watching them closely. She waited for the catch, the rub, the trick, the other shoe to drop. Nothing happened. Her mind swirled with confusion. She couldn't bear it any longer. Crossing her arms defiantly, she asked, "Is that it?"

"Hmm?" Maman replied, now jotting calculations in the vineyard ledger. *Was she preparing for their visit to the convent and distribution office in New York? Why was she so calm about Pippa's plans? Did she care so little?*

"What?" Papa peered over the edge of his *San Francisco Chronicle.*

"I don't understand why you haven't raised any objections."

"To what specifically?"

"To my living in Paris!"

"Oh." He exchanged another indecipherable glance with Maman.

Pippa counted out on her fingers. "I'm unmarried. I'll be alone. I'll be in an unfamiliar city working with strangers."

"At least you speak the language," Johnny offered brightly.

"Sounds like you've thought of everything," Papa added wryly.

"Wait—is this about Billy?" The suspicion struck like lightning.

"Whatever do you mean?" Maman asked.

Pippa wagged a finger. "You never liked him, Maman. And you never trusted him, Papa."

"That could be said of any man who dares to court our daughter." Philippe butted Maman's shoulder, chuckling conspiratorially.

Maman returned a rare smile and shrugged. "We thought a change of scenery might do you good."

"Wait, what? You knew?"

Maman's lips pressed into a thin line while she hesitated. "I meant a change of scenery for us all. Time in France with family should do us a world of good, don't you think?"

Skepticism crinkled Pippa's brow. "Did Marie tip you off?"

"Marie has been our friend for nearly three decades. Of course she tipped us off."

Pippa huffed, indignation rising, steam threatening to blow from her ears.

Maman patted Pippa's knee. "Luc and his fiancée—or wife by the time you leave for Paris—will help move you into your new home."

Pippa harrumphed. She still had one ace up her sleeve. "You needn't worry about my finances. I'll have a steady flow of cash from my investments."

"Is that so?" Papa sounded impressed.

"Indeed," Pippa said haughtily. "I have let out Aurora's house. Your new neighbors move in next month."

"Is that so?"

"A teacher and his family."

"But I thought—" Johnny began before Papa interrupted.

"Sounds promising."

"But—" Johnny persisted before Maman's glance silenced him.

"Pippa, there will be a teacher there, but he won't be living with his wife and children. He'll be supervising five boys from St. Isidore's Agricultural School," Papa said.

Johnny's chest puffed up. "And I'll be assisting him."

"What!" Pippa exclaimed.

"You needn't fuss. We saw your solicitor's advertisement in the paper. We had just reached a deal with the archdiocese to house five of their boys displaced by a family who lost their home in the Rutherford fire. They'll attend Las Amigas schoolhouse and help with the chores at the vineyard until beds become available at St. Isidore's."

"And you didn't think to tell me?" she shrieked.

Papa lowered his voice. "You didn't think to tell us either. Besides, your solicitor knows."

"It was my own personal business!"

"Well, now it's family business. We will look out for the place and you'll receive a generous check each month. It's all settled."

Pippa diverted her gaze to the window. Her indignation slowly evaporated as she watched the passing landscape, painted in brown, gold and scarlet, dotted with grazing sheep and cattle. She sighed, supposing she would have to release the only arrow of surprise she had left in her quiver.

"I have applied to study at the *École des Beaux-Arts* in Paris. I will matriculate in August if they accept me. My interview is in February."

To Pippa's satisfaction, her parents were flabbergasted. "I thought that was Billy's dream," Maman said.

"It's mine now," Pippa said unapologetically.

Papa tapped the tip of Pippa's nose with his finger, as he had when she was a toddler. "You, Miss Lemieux, are going to do just fine." Pippa's ebullient smile spanned from ear to ear.

———

ROYAT, FRANCE

On Thanksgiving Day 1918, Adeline Donnelly had indeed counted her blessings. She had successfully faked a German prisoner's death, carried out a plan to transport him over the Swiss border, survived a bullet, dodged the risk of infection, returned to Base Hospital No. 30 at Royat and celebrated jubilantly with her colleagues when the armistice was signed. Only one question troubled her: Had Heinrich even made it to Köln?

Two weeks before Christmas, and four weeks before the hospital would be disbanded and the remaining staff would be transferred to Saint Nazaire, Adeline waited at the entrance of the majestic, white-columned former Metropole Hotel. Surgical Team No. 51 was expected any minute now. They were bringing a few special guests: convalescing shell-shocked soldiers, many of whom had been concussed or buried in dirt for hours when the last artillery shells had hit at the Battle of Amiens.

As the ambulances rolled up, Adeline stood on tiptoes to catch a glimpse of her stepfather. His kindness and humor would surely be a balm for what ailed her.

The corpsmen carried the writhing soldiers in on stretchers. Adeline directed them to the room that had been scrubbed and prepared with five cots and fresh linens in a particularly quiet wing of the hospital. Sally Dunn met them there, a clipboard clasped to her chest.

"They reassigned you as well?" Adeline asked, pleased to have the company of her friend and head nurse, especially since she was not familiar with the treatments for nervous conditions.

"Yes, back to basics with this crew," she said merrily. "You know, bedpans, walks, soft music, conversation." Adeline agreed. Although it was disconcerting to watch the men tremble involuntarily, she was relieved to skip the trips to the incinerator.

"You're handling this well." Sally rested a hand on her friend's arm.

Adeline perked up. "I'm always eager to help and to learn. Have you seen Matthew—I mean, Lieutenant Colonel Donnelly?"

Sally gently guided Adeline from the room. "My dear," she began in a hushed tone, "didn't you recognize him?"

Adeline clenched with alarm.

"He is—he's one of our new patients." Sally broke the news with a sympathetic glance into the room. "There, by the window."

All the blood rushed from Adeline's head.

"Oh, my dear, did they not warn you?"

She shook her head and collapsed against the wall.

When she drummed up the nerve to go back in to the room, she saw Matthew lounging in the corner chair, near the window that looked over the towering former hotels that formed Base Hospital No. 30. His head craned toward the glass, but focused on nothing, eyes rounded in perpetual shock. His legs shimmied, stretching straight, toes pointed, ankles rigid. He crossed his wrists over his lap and stammered, "Wh-wh-where is i-i-it?" He repeated the phrase over and over, spittle collecting on his lips.

"Was he near a blast?" Adeline whispered to the corpsman nearby, her heart threatening to burst from her chest.

"No ma'am. He was behind the line, sewing our butchered boys back together."

"I don't understand. He's exhibiting shell-shock symptoms."

"Nerves, ma'am. Purely emotional is my guess. The strain was too much."

Adeline stood motionless before she exhaled. *What on earth was she to do?* She must write Maman, but first she must assess the damage, study his physical and psychological symptoms, and report back. She would tell Maman about his symptoms and possible treatments—as a nurse would to a physician, not to a man's wife. Maman would expect no less.

Over the next three days, Adeline spent every spare moment she had speaking with the stammering Matthew, observing the specific trembling of his limbs, his hysterical dancing gait, the nose-swiping tic he employed when distressed, the slow but steady easing of the tissue around his eyes as his expression relaxed slightly from one of intense surprise to one of mild fright.

Adeline interviewed the surgeons, nurses and corpsmen of his surgical team and learned that his symptoms had started soon after he had lost three boys over the course of one afternoon. He had missed a piece of shrapnel lodged deep in the third boy's quadricep. He had succumbed to infection, which had turned to sepsis. Matthew had blamed himself. He had lived in this state for over a month with little improvement. *Why had no one told her? Because she had been recovering from a gunshot wound in Saint Martin.*

Her despair was acute. Her strong, handsome, accomplished father had been reduced to a state of utter infantilism. She could not account for it, but she was determined to treat it.

The letter to her mother was like a hot coal in her hand. It contained a full account of Matthew's tribulations. She still withheld all mention of Heinrich Sommer and her own accident. In time, perhaps she would confide in her mother. For now, they had all agreed to keep silent on the matter.

She tensed as she dropped the letter in the mail tray.

"Donnelly?" a squat, bearish man in a postal uniform asked.

"Yes?"

"A letter for you."

Her spirits lifted. Perhaps it was news from San Francisco. The envelope was thick and the return address listed Luc Lemieux of Clos du Saint Martin in Vouvray. She stepped into the brightly painted corridor and ripped open the envelope. It contained a letter and a smaller envelope, still sealed.

Adeline rallied when she read Luc's letter. He and Ondine would be married on Christmas Eve. Could she and Matthew escape for the holiday to join them? The letter went on to inquire about their health but made no mention of the smaller envelope contained within.

Adeline turned the mystery mail over in her hands. It was addressed to her, care of Luc Lemieux. There was no return address. She carefully tore it open and unfolded the sheet therein. She froze. *Pour Ma Blanchette* was written in elegant script at the top of the page. Beneath it, the artist had traced a pair of hands—one a man's and the other a child's.

Adeline gripped the doorjamb, pressing the precious memento to her heart, revisiting every caress, every whisper of their two nights together. Heinrich was all she had ever wanted in a lover, but it was their unexpected friendship that had transformed her.

Adeline had been in her mother's womb when her father, Bastien Lemieux, had abandoned them. She had grown up with a mother who adored her, but even Maman's ferocious love could not plug the hole whittled by her father's indifference.

She had promised herself when she became a nurse that she would never allow herself to grow impervious to others' pain. This conviction, stoked by her own lack, had compelled her to give Heinrich up to Werner, so that dear child could experience a father's love in the wake of his own mother's senseless abandonment.

Adeline convulsed into a sob. All was as it should be! At another time, in another place, perhaps a Franco-American nurse and a German medic might forge a life together. *At another time, in another place . . . far from here.*

———

KÖLN, GERMANY

Heinrich and Werner Sommer strolled through the Christmas market near Köln's town hall. The immense, ornate twin towers of the Gothic cathedral rose higher than any other in all of Europe and, in the twilight hours, appeared to glow from Heinrich's vantage point below. The Alter Markt itself, set on the winding streets of the old town and lined with decorative huts showcasing toys, treats, handmade ornaments and clothing, seemed unscathed by war. The citizens of Köln, however, were strikingly gaunt and shabbily dressed.

Heinrich watched the British soldiers posted along the streets. The dragoons had crossed the border on the cold morning of December 3, threading their way through desolate streets and past the black ash and debris of bonfires lit only days earlier by German soldiers ordered to retreat across the Rhine. By the time the British reached Köln on December 6, their drums had ceased to beat, the batter heads soaked from the driving rain.

The prevailing sentiment tonight was one of relief, not only because the killing was over, but because the arrival of the Allied forces had quashed the Reds and ended weeks of looting by the defeated, demobilized soldiers and sailors. Heinrich, for his part, was grateful to be alive, to have evaded the French and Swiss border guards, to have found his son safe and sound.

Smiles and laughter, so foreign to his ears, were the order of the day this Christmas Eve. In the New Year, the citizens of the Rhineland would return to their studied indifference toward the occupying forces and brace for more humiliation as the details of the peace treaty were hammered out.

Heinrich chose to dwell in the present moment, with the indescribable joy he felt to see Werner's radiant fascination as he tinkered with a set of colorfully painted wooden toys. He was several centimeters taller now, at almost six years old, with a shock of yellow hair and a keen curiosity. Heinrich ruffled the boy's newly clipped hair, trying to tamp down the cowlick at the crown of his head with no luck. Anna had always been the barber in the family. Heinrich would simply have to practice such domestic skills when he wasn't working to provide for them and save money so he could one day return to medical school.

At the bakery, the white sugary glaze of a cruller clung to Werner's lips. Heinrich explained, "The *Heinzelmännchen* arranged all of this." He swept his arm wide, motioning to the baker, butcher, shoemaker and other artisan's huts surrounding them.

"Gnomes, Vater?" the boy asked in disbelief.

"Yes. They wake early in the morning to shake off the snow and set to work. They make the sausages for the butcher and raise the dough for the baker and carve the *klompen* for the clog maker."

Werner's eyes expanded to the size of saucers. "What do they look like?"

"Short little creatures, bushy beards, tall, pointed caps," Heinrich said between bites of his warm, sugary doughnut.

Werner giggled and licked the icing off his fingers.

———

After attending the Christmas vigil, father and son toured the vast cathedral, strolling to the shrine of the Magi with its magnificent medieval goldwork dating back to the thirteenth century.

"The three kings who brought the baby Jesus gifts?" Werner asked, wide-eyed.

"Indeed. Their relics are buried here."

When they reached the lady chapel, Heinrich slid the plain silver wedding band from his right hand and placed it in the collection plate. He knelt beside Werner at the altar and pulled him close. The boy's ribs were as fragile as twigs beneath his fingers.

"Do you want to light the candles?"

"One for Mama?" Werner asked.

The boy did not understand why Anna had left them, only that she would not return. Heinrich hardly knew how to explain it himself, save for reassuring Werner that they had each other and he was safe now. Heinrich swallowed hard, shoving down a mixture of grief and fury. *How could a woman abandon her son?* He had been such a fool to fall for her empty charm in the first place.

"Of course, for Mama."

Werner stepped up to the thick marble railing and reached for a long match. Heinrich helped him light it. Together, they lit one for Anna.

"Choose six more," Heinrich whispered.

"For whom, Vater?"

Heinrich listed the names slowly so Werner could repeat them. "Pierre, Michel, Ondine, Marguerite, Luc." Werner brightened as he successfully lit the cluster of votive candles before him. "And the sixth one, Vater?"

"We save the best for last, Werner. Adeline."

"Adeline?"

"Yes, Adeline saved me and sent me home to you."

"Adeline," Werner repeated, as if the mere mention of her name were a holy secret.

A lump caught in Heinrich's throat. "One day you will meet her, Werner. I promise."

"Adeline. Is she an angel, Vater?" His eyes blazed like blue beacons.

Heinrich kissed his little boy's hand. "To us. She is to us."

CHAPTER 18

Christmas Eve 1918

VOUVRAY, FRANCE

Luc Lemieux married Ondine Marchand on December 24 at two o'clock in the afternoon at the Église de Tous les Saints in Vouvray. The bride's and groom's families were both in attendance.

While Luc waited near the altar for the ornately carved doors to open and his bride to appear, he calmed his nerves by studying the members of the congregation. Their clothing was muted, in somber tones of gray, navy and brown, with occasional hint of color. Grandmère beamed, pleased as punch to welcome her daughter and grandchildren back to the family home. She celebrated the occasion with a sprig of red holly berries on her lapel. Maman looked stylish in a new taupe silk dress with a trim little jacket and sash, and Papa handsome in his navy suit, plaid shawl-collar waistcoat and cobalt silk tie.

Beneath the miniature portrait of Lydia, painted by Pippa and tucked neatly in Luc's left breast pocket, he felt a stab of grief. The influenza had killed millions of innocents across the world and had only recently begun to taper off. If only he had been able to see Lydia and Aurora one last time . . .

Luc bit his lip, his gaze drifting to his remaining sisters. In Lydia's honor, Pippa had braided a yellow ribbon through her hair. She had grown into a striking young woman, her golden hair just a shade darker than Ondine's. Luc made a mental note to warn his sister off the soldiers who might pursue her once she arrived in Paris. He would have none of that. He knew what rascals his fellow soldiers could be. Adeline had twined her arm through Pippa's as the pair whispered and eyed Luc at the altar. He shook his head in disapproval, but true to form, they only giggled.

On the other side of Adeline, Pip and Mim Chevreau bolstered their son-in-law, Matthew, as he gripped the pew in front of him. Since he and Adeline had arrived the day before, the family had quickly adjusted to his involuntary twitches, which Adeline had quietly explained were the result of a mental breakdown of some sort. Michel had warmed to Matthew instantly, sitting cross-legged on the floor, mesmerized by the surgeon's tales of his medical adventures at the front. Matthew still stuttered but took great care to deflect all attention from his own tribulations and revel in the festivities. Adeline, generous soul that she was, had forgiven Michel after she learned more details about their traumatic attack by the German soldiers.

The heat of shame rose on Luc's skin. He had not considered what Adeline and Matthew might have endured in the operating rooms, hacking off limbs, carving out the most minute shards of shrapnel, wading in blood and filth and bile to save souls. He was wrong to have called Adeline a traitor. He would never approve of her relationship with the German, but Luc had to concede that Heinrich Sommer was an honorable man. He had rescued Ondine's father, and in doing so, he had saved Ondine and Michel.

The organ began to blare, and Johnny, his best man, was at his side whispering excitedly, "Are you ready?" The swinging doors released a swath of sunshine into the church, momentarily blinding Luc and the congregants. The bride, escorted by her father, had glided halfway down the aisle before Luc realized he had forgotten to breathe. He sucked in long ribbons of air.

He would never remember what Ondine wore that day, only that the gown and veil were simple and white and stunning. From the creamy, supple skin of her slim neck to the rosy apples of her cheeks, to the pink pout that had taught him mercy, to the shimmering sapphires that now returned his devoted gaze, Ondine was all woman—and Luc was undeniably all hers.

After the ceremony and a grand meal of fresh-caught trout, roasted squab, buttered asparagus, potatoes, and a delectable assortment of cheeses and cake, Sara and Philippe toured the vineyard. The sun hovered near the horizon on this brisk, December day. Sara drew her wool shawl over her shoulders.

"Luc did a fine job this harvest. Jacques would be so very proud," Philippe said.

Sara smiled faintly in agreement.

"Penny for your thoughts," he offered.

Since Lydia's death, Sara had fallen into a muddle, but her return to Saint Martin had ushered in a flood of vibrant, once-submerged memories—some delightful, others distressing.

"Aurora has been on my mind. Lydia, too, of course, but Aurora took Luc and me in and gave us a home all those years ago. Without her, you and I never would have met, would never have reconciled and married and built this business . . . this life together."

"Ah, Aurora. She was a second mother to me."

"And to me. Do you remember that first dinner party she held at her home for all the wine men and their wives, to introduce me? When was that? 1897?"

"Good Lord, last century! Can we be that old, Mrs. Lemieux?"

"Speak for yourself," Sara teased. "Aurora was scheming to marry me off even then."

"To either me or the priest, Father what's-his-name." Philippe chuckled.

"I was afraid of you but wanted so desperately to impress you."

Philippe tapped a finger to his lips. "Something you said that evening has always stuck with me."

"Oh no, what was that?" Sara cringed.

"You said that the land is constant and loyal, something a person can cling to. Then I asked why *you* cling to the land."

Sara nodded as she recalled fragments of their lively conversation. "And I replied, 'Because the land does not disappoint' or some such nonsense."

"Nonsense?"

466

Sara's mouth twisted, a sour taste on her tongue. "Well, the land hasn't disappointed, but Congress certainly has. How can they restrict Americans' rights to make, sell and drink all kinds of alcohol? It's barbaric. It would never happen in France," she declared.

"Absinthe, yes, but all wine? Never," Philippe agreed.

"We worked ourselves down to the nub to leave a legacy for our children and now it's threatened by this ridiculous bill!"

Luc appeared from nowhere and wedged himself between them, draping his arms across their shoulders. "Speaking of prohibition, you two, I have a proposition."

Sara and Philippe exchanged a skeptical glance that did nothing to dampen Luc's enthusiasm. "Two words: St. Pierre."

Sara stopped in her tracks. "Which is what?"

"A tiny French colonial island twenty-five kilometers off the coast of North America." Luc dropped his arms and looked expectantly at his parents.

"Never heard of it," Philippe said.

"Precisely. It's part of a small archipelago of islands located between New York and Greenland and is inhabited entirely by cod fishermen and their boats. Now that the war is over and overseas trading has resumed, my sources tell me it is fast becoming a way station for booze and wine—even *Champagne*. Some schooners can carry over five thousand cases of bottles."

"To where?" Sara asked, flabbergasted.

"The east coast of America, of course."

"Smugglers?" Philippe looked intrigued.

"No!" Sara interjected. "I will not break my promise to the Reverend Mother."

"Of course not. The convent won't be involved. We'll ship our wines to a distributor in St. Pierre, where importing alcohol is entirely legal. We pay our share of the shipping, the distributor fills the customers' orders, and we receive payment. The rumrunners will deliver it to the ports and inlets along the eastern seaboard. The feds won't be able to touch us, Maman." Luc guided his parents over to the painted bench at the edge of the vineyard.

"The European economies are in a shambles, Sara," Philippe said. "Demand for high-quality chenin blanc has all but dried up here, but there will always be demand in the wealthy cities of America."

To Sara's surprise, Luc pulled a folded sheet of paper from his pocket. "Check my calculations, Maman." *On his wedding day? Clearly this was not a passing fancy.*

Sara reviewed the figures. Luc had done his homework. He had worked out an answer for every objection she could have raised. She sighed. Part of her felt too drained to launch another enterprise. The other part, the one that had always craved adventure, inched its way to the front of the line.

"You know Aurora would approve," Philippe nudged, teasing Sara's lips into a smile.

"Aurora would be leading the charge," Sara agreed. "But what does your new wife think?"

With a bashful smile and color rising in his cheeks, Luc replied, "Ondine is still learning the business, but she has never shied away from a challenge. She said she'll agree to it if you approve, Maman."

"Only Maman?" Philippe crossed his arms, clearly amused.

Luc shrugged and slid his hands into his pockets. When he finally lifted his head, his intense brown gaze met Sara's. "I told Ondine she reminded me of you, Maman. Just as you fled France with my mother and me to escape what happened, Ondine fled Paris with Michel to escape the Germans. You both left with nothing but had the pluck to persevere." A shadow passed over his face. Sara had instinctively guessed there was more to Ondine's story than the couple had divulged.

Luc cleared his throat before continuing. "You and Papa and Jacques and Grandmère replanted the vines and worked every harvest for eighteen years so I could one day claim Saint Martin as my own." He squatted down in front of Sara and clasped her hands. "I can't let it fail now, Maman. It's the only thing I'm halfway good at," he added with a laugh.

"That is quite a speech." She had to give the newlyweds credit.

Philippe, too choked up to utter a word, squeezed their joined hands in his.

"What do you say, Maman?"

As she admired the beautiful young man before her, her heart tripped over the memories they had made together. The day he first toddled into the barn at Eagle's Run and Sara had rushed to protect him from the earthquake. The time she searched for him frantically, only to find him tucked away, laughing with Pippa, beneath the canopy of an apple tree. The moment his train pulled away from the Napa Depot, hurtling him down the tracks toward his new life a world away in Vouvray.

Little Lydia's sweet, lilting voice suddenly sliced through Sara's reverie with the sage observation she had made about Aurora before she died. *People are her treasures.*

Sara swallowed her grief and placed her palm against Luc's cheek. "As much as I love Saint Martin, I will always love you more."

"I know, Maman."

"Go on," she said, shooing him away with a wave of her hand. She nestled into Philippe, comforted by his warmth on this brisk Christmas Eve. "Go back to that lovely bride of yours and tell her we have a deal."

FIN – THE END – ENDE

About the Author

Kristen Harnisch is the author of the award-winning, internationally bestselling novels *The Vintner's Daughter*, *The California Wife* and *The Vintner's Legacy*. She drew upon her extensive research and experiences living in the San Francisco Bay Area and visiting the Loire Valley to create the stories for the three historical novels in the series. Ms. Harnisch earned a degree in economics from Villanova University and currently resides in Connecticut. Visit her online at www.kristenharnisch.com or follow her on Twitter @KristenHarnisch or Instagram @kharnischauthor.

Also by Kristen Harnisch

The Vintner's Daughter

In 1895, ambition, betrayal and love take spirited Sara Thibault from her home in the Loire Valley to turn-of-the-century Manhattan to California's wine country, where she must confront the one man who could either return her family's vineyard to her—or send her to the guillotine.

The California Wife

In this sweeping, poignant stand-alone sequel to *The Vintner's Daughter*, the Lemieux family's ambition to establish an American wine-making dynasty takes Sara and Philippe from pastoral Napa to the Paris World's Fair and into the colorful heart of early twentieth-century San Francisco. However, fate has other plans in store for the Lemieux family in the spring of 1906, when a massive earthquake rocks northern California. Will the unstoppable events overwhelm Sara and Philippe's future, despite their devotion to each other?

Author's Note

The Vintner's Legacy, like all my work, is a blending of fact and fiction. Readers often ask how I draw the line between the two.

In the story I took a few creative liberties with timing. The American Expeditionary Forces' (AEF) Services of Supply actually moved from Paris to Tours on January 13, 1918, not in late 1917. The Hello Girls—over two hundred female bilingual wire experts recruited into the U.S. Army Signal Corps by General John Pershing to keep him connected with the troops under fire—first arrived on French soil in March 1918, not in late 1917. They were mostly stationed at the American Headquarters in Chaumont, or on the front, but it seemed reasonable to imagine that some of them may have worked in Tours. I recommend *The Hello Girls: America's First Women Soldiers* by Elizabeth Cobbs if readers would like to learn more about these patriots.

Homing pigeons were indeed used by the U.S. Army Signal

Corps under the initial guidance of British fanciers who, along with the French, had used them since the start of the war to communicate with the citizens of German-occupied Belgium and northern France. I did not find any evidence that pigeons were used in the operations at Chateau-Thierry or Belleau Wood, but it was not beyond the realm of possibility. *Pigeons in the Great War* by A.H. Osman offers unique insight into the care, training and battle heroics of these fearless feathered friends.

At the beginning of the book, I list the cast of characters which includes real historical figures whose words and (in some cases) deeds in the novel are fiction. Captain Eugene Kilgore, M.D., commanding officer of Base Hospital No. 30; Major Alanson Weeks, M.D., of Surgical Team No. 50; and Lieutenant John Homer Woolsey, M.D. of Surgical Team No. 50 were real men who served in Royat-les-Bains and Juilly during the dates mentioned in the novel. The fictional nurses of Surgical Team No. 50—Adeline Donnelly and Sally Dunn—should not be confused with Agnes Dunn and Alta Ireland, the real nurses of the team who deserve recognition for their service.

My primary sources for details of Base Hospital No. 30 and Surgical Team No. 50's service were: *The Thirtieth in Two World Wars: The Story of the University of California Medical School Unit* by Meyer Schindler, M.D. and the four-part guest post for the UCSF Archives and Special Collections website blog: *Base Hospital No. 30 – One Hundred Years Later* by Aaron J. Jackson. For details about war surgery and nursing—along with descriptions of the hospital at Juilly—I turned to *Stretchers* by Frederick Pottle, M.D., *A French World War I Scrapbook* by army nurse Alma A. Clarke, part of the Bryn Mawr College Special Collections, and *A Hoosier Nurse in France: The World War I Diary of Maude Frances Essig,* by Alma S. Woolley.

To portray the harrowing war experiences of the French and German soldiers as accurately as possible, I researched firsthand accounts of their stories in *Poilu: The World War I Notebooks of Corporal Louis Barthas, Barrelmaker* and *German Soldiers in the Great War: Letters and Eyewitness Accounts* by Bernd Ulrich.

While researching the Battles of Chateau-Thierry and Belleau Wood, I found that historians and eyewitnesses sometimes contradicted each other. To decipher the actual troop movements and engagement of the U.S. Army Doughboys and Marines—along with the French Tenth Colonial Division and the Kaiser's 231st Division—I drew my own conclusions from the following sources: *Thunder and Flames: Americans in the crucible of combat, 1917–1918* by Edward G. Lengel, *With the Help of God and a Few Marines: The Battles of Chateau Thierry and Belleau Wood* by Albertus W. Catlin, *Order of Battle of the United States Land Forces in the World War, 1931–1949* by the U.S. Government Printing Office, *The American Army in France, 1917–1919* by James G. Harbord, *The Story of the Doughboys: the AEF in World War I* by Laurence Stallings, *Imperial German Army 1914–18: Organisation, Structure and Order of Battle* by Hermann Cron and Duncan Rogers and the U.S. Army Center of Military History Pamphlet "Into the Fight, April–June 1918" by Dr. Mark Grotelueschen.

Based on my research of the battles, the fictional characters of Luc Thibault, Heinrich Sommer, and Pierre Marchand, and the real soldiers Colonel Paul Malone, Major Charles Elliott, Major Edmund Waddill, Major Berton Sibley and General James Harbord, would have crossed paths as written on these crucial battle dates and in these locations, although the dialogue between them is solely my invention—within the historical context of what transpired.

The unprecedented use of modern weaponry such as rapid-fire machine guns, heavy artillery and flamethrowers in the Great War mutilated men on a scale never seen before. Endeavoring to ease fears of soldiers disfigured in combat as they tried to re-enter society, American sculptor Anna Coleman Ladd opened The Studio for Portrait Masks in Paris and hired artists to fashion prosthetic masks for the facially wounded. Ms. Ladd's innovative studio inspired the storyline for Pippa Lemieux and Billy Hudson. To learn more about Ms. Ladd's amazing work, I recommend Caroline Alexander's February 2007 Smithsonian Magazine feature article, *Faces of War*. There are also some fascinating videos of Ms. Ladd's work online.

St. Isidore's Agricultural School in Rutherford, California was my invention but was inspired by the real existence of St. Joseph's Agricultural Institute, established by the Roman Catholic Archdiocese of San Francisco in the heart of Napa Valley. From 1902–1928, the school taught poor and homeless boys from San Francisco how to work the land and learn a trade. For more historical context, I suggest reading *Frankie's Journey – The Silk Road to Napa* by Stephanie Farrell Grohs and Lauren Coodley.

In *The Vintner's Legacy*, I tried to craft as accurate a portrayal of historical events as possible. If there are any errors or omissions, they are mine alone. I am truly indebted to the aforementioned authors, eyewitnesses and historians for their carefully written accounts of what transpired between 1917 and 1918. Thank you.

For more information on sources, please visit www.kristenharnisch.com.

Acknowledgments

In the Great War spanning 1914–1918, nearly ten million soldiers died from battle wounds or disease and twenty million were wounded. Over seven million soldiers were imprisoned or recorded as missing in action. Over six million civilians died from direct military action, disease and famine. As I face these staggering statistics, it is with awe and humility that I must first thank the courageous men and women who endured such searing physical and psychological suffering—and especially those who sacrificed their lives and futures to fight for their countries.

The research for *The Vintner's Legacy* took over two years to complete and lasted throughout the writing of the final draft. For this fascinating but daunting project, I once again turned to the trusty team of researchers at the Darien Library in Darien, CT. In particular, I would like to thank librarians Blanche Parker and Tina Bothe for tracking down with efficiency and verve the stacks of books and archived documents I requested from around the country.

While exploring the history of World War I and writing the novel, I continually relied on the wisdom and guidance of my father, retired admiral Frank Lacroix, whose extensive knowledge of war history and military tactics, along with his suggestions of key source materials, helped shape the story of *The Vintner's Legacy*. I deeply value his time and his faith in me.

I must thank the U.S. Army Center of Military History and Dr. Mark Grotelhueschen, Dr. Brian Neumann, Gene Snyder, Shannon Granville, William Story and Cheryl Batten for managing to provide me with the 2D Division Order of Battle map during the middle of the coronavirus lockdown when they were not allowed into their offices!

I also would like to extend my gratitude to The Napa County Historical Society, an invaluable resource for all things related to Napa Valley and its winemaking history, and to The Darien [CT] Historical Society, whose 2019 exhibit, *Over Here: Darien's WWI*, displayed artwork, government propaganda posters, uniforms, equipment and soldiers' letters which enhanced my understanding of America's role in World War I.

Thank you to William "Trip" Wilson, our neighbor in Wenham, Massachusetts, for allowing me to pore over his collection of letters and telegrams from 1919 that gave me insights into the lost art of the handwritten note and the cares of a young couple in post-war America.

I am also grateful to my research assistant, Sarah LeHan, and my readers of the early drafts: Maryellen Lacroix, Frank

Lacroix, Ellen Harnisch, Autumn Howard, Eileen Murphy and Pat Donelan, and to Manda Pepper Langlinais, my proofreader. Thank you to copyeditor extraordinaire Sarah Wight, who painstakingly verified the facts and timelines of the manuscript and the consistency of my characters and storylines, just as she did for my two earlier novels. My gratitude extends to Lance Buckley and Beth Mathis for the beautiful cover and interior designs.

To Cynthia Cooke and Aimery de Moucheron, whose nineteenth-century pigeonnier, located on the grounds of their family's historic château La Poterie in Château-du-Loir, France, served as the inspiration for the pigeonnier I describe at the fictional estate of Saint Martin. I offer the de Moucheron family my sincere appreciation for your French hospitality and the welcome you have given our La Poterie Writers' Retreat and Workshop over the past several years.

I am indebted to the local bookstores and readers here in America and throughout Europe and Canada who have embraced *The Vintner's Daughter* series. Thank you for reading, reviewing and recommending my stories!

To my agent, April Eberhardt of April Eberhardt Literary, and my foreign rights' agent, Gregory Messina of Linwood Messina Literary Agency in Paris, thank you for continuing to champion my work across the globe with enthusiasm.

To my husband, David, and my children, Ellen, Ryan and Julia: your patience, encouragement and love overwhelm me. Thank you.

CPSIA information can be obtained
at www.ICGtesting.com
Printed in the USA
LVHW041450230623
750517LV00005B/133

9 798985 650945